ONWARD VIRGIN SOLDIERS

Born in Newport, Monmouthshire, in 1931, Leslie Thomas
is the son of a sailor who was lost at sea in 1943. His boyhood
in an orphanage is evoked in *This Time Next Week*, published
in 1964. At sixteen, he became a reporter before going on to
do his national service. He won worldwide acclaim with his
bestselling novel *The Virgin Soldiers*, which has achieved international sales of over four million copies. His most recent
novel, *Dover Beach*, is available now in William Heinemann
hardback. In 2005, Leslie Thomas was awarded an OBE for
services to literature.

ONWARD VIRGIN SOLDIERS

Leslie Thomas

arrow books

Reissued by Arrow Books in 2005

3 5 7 9 10 8 6 4 2

Copyright © Leslie Thomas 1971

Leslie Thomas has asserted his right under the Copyright, Designs and
Patents Act 1988 to be identified as the author of this work

This novel is a work of fiction. Names and characters are the product
of the author's imagination and any resemblance to actual persons,
living or dead, is entirely coincidental

First published in the United Kingdom in 1971 by Michael Joseph
First published in paperback in 1973 by Pan

Arrow Books
Random House, 20 Vauxhall Bridge Road,
London SW1V 2SA

www.rbooks.co.uk

Addresses for companies within The Random House Group Limited
can be found at: www.randomhouse.co.uk/offices.htm

The Random House Group Limited Reg. No. 954009

A CIP catalogue record for this book
is available from the British Library

ISBN 9780099490050

The Random House Group Limited supports The Forest Stewardship
Council (FSC), the leading international forest certification organisation.
All our titles that are printed on Greenpeace approved FSC certified paper
carry the FSC logo. Our paper procurement policy can be found at:
www.rbooks.co.uk/environment

Mixed Sources
Product group from well-managed
forests and other controlled sources
www.fsc.org Cert no. TT-COC-2139
© 1996 Forest Stewardship Council
FSC

Typeset by SX Composing DTP, Rayleigh, Essex
Printed and bound in Great Britain by
CPI Cox & Wyman, Reading, RG1 8EX

For Carl Foreman

True patriots, we; for be it
understood,
We left our country for our
country's good!

George Barrington, an Englishman, 1796

1

It was an early-rising wind, pinched, niggardly, seeping from the harbour, that woke him. It tapped around the Chinese house like a blind man's stick, agitating the thin window frames and the tin door, and getting under the frail roof.

Had it been an English wind, Brigg thought, a wind turning up at five in the morning in Aldershot Barracks, it would have barged about like a drunken corporal, banging on doors, belching around concrete corners, and staggering across the parade grounds. When the men had to turn out at seven it would doubtless have acquired some ill-met rain. Between them they would have given Aldershot that crouching, grey, guilty aspect so familiarly miserable to the British soldier at reveille.

But here the Chinese wind was a sneak. Not as chill, but probably pulling along a morose rain, like its own grumbling grandmother, it was Oriental in every sly sound and shift. If winds were coloured it would have been yellow. Appropriately, two of the freighters in the harbour began to cough, first one then the other, like competing consumptives. Brigg knew it was time to get up and go back to the camp.

On a ledge over the wide bed, next to a bored Buddha, was a Micky Mouse alarm clock. Brigg was ready for it when it went off. His hairy arm reached up and over his head to the grinning clock. Then, two other arms, pale arms, bent lilies, curved up, one from each side, and young fingers sought the button surmounting Mickey's head. The trio of hands, all right hands, performed a calm, desultory dance around the agitated clock and about each other. Then the clock stopped of its own accord and the hands, gratefully, fell back to their owners in the bed.

Pearl was lying on Brigg's right, Ruby on his left. The thought passed him that when they had gone to sleep they had been on opposite sides. It did not occupy him greatly. Chinese girls were born nocturnal wanderers. One thick July night he had closed his eyes with both and had awoken with neither, Pearl being curled on the balcony and Ruby snoring tunelessly on the kitchen floor. Now they lay close and naked to him, their small white bodies adhering to his, like piglets and a sow.

He was fully awake now. He turned first to Ruby, then to Pearl, and kissed each chastely on the pale young cheek.

'Whose turn?' he asked loudly, looking up to the soles of the flat plaster feet of the Buddha projecting coyly over the ledge above his head.

'Love or coffee?' Ruby mumbled with her eyes still tight and her forehead and nose pressed into his warm ribs.

'For Christ's sake,' whispered Brigg. 'Coffee, of course. You kids never realize how old and tired I am.'

'Thirty-nine,' contributed Pearl, her murmuring mouth wet against his other set of ribs. 'You too old for bloody coffee soon,' she grumbled. 'You no have any love last night. All drunk and asleep.'

'It's my age,' agreed Brigg propping himself on one elbow. 'Anyway, I *can't* have anything more than coffee this morning, loves, because I've got to get back to defend Hong Kong. Today the Chinese may strike across the border! And it's an hour and a bit from here. If I get the ferry right.'

Pearl detached herself from him, pushed herself away, and rolled beautifully from the low bed onto the floor. She crouched for a moment like a spy getting her bearings then rose gracefully and began pushing her hands through her black hair.

Brigg rolled his eyes towards her. Her back was towards him, white and small as a child's. He reached out and with smiling luxury ran his index finger down the soft crack of her backside.

Impatiently she touched his hand aside. 'You no point,' she pouted. 'It rude.'

He laughed soundlessly and patted her friendly buttocks. She gave him a tired but genuine smile, reached for a thick patchwork robe, and, having wrapped it inelegantly about herself, padded off towards the kitchen.

Ruby stealthily opened one oblong eye and looked across the ridge of Brigg's body. 'She gone?' she said. 'Good. Pearl make coffee, Ruby make love.'

Brigg grinned into her miniature face and cradled her like a large father. He could feel the roughness of his own hard body against the minuteness of hers. The small eggs of her breasts lay in the hairy nest of his chest.

'Can't this morning, love,' he whispered. 'No time.'

'Plenty time last night,' she sulked. 'You bloody drunk.'

'I'll have to stop mixing my pleasures,' he acknowledged. 'Anyway, you both got paid. What are you moaning about?'

'No like pay without work. Not honest to goodness,' she said digging her fingers into his soft parts. She touched him between his legs as though making some kind of quality test, then she gave up, dropped him, and sighed.

'I'll see you next week, next Thursday, and I won't get plastered then. Promise.'

'Plastered? What plastered?'

'Drunk. You know.'

'Aaaah, *plastered* is drunk?' She said it as though she had discovered some extraordinary new truth.

'That's it.'

She laughed and called to her sister excitedly. 'Plastered! Plastered is drunk! Ha!'

Unimpressed, Pearl came to the thin partition of the kitchen. 'Coffee come,' she said.

'Brigg not,' Ruby complained suddenly sulky from the bed. 'Too tired.'

'Army live too far away,' said Pearl. She began to stir the Nescafé in dainty beakers. Then she laughed. 'We come live with Army. With you.'

Brigg snorted rudely into Ruby's face. Resignedly she wiped her cheek with the back of her hand. 'I can see the Old Man being very pleased with that,' he said. 'God, it was difficult enough to get Ho-Ho, and she's just a housekeeper, fifty and crammed with gold teeth.'

'Who Old Man?' asked Pearl.

'Who? Oh, the Old Man. The Colonel. The CO. The boss.'

'Oh, Army boss not like us?' She sounded amazed. 'I think he might be difficult.'

Ruby, impatient as a child with a disappointing toy, tugged at his private parts. 'Maybe we marry you and come live with Army.'

'Both of you?' laughed Brigg, firmly taking her hand away. 'Not likely. Anyway, you're on the game. I'm not marrying anyone on the game.'

They took no offence at this. Ruby tweaked his penis affectionately again. Pearl brought the coffee to the bed. 'Our father not like us marry British Army soldier,' she sniffed. 'Not good for family name.'

The buildings of Hong Kong were piled on the hills about the harbour like large people who have found vantage points and are waiting patiently for some spectacle to occur. Along the water's edge they were thick as the front ranks of a crowd, but the tall white places on the slopes were quieter and indistinct in the breaking morning.

A junk, its sail like a spread hand, moved poetically along the hull of a cheerless warship at anchor, wallah-wallah boats, the wet taxis of the waterway, moved like beetles on a pond, and labouring ferries rattled from landing to landing. The merchant ships that Brigg had heard on waking lay in the dull water coughing like dirty old men, irritable and ill.

January was the sickly month of the year in Hong Kong. The sun might appear later that day but only as a concession. Rain was more likely. All five channels of Hong Kong Television had forecast it. In

English and Chinese. Black and white and colour. Brigg went to the ferry landing stage, the damp of the air like muslin against his face. His eyes felt small and sore after the drunkenness of the night and he was annoyed because he had heard the two girls giggling their childish Chinese giggles about him as he went from their house. He didn't mind paying for it, that was the soldier's way, but paying for it and then not bothering to have it was careless. However, the twins had that morning accepted his jokingly suggested half-rate, which surprised him because all Chinese were extremely sharp business people.

Twenty years before he had first pressed money, all the money he had, into the gentle, but uncompromisingly extended hand of an Oriental girl. Dear Juicy Lucy, honest and sweet, dividing her time between bed, the dance floor, and the Christian Rehabilitation Centre For Young Women. She had returned the money when she discovered that she was initiating him. He smiled dryly as he remembered trying, in confusion, to press it into his back pocket and discovering only his bare arse. Now he was again a soldier of sorts, if nothing else. Here on this indifferent Hong Kong morning was the treble-striped ghost of that callow conscript exploring sin in Singapore.

Now at a purposeful slow march towards the caverns of middle-age, he was thicker across the chest and in the skin; quiet in the eye; burying much behind the firm army face. It was the sort of face that the army liked to have; responsibility replacing the brazen aggression of the older recruiting posters. The Professional of the comic strip advertisements, the

6

kind and capable man behind the gun, at home in the most dire jungle, playing tennis, or sharing martinis with uniformed nurses. That's how he looked. Clean-cut military ambition all over him. How he felt was different and indifferent. He was in it, Sergeant John Brigg, Buller Barracks, New Territories, Hong Kong, because nobody bothered him very much, because it was easy and because he could think of nothing more important he wanted to do.

At the landing stage there were thirty or forty school children, badged blazers, ink splashed satchels and choking ties, humbug striped, pushing and chattering. To Brigg they seemed the identical clutter which crowded the morning bus at Aldershot, except that here they mostly had stained faces or elongated eyes. Chinese, Indian and English businessmen stood aboard the ferry, unsuited, suited, unspeaking, reading the *South China Morning News*; irritated perhaps by half-digested breakfast, oblivious to the theatrical hills and the harbour of Hong Kong. Dreaming, perhaps, of somewhere else.

The wind chopped busily at the skin of the water. Under the nose of the British warship the ferry went, giving small nervous jumps as it travelled, like an urchin passing a policeman. Brigg saw there was another destroyer moored alongside the first. Asleep in each other's grey arms, there came no movement from either. He wondered how long it would take for them to wake and sail if they were called to action. Probably as long as it would take to organize the army in Hong Kong. Hardly longer. He wondered, not for the first time, why they were there at all. The soldiers and the ships.

A Boeing jet wobbled uncertainly through the cleft in the interior mountains and he could see another dropping down over the distant dragon-backed islands. The nearer Boeing straightened itself in a relieved way when it was over the city. From the ferry he watched it alight gingerly on the long platform in the sea that was Hong Kong's airport.

As the ferry pushed towards the town landing stage he saw the bright blue roof of Sergeant Murdoch's Volkswagen moving with the rush-hour traffic along the front. Some of the schoolboys were bouncing around with a football. It jumped, bright orange, among the aloof adult passengers, the boys shouting as they tried to capture it. One big English child had grabbed it from a smaller Chinese and now triumphantly his fist rose above the others and punched the ball against a stanchion. It flew with new impetus towards the rail of the ferry. Brigg thrust his hand out to try to save it, but it was gone. It dropped over the side of the vessel and floated brightly away like a buoy in the dull water. The Chinese boy began to cry.

Sergeant Murdoch leaned out and opened the Volkswagen door when he saw Brigg jogging from the ferry. Three Chinese boys were throwing the large English schoolboy to the boards of the landing stage.

'Look at that,' said Murdoch. 'That's how they'll beat us. Three to one.'

'Three thousand to one,' corrected Brigg as he got into the car. 'He threw their ball over the rail of the ferry.'

'Three to bloody one,' repeated Murdoch. He

moved the car away through the taxis and carts and cars at the pier head. 'Timed it all right this morning.'

'From bed to barracks in one hour flat,' agreed Brigg. 'Good job you're camping out too.'

'There ought to be a law that every Englishman should have a Chinese wife. This one's bloody fantastic. Comfort, consideration, cunt. What more could a man want?'

They were driving by the cricket ground, sacrosanct, green and open in the middle of the thick, untidy town, like a lily pad in a conglomerated pond.

'I've heard that my missus makes out I'm living in the camp with her,' said Murdoch. 'She won't even admit I've gone.'

Brigg said: 'She's not fooling anybody. Everybody knows. It's all around the backyards.'

'Too bad,' said Murdoch. 'Minnie ought to bugger off back to England. She's a schoolteacher you know, this Chinese girl.'

Brigg said: 'You told me before. Quite a few times actually. Has the Army noticed it yet? Has the CO said anything?'

'Not a sausage. I'm waiting for something to happen. The trouble with lodging out on the quiet, unofficially, is that you don't get any ration allowance.'

Brigg said: 'As long as you get your rations.' He did not like Murdoch much, but the Friday morning lift was convenient.

'Been getting yours?' asked Murdoch. 'Siamese twins last night?'

'They're Chinese twins,' amended Brigg evenly. 'They're not joined up or anything like that. Not that I've noticed anyway.'

'Gets crowded in bed, I expect,' pursued Murdoch. 'With all three of you.'

'Like fucking in a bus queue,' said Brigg casually, looking out of the window.

The car was pulling uphill now. It was ten years old and it protested as it curled around the rough streets and up the slopes leading from the town towards the free ground New Territories. Murdoch swore at it. 'This thing's like a bloody coolie's grandmother,' he said. 'I was thinking we ought to club together and get a new one.' He looked hopefully at Brigg from the border of his eye.

'Why not have one each,' said Brigg.

'A car each?'

'No, a coolie's grandmother each.' Brigg did not mind how he niggled Murdoch because Brigg arranged the guard duties at the garrison. The lift was a reciprocal arrangement.

'Those twins are no grandmothers, are they,' said Murdoch changing gear and subject. 'Christ, when I saw them the other night at the Jiggery Pokery Club they looked like a couple of kids. It can't be too bad screwing them.'

'They're eighteen,' said Brigg without emphasis. 'It's not too bad.'

'What do they do for the rest of the week?' asked Murdoch. 'Don't tell me they wait for Thursday night and Sergeant Brigg.'

'Oh, they keep themselves busy,' said Brigg waving his hand. 'Knitting and doing their homework. That sort of thing.'

'I bet,' laughed Murdoch nastily. 'They're down at that bloody club every night. I know because I pop in

10

there occasionally . . . Just for a change.'

'That's what everyone goes there for,' agreed Brigg. 'A change.'

'The place gets chock-a-block full of Vietnam Americans,' grumbled Murdoch. 'Shouting their mouths off. God, they don't know what war is.'

Brigg sniffed. 'They must be getting a strong hint by now,' he suggested. 'If soldiering is reckoned to be some sort of art, or craft if you like, then they must know a bit more than we do. Our Army wouldn't know a fart from a flame-thrower these days.'

'What about the war?' inquired Murdoch argumentatively. 'What about that?'

'History,' Brigg told him. 'Ancient history, mate. Can you imagine our little lot up at the camp getting shoved off to somewhere like Vietnam. Imagine it! The Colonel would want to take that bleeding horse of his for a start.'

Murdoch backed out. 'Well the Yanks enjoy their Rest and Recreation all right,' he sneered. 'They do in the Jiggery Pokery, anyway. From what I've seen.'

Brigg said nothing for a while. Murdoch had a little moustache, like a permanent complaint under his nose to go with his barrack-room lawyer's whine. Eventually he shrugged: 'Oh, they enjoy their R and R right enough. Can't say I blame them.'

'It's not the R and R I would worry about,' said Murdoch bending confidentially into the classic arch of the gossip. 'It's the V and D. That's what would worry me.'

'Oh, wrap up,' thought Brigg. But he said amiably, 'You shouldn't go to the club then, Murd. Even for a change of scene . . . You stick to your Chinese schoolteacher, mate. Then all you'll get is the odd fall of chalk dust.'

The Chinese in the New Territory villages were going about their busy but ordered lives, carrying and loading, suckling children, making food and little fires, and listening to metallic songs from Radio Canton, across the border in their homeland. Colonel Alfred Simmons, commanding Buller Barracks, noticed them only as a vague brown and grey Oriental frieze. His staff car took him steadily along the rural road, past the big duck ponds and the spreading vegetable fields, the minor mountains hunched at his left and right, the sea lost somewhere miles down the valleys at his back. He had driven thus in India, in Egypt, in Cyprus, in Aden and in Aldershot, with the landscape and the people being for him only the most shadowed of patterns. He had travelled the world and he had not touched it, neither had it touched him. In four years and three months he would retire.

He was the sort of officer whose prized, early-wartime, Sam Browne belt seemed more like a truss than a symbol of authority. He was short (but, as he told himself, so was Field-Marshal Harding) and he was ungainly (so was Napoleon) and the belt held him together around the middle. His face was round, puzzled but kind, indented with distant blue eyes and marked by a button-sized turned-up nose of almost infant charm.

All his life he had been involved with the routine of wars, the logistics as they were now mysteriously called, the workings of an army; but the savagery of warfare had always, and only by chance, gone on

12

behind his back, out of his hearing, or before he had even managed to arrive on the field. Other men told of amazing escapes in action; all he had known were amazing escapes from action.

He had been called to London from France (to plan a parade) three weeks before Dunkirk, and had missed Normandy on D-Day, and many of the terrible subsequent days, because he had fallen innocently from a peaceful pear tree at his home in Hampshire. By the time his leg was knit and he arrived on the invaded continent it was D-Day Plus 182, and there were uncaring children playing on the wrecked beaches. He was an uncertain, but peaceful man, one who had never got to grips with his profession. He had never known war.

On this morning he turned no more than a mild glance on a Chieftain tank which had split its right track and slewed dismally off the road into a Chinese village eating-house. A hundred silently interested Chinese and half a dozen awkward British soldiers stood watching the monster eating into the thin wooden building, all regarding it patiently as though waiting for it to finish its breakfast.

'That'll please Command Workshops, sir,' said Turner, his driver, who made a point of speaking at least once during the morning journey from the Colonel's billet to the garrison.

'Seems like it's broken down,' said Colonel Simmons absently.

'Oh, they'll be *well* pleased, sir. They're playing in the final against Royal Marines this afternoon.'

'What final is that, Turner?'

'Football, sir.'

'Oh, football. Ah, well, they'll have to wait until they've mended the tank, I suppose.'

'And the chop-chop house, sir.'

'That too,' sighed the Colonel patiently. 'Yes, yes. They'll have to replace that, I suppose.'

Turner knew the conversation was terminated. He persuaded the car from the haphazard main road and on to the tarmac drive into the garrison. It was eight-thirty, the indifferent morning had gathered itself a herd of frowning clouds across the Hong Kong mainland, and the new guard was drawn up at the garrison gate. They were there every morning, Monday to Friday, as he arrived, a line of eight British professional soldiers hung with the arms and appendages of the seventies. The sergeant of the guard called them to stern attention as the car droned in. The Colonel saluted them casually from his window, almost a wave, as though he had spotted a vague acquaintance in the street. Had they been mounted on dromedaries, or arrayed in comic hats and clowns' ruffs, he would hardly have noticed.

Major Fortune, his adjutant, was sitting in his office. The Colonel always felt there was something fractionally wrong with Fortune. He was a little too lively for such a tall man, his fair hair was a shade too shaggy, he had too many jokes that the Colonel did not understand. One Saturday afternoon in the lounge of the Peninsula Hotel in Hong Kong he had seen Fortune wearing a long light suit with a flowered shirt and tie. The Colonel had hidden behind a large Korean vase so that his aide would not see him.

'Don't you think he's a bit too . . . er . . . ladylike?' he had nervously asked his wife that evening.

'*Miss* Fortune!' Grace had exploded. Her husband showed his quiet annoyance. 'No, dear,' said Grace consolingly. 'He's just up to date, that's all. He's nice and trendy.'

'Trendy?' the Colonel had repeated. 'Is that what he is?'

Grace touched her brittle blonde hair. She was pleasant and she tried to keep young. 'I like him,' she confessed. 'I think he's very refreshing. And not a bit stuck up like some you've had. And why shouldn't he be a little trendy? You advertise for Soldiers of the Seventies – and then you grumble because you get them. It's a shame the War Office won't allow them to grow their hair a trifle longer. Down to the bottom of the neck anyway.'

'God forbid,' breathed her husband. 'And *I* don't advertise for them. The flaming War Office does.'

'So they do,' agreed Grace.

He grunted. 'But I wish we had a few more soldiers of the forties, that's all. You can't run an army on curly locks and damned shirts like Kew Gardens.'

'He makes a nice adjutant,' she insisted.

'An adjutant is also a species of large Indian stork, you'll recall,' grumbled her husband. 'This one is more like a tall parrot.'

Fortune seemed more agitated than usual this morning, hopping stiff-legged about the office. The Colonel thought again of the large Indian stork. He frowned around for his coffee.

'Sorry, Colonel,' said the young major. 'It's not made yet. Nobody's had time. These signals . . .' He proffered a fan of white forms as though inviting his superior to select one at the commencement of a conjuring trick. '. . . They keep coming in.'

'Signals?' asked the Colonel incredulously. 'On a Monday? What's happening?'

'We're to have a visit from the Secretary of State for Defence,' said Fortune like a man coming straight to the point with dread news. 'He's to spend a weekend here in the garrison while he's in Hong Kong.'

The Colonel sat down: 'Oh, for Christ's sake,' he exclaimed. 'What the hell does he want to come here for? Can't the man go and poke his nose in on the navy or the bloody air force?' He picked up the signals and studied them miserably. 'Six weeks,' he muttered. 'That doesn't give us much time. I mean, for God's sake, we're trying to do a job up here, a couple of miles from the most powerful potential enemy country in the world and we have to take our minds off it just to accommodate some flaming politician.'

'Exactly, sir,' agreed Fortune. The Colonel glowered at him nevertheless.

'And it's not just the VIP,' continued the Colonel. 'It's all the hangers-on, the security buggers and all that sort of rubbish. They'll all put their spoke in, you can bet your life.'

'I wouldn't, sir,' contributed Fortune.

The Colonel glanced at him sourly: 'You wouldn't what?'

'Bet my wife,' said Fortune, dropping his voice dejectedly.

'Christ, is that one of your trendy jokes?'

Fortune blushed. 'Trendy? No, sir. It was just an observation. Agreeing with er . . . your observation, sir.'

Colonel Simmons did not bother to reply. He held up the signals like a white bouquet before him. He let his annoyance drain from him, for he was a mild man and ashamed of raising his voice. He read all the signals carefully, shuffled them and went through them again.

'Sorry, Fortune,' he said quietly.

'What, sir?' asked Fortune.

'Sorry, I said,' replied the Colonel his annoyance flickering again. He damped it immediately. 'Sorry for having a go at you.'

'Oh, that's all right, sir. Nice of you to apologize.'

'Well, for heaven's sake,' protested the Colonel hitting the papers with the back of his hand. 'This sort of thing on a Monday morning. Right after the weekend.'

'Very annoying,' agreed Fortune. 'They even want to know if there's been any activity over the Chinese border.'

'I know,' nodded the Colonel. 'Have you been up there recently, Fortune? Have you seen anything?'

'Not for some weeks, sir. Not since before Christmas. I took my parents up to have a peep at China one Sunday when they were here on their trip. But it's not the sort of place one goes a lot. It's a bit touristy.'

'Quite so,' agreed the Colonel. 'I can't remember when I last went up there. Not that you ever *see* anything. Only that turgid river and that wire sheep fence. There's just *nothing* there, is there? If an ox cart appeared I think I'd go wild with excitement.'

'Intelligence said there was an increase in the number of flags on the other side just over a month ago,' said Fortune. 'And the Chinese this side were singing a lot of songs.'

'If I remember correctly,' said the Colonel, 'nobody in this garrison could even remember *seeing* any flags, when Intelligence got round to asking us about it. And who in God's name knows what the Chinese around here are singing about? Apart from the other Chinese.'

'Could be a sort of musical version of the Thoughts of Mao,' said Fortune helpfully.

'And they might be singing God Bless America in Cantonese,' grumbled the Colonel. 'All right, let's think about it later. I suppose we'll have to put on some sort of a show. What else is there this morning?'

'Routine stuff, sir. There's the inter-services final this afternoon and you have been invited. Command Workshops are in it.'

'Doubt if they'll play,' said the Colonel assuredly.

'No, sir? Really? Didn't know you kept up with soccer, sir.'

'Nothing to do with keeping up, Fortune. Some silly ass has put a tank straight into one of the Chinese eating-houses in the village down the road. Command Workshops have got to get it out.'

Fortune said: 'The tank. Oh, yes, it's on the Military Police report. Track went or something. But that won't stop the match, will it, sir? I mean it won't take the whole resources of Command Workshop to get that seen to.'

'It will *this* Command Workshops,' replied the Commanding Officer, confidently. 'They took three weeks to fix my damned table lighter. What else is there?'

'Postings,' said the adjutant holding a list towards the Colonel. 'One sergeant, nine other ranks from home, sir. The sergeant, Sergeant Wilcox, is the armourer we requested.'

'Thank God for that,' breathed the Colonel. 'With this big noise coming we're going to need him. This lot are only allowed rifles once a week and then they can't look after the wretched things. People getting their fingers jammed and that sort of idiocy. I'm relieved he's here. I'll give the new chaps my pep-talk tomorrow.'

'Right, sir. There're a couple more things. A dispute between three of the men and RSM Love's daughter. They say she hurled stones and abuse at them.'

'Again?' sighed the Colonel.

'She says they were making fun of her,' replied Fortune resignedly.

'Oh, Christ. The women on this garrison are more trouble than all the men. What is it they call her? What's her name?'

'Violet, sir. They call her Violent Love.'

'What in the world am *I* supposed to do? I ask you – what *can* I do? That girl is seventeen and she's bloody enormous – fourteen stone if she's an ounce. And prancing about a military base in those ridiculously tight trousers . . .'

'Jeans, sir,' replied Fortune.

'That's right. Those. Ridiculously tight. She bulges all over. She's like the Michelin man. And that huge ballooning jumper with the dog on it . . .'

'Snoopy, sir.'

'I don't give a damn who it is,' asserted the Colonel.

19

'All I know is it's stretched across an eighty-inch bosom. And then *I'm* supposed to stop the men taking the rise out of her. Be better if RSM Love shipped his daughter home.'

'Perhaps they can't find a big enough ship,' offered Fortune.

'Ha! I say, that's not bad for you, Fortune! Not bad at all.' He quickly became stern. 'Mind, you shouldn't be making jokes at the expense of other ranks or their dependants. I don't want to tell you that again.'

'Sorry, sir. There's one more item. A report from the sergeant of the guard that Mrs Murdoch had a Chinese peeing through her window last night.'

'Peeing through her window! Oh, come on, Fortune.'

'Probably a typing error,' agreed Fortune. 'I think it should read "peering", or "peeping". That is looking, rather than urinating.'

The Colonel stared. 'That is more like it. If the Chinese have a weakness it's their curiosity not their bladders.'

'Quite so, Colonel,' agreed Fortune. 'The guard searched the area of the married families' quarters, but found nothing.'

'Where was the woman's husband?' asked the CO.

'He's the sergeant . . . Sergeant Murdoch . . . who is living . . .'

'Oh, don't spare me,' interrupted the Colonel. 'I remember. He's living out of barracks, isn't he? Unofficially?'

'I believe so, sir.'

'You damn well know so,' said the Colonel without emphasis. 'Everybody else knows. That's obviously going to cause some complications at some time. We must keep an eye on the situation. Is that all?'

'One more thing, sir. Rather distressing really . . .'

'Now what?'

Fortune produced a bare bayonet. 'This, sir. A Chinese boy from the village handed it in at the main gate. One of the men must have lost it during the last military training period.'

The Colonel sat back heavily. 'Oh, for God's sake, Fortune. What is this place coming to? A *soldier*, a British, *regular*, soldier, losing his bloody bayonet! And handed in – by a Chinese child!'

'We're checking to find out who lost it,' promised the adjutant.

'Let me know,' said the Colonel. 'I want to know as soon as possible.'

'Naturally, sir. Would you like your coffee now?'

'I think I'd better,' muttered the Colonel looking sadly at the papers on his desk. Fortune went into the next room, beyond a glass partition. 'There's nothing else, is there?' called the Colonel irritably. 'The wives aren't marching for Women's Lib, are they? The medical officer hasn't taken arsenic? Nothing trivial like that?'

'Not as far as I know, sir,' called Fortune around the door. 'But it's quite early yet.'

Buller Barracks squatted in a plate-shaped plain among the Chinese duck farms and patchy market gardens of the Hong Kong New Territories, in the earthy hills that ran to the Chinese border. It was rural and removed from the crowded energy of the city. The Kowloon–Canton Railway, a thin relic of the old imperial days of China passed through a station just over a mile away and this, apart from the serpentine road, was the communicating link with the town and the port. Strategists, far removed from the locality in London and Peking, viewed the tenuous position of the garrison with apprehension and amusement respectively. To the soldiers the road and the railway meant lifelines to the delights of the Oriental bath-houses, to the exciting rigours of the Jiggery Pokery Club and similar establishments, and the confident comforts of the YMCA.

During the early weather of the year, however, the indifferent few weeks, and on weekday evenings through the rest of the year, few of the soldiers adventured to Hong Kong itself. They occupied themselves in their military village with football and general knowledge quizzes, home education, and evenings of recorded music. There was a model electric railway club, a philatelic circle, a small tuneless choir, a debating society full of loquacious drunks, and a pop group called The Ding Dongs who rang a brass bell and dressed as firemen.

One man, Private Burgess, occupied his whole spare time lifting weights and performing exercises. His dawn run, in red singlet and shorts, was the earliest activity of any day at Buller Barracks, and almost any evening he was to be found doing hand-stands against the chapel wall. He was forty-two, fine and muscled. The odds on him suffering a heart failure within the next year were quoted in the camp at four to one.

Outside-duty-activities were, for the most part, however, the resort of the unmarried soldiers. The married men went home nightly to their wives and television sets.

Around the barrack square, in pointless patterns, were ranged garrison officers, barrack rooms, mess-halls, NAAFI canteen, the school, the church, and behind these the suburban brick and wooden bungalows that housed the sergeants' wives, families and television sets.

It was a place, not of Hong Kong, but London, Wolverhampton, or Edinburgh, hugging itself with hopeful security, keeping all alien interests – except necessary working Chinese – outside its gates. The guardhouse at these gates was demonstrative of the British Army's historic habit of making an Anglian ghetto for itself in a foreign land. It was entirely symbolic, this low-roofed guardhouse, with its red fire buckets, its mirror to see that the soldiers were nicely dressed when they occasionally ventured out, and its baffled, lonely sentry looking out in the general direction of the threatening millions of China. Symbolic, because the camp was not contained by any perimeter fence or wall, and any intruder could gain entry with no difficulty whatever. But the British, as ever, kept their watch at the gate and relied on a sense of fair play in the foreigner.

Some of the old military school, Regimental Sergeant Major Love, other senior NCOs, and a clique of life-term lance-corporals, viewed this lack of an encompassing fence with some professional concern. It was like a football pitch without goalposts. But the Defence Ministry, beyond the world in London, met suggestions with the thin retort that it would be far too expensive and would hardly keep out a Chinese invasion anyway, which made the presence of the guard at the gate even more suspect.

Intruders did penetrate the garrison at intervals and at will; indeed it had been drawn and photographed, both the inside and the outside of the buildings and establishments, and these details were now filed for future use at the Hong Kong Expansion Department of the People's Republic Development Board in Peking.

Gossip, bitchiness, male and female, cliques and feuds, ironically bound together the military village like some split and damaged beehive, incoherent yet coherent at the same time. Beneath the individual roofs the career soldiers, The Professionals as the recruiting posters called them, lived lives as minor and sedate as any collection of greengrocers, insurance agents and town hall clerks in any market town in Britain. Hong Kong Television's vanishing dot at the end of the daily transmission (on five channels – better than at home) was also the conclusion of the military day, with the exception of a goodnight cup of chocolate, a poorly aimed kiss, and some fairly routine sexual intercourse.

At seven each morning reveille sounded over the British stronghold. It was sent forth, not by a brassy bugler with shining sashes, a blatant bugle, and a face upturned to the rising sun, but by a relayed gramophone record sent spinning by the bored sergeant of the guard, and sounded from loudspeakers poking their trumpet noses from corners and angles in the camp. This second-hand rouser had ceased to surprise or offend even the most old-fashioned of the soldiers, for it had been playing to them for too many dawns.

On the obverse side of the record was Lights Out which was played a full two hours before the televisions were switched off.

In the middle of the day a regular and singular sound came to the garrison, the metallic, chain-gang, clanking of the soldiers beating their enamel drinking mugs with their stainless steel eating irons, as they wandered back to the barrack blocks after the midday meal.

Everyone did it, unthinkingly; a trudge, trudge, trudge, clank, clank, clank. It did not pause during shouting or conversation, it sounded over the calls of horseplay and the demanded orders to the Indian ice-cream man who, each lunchtime, parked his patriotically red, white and blue van on the side of the parade ground.

Lance-Corporal Harold Harrison, ten of his twenty-two year engagement with the Army now history, clanked into the barrack room which he shared with ten others. He was a slow, uncouth man, eyes dull and nowhere. He sat on the edge of his bed, thrust out a thick tongue and tried to view it by squinting ferociously down his nose. Making no sign as to whether the experiment had been a success or otherwise, he levered himself on to his bed and opened a medical text book which he had secreted beneath his grubby pillow.

Clanking through the door from the concrete balcony of the barrack block then came another career soldier, a man fallow and fat, with a wet, unhealthy moustache, a man like a white walrus. His name was Wilson.

Harrison half turned on to his side. 'Get a shufty at

this, Nancy,' he said to Wilson who had stopped beating his knife, fork and spoon tattoo. He held up the open book. 'Look. The fallopian tube!' he said lasciviously. 'And the urinary canal!'

Wilson stared at the drawing unimpressed. 'Honest,' he said. 'I just don't get it. It's only a drawing. It could be any bleedin' thing. It could be a pig's bladder. How you can think that's sexy beats me, mate. If it was a couple of tarts working away with a dill-doll, I'd get as excited as the next bloke. But that's just a book for doctors and nurses. It's just drawings. It's just drawings. It's not porny, mate.'

'You stupid clitoris,' said Harrison. 'That's the point. It's the words. Vagina! Womb! Don't they do anything to you? And fallopian tube! Christ, that drives me bloody crazy!'

'Well it don't me, Hairy, so you just enjoy yourself in your own way. You give your lips a good lick but don't try to get me interested in it, because I don't see nothing in it. Don't tell me that sexual intercourse is anything like a good fuck!'

The others came into the barrack room, sounding like a tinny procession of eastern priests. Pardoe, the Welshman who sometimes in the evenings played the spoons; Bainbridge, the corporal in charge of the room who walked with a trail of talcum powder falling from his trouser legs. Kenton, who concealed short-sight to stay as a soldier; Walton, an eighteen-year-old farmer's boy who dreamed of wild duck and widgeon and early mornings with a gun; McBride, the lonely Scot; Renwick, at fifty the oldest lower-ranker in the camp; and Joss and Wilberforce, a pair who talked their own language in the Latin names of flowers.

Lance-Corporal Ferris, a sad and angular man, who kept a secret dog under his bed in the barrack room, clanked in. Everyone in the garrison, from Colonel Simmons down, knew that Lance-Corporal Ferris had a secret dog, a fawn monster which he had adopted as a whining stray and which had lived under his bed ever since.

It had grown so spectacularly that it had been known, during a restless night, to have thrown Ferris from his bed as it turned below. Ferris brought a pint of beer for every man in the barrack room, once a week, so that his secret would never be revealed. Now he entered the barrack room slowly, stopped striking his cutlery and his mug at the door, and sat down guilt-faced on his bed. His hand went to his pocket and he produced a lump of food, salvaged from the mess hall, and held it below the level of the bed. The snout of his secret dog thrust itself out and took the offering at one gulp.

'That dog's got to go, Ferris,' said Wilson unkindly. 'It's a night-time niffer. It's not healthy in a room with humans.'

'Dog?' asked Ferris. 'What dog?'

'Oh come on. Don't give us that crap again. That blinding great pooch what's right now sticking its nose through your legs like a darkie's dick.'

'Listen, Nancy,' said Ferris in a strange half-plea, half-threat. 'If I have to get rid of this dog, then there's no more buckshee beer.'

'Aw, shut up,' said Harrison leaning towards Wilson. 'It's not his dog what makes the niff. It's that bugger Treacle Thompson, on the end. I swear it is. Can't think why we've got to have him in here at all.'

'Because I was told to come in here by Sergeant Brigg,' said Thompson walking through the door. 'I've got to sleep somewhere, Harrison. I'm in the Army too, you know.'

'Shows how 'ard up the Army is,' snorted Harrison.

Thompson quietly put his mug and eating irons in his locker. He had been beating them too, but in an oddly tuneful way like a toy drum. He was an undersized, red man, his face rough and pocked, his hair sparse and tufted, his eyes blue and brave. Nothing could hurt him. That day he was in love.

2

In his office, adjoining the orderly room, Brigg had hung photographs of people who had been notable failures. Wilcox followed him in after the lunch break and stood examining each one like a witness at an identification parade.

'Failures,' announced Brigg going behind the desk. 'It's a hobby. I collect them.'

Wilcox twisted his face to a wry grin and examined the gallery. He was taller than Brigg, thirty-eight, a year younger, with a hard but humorous face topped by a fringe of vigorous hair. He examined the photograph of Lawrence of Arabia, the thin mystic countenance looking from beneath his robe like a fugitive peeping from under a tablecloth.

'A failure?' inquired Wilcox.

'One of the best,' said Brigg. 'Even when he'd worked it out for himself that he was a failure people kept making a big deal of him. The poor sod was even a failure as a failure. He once shot the brains from his own camel, you know.'

'Careless,' Wilcox tut-tutted.

'Charging along with his Arabs,' Brigg said. 'And shooting away, and I suppose the camel's head was swinging about and – bang! That was that.'

'No synchronization,' said Wilcox the armourer.

'That problem would only arise with a camel – or possibly a giraffe. And even a giraffe keeps its head up in the air, so unless you were shooting at aircraft . . .'

'This,' interrupted Brigg running his finger past actors and admirals, horizontal boxers, ugly courtesans, and stopping beyond a lady missionary devoured by converts, 'this is a Dutch explorer.'

'What did he fail at?'

'Exploring. Losing ships and men in storms and battles and what-have-you, and getting to some place only to find that some bastard Spaniard or Englishman had discovered it the week before. I pinched the picture from one of Charlie's school books.'

'Poor kid will probably end up on jankers, knowing what Army schools are like.'

'They haven't noticed, I don't think.'

'And Charlie?'

'Probably. But he won't say anything till he's ready. He'll use it as blackmail.'

'Jesus, what a kid. I'll never forget him from the Aldershot days.'

'He's different,' admitted Brigg. 'Too different sometimes. He's been hypnotising the girls at school. I was hauled up before the CO last week and told that the little bugger had been putting the other kids in trances behind the school lavatory. He says he learned it from a book.'

'That sounds like Charlie,' laughed Wilcox.

'Okay, it's a laugh,' sighed Brigg. 'But they found Staff Sergeant Billing's girl stretched out stiff among the dustbins. Charlie said he didn't have time to bring her around before the bell went for lessons. Christ,

30

they had the MO there trying to wake her up, but in the end they had to do a deal with Charlie. No punishment if he snapped her out of it.'

'And he did,' suggested Wilcox.

'I'll say. The Medical Officer was bloody livid.'

'Who looks after him?' said Wilcox. 'Who's his mum?'

'I've got a Chinese housekeeper called Ho-Ho,' said Brigg.

'Any Ho-Ho?' said Wilcox raising his eyebrows.

'No thanks. You should see Ho-Ho,' said Brigg.

'How's the general ho-ho situation?' asked Wilcox.

'The ho-ho . . .?' began Brigg.

'You know! Ho-ho. Do you want me to draw a dirty picture?'

'Oh, that? Well, yes, that varies. It's not so free-and-easy as it was at Aldershot. The men tend to er . . . cherish their wives a bit more out here. Being as there's not a lot of anything else around – unless you don't mind spending out on the girls at the Jiggery Pokery Club.'

'What about the tourists? Rich American widows and that,' insisted Wilcox.

'For poor British squaddies?'

'You've got civvies, haven't you? You don't have to wear uniform. How will they know?'

'Never thought about it,' admitted Brigg. 'I suppose you could try.'

Wilcox's glance went to the failures again. 'Who's the anaemic looking youth?' he inquired. 'The one with the shrunken head and the big hat?'

'Me,' said Brigg. 'Eighteen. The virgin soldier.'

'What a big lad you've grown into,' said Wilcox

unembarrassed. 'Your beret fits better now. And what are you doing marching like that? – you've got the right arm *and* right leg stuck forward together like a clockwork toy.'

'It took me years to spot what was wrong with that picture,' shrugged Brigg. 'Bloody pathetic. The whole bunch. And always taking photographs of each other in warlike poses.'

'That makes you a failure?' said Wilcox.

'That, mate, was just the start. The apprenticeship. Only I could run joyfully from the Army at twenty and crawl back again, beaten, at twenty-seven. That's why I'm up there. And *I'm* the one who has a wife who gets herself killed in a car with another soldier – and in a lay-by. Always thought they were appropriately named.'

'How long have you got to do?'

'Life,' said Brigg. 'I'll keep signing on for life. Hah! Makes you laugh, doesn't it? In those days I used to mark the dates off the demob calendar. That's the funny thing about the Army now – now there's no conscripts – don't you think? At least conscripts were young and they gave it a bit of go, a bit of verve, even when they hated every minute. And they always had that *something* to look forward to – getting out. Half the mob here now are in limbo – like me – and we'll go on for bloody ever. This is the only thing we've got.'

'I wouldn't know anything else,' said Wilcox, as though anxious to take some guilt. 'I've been in it since I left school. But I don't worry about it as much as you, mate.'

'God, how snide I used to be about regulars,' said

Brigg. 'Smarmy little bastard. Nowhere to go, I said. No mummy, no daddy. And here I am with the worst of them.'

He sat down resignedly behind his desk, gathered half a dozen army forms and dropped them decisively into the waste paper basket. 'I keep them there,' he explained seeing Wilcox's expression. Nobody ever clears that out except me. Anybody who comes in after hours, cleaners or the guard, always goes through the desk.'

'Same everywhere,' agreed Wilcox. 'Well, I'm here for two years' minimum.'

'And a great job you'll do,' grinned Brigg. 'Guarding the Crown Colony for Her Majesty against the slant-eyed devils of Mao, who could walk in here any morning before breakfast.'

'Well, until they arrive I'm going to be in the armoury. Same as Aldershot. Routine but safe.'

'They won't give you much to do here,' forecast Brigg. 'The soldiers only get their bang-bangs on Saturday mornings and for guard and the Queen's birthday parade. You'll have plenty of spare time.'

'The mess seemed a bit quiet last night,' said Wilcox. 'If we hadn't been there they wouldn't have sold more than a couple of pints.'

'Last night was gala night compared with some,' said Brigg. 'They all go home to their little houses to watch Z-Cars or The Virginian. Only the homeless, the old soaks, and the dreary ones go to the mess.'

Wilcox rose. 'Today, Briggsy,' he said, slapping Brigg on the arm, 'you've cheered me up no end. I thought maybe I wasn't going to enjoy it. Anyway I'm going off to my armoury. Tell Charlie to look after you. Maybe put you under the old 'fluence now and again, you miserable bugger.'

That day, that far off day, in England, he remembered, October sun was spinning through the window. It was getting tangled and diffuse in the suburban side-net curtains, but entering free through the middle panes. Two lucky wasps and a muscular fly clung to the glass and pushed their stomachs to the unexpected late heat. The morning's rain had washed out the sky and across the London street, trees and resigned grass sweated in the cemetery.

That day, Brigg had stood in the window and watched his son walking like a spirit among the graves across the road, his football beneath his arm, held like a muddy parcel, his wet boots trudging through the cemetery grass.

The boy took no notice of the graves through which he journeyed until he came to one which had subsided on one edge and tipped heavily. Brigg watched him put his foot on the marble and attempt to straighten it. It remained nose up, like a capsized and petrified boat. Glancing around, the boy dropped the football and then jumped zealously with both feet on the deformed marble. He jumped on and off several times then stopped, perplexed because it remained unmoved. Again he looked over his shoulder as though worried he might be observed. He jumped once more and then gave up. Picking up the ball he went towards the cemetery gate.

Brigg watched him. The face, as always, pale and concerned, the fringed fair hair smooth with sunshine. Glenda had insisted that they call him Leofric because that was the name of the hotel in Coventry where they had spent their four-day honeymoon, and where, in fact, the boy had been conceived.

She had taken a rare fancy to the name of the hotel and the boy had to be called Leofric. 'Thank God we didn't stay in London,' Brigg had said. 'He could have been called Regent Palace.'

Charlie, as Brigg now called him, had, without doubt, been planted at the Leofric Hotel on the final night of the honeymoon. After four days and nights there he was left with exactly enough money for two single rail fares to London. No more. Not even enough for the extravagance of another packet of Durex. If he had purchased another packet it would have meant that he, anyway, if not Glenda, would have had to walk at least two stations. So he did not buy the extra contraceptives and neither did he withdraw in time.

After Glenda had been killed with Staff Sergeant Pollock in his car, Brigg changed the boy's name to Charlie. Glenda was one of those women who hang a name like Leofric around a kid's neck; or Cheyenne, Darren, or something televisionic like that. She had insisted on calling the boy Leofric, in full, and Brigg himself had to confess that Leo was pointless since his son looked more like a whippet than a lion. He began calling him Charlie immediately after the funeral. In fact, when they got back to the barracks in Aldershot from the crematorium, he had said something like: 'Let's have a cup of tea, Charlie.' The boy had acknowledged the change without any outward reaction. He was Charlie Brigg from then on.

From the sunlit window, an upper bay in London,

Brigg saw the boy wait on the pavement across the dull, dumb road. He waited nervously as though the street were full of traffic, his white face turning first left then right. There were no cars. Then Brigg heard a vehicle approaching and saw the boy hunch as he timed his run. Brigg screwed up his eyes and heard the car screech and honk and then cough nastily and drive on. Downstairs the front door was opened and banged and he heard his mother-in-law call, 'Is that you, Leofric?' The boy shouted something back.

He came into the untidy sitting-room. He saw that Brigg had been observing him from the window and began to bounce the football uncomfortably on the worn fawn carpet. It got away from him and rebounded with a wet heaviness around the room. Brigg trapped it with his foot and looked at the boy.

'That car nearly got me,' said Charlie guiltily.

'You nearly got *it*, you mean,' said Brigg. 'You *waited* for the bloody thing. I saw you.'

The boy regarded him steadily. 'You always tell me to stand on the kerb and look both ways. That's what I was doing.'

'Right,' agreed Brigg. 'But the idea is to see that there is nothing coming along the road before you cross, not to wait until there *is*. Christ, haven't I got enough bother?'

'I miscalculated,' said Charlie. He sat down, his butter-pale face sticking from his muddy track suit like a bean from a pod.

'You got soaked,' said Brigg. 'I told you not to go.'

'It's only mud. I got in the park shelter when it was raining.'

'Did you play with anyone?'

'Just by myself. There's nobody else over there except the old man because they're all at school. I just ran about with it, in and out of the trees, and the old man, who sits in the shelter, was goalkeeper and the shelter was the goal, so that wasn't too bad.'

'That *very* old man?'

'That's the only one who goes there.'

'He must be ninety.'

'Well he didn't mind. I got him to move up to the middle of the seat in the shelter and he was the goalkeeper. He likes having a game as well, even though he can't dive after the ball. We often have a game like that. Once I knocked his pipe out of his mouth, but he was all right about it.'

'Do you want a biscuit or something?'

'I'll have a cup of tea if you're making one.'

Brigg said: 'I wasn't, but I will.' He went towards the kitchen. The boy seemed anxious.

'How long are we going to be here?' he said. 'When are we going to Hong Kong?'

'On the twenty-second,' said Brigg. He went into the kitchen and filled the kettle.

'How many days is that?' It was strange how he floundered when it got to dates or numbers.

'Five, including today.'

'We have to go back to Aldershot first, don't we?'

'That's on the twenty-second, like I said. Then we start the next day for Hong Kong. Why, do you want to get away quickly or something?'

Charlie said quietly: 'Well, I wouldn't mind. I wouldn't mind clearing out today, really.'

Brigg stopped and came out of the kitchen. 'Today! We *can't* go today, for God's sake. What about your gran'ma? She'd be a bit . . .' He went around to the front of the boy and looked closely at him. 'You in some bother?' he asked.

'A bit,' admitted Charlie not looking up. 'Not a lot. Just a little bit. But I'd like to get out if we can.'

'It must be a lot if you want to clear out.'

'No. It's just that the vicar bloke over the cemetery knows gran'ma and I had a bit of an accident over there that's all.'

'An accident? In the cemetery?'

'That's right, Daddy.'

'Don't go giving me that "Daddy" rubbish, Charlie. You only try *that* when it's serious. What was it?'

'It was an accident,' the boy repeated defensively. 'It could happen to anybody who just *happened* to be going through the cemetery with a football.'

'Not many people do.'

'It's a long way round from the park if you don't take a short cut through the cemetery.'

'What happened, Charlie?'

'I was just bouncing the ball along the cemetery path. Just gently. And I came around the corner by that chapel place and I saw a whole funeral. People all in black and crying, and these men carrying the, you know . . . the box . . .'

'The coffin.'

'That's right, the coffin. And I was bouncing the football, like I said, and I was so surprised when I saw them that I let it bounce away from me. Just like it did in here just now.'

Brigg watched him carefully. There was a break while the boy waited for him to say something. He didn't.

'Yes,' confirmed Charlie seeing he wasn't going to gain a pause. 'And it sort of ran away across the path over the gravel and kept bobbing about the legs of the people in the funeral.'

'Oh God,' Brigg said seriously.

'Yes. And then one of the men with the box – the coffin – gave the ball a kick. Honest! That's what he *did*. It was on purpose, too. Christ's honour. I saw him kick it. Everybody was getting all upset, especially the vicar bloke and the crying people, and this man give it a *kick*.'

'Go on.'

'It went in the hole.'

'The hole?'

'You know . . .'

'Not the grave!'

'That's right. The grave. I mean, *he* kicked it, didn't he? I didn't. And that's where it landed up. In the . . . thing.'

Brigg sat down. He could hear the kettle steaming impatiently in the kitchen but he took no notice. The boy heard it too and half turned.

'There's steam coming out of the kitchen door,' he said.

'Never mind that,' muttered Brigg. 'I suppose *you* went and asked for your bloody ball back?'

'Well, I didn't actually *ask*. I felt like running because they were all sort of wailing and threatening and I saw that the vicar was the same one who comes around to see gran'ma, but he has his ordinary civvies on then. Nobody seemed to do anything. We all just stood there. But they couldn't put the thing, the coffin, in the hole with my football in there, so one of the working men who was there, one of the shovellers, he got down into the ground and threw the ball out to me. And I came home.'

Brigg went and made the tea and brought two cups back into the room. They drank the tea and for several minutes neither the man nor the boy spoke. Then, eventually, Brigg said inadequately: 'Charlie. Try and behave yourself in Hong Kong, will you?'

3

Some sunshine came over from China at mid-morning on the Friday. It moved over the blank hills and the speckled duck farms of the New Territories and found the British soldiers of Buller Barracks drilling. Because it was a weekday, and the middle of the morning, it was for them an unfamiliar experience. In platoons, under their sergeants and corporals, they stamped and marched, wheeling before the puffy, bawling RSM Love and an embarrassed array of junior officers who had no other function other than that they were required to be there. They stood awkwardly, like a clutch of shady bookmakers, making short jocular remarks to each other or occasionally giving barren little laughs and scratching their legs with their canes.

From one corner of the barrack square, from an alley between two blocks of garrison buildings, two of the Army's wives emerged and stood, for a moment, watching the parading.

'Looks like we'll have to walk all the way round, Hilda,' said the larger, older, woman. 'Didn't think they'd be capering up and down at this time of the day.'

Hilda Harvey, the tired young wife of a records' office corporal, nodded. 'Edwin says we should never

41

take a short cut across the parade ground anyway. He says if Mister Love sees us, or anything like that, then he could get into trouble. It's sacred or something.'

Doris Boswell, the spreadeagled wife of the garrison's chief cook, blew out her cheeks defiantly. The cheeks were strewn with broken veins, her eyes were glittering like a gipsy's, plugged deeply into her face. 'I'd like to see RSM Love or any other bugger stop *me* going across the square,' she answered sourly. 'I'd have my Phil sticking sennapods in his midday curry before the week was out. He'd have more to think about than his precious barrack square then, I can tell you.'

'There's always ways of people getting back at people,' agreed Hilda simply as she hunched and hurried along at her companion's side. Then, anxious to make her contribution, she added: 'I suppose I could try and get my Edwin to knock a couple of years off Love's service in the records. But I don't think he would do it. He's very conscientious.'

'Sennapods is best,' sniffed Doris Boswell. 'More sudden. It might be months or years before he found out that his records was all messed up. It would only be minutes before he found his pants was.'

She chortled coarsely and started off around the perimeter of the square with the younger woman continuing uncertainly alongside. They had dowdy coats hanging from their shoulders, unbuttoned down the fronts because of the sudden sunshine. Their shopping baskets were laden from the NAAFI store and crowning hers Doris had a thick mail-order catalogue. They could have been plodding from any suburban shopping parade in England.

'Can't say I'm looking forward to this coffee morning thing,' grumbled Doris perspiring mildly as she tried to make up the time lost from not being able to cross the square. 'That Mrs Love's such a daft bitch and she's mean with the biscuits. God, no sooner do you get your fist in the tin than she's trying to snap the lid closed.'

'Better to go, I suppose,' counselled Hilda. 'They think you're stuck up if you don't. And there's enough nasty tongues waggling around this place already.'

'Stuck up!' shouted Doris. 'I *am* stuck up!' She stopped and wiped her large ugly face and watched the drilling soldiers malevolently. 'Christ, dear, I've been with my old man in some of the best postings in the Army. Paris, Berlin, all over the show. I'm *entitled* to be bleeding stuck up.'

'I suppose you *are*, really, Doris,' said Hilda meekly. 'This being our first overseas posting, I wouldn't know.' She paused slightly then asked: 'Have any of your family ever died of heart attacks, Doris?'

Doris Boswell stopped and stared at her through broken blood vessels and slight sweat. 'What d'you mean?' she demanded truculently. 'What exactly d'you mean by that?'

Hilda shivered under the challenge and drew her coat closer to her. The two women stood face to face four feet from where a corporal was bawling orders to a squad of men. The women did not hear him.

'*Squaaaaaaaaaad!*' he bellowed. '*Squa-d!*'

'Just changing the subject, that's all, Doris,' said Hilda.

'*Squad, atteeen-shun!*' The squad rattled together.

'I thought you was reckoning I was going to have

heart failure,' said Doris loudly. 'Christ, I'm only puffing a bit.'

'*Right, tueeeern!*'

'Not at all, dear. It was only out of *interest*. It's just that heart attacks run in *my* family. We just heard about Edwin's Uncle Alex yesterday.'

'*By the right – queeeeeek march!*'

'Heart attack?'

'*Left-right, left-right . . .*'

'Dropped dead at his paper-stall. What runs in your family, Doris? Anything?'

'*Left-right, left-right.*'

'Drowning,' said Doris morosely. 'We've had three drowned in our family. Two by accident and one did it off his own bat. That's what runs in our lot.'

'*A-bout TURN! Left-right, left-right . . . Come on now, open those legs! You've got nothing to lose!*'

The platoons marched by and the gossiping women meandered on. 'Why do they say that?' asked Hilda.

'What?'

'You know. Open those legs. You've got nothing to lose. I've heard them shout that before.'

Doris looked at her sympathetically. 'Ask your old man,' she suggested. Then she added to herself: 'I don't suppose he's got much to lose either.'

Wilcox eased himself onto an uncomfortable upright chair in the sergeants' mess, carefully, as though nursing a wound, and moved his damp toes around inside his boots. Brigg brought two beers and put them on the Formica topped table.

'Sod that for a game of soldiers,' murmured

Wilcox. 'I thought you said there wasn't any of this caper here.'

'They must have heard you were on your way,' grunted Brigg amiably. 'So they sent the Defence Minister right on your tail. Nobody goes much on all this parading business, I suppose. Some of this lot would rather walk hand in hand than march, believe me. But sometimes they think we ought to make a stab at looking the part. They're even talking about getting a loan of a Guards drill sergeant from Singapore, on special secondment, just to get this shambles into some sort of order. And an unarmed combat man.'

Wilcox nodded. 'I can imagine,' he said. 'They're not exactly Royal Tournament stuff, are they. I've been in the cake a few years but I can't say I've ever seen two platoons collide head-on before.'

'Good men, though,' incanted Brigg over his beer. 'Did you see how they just kept on marching, not a single faltering step, even when on a collision course. Straight at each other! Those are the fighting qualities the Army needs today.'

Wilcox sighed: 'It will probably be all right on the day. You can hope anyway.'

'Oh, I should think so. There's more than a month yet,' agreed Brigg. 'What does a politician know anyway? Bit of bull-shine and the old man up there on his horse.'

'He's got a horse?'

'God, yes. Thinks he's the Duke of Wellington. Damn great meaty thing it is too. It takes three squaddies and a fifteen hundredweight to clear up the dollops on the square after he's been riding that thing around.'

'A horse,' breathed Wilcox with quiet wonder. 'Who would have thought it? He hasn't got a plume in his hat as well, has he?'

'No. He'd like to have, but the horse is the best he can manage. All strictly unofficial, mind. It's his own thing – his private property and he has to feed it out of his ration allowance. You wouldn't think the CO of this dump would merit a bike.'

'Where does he keep it?'

'With the mule company.'

'Don't tell me there's a mule company.'

'Last one left in the British Army,' nodded Brigg. 'And it's here in Hong Kong. It's to help us stem the invasion of the Chinese hordes when it comes.'

'That ought to drive the yellow bastards back. Mules.'

Wilcox laughed into his orange beer and muttered, 'Mules,' again. He drank philosophically, still moving his head from side to side, the beer glass going with it. Then he said: 'Maybe we could borrow a couple of their mules to go into town tomorrow night.'

Brigg said: 'I doubt it. They're a bit touchy about their mules and who uses them. Anyway, I'm not going into town tomorrow night. It's not my night.'

'Listen, it's not a weekly bible class, mate. What's stopping you?'

'It's just I don't go Saturday nights because it's just a bloody free-for-all. Everybody's out then. It's all you can do to get to the bar, let alone a bed. The Americans change over on a Saturday too, one mob arrives and the next goes back to Vietnam. The ones who arrive are straining to get out on the town. And I don't like that much competition. It gets very pricey too. Everything. And noisy.'

'You poor sod,' said Wilcox shaking his head. 'You poor old sod. Too noisy and too expensive for you, and too many nasty, randy, Yanks. So you go down in the week with the old folks when it's nicer, and a bit cheaper.'

'All right,' agreed Brigg. 'We'll go tomorrow night. And I hope you end up with a couple of combat marines. That'll serve you right, mate.'

The two women chimed the doorbell. Violet Love opened it, hugely self-conscious, and whispered: 'Come in. Mum's expecting you. Everybody else is here.'

'Thank you, Violet, dear,' said Doris Boswell wearily. 'We had to walk all the way around the square because they were playing soldiers.'

'That's made us ten minutes' late,' confirmed Hilda Harvey. 'We'll tell your Mum we're sorry.'

'She won't mind, Mrs Harvey,' said Violet with fat cheerfulness. 'She's just handing out the biscuits.'

'Better hurry,' muttered Doris to Hilda as she rolled her coat off her back. Violet left them in the hall and waded with the massive daintiness of fat people among the front room visitors.

'God help us,' whispered Doris to Hilda as they hung their coats. 'That girl's bigger than ever. I swear somebody pumps her up every morning.'

'Poor thing,' said Hilda sympathetically. 'Heart disease will get her. You just watch. Like my family.'

'She'll never drown like mine,' sniffed Doris. 'Not with that lot on her chest.'

They went into the front room, Doris first, Hilda tentatively behind her. A dozen of the garrison wives were chattering above the rims of coffee cups. Without a word Doris launched her Littlewoods' mail order catalogue among them. It bounced about like a raft, from hand to hand. Mrs Love, a square, small woman with an icy smile and brittle eyes, circulated with a biscuit tin, red and round, its lid opened a mere two inches as though she were displaying some precious treasure cosseted within. 'Glad you could come,' she said with a flat, organizational tone to Doris and Hilda. 'They're using the square, I hear. Very annoying. Although you're a bit naughty walking across it, just like that, ad lib. If any of the men did it, they'd get it in the neck from Violet's daddy.'

She motioned the biscuit tin, uncertainly, towards Doris. 'Biscuit, Mrs Boswell?' she inquired. She opened the tin jaw of the container and looked up to catch the deep, common eyes of the other woman. The antipathy in their expressions locked for a moment.

'Thank you, Mrs Love,' said Doris thrusting her hard hand into the maw of the biscuit tin. The other woman had not extended the crack, but Doris was now in up to her tough wrist and she rummaged round in the tin like someone who has posted a letter by mistake and tries to retrieve it from the letter box.

'There's not a lot of variety, I'm afraid,' warned Mrs Love.

'I'll just have a feel around, dear,' returned Doris icily. 'Could you open up a bit more, Mrs Love? I think you're cutting the tendons in my wrist.'

'Oh, *so* sorry,' piped Mrs Love. 'Here, take your

pick.' She reluctantly opened the lid wide and Doris, having sorted through the contents, emerged with a handful of gingersnaps. Mrs Love looked at the biscuits and then at Doris. 'Are you sure that's sufficient, Mrs Boswell?' she inquired.

'It'll do for this cup of coffee, Mrs Love,' said Doris cheerfully. 'Why isn't your little girl working in the NAAFI shop today? I thought we hadn't noticed her down there.'

Violet Love blushed. 'I'm hardly "little", Mrs Boswell.'

Doris snorted. 'Well, I meant, *young* girl. You're still young, aren't you, Violet?'

'I suppose I am,' smiled the girl genuinely. 'I've got all my life in front of me yet. Someone told me that the other day.'

'I think that's right,' said Doris eyeing her. 'How do you like it in the shop?'

'It's very nice, really. But there's a lot to learn. And Mr Fielding says it would be better if I didn't go in when the shop is very busy. He'd rather have me there when there's not too many customers.'

'Well, it's only a *small* shop,' said Hilda absently. She stared, embarrassed, at Violet and then saw Doris watching her. 'Never mind,' she added hurriedly. 'It's nice that you can help your mum this morning, isn't it.'

The girl hung there for a few moments, her great, white, swollen sweater trembling above the small, seated Hilda like some alpine threat. She put her hands behind her back and swayed girlishly. 'Got a boyfriend now,' she announced softly. Her large walnut eyes rolled in her mother's direction, but Mrs

Love was bent anxiously over an array of coffee cups waiting to be replenished.

'How nice,' said Hilda genuinely.

'Someone in the garrison,' whispered Violet. She leaned towards Hilda who moved nervously away. 'But,' she said, 'we've got to keep it a secret. But, all I know is I've *got* him.' She straightened triumphantly and made off across the room like some dirigible accidentally released from its moorings.

Hilda said: 'I know she's big, but it's nice to think she's found someone. And all secret as well.' She giggled. 'We kiss in the shadows,' she said poetically.

Doris rammed the last gingersnap into her mouth. 'And it must be a bleeding great shadow,' she said unkindly.

When the normal Saturday morning parade was done and the soldiers had limped and shuffled from the square, in the direction of beer or bed, the rest of the day being free, Colonel Simmons reined his horse, Melksham, before the squad of men newly arrived in Hong Kong. They were formed up beside the unit transport sheds.

Wilcox, the senior NCO of the party, called them to attention and then wheeled to salute his commanding officer. Disconcertingly, he found himself looking directly up the long tubular nose of the horse. Its putrid breath struck him in the face. He came down from the salute and stepped one smart pace back. The horse eyed him down its narrow face. Wilcox elevated his head to the Colonel.

'Party ready for inspection, sir!'

'I've seen them, Sergeant,' said Colonel Simmons

casually. 'This is just a welcome-chat. Stand them at ease, please.'

'Sir!' acknowledged Wilcox. His eyes again travelled up the snowy snout of the horse, unfamiliar and fascinating. He tore himself away and turned towards the squad, instructing them to relax.

'Thank you, Sergeant,' said the Colonel, briefly raising his hand to return the NCO's salute. 'Just a chat, that's all.'

'Sir,' returned Wilcox.

'You're the new armourer, then?' said the Colonel from his lofty place. 'Sergeant Wilcox.'

'Correct, sir,' replied Wilcox.

'Good. Time we had the armoury reorganized and the weapons put into good order. We're always having trouble there, Sergeant. People getting their fingers and thumbs jammed in mechanisms, and that sort of ludicrous thing. On one Saturday last year we had five separate cases of the black man's pinch. Very painful it can be too.' He leaned first to the right and then the other way, around the neck of his horse to see if any of the squad were grinning at his jest. None was.

'Only a joke, of course, about the black man's pinch,' the Commanding Officer explained emphatically. Wilcox glared at the squad and there was an obedient titter of belated appreciation. The Colonel laughed too. 'Just my joke,' he repeated.

His face straightened. 'We are here,' he said sternly, 'in this colony of Hong Kong to do a job. We are doing it well, and we shall continue to do it well. And you are the men I shall look to in the future to help with this job.

'You may well ask what this job is. It is simply the

keeping of this Crown Colony for Her Majesty the Queen. Now a word about venereal disease. It is prevalent, even rampant in Hong Kong at the moment, due, I am sorry to say, to the large influx of American servicemen who come here for Rest and Recreation, and have too little of the former and too damn much of the latter. They come in from their business in Vietnam and when they've gone they leave this nasty complaint behind and our chaps, trying to do a decent job here in Hong Kong – and damn it all, *we* have to live in the place, and defend it – our chaps here quite often pick it up. I've had a word with the American liaison officer here about this but, I must say, quite frankly, just between us, his attitude was not what one would expect, certainly not cooperative. So I can only ask you chaps to be jolly careful. I always say that man does not live by bed alone. Hah!'

There was an uncertain, but generally appreciative reaction from the squad, and Colonel Simmons again leaned alternately both sides of his horse's neck, right then left, to get a good view of the men directly in front of him.

'Would you like me to move the squad back, sir?' suggested Wilcox. He had never had to deal with an officer on horseback before and he found himself bowing sideways to get a view of the Colonel.

'Don't fret, Sergeant,' said the Colonel kindly. 'It's this animal. He's got such a damn big head.' The horse, as though seeking to divert attention from its front, deposited a mountain of steaming ginger dung on the square. Hearing it flop on the concrete, the CO turned briefly, and then said to Wilcox, 'Get a fatigue party to er . . . wipe that up afterwards, will you, Sergeant.'

'Yes, sir.'

'Anyway, I simply thought I would welcome you all here. You'll find there are some pleasant outings to Hong Kong. Up to the Peak and along the Aberdeen fishing harbour, and suchlike. Dinner on the floating restaurants is fun, and there's lots of good shopping.

'Here in the garrison there are a number of off-duty activities, debating, quizzes and that sort of . . . er activity, which you might like to enjoy. And when the weather gets a bit better, next month or the month after, you'll find it's a damned nice place to be.

'There is only one thing more, chaps. Watch the water, will you. Hong Kong is jolly short of water and, in fact, we have to purchase it from our neighbours across the border, the Red Chinese. We don't really like doing it, but there it is. Anyway, we don't want to buy more than we can help from that bunch, so we try to conserve it as much as possible.

'I think that's about all. Have a good stay with us and work hard. Right, Sergeant, carry on, will you.'

'Sir,' agreed Wilcox, bringing the squad to attention. He saluted and Colonel Simmons saluted in return. Then he trotted away, leaving the pyramid of dung smoking like a camp fire just in front of the squad.

'What a load of shit,' observed Wilcox quietly.

4

There was a certain miserable timelessness about Saturday afternoons in the military village. There were no duties except for the bored men guarding the pointless main gate, or those on guard at the garrison armoury, or those who were confined to barracks and on punishment fatigues. The soldiers lay in the sheeted pits of their beds, snoring and sweating, journeying through dreams; those who had drunk greedily in the late morning occasionally cursing or calling out unintelligible desires. Generally they were twelve to a barrack room, except specialist corporals and those above the rank of sergeant who had their own rooms on the ends of each floor of the barrack blocks about the main square.

There were some who refused to be ensnared by the dismal drugged sleep of the vacuum afternoon and instead kicked a football about the recreation field, watched other teams playing, or went to the heated swimming pool. Others, mostly those freshly arrived, took advantage of special tours offered to Tiger Balm Gardens, the Fung Ping Shan Museum, or Victoria Peak. Further contingents went on the train into Hong Kong and drank tea or beer in the services' club, relaxing before the Saturday night rush on the whorehouses and massage parlours, and a few wandered the close shopping streets listening to Americans bargaining for mass-made Oriental treasure with contempt founded on envy. On this particular Saturday a small group of languid men who did not want to stray far had walked to the Chinese village down the pitted road from the camp to see the tank which had buried itself in the eating-house and was still not removed.

In the military houses officers and non-commissioned officers, their wives and families, had withdrawn, for the most part, into their cherished suburban privacy. Some of the younger married couples were dozing after a bout of sex; in other homes sergeants loosened their collars and lounged back to watch televised racing from the Hong Kong track, curtains drawn for privacy and from habit more than any aid to viewing. Children dug the hard ground their fathers left untouched in the gardens, playing and occasionally kicking each other. Military games were popular with the boys and with that unique sense of history possessed by children, the enemy was always German or Japanese. Wives washed or wept, or told the Chinese housekeeper to do the former leaving themselves free for the latter. Others sat with solid faithfulness in the same dimness as their chair-laid husbands and read again every last sentence and word of the *Overseas Daily Mirror* in its mustard wrapper.

Mr Love was not the regimental sergeant major of the powerful jaw and the baying voice. Nor was he tall, distinguished, military or broad.

His boots were ever shiny, his brasses bright and his peaked cap set at a belligerent angle. But he was one of those pink, puffy-faced men with shadowed chins; soft-structured men whose strength seems to have gone elsewhere and left them with a rubbery shell.

On Saturday he made a point of being last to his house. He liked to stride the off-duty barracks on his own, like some smug cat, wandering around the backs of the blocks, walking quietly up to the gate sentry and, saying nothing, just sniffing as though he could be smelling China or the man on duty. Stick under arm he went about his domain, watery eyes jumping about. He considered himself to be the only *soldier* in the entire garrison, a knowledge which rubbed and hurt him inside. He was the only man at Buller Barracks who knew nothing of Ferris' secret dog. Had he known he would have had the animal killed the same afternoon.

Having performed his tour on this Saturday he was about to go to his house when he saw a square of paper shuffling at the distant corner of the barrack square. More distant still was a soldier, late from the mess hall, beating a lonely tattoo on his mug with his cutlery.

'That man!' Love's voice was a peculiar breathless whine, pitched high in the air and carrying astonishing distances. At the second cry the soldier, Pardoe, stopped as though struck by an assegai. Even at that distance he only swore well below his breath. He started to move towards the RSM, almost collided with the sacred area of the square, glanced up in fright, changed direction, and marched quickly to the far place where the sergeant-major stood.

'Sir?' inquired Pardoe coming to attention.

Love regarded him sourly. 'What were you doing?'

Pardoe's face clouded with doubt. 'Nothing, Mr Love. Just going back to the barrack block, that's all.'

'Making all that bloody racket,' sneered Love. 'I could hear you, laddie. Don't lie to me.'

'No, sir,' said Pardoe. His voice became very Welsh. 'I was just tapping the mug with the eating irons, sir.' He held out the implements.

'What for?' demanded Love.

'Nothing, sir. Just . . . well, keeping time.'

'What's your name? Pardoe, isn't it?'

'Yes, sir,' admitted the soldier miserably.

'You are not a bandsman, Pardoe, and banging those things together is damaging Government property. The British taxpayer pays for those implements, son. And you destroy them.'

Pardoe glanced dismally at the ugly mug and the heavy metal cutlery. 'Sorry, sir,' he said.

'Indent for a new set on Monday,' ordered Love. 'The prong of that fork is bent. Don't look at it, sonny. Can't you take my word! Indent for another. It will come off your pay. Perhaps you won't desecrate Government property in future. Now, look across the square, laddie . . .'

Pardoe looked blankly across the parade ground. 'Sir?' he said.

'What do you see? You see a piece of litter, don't you?'

'Er . . . er . . . yes, sir.'

'March smartly to that litter, Pardoe, and pick it up. Dispose of it, Pardoe. Dispose of it.'

He watched the Welshman circumnavigate the square and capture the piece of paper. He then thrust his stick under his arm and made for home. His garden, like the others, was a riot of weeds, but his eyes and his nose were on a different plane as he went through the gate which he considered to be the barrier between his private and his military life. He closed it with a heavy thrust as Violet looked from the window and saw him coming. That face, she thought, is like a dull, dead, pink rose. How she hated it.

'Right,' he bleated at the door. 'Where is lunch?'

'Mother's out,' said Violet. 'I've cooked your lunch. If you sit down I'll give it to you.' She wasn't afraid of him but he thought she was.

She brought in the food and put it in front of him, stood back and watched him pick it about with a fork. 'That's your lunch, not a mine field,' she said in her mind.

'You've been causing trouble with the men, I hear,' her father said. 'I've got a hard enough job here, my girl, without having you undermining it. Understand?'

'They were rude to me,' she said evenly. 'And they got a handful of gravel for their rudeness. Can I go now? Your pudding is in the oven. All you have to do is to take it out and turn the oven off. Mother will be back by three.'

'All right,' he said not looking up. 'Get out.'

Violet went from the house by the back way, walking properly through the gate but, once on the road, out of sight, progressing at a balloonish hop. Like an extensive fairy she took the downward military road.

The afternoon was overcast, but warm in the absence of the Chinese wind. There were few people about. At one point she walked on rising ground and from that elevation she could look out over the entire garrison lying in the natural basin below. Its square was as vacant as a desert, the roads between the buildings were dry and empty channels. She could hear the shouts of men pursuing a football beyond the haunch of the hill to her left, and in the middle distance she could see the knot of soldiers standing around the tank embedded in the Chinese village. At the main gate to the camp the sentry made his own, slipshod, unceremonial marching pattern. Two dogs were sniffing each other without much expectation at the corner of the NAAFI bar. Otherwise, nothing. It was Saturday afternoon. The army was not working.

Violet went down the concrete road with nonchalant guilt. It was difficult for someone of her size, and at full sail in a white sweater to make any worthwhile attempt at concealment. She tried to look as though she was going somewhere else.

At the junction of the cookhouse with the main other ranks' mess hall, she apprehensively rolled her big head first one way then the other, and then sprang determinedly into a grim doorway, avalanching down the steps the other side. She had descended into a steamy, tiled room, hung with the smell of fat and gravy. Great baking and roasting tins, recently from the ovens and now larded and lined with the sludge of Bisto, were piled about the room. On the far wall, his insignificant arms lost in a great, hot sink of thick water, was Treacle Thompson, the miniature soldier.

She kissed him awkwardly over the volcanic sink, its water green and steaming.

'My bastard dad again?' she asked knowing it was. She looked disgusted, despairing at the awesome assemblage of metal and muck. It stood in layers to the roof.

'Who else?' Treacle shrugged. 'He's really got it in for me, Vi. This fat is even getting in my eyes.'

'He's got it in for everybody, the rotten shit,' she said. She looked at him pityingly. 'And especially you, love.'

Treacle grimaced. He brought a long narrow meat tin to the surface of the foul water with a certain flourish, like an engineer explaining the idea for refloating a sunken submarine. He sailed it on a melancholy voyage through the slime to the edge of the sink.

'Four Saturdays on jankers, and always here in the Tin Room,' he muttered. 'And all for something that was just an accident in the first place. So the bayonet fell off the end of my rifle and I didn't notice it, that's all. It's the armoury's fault. The catch wasn't working.'

'I know, I know, darling,' she sympathized tenderly. 'And it wasn't as though it was lost. That little Chinese boy brought it back to the camp anyway.'

Treacle sighed. 'That's what put me in here,' he said. 'Losing a bayonet is bad enough, but having it found by a Chinese is much worse. The way he went on you'd have thought that kid was going to take over the whole of Hong Kong with my bayonet.'

'My old man went on something dreadful about it at home,' said Violet. She stared at him: 'The pig wanted to have you shot.'

'I don't think he can go that far,' said Treacle uncertainly. 'It might have been better if he could. If it wasn't for you I don't know what I'd do.' He looked at her and, moving against her, buried his pimpled, steamy face between her huge breasts leaving a plate-sized grease mark on the front of her sweater. 'Treacle, do this, Treacle, do that. Run here, jump to it, there. They never leave me be. I came into the army to escape being nagged.' He glanced at her anxiously as though he had said too much. But she did not react. 'I always thought everybody was equal in the army apart from some being colonels and some being sergeants and that sort of thing. They make out that it's one big happy family. *And* it's about time I got a stripe too. I'm the longest serving private in this unit, d'you know that?'

'I believe you,' she said with simple sadness.

'It's not the glory I want,' he insisted. 'But I'd feel a lot better as a lance-corporal.'

'Have you asked anybody about it? About a stripe?'

'Yes, I did as a matter of fact. I mentioned it to Sergeant Brigg, who isn't bad, and he made some excuse about changing my rank upsetting the establishment in the garrison, or something.'

'Well perhaps he's right,' said Violet consolingly. 'He seems a very nice sergeant compared to some.'

'Yes? Then why did he say afterwards that he wondered if the weight of the stripe on my arm would be too much for me?'

'He was just joking,' she said soothingly.

'They're all the ruddy same. I've grown to expect it now.' He launched another meat tin down the slipway of the draining board and into the sink. It floated and spun on the hot slimy water, until Treacle sank it with an undersized but triumphant fist. 'Treacle, do this, Treacle, do that, all the time. Treacle come out to see

61

the moon, and you go out and they throw the contents of the sergeant's piss-pot all over you. I'm sick of it.'

Her fat lips hardened together in a strong line. 'You shouldn't *let* them do it to you,' she asserted. 'For a start it's time this Treacle business stopped. Your name is Robin and you should make sure they call you Robin.'

'Nobody will. I've asked them. They say things like, "All right, Robin, Treacle". All that sort of remark.'

She touched the sparsely ginger-haired arm, projecting thin from his army shirt. 'Have you got another name?' she asked coyly. 'A middle name.'

'Halibut,' he said miserably. He looked at her eyes to see if she laughed. He saw only amazement.

'But that's a . . .'

'A fish,' he finished for her. 'I know. I know. Now you see why I don't mind being called Treacle.'

She did not pursue it but surveyed the baking tins. 'I'll help,' she said. 'Nobody's likely to come in here this afternoon, are they?'

'The orderly sergeant will be in about five to see a nice clean pile of tins,' he said. 'I can't see them bothering otherwise. Are you sure you don't mind, Vi?'

'I love you,' she explained. 'If I help you'll be done in half the time.'

'Thanks, darling,' he said earnestly kissing her. 'I'm glad you're here anyway because I want to tell you about tomorrow. I'm going to shake them up tomorrow.'

'There's not room for two of us at this sink,' she interrupted pushing her great hip against him. 'You sit down for a minute and tell me about tomorrow.'

*

Brigg's housekeeper Ho-Ho had a face like flour, riven with an alarming battery of gold teeth and eyes like sampans. Between her and the boy Charlie there was a war of skirmishes, sometimes half-mended by periods of peace and an acknowledgement of mutual regard and suspicion. The woman moaned and chattered about the boy. The boy made up bizarre stories about the woman. He told his father he had once seen her flashing her gold teeth in the sun as a signal to Communist China. Brigg rarely understood either of them.

Brigg left the sergeants' mess at two o'clock on the Saturday afternoon, leaving Wilcox lolling asleep in one of the cane chairs. Wilcox was the last sergeant there. The Chinese barman was wiping the bar and tutting impatiently at the crumpled British soldier. Brigg walked quietly through the camp towards his house. He was the only unmarried sergeant with a son. His house was like the others, a carelessly blank white front with small windows and a moon-shaped porch set back into the wall. He had thought, when he first arrived, that an appropriate embellishment might be a large round stone, like the one in the garden of Joseph of Arimathea, which could be rolled back and forth. He had mentioned this conversationally to the garrison padre, the Reverend Captain Church-Smith, who, by his limp smile, had apparently been unable to appreciate the point and had never looked in Brigg's direction since.

Brigg had watched Violet Love trudging secretly to her lover's rendezvous with Treacle.

He continued his pace, but considered her as one

might consider the curiosity of a slowly moving traction engine. Under his breath he sang:

> 'Oh, Violent Love,
> All loves excelling.'

His song was joined by the voice of Ho-Ho bawling from the house. 'SARJ BLIGG! SARJ BLIGG!'

'Oh, Christ,' muttered Brigg. He opened the undersized gate and marched through the few yards of the morose garden. The maroon front door was open and Ho-Ho's pleas came up the dull passage, quickly followed by Ho-Ho. She wore a flowered dress, many sizes too big, that had once belonged to his wife. When he arrived in Hong Kong he discovered that he still had the dress although he had got rid of all her other possessions. He had given it to Ho-Ho and regretted it from that moment. To see the small, ageing Chinese woman enshrouded in the large gay pattern was like looking at the shrivelled body of Glenda herself.

'Sarj Bligg,' said Ho-Ho, bringing her voice down to the confines of the passage. 'Boy bad.'

'I know he is,' agreed Brigg. 'What's he doing now? Charlie!'

The boy appeared at the end of the passage. 'I'm not bad,' he said glaring at the housekeeper. 'I'm not *that* bad, anyway.'

'He do devils,' said Ho-Ho, pointing a parchment finger at him. Then she screamed: 'Devils!'

Brigg frowned at his son. 'Have you?'

'Have I what?' asked the boy.

'Been doing devils.'

'Devils,' nodded Ho-Ho patently glad that he realized the implications.

'It's got nothing to do with devils,' argued Charlie. 'I was trying to put her *under*, that's all. Put her in a trance.'

'Oh, you're on that again, you little bugger,' said Brigg. 'Haven't you caused enough bother at school?'

'It's my *hobby*,' protested the boy. His face was thrust up at Brigg. 'You're always telling me to have a *hobby*. When I get one all I have is trouble.'

'Only *you* could have a hobby like that. Hypnotism!'

'I'm getting good at it, but nobody will let me have any practice.' He glanced at Ho-Ho who muttered, 'Devils,' sulkily through her metallic mouth.

'Don't practise on Ho-Ho,' said Brigg. 'The Chinese are very funny about things like that. Apologize to her. We'll never get another woman who'll put up with you.'

'All right,' muttered Charlie, quickly acknowledging the truth. 'Sorry.'

Ho-Ho made a small flighty movement. 'He's sorry, Ho-Ho,' said Brigg. 'No more devils.'

The woman nodded an ungracious acknowledgement and returned at her padding pace down the corridor to the kitchen.

Brigg walked into the front room with the boy. He sat down. 'Can't you keep out of trouble for just a bit,' he said. 'Nobody else seems to get into scrapes like you.'

'It's my interests,' said the boy. 'Nobody understands them.'

Brigg said: 'Well you'd better quit this hypnotism thing, for a start. Fancy doing it on Ho-Ho.'

'She wasn't any good anyway,' Charlie grumbled. 'I suppose it's because her eyes are too narrow.' His enthusiasm gathered. 'You see, you really need people with sort of wide-open staring eyes if you're going to put them really *under*. And somebody who hasn't got much of a strong will. What are you doing this afternoon, Dad?'

Brigg glowered at him. 'It's nice to know you've got such a high opinion of me,' he said.

The boy looked surprised. 'I didn't mean anything,' he argued. 'I wondered if you were going to take me out, that's all.'

'Oh, I see,' nodded Brigg. 'All right. I'll get changed.'

'Put your red shirt on, will you,' smiled Charlie. 'Then we can go and have another look at China.'

'Red shirt?' asked Brigg. 'Oh, I see. Big joke. Anyway we saw China last week. It's still there.'

'I know. But I like looking at it and I like seeing the Chinese soldiers on the bridge. It's not often you get a chance to see Chinese soldiers.'

'We may see a few more than we want before we're done,' grunted Brigg.

'D'you think so?' The boy looked excited. 'What's so marvellous about that?'

'Would you have to resist them, Dad?'

'I suppose that would be the general idea.'

'There's millions. You wouldn't have a chance.'

'I know,' said Brigg.

They took the train to Sheung Shui, the final alighting place for passengers on the Kowloon-Canton Railway unless they were continuing into China. Not many did. Brigg and the boy left at the station and took the bus up the broken road towards the border. The boy sat quietly all through the journey watching the New Territories' peasants with their bundles and their sticks, their chickens in cages, and their caramel-coloured children. The children and the younger people chattered incessantly as the bus rolled and rumbled on its rough route, but the old people, their faces like dried fields, sat silent and hunched. The boy watched them carefully, examining each riven face, but all the eyes were dead and dull and not one returned his interested stare.

They left the bus at a walled village near the border. The houses were crouched beneath their collective parapet, as though unconvinced that their neighbour, the enemy they had feared centuries ago, had neither gone away nor mended his ways. This was looking at the land of old China. The man and his boy walked beside the village, staring up at the dragon curved roof of its little hall of ancestors curling above the walls. Brigg watched Charlie taking in every sight. The boy's eyes were quiet and attentive but he asked few questions, possibly, Brigg thought, because he doubted if his father would know the answers.

The path climbed up the leg of a medium hill, until they could see easily into the enclave of the settlement, view the Chinese people moving among the close dwellings, see huddles of children, loitering dogs, and open fires. Chinese music from transistor radios sounded less violent, the cool rural air seeming to dilute it. An American pop song howled out through the local sounds, as the voice of some unbeliever might break through a religious incantation.

'There's some dead 'uns up here, Dad,' warned the boy quietly. They had been on these excursions before and had walked awkwardly by the lined up funeral urns of the village, set out neatly on a hillside, waiting until the spirits gave the blessing for the burial.

'Make sure you keep your hands off,' said Brigg like a man in a museum. 'We don't want any nasty accidents.'

'If you broke one of those pots, a dead Chinese would roll out, wouldn't he?' whispered the boy excitedly. 'I wonder how he would look.'

'Surprised, I should think,' answered Brigg. 'Anyway, don't let's even give it another thought. Just don't touch.'

'Fancy having to leave them like this, for years, until the spirits give the okay for anything to be moved,' said the boy.

'A bit like the British Army,' grinned Brigg. The boy laughed and the man laughed aloud too. Then they realized the offence they might cause so near the burial urns and hushed themselves.

They walked higher. The man's arm on boy's shoulder. Eventually the hill rolled out flat and they stood there looking out on the fields and farms and smoking villages, a ten-thousand-year-old landscape of green and grey. The large hills shouldered their way above the mounds and flat paddy fields; the sky, now broken into pools of dubious blue, the sun strolling intermittently across the land. A minor wind touched them and water in the harvested paddy fields lay leaden or silver depending on the passage of the sun.

Villages squatted on the brief plains, or in the

68

unspectacular valleys beneath the less muscular hills. Each had its wall, each housed its clan. Dry trodden paths sauntered over the countryside visiting each village in turn, and eventually joining the main road between the border and the coast. Around them like washed blankets left to dry were the market gardens, and beside the fragmentary lakes and ponds the speckled duck farms. There were people working on the plots and around the farms, but the empty paddy fields, the rice taken, lay idle under the cool sky.

'They managed to bash a tank into the village down the road, Dad,' said the boy conversationally.

'Right into the eating-house,' nodded Brigg. 'I thought they were going to get it out today.'

The boy said: 'They can't, after all, because they've worked it out that if they pull the tank out now, the eating-house will fall down.'

'That could be a bit inconvenient,' agreed Brigg.

'So they're leaving it there until next week, so they can do something to make the eating-house stay up.'

Brigg touched the boy's arm and they walked around the bevelled lip of the hill towards the east. 'The Chinese don't mind,' said Charlie. 'I suppose it brings in more people. Not every eating-house has a tank for one wall. Treacle Thompson and his cubs were going down there this afternoon to help the eating-house man tidy things up a bit and make it all safe.'

They had reached the limit of the hilltop path now. They stopped and looked across into the Chinese People's Republic. It was an utterly peaceful land-scape, the River Shumchun moving through the fields and a timid fence marking the frontier. China seemed unoccupied. At the furthest point were some dark, pointed hills, but the pastures that progressed from the river and the fence were vacant. Stripes of sun and cloud moved across them making them into a huge football shirt. The boy sniffed.

'Looks just like Aldershot,' he said.

'How can it?' said Brigg. 'Aldershot's a town. There's not even a wall over there.'

'I mean all around Aldershot,' corrected Charlie. 'The fields and that.'

'Hampshire,' said Brigg pedantically. 'I suppose it does really. A Chinese Hampshire.'

'Can we go and see the Chinese soldiers on the bridge?'

'Can we skip that today, Charlie? I want to get back a bit early. I'm going out tonight.'

The boy grimaced. 'Saturday night?' he said. 'I thought we could watch the telly.'

'Who needs a wife when you're around?' said his father. They began to descend the hill. 'I'm just going to take Sergeant Wilcox around a bit, that's all. Show him a few places of interest.'

'The Jiggery Pokery Club,' guessed the boy.

'How do you know about that?'

'Everybody does.'

'Everybody where?'

'At school. Will you take me there one day?'

'One day,' sighed Brigg. 'When they have a kids' matinée.'

'What do they do there?'

'Oh, drinking and music and that sort of thing. The usual.'

'Dancing?'

70

'Yes, there is a bit of dancing.'

'Do you dance?'

'I've had the odd waltz.'

'Will you dance tonight?'

'God, don't you go on once you get chewing at something!'

'Sorry.'

'I *might* have a dance tonight. That's if we go there.'

'Who will you dance with? Not with Sergeant Wilcox.'

'Oh hell, of course not. I suppose you think that's funny. I'll dance with one of the women there.'

The boy stopped as though he was reluctant to abandon the interrogation. They were adjacent to the burial urns now and Brigg apprehensively touched Charlie away from them. The boy looked at him challengingly.

'What are the women there for?'

'For dancing,' said Brigg embarrassed. 'For heaven's sake.'

'What sort are they?'

'What does that mean?'

'Well, are they, like, Chinese?'

'They'll hardly be Eskimos. Chinese and various sorts. Anyway, I don't know what all this is about. For God's sake, you're only nine years' old.'

'I'm ten soon.'

'That won't make much difference.'

'It will to me,' said the boy. Then he asked quickly: 'Do you want to run? We can if you want. We'll get the bus that's a bit earlier and we can catch the five o'clock train.'

Brigg smiled at his son's serious eyes. The boy

looked away shyly. 'I thought you wanted to hurry, that's all,' Charlie explained. 'If you're going out, you'll want a bath and shave and everything. You can't go to the Jiggery Pokery without getting cleaned up.'

His father said nothing more. Sometimes arguing with him was like talking back to a reciting poet. He pushed the boy gently and they went down the root of the slope until they reached the road beside the walled village.

'I think the man in the eating-house ought to buy that tank from the Army,' said Charlie. 'He'd get lots of people going there for food, just to see the tank.'

'I don't think we'd want to sell it to him,' said Brigg. 'The government are a bit funny about selling tanks to the Chinese.'

'It would save the Army the trouble of getting it out,' pointed out the boy logically.

'They'll get it out,' Brigg assured. 'Somebody will be in trouble otherwise.'

They heard a car coming along the single road, labouring up an incline hidden from them, travelling unhappily as though in the charge of someone unused to it. It appeared, red and low, like a ladybird, at the extreme corner of the village walls, and, taking new encouragement now it was on the flat, drove more surely towards them. The man and the boy moved to the side of the road. They could see that a woman in pale blue was driving the car. She slowed and stopped.

'Pardon me,' she called from an opening an inch wide at the top of the window. They could hear that she was an American. Brigg walked towards the car.

'Does this road go down to the main highway?' she asked. She was stretching up from her seat, with her mouth at the narrow aperture.

'Yes, it does,' answered Brigg. He grinned.

'I'm sorry,' she said. 'But I can't open this darned window any more. It's jammed. I guess I'm not used to these.'

'I'll try and shift it for you,' offered Brigg, but then Charlie, standing beside his father, quietly watching the woman inside the window, said: 'If you want to talk why don't you open the door?' He pushed his hands into his pockets and sniffed mildly.

She laughed and opened the door. 'Didn't think of it, that's why,' she confessed. 'It *is* easier like this.'

Brigg said: 'You looked like a prisoner trying to get a last message out.'

She was wearing a blue trouser suit. Her hair, dark and straight, parted like curtains over an earnest face set with notable eyes. He thought she must be in her late twenties.

'Are you going the same way?' she asked.

'We were rushing to catch the bus,' put in Charlie. 'He's in a hurry.' Brigg cautioned him with a finger on the shoulder and the woman laughed.

Brigg said: 'We're going to Sheung Shui to get the train. We have to get a bus from here.'

'Well, I'm going back to Hong Kong city,' she said in the peculiar American way. 'Can I give you a ride?'

Brigg felt Charlie's bony elbow knock his hip encouragingly. 'It's very good of you,' he said. 'We're going to the Army camp. Buller Barracks. It's more or less on your way.'

'Get in, then,' she invited. 'That's if you can stand

the way I'm ill-treating this poor little British automobile. I guess I'm just not accustomed to a gear-lever.'

Brigg sat beside her and Charlie sat in the rear seat where he whistled quietly and tunelessly.

'You're a soldier?' said the woman. They were reaching the end of the rural track now and turning south on the main road.

'Yes,' nodded Brigg. 'This is my Sunday best.'

'My husband's a soldier,' she said. 'Just now I'm waiting for him to come from Vietnam. His furlough should have started this weekend, but they've done something awful and all the schedules are wrong. So he won't be here for three weeks. And I just have to wait around.'

'You came specially from America to Hong Kong?'

'Yes,' she said quietly. 'I haven't seen him for a year.'

'Armies are not very good at family relations,' he said. 'The British Army doesn't do much fighting these days, so it takes its wives with it. I think some of the soldiers would prefer the fighting.'

She giggled engagingly. 'Is the British Army a good army?' she asked. 'Somehow I always picture them with red coats and fur hats – and with those pointed axes.'

'We only keep them for Sundays,' laughed Brigg. He heard Charlie laugh behind them. 'As for whether it's any good or not, I don't know. Good at what? Being an Army? It's all right I suppose, in parts, like the curate's egg. We've got keen soldiers, born soldiers some of them, and there's others that are not so good. It takes a war to find out what an army is made of.

And I, for one, don't find myself *that* anxious to find out.'

They drove into Sheung Shui and passed the railway station, then took the southern road, until they reached the garrison crossroads. Brigg thanked her and he and the boy walked back to the garrison past the village with the tank's nose still inside the eating-house.

'That was a nice American,' said Charlie eventually.

'Nice of her to give us a lift,' said Brigg.

'You should have asked her to go out with you tonight. Better than the Chinese women at that club.'

'You keep quiet about the club, my boy,' said Brigg tersely, 'or you'll be in trouble. Understand?'

'Understood,' agreed the boy and Brigg knew he meant it. Then he went back to his question: 'Why didn't you ask her?'

'Because, for a kick-off, she is a married woman,' said Brigg, wondering why he had not asked her. 'And she's waiting for her husband to come on leave from Vietnam.'

'But he's not come yet,' said the boy with steady logic.

'You have ideas that strike me as being a bit advanced, sometimes,' said Brigg. 'I don't like the look of your future.'

'You might have had a good evening instead of dancing and that at the Jiggery Pokery Club.'

'Drop it,' warned Brigg. 'I won't tell you again.' He changed the topic. 'Listen,' he said. 'You know when we were talking about the tank and the eating-house, earlier? I meant to ask you something.'

75

'What was that?' asked the boy.

'You said about Treacle Thompson going down there to help clear up. What was it you said about . . . cubs?'

'Cubs,' nodded Charlie. 'Didn't you know, he runs the cubs?'

'Cubs?'

'Yes, you know. Like little boy scouts.'

Brigg grimaced. 'For God's sake,' he said. 'Cubs.'

The boy and the man walked back in the failing light towards the pointless sentry on the useless garrison gate.

5

The Jiggery Pokery Club had been built by émigré Welsh Baptists at the end of the nineteenth century. It had been their church and with their inward eye still on the chill tombstone buildings in their home valleys, they had constructed it with a pointed door and roof and a cold, aloof face looking on to the exotic Chinese street. It looked something of a curiosity sitting so soberly among the cheap bright plaster and corrugated tin of that neighbourhood, some self-holy Celtic finger held aloft in a pagan world.

As more Baptists left their homeland so the community prospered, the sly Welsh proving a commercial match for the wily Chinese. Although the church was always adequate for their numbers, they decided to build another, and better, because the Hong Kong Methodists had done so. The original church became a church hall, and then a warehouse, a factory for making Chinese crackers, an officers' club (during the Japanese occupation), a prostitutes' rehabilitation centre (after the Japanese occupation), an Indian cinema, a dried fish market, a dancing academy, a photographic studio, and, eventually, the Jiggery Pokery Club.

Throughout all this diverse existence it had retained its episcopal hat roof, its raised-eyebrows' windows, and its church door, open and elongated like the mouth of a hymn-singer holding a high note. Its career as a night club had brought it more patronage and more activity than any of its other previous lives.

'Funny,' said Wilcox as they walked along the dirty, broken street. 'Fancy having a place like this in a church.'

'Not many people notice that it's a church,' said Brigg. 'It's always dark when they get down here and they don't notice the outside, only the neon sign. If they came down here in daylight half of them wouldn't be able to recognize the place.'

Cheesy light issued from the front door and there were silhouettes leaning against the iron railings that descended to street level. The engine room sound of a bad band with an over-elated drummer came out with the light. There was a girl with a beautiful river of black hair with her brown arms looped around an airman at the door. Her backside under bright silk trousers wriggled as she laughed. Wilcox nudged Brigg when he saw her but Brigg shook his head and pointed to his own grimacing face. It was rarely they had a good back *and* a good front. Half a dozen idle men were also standing along the railings and three or four young Chinese girls. There they looked strangely like children outside Sunday school.

'You choose the nicest places,' said Wilcox wrily.

'You wanted to come, not me,' argued Brigg. They had reached the ecclesiastical door now; the noise and the smell of the interior flooded out to them. 'I told you I only come during the old folks' nights during the week.'

'Will we get in?' said Wilcox doubtfully. 'I hope I didn't put my nice clothes on for nothing.'

'Everybody gets in,' said Brigg. 'As more come in the front so they heave the drunks out at the back.'

'It looks like a living death to me.'

Brigg hesitated. 'Do you still want to go? We can go along and have sausage and chips at the YMCA if you like?'

'No, I don't think I'm strong enough for that,' said Wilcox. 'We'd better dive in.'

Brigg went first, into the heaving people, the thick, hot smell and the noise. The main room was riotous, with the band's efforts bouncing from the sombre walls and a sheet of smoke waving between the dancing heads and the roof, high and arched and shying away from the mingled flesh below.

Like a man leading a patrol through perilous country, Brigg led the way around the right hand perimeter of the wall. They paused and Brigg got on tip toe to ascertain the route.

'You could get suffocated in here,' said Wilcox looking down the breast crevice of a big olive Eurasian girl sprawled in the chair below his face.

'People have,' shouted Brigg. He was setting off again through the congregation in the direction of the bar. They reached it just as two American sailors fell from their stools. Brigg solicitously steadied them on their way and watched them become drowned by the mass. Appreciatively Brigg and Wilcox climbed on to the warm seats. Six barmen were working like stokers, wrung with sweat and beer. Brigg called, 'Humphrey,' and one of the barmen turned his labouring frown to an Oriental smile and came towards them.

'Sarj Bligg. You come bad night.'

'I can see,' said Brigg. 'Two beers, Humphrey.'

The beers came quickly and Wilcox drank his while reading a stone tablet set irrevocably behind the bar and cut to the everlasting memory of Richard Lloyd Hughes and his wife Gwyneth of Caerphilly, founders of this church, who departed life in 1901 and 1905 respectively, in the certainty of peace, perfect peace.

Someone was shouting a song over the frenzy of the band now, but, as though by some act of mercy the voice was suddenly terminated and the musicians converted to something slower and lower.

'He soon shut up,' commented Wilcox looking across the heads to the band dais.

'They threw him off the stage,' Brigg predicted confidently. 'They do that. If somebody wants to get up to sing they let him and if he messes it up they grab him and sling him off the platform.'

From Brigg's left, a youthful, long-faced American leaned across to them. He was wearing a Hong Kong flowered shirt, his eyes were wearily ringed and his fair hair had fallen in a rough wet fringe. There was a thin line of sweat across his upper lip.

'Say, gentlemen,' he began uncertainly. 'Are you familiar with this place?'

Wilcox eyed the young man suspiciously. Brigg said: 'Well sort of.'

'I heard your British accents and I thought you would be,' he said enigmatically. 'You understand, I have a problem and I need a little help. I'm just in from Vietnam.'

'What's your trouble?' asked Brigg. 'Apart from Vietnam.'

'I need a woman.'

'You're right on course,' Brigg assured him.

'Sure, sure. I can see that. It's pretty difficult to forget what they look like even when you've been out of things for a period. But I don't just want to make a grab, see. I want a special sort of woman.'

Brigg was silenced by this confession. Wilcox leaned across and whispered. 'Perhaps he fancies a nice nun.' Brigg shrugged him off. 'What special sort?' he asked the American cautiously.

'Well, one that's . . . that's . . . trustworthy. You know? It seems like it's crazy, I know, but I don't want any disappointments or any trouble . . .'

'That's women,' shrugged Brigg. 'Disappointments and trouble.'

'I've had enough trouble,' said the young man not seeming to hear him. 'I'm up to my ass with trouble. So I want this woman to be . . .'

'Trustworthy – with big tits,' grunted Wilcox sourly. Brigg nudged him again.

'She's got to be a *decent* woman,' said the American letting go a profound breath, as though at last he had pinned it down.

'Decent,' nodded Brigg understandingly.

'Oh, sure, I want to screw her and everything, but I want to *talk* to her afterwards and I want to sleep sound as well and know she's not going through my pocket book, and I want her to make me some breakfast.'

'He doesn't want a whore, he wants a caterer,' suggested Wilcox. He stared at the epitaph panel across the bar. 'Or . . .' He turned to Brigg. 'How about Gwyneth Hughes?'

'Who's that?' asked the American immediately hopeful, looking around Brigg at Wilcox. 'Who did you say?'

Brigg calmed him. 'No,' he said placatingly. 'She's too quiet. And she's not here any more.'

'Don't you go and tell him about the twins,' Wilcox whispered fiercely in Brigg's ear. 'I may not have been in Vietnam, mate, but I need it as much as he does.'

'Don't worry,' Brigg said gently nudging him away again. 'I don't know,' he said doubtfully to the young man. 'Wait a bit.' He turned to look for the barman. 'Humphrey,' he called.

The Chinese, his smile as pale as the beer, came the length of the bar. 'Sarj Bligg? Two more?'

'Er . . . yes, please.' He hesitated, then turned to the American. 'Will you have one?'

'Thanks. Will you ask him? Maybe he knows?'

'I was going to,' said Brigg. 'Three beers, Humph.'

'What else you want?' asked the Chinese.

'Humphrey, this gentleman wants a nice, quiet, pleasant woman. Got any ideas?'

Humphrey's forehead contracted. His eyes went to splinters. 'He also want jig-a-jig?' he inquired.

'Yes, that as well, but he wants someone to . . . er, live with . . .' Brigg could feel the American nodding eagerly at his choice of words. 'To live with,' he repeated. 'Somebody nice who will look after him. He's been in Vietnam.'

'How 'bout my wife?' suggested the barman. He burst into huge laughter, but then saw the young man's serious and disappointed face. 'Ah so,' he said suddenly sage and wise. 'He want mummy. Yeah, sure. Ah so.'

82

'Also jig-a-jig,' Brigg reminded hastily. 'Nobody too flaked out.'

'Wait a tick,' said the Chinese quaintly. 'I see what can do.'

'Does he keep a stock in the cellar?' asked Wilcox.

'Dry up,' suggested Brigg. 'I'm trying to help this lad.'

'And I sure appreciate it,' said the youth earnestly. 'I truly do. I'm glad you understand.'

'I understand all right,' grunted Brigg. 'I've been looking for a woman like that all my life. If he gets one for you, maybe he can fix me up too.'

The American laughed tentatively. 'Well, I appreciate it,' he repeated nervously.

'Call it my contribution to the Vietnam war effort,' said Brigg.

'She'll be . . . er . . . clean, won't she?' said the youth with new anxiety. 'I mean . . .'

'He'll get her from the Chinese laundry,' muttered Wilcox into his beer.

Brigg said: 'There's no guarantee. It's going around, you know.'

'Yeah, I know.'

'They say it's coming from Vietnam,' said Brigg apologetically. 'But I expect Humphrey will know what he's doing.'

They added nothing more. The three of them sat at the bar waiting for Humphrey to return. The American's head was low over his drink and he quietly drew the outline of a woman in the sheen of spilt beer on the counter before him. Brigg watched him and noted that the figure was big-busted, matronly.

Humphrey did not keep them waiting long. To

Brigg's surprise he emerged from the other side of the hall, pulling along a plump, orange faced girl in a white European peasant dress done up like a sack about her middle. The little group, the girl, Humphrey, Wilcox, Brigg and the young man, stood still and awkward, for a moment in at the edge of all the frenzy. Then Humphrey asked, 'She do?' The girl smiled readily, revealing one black tooth, but well back at the side of her mouth.

'Well . . .' said the American shyly sliding from his stool. 'I guess she certainly will.'

'She looks nice and placid,' commented Brigg. Wilcox nodded slowly, knowledgeably like a farmer at a market.

'She Siamese,' offered Humphrey. 'She sew clothes, cook and all stuff like that.'

'Gee, Siamese,' enthused the American. 'That's a nice country.'

Brigg looked at Humphrey questioningly from the edge of his eye.

'Also good jig-a-jig,' Humphrey added assuringly.

'That seems like a pretty reasonable bundle,' muttered Wilcox into his beer. 'Bit thick down the bottom end. Thighland, I suppose you could say. But for darning socks . . .'

Brigg was closely watching the American and the girl. He was touched by the young man's gentle shyness and concern. The girl stood facing him, her face frank and happy, her smile puzzled. The American reached out awkwardly and touched the flimsy shoulder of her dress with her own substantial rounded shoulder beneath it. It was at once an introduction and an invitation.

She mounted his bar stool like a small obedient circus elephant, smiling all the time. Brigg said: 'We were just going, anyway. You can take this stool.'

'Thanks,' said the young man anxiously. 'And thanks for what you did. That was real good of you. Say, let me pick up your check.'

Brigg shook his head. 'All part of the service,' he said. He dropped the money for the drinks on the bar, and Humphrey, who had returned to the other side, picked it up. 'Just drop Humph a couple of dollars.'

'Sure, sure,' nodded the American.

They made to move off through the crowd. 'Cheers,' said Brigg. Wilcox made a small wave to the girl.

'Cheers,' echoed the American strangely. 'And thanks again.'

Brigg and Wilcox continued their patrol. 'I hadn't finished my drink,' grumbled Wilcox. 'You ought to have a bleeding set of bow and arrows.'

'She was all right, don't you think?' Brigg said.

'Bit tubby, but pretty apart from that black tooth.'

'Tubby,' agreed Brigg. 'But a thin bird is no good to a man just back from a war.'

'What about us? We didn't come here to do friendly turns for every other bugger. Can't you see the twins?'

'I've been looking,' said Brigg. 'I can't spot them.'

'They'll be fixed up,' grumbled Wilcox. 'We'll be too late to get them.'

'Don't worry,' Brigg assured. 'I know how they work. They don't fix up with anybody for the real thing until the end of the evening. It's midnight or more before they pounce.'

Then he saw them. They were at an alcove table,

reserved for the most profitable customers, with two expansive businessmen, large, with well-made suits and flashing wrist watches.

'The twins,' said Brigg to Wilcox indicating at the alcove. 'Let's wait here a minute.'

'Oh, yes,' breathed Wilcox. 'That's not bad at all.'

'Pearl is on the right and Ruby on the left.'

'I'll have Pearl,' said Wilcox. 'Or Ruby.'

'Wait till you're asked,' said Brigg.

'I don't much like the look of the opposition,' muttered Wilcox.

'Nor do I,' admitted Brigg. 'That sod with Ruby has got so much jewellery on his wrist he can hardly lift his glass.'

'What are we going to do?'

'What do you want to do, walk over and say "We are two impoverished soldiers and we want these two birds, so you rich blokes can just fuck off"?'

'Maybe if you phrased it a bit different . . .'

'They wouldn't be impressed.'

'I could handle those two hulks by myself,' grunted Wilcox. 'Look at them, all thick and flabby and flogged out because of too much expense account screwing.'

'Lucky bastards,' said Brigg.

'They wouldn't give us any bother.'

Brigg sighed. 'It's not the men I'm worried about,' he said. 'They could be handled, as you say. It's the twins, you idiot. They'd have us chucked out if we tried anything like that. They've got their reputations to think about.'

'So what do we do?'

'Stand here.'

'All steamed up like this?'

'Afraid so. I told you it was the wrong night. Charity night is Thursday.'

'Ah well,' said Wilcox philosophically. 'There's plenty more around, I suppose.'

'Is there?' said Brigg. 'There's plenty more blokes around too. Start poaching now and you could get me into trouble.'

'But surely . . .'

'If you want to get fixed with Chiang Kai-shek's grandmother I expect you could,' said Brigg. 'But there doesn't seem much for two young, handsome, virile lads like us.'

'But I notice you managed to get the Yank sorted out.'

'Humphrey did that.'

'Couldn't you ask him for us?'

Brigg snorted. 'Go and ask him yourself. Tell him you want your shirt washed.'

'Just my luck,' muttered Wilcox. 'I suppose we'll just stay here and get pissed.'

'I expect so,' nodded Brigg. 'I must be getting old, the smoke's hurting my eyes.'

'Well if you go blind it won't matter too much what you land up with,' said Wilcox miserably. He nudged Brigg. 'They're going to dance.'

The twins and their escorts, the two slight girls and the two big, sweating men, had risen in the alcove and were walking through the crowd towards the dance floor. They passed within touching distance of Brigg and Wilcox, but the girls made no sign of recognition.

'Are you sure you know them?' asked Wilcox suspiciously when they had gone by. The two pairs were dancing close together at the edge of the floor now.

'Know them? I sleep with them,' answered Brigg.

'They don't seem to remember.'

'Aw, come on, Willy, you know what hostesses are like. If they're with somebody they're not going to let on they know somebody else.'

'Especially when the first somebody has got a lot more dough than the second somebody,' agreed Wilcox cynically. 'Christ if we end up with sausage and chips at the YM I'll commit suicide.'

'Let's sit it out for a bit,' counselled Brigg.

'Not that we've got much choice.'

Wilcox ordered two beers from the waiter who arrived through the crowd like a magician materializing through a blank wall.

They stood and drank and looked around, pushed by passers-by, their heads in the cloud smoke, their ears battered by the assault of the band. Their eyes dropped as though on the same puppet string when a pair of exposed brown breasts floated by their view.

'There's old Murdoch,' commented Brigg nodding at the dance floor. 'Have you seen him in the mess?'

'No,' answered Wilcox grumpily. 'But he seems to have a bird.'

'His wife still lives up at the camp and he lives with a Chinese schoolteacher in the town.'

'That's handy,' said Wilcox immediately interested. 'What's the wife like?'

'Not bad. But a bit pathetic really. She pretends he's still there with her, and everybody knows he's not.'

'That piece he's got hold of there doesn't look much like a schoolteacher.'

Brigg shrugged. 'No, it wouldn't be. He comes here for some extra fun on top of his extra fun, if you know what I mean.'

'I wonder what his Chinese schoolteacher is doing?' said Wilcox thoughtfully.

'Go and ask him,' suggested Brigg. 'But don't annoy him. I have to rely on him for a lift back to camp when I come down in the week.'

Wilcox touched Brigg's sleeve. 'Wait a minute. One of the twins just winked at me. Over his shoulder.'

'It was probably just his cuff-links flashing in her eyes,' suggested Brigg.

'You're a pessimistic bastard.'

'I'm realistic,' returned Brigg. 'The girls have got to earn a living, and they'll earn more from one of them than the pair of us put together.'

'Money, money, money,' muttered Wilcox.

'No sense of values,' agreed Brigg. 'But there it is.'

The band wavered to the end of its slow noise and the mass of dancers on the floor broke as though a restraining string had been cut. The twins and their two men again passed close to Brigg and Wilcox. This time Pearl pushed out a dainty hand and secretly waved her fingers at Brigg. At the same instant there was a shout and a scream and an explosion of breaking glass from the direction of the bar.

'Ah,' breathed Wilcox stretching up. 'Someone's started a punch-up.' He looked relieved and interested.

'Is it a good one?' said Brigg craning over the heads of the people around him.

'Sounds like it. Can't see very much.'

'I hope our Yank friend isn't in it,' said Brigg. 'He doesn't look very strong.'

'Oh, Christ, you're not worrying about him! You sound like his dad. He's been in a war remember.'

'That's a war,' sniffed Brigg. 'This is a fight.'

The battle spread spectacularly. A large Chinese floor lamp tottered near the dance area, swaying and shaking as though it were dancing too, before falling into the crowd. Part of Humphrey's bar collapsed. The sliding and breaking of bottles and glasses sounded over the shouts of the growing number of combatants. Men were fighting everywhere, hitting out at previously peaceful neighbours, like people recklessly throwing fuel on to a bonfire. Women were screaming or laughing, crawling or already lying under the tables. Brigg glanced towards the twins. In their perched alcove, with their escorts, they had a fine view of the engagement. The band terminated with short jabs of sound and a clatter of escaping musicians.

The noise grew explosively in the crowded room. As though it were in the saloon of a liner in an ocean storm, the crowd swayed first one way and then another. Only the screaming drowned the swearing.

Brigg and Wilcox were on a small comparatively peaceful island at one side of the room. They observed with interest and enjoyment in the manner of guests at a specially staged production. The movement of the battle had cleared the view in front of them and Brigg saw the young American still sitting at the bar, his arm protectively around the chubby Siamese girl. As he watched a man in a big yellow shirt punched the American in the ear. The young man pitched sideways towards the girl. Brigg began to move forward.

'Leaving?' asked Wilcox.

'No. Our Yank friend's in bother.'

'He's not *our* friend. He's *your* friend.'

'Somebody's just hit him in the lug. Are you coming?'

'I'd better, if you're going,' said Wilcox. 'I'll get frightened by myself.'

Brigg glanced around once more at the twins. They and their bulky escorts were still safe in their alcove, like aristocrats on a hill observing a battle in the valley below. Brigg and Wilcox worked their way about the fringe of the fight, ducking and quietly pushing away groups of men in clinches far tighter and more passionate and more sincere than any of the women of the place had ever known.

As they went forward Brigg saw the youthful American recover from the blow. He turned on the bar stool and jabbed out a short heavy punch which struck his yellow shirted assailant between the eyes and dropped him poetically. His yellow shirt went down like a dipped flag. Brigg snorted approvingly. He saw the American swivel on his stool again, using it like a jousting saddle, to repel another attack. He was obviously beginning to enjoy it. His feet came around with the next manoeuvre of the stool and shot out to catch a marauding sailor amidships and sink him into the stormy crowd. Brigg heard the American hooting and guessed he was drunk too. The Siamese girl had remained on her stool and was regarding it all phlegmatically, occasionally wiping her pretty nose with a plump finger.

A man, flushed with recent victories, tried to hit Wilcox with his elbow. Brigg turned to help but Wilcox had quietly countered the blow and appropriately hit the attacker on the chin with his elbow. They moved forward another couple of yards, pushing people aside like débris, although the going was now more difficult, the fighters more congested. Brigg began to wonder how long it would be before the police, civil and military, would arrive. They usually let a situation like this exhaust itself before entering, since it made their job less difficult and dangerous and more enjoyable.

He looked towards the bar once more and saw the whooping young American swing his right arm like a boom in preparation for the delivery of a bolo punch on an opponent who had appeared on the other side of the bar. Brigg touched Wilcox and they stopped and watched with fearful anticipation as the huge looping punch came around, and the swivelled bar stool swung with the same hard impetus. On his axis the American curved the blow towards the man behind the bar. The man ducked it easily. The arm travelled on as the stool swung violently. The blow struck the placid Siamese girl and sent her tumbling backwards into the crowd.

'God,' murmured Brigg. 'He's thumped her.'

'No socks mended for him,' grunted Wilcox, pushing away a small Chinese who was pawing at him aggressively.

'We'd better get him out of here,' said Brigg moving quickly.

Wilcox grumbled but moved after him. The youth was trying to trace the girl among the piles of convulsive bodies around the bar, like a man searching bomb-debris for a loved one. 'Phyllis,' he was calling. 'Oh, God, Phyllis.'

'Phyllis?' Brigg queried, screwing up his nose. He reached the boy now. 'I think you'd better come back some other time.'

'Oh, Jesus!' howled the American. 'D'you think I killed her?'

'Probably,' interjected Wilcox cruelly. 'And in that case you'd better get out.'

'No! No! I just can't!' The youth was on his knees again, trying to sort out prostrate fighters. Brigg saw the girl crawling quietly away around the skirting of the bar. Then Wilcox pulled on his shoulder. 'They're hopping it, with the girls.'

'Bligg! Bligg!' Brigg could hear the calls above the now flagging noise of the conflict. Then he saw them, on the far side of the room, the two large and prosperous men, stepping carefully through the human wreckage, each with a twin across his shoulder. The men were laughing violently, the small girls were struggling and calling.

'The rotten bastards,' said Brigg solemnly.

'To the rescue,' said Wilcox with relish.

'No unnecessary fighting,' warned Brigg primly as they began to push and stumble across the room. 'We'll ask them nicely first.'

Wilcox was emitting small squeaks of anticipation as he hurried, like a runner crossing difficult terrain, but knowing that he is for the prize.

They confronted the men two yards from the

main door. 'Excuse me,' said Brigg politely. 'But you mustn't take the young ladies out of the building.' The men's big sweaty faces expanded with surprise.

'Vot?' one of them asked. 'Vot iss?'

'The ladies,' repeated Brigg pointing to the girls across their shoulders. He rounded his words carefully. 'They do not want to go.'

The man nearest Brigg creased his face into a gigantic frown. He shouted at Brigg in a large foreign voice. He spat as he shouted and it was a long sentence.

'What language was that?' asked Brigg of Wilcox as he wiped the spittle from his face.

'I don't know. Let's kick them in the balls.'

'All right,' agreed Brigg calmly. 'I'll do this one.'

They kicked together, both hitting the target brilliantly. The assault was effective in that it resulted in the two big men subsiding in breathless and surprisingly quiescent agony to floor level, like two camels dropping down at the end of a journey. Brigg and Wilcox walked around them and courteously helped the Chinese girls from their backs.

With no undue haste nor delay Brigg and Wilcox led the girls to the exit. Ruby and Pearl were frightened and dumb. A police siren was howling along the street. In the foyer of the club Sergeant Murdoch was trying to stem a bleeding nose with a khaki handkerchief. He saw them and muttered cryptically: 'Trust you, Brigg. Trust you.'

They walked outside. The air was damp and cooling. At the ecclesiastical railings their young American was kissing a nasty bump on the side of the Siamese girl's sorry face. His hands were massaging her motherly breasts and he was saying: 'I tell you, Phyllis honey, it was an accident. It was an accident.'

6

They took a taxi at the end of the street. At the open mouth of the Jiggery Pokery Club the oval helmets of the military policemen shone like eggs as they passed in and out of the light, bringing people with them, carrying them, dragging them, like men carrying out a rescue operation from some catastrophic place.

The twins sat between Brigg and Wilcox, together and chattering in their chiming Chinese. The two men conversed without difficulty above their heads.

'Let's hope we get the half-past ferry,' said Brigg. 'It's a long wait otherwise. My passion might cool.'

'Very romantic, a boat ride before a screw,' suggested Wilcox. 'It's not much of a night for it, though.'

'You're not *still* grumbling?'

'I meant the boat ride.'

The taxi ran along the harbour front. Big ships in the bay sat in pools of their own light. A small vessel moved in the darkness, its red lantern only to be seen, as though somebody were making a sweeping statement with a hand that held a cigarette. Lights were thin on the hills but closer and more brilliant lower down. In the town and the harbour, almost empty in that part, they were illuminating only a late night wasteland of pavement, wall and water.

'How are they going to manage this?' asked Wilcox.

'I was wondering that myself,' admitted Brigg. 'There's only one bed unless they've got a camp bed. If they have it's yours.'

'Thanks. Haven't you ever been there in a foursome before?'

'Never,' said Brigg truthfully. 'You're being honoured, take it from me.'

'So *you've* been paying twice.'

'Not really. They regard me as a sort of hobby.'

Ruby prevented Wilcox's reply. 'Who have who?' she inquired bluntly.

'Who have who?' repeated Brigg inadequately.

'Sounds like an old Chinese firm,' said Wilcox.

'Look,' said Brigg patiently. 'They don't understand your jokes. I fix you up with something choice and you rattle on like a bleeding pantomime comic.'

'Sorry,' said Wilcox seriously. 'No more jokes.'

'Who with who?' asked Pearl. 'What his name?' She dug a small unceremonious finger towards Wilcox.

'Wilcox,' answered Brigg. 'Sergeant Wilcox.'

Pearl contracted her cheeks. 'Wilcox,' she repeated doubtfully. 'You make sexy joke?'

Brigg laughed. Wilcox moved uncomfortably. 'No, funnily enough, dear, that's his name,' said Brigg.

'I like Wilcox,' announced Pearl.

'I like Wilcox,' decided Ruby also. 'Wilcox new.'

'Oh, Christ,' muttered Brigg.

Wilcox put his arm easily about both girls in the middle of the cab seat. He grinned at Brigg. 'I reckon you're going to end up having a quiet wank,' he said.

*

The Chinese house was still. There was no wind from the harbour that night. But the insidious damp of the waterfront was about the streets. The stairs like the rest of the house seemed thin and impermanent like some structure built on a stage. Wilcox surprised himself by poking his finger through one of the walls while they were waiting for Pearl to unlock the inner door.

Ruby turned on the uncertain light and Pearl went into the kitchen alcove and moved about making coffee.

'It's quite a *big* bed,' said Wilcox, reassured.

'Takes three comfortably,' said Brigg. 'I don't know about four.'

'We'll see,' sniffed Wilcox.

'That's what I'm concerned about,' answered Brigg. 'Seeing I like my bit of privacy.'

'Well I'm not standing out in the street until you've finished,' said Wilcox. He put his hand on Brigg's shoulder. 'I tell you what,' he promised.

'You won't laugh, if I don't laugh?' suggested Brigg.

'No. We both turn our heads outwards,' explained Wilcox. 'You look at that wall and I'll look at that one. Simple.'

Ruby solved it for them. 'Help with scleen,' she asked. 'Please to help with scleen.' From a corner she began to manoeuvre a fine and elaborate Oriental screen. It was silken and loose-hanging, suspended between two carved uprights on squeaking wheels.

'I'll take it,' said Wilcox moving quickly towards her. 'Don't go tiring yourself.'

He and Brigg led the long, unfolding screen across

the floor like a sick racehorse. It squeaked pitifully, so they lifted it and, to Ruby's directions positioned it along the length of the bed so that the bed was divided into two roughly equal halves.

This was not accomplished without some self-interested manoeuvrings, first by Brigg and then by Wilcox, one inching it a short distance to the right and the other nudging it back so that he regained the taken territory and a little more.

'I need a bit more room than you,' argued Wilcox.

'Why? We'll both be doing the same thing.'

'Not quite,' said Wilcox. 'I may well want to use my famous side-shuffle and ram technique and that requires a slightly wider area. I mean, I don't know – and don't take offence – but you seem to me to be a straight up-and-down man yourself.'

'How do you know!' snorted Brigg. '*Your* side-shuffle and ram technique! For all you know, *I* may be the greatest thing since Houdini. *I* may need this bed and *another* for *my* gymnastics, mate.'

'Last time, you go sleep, Bligg,' said Ruby cautioningly. Wilcox laughed and she moved the screen to the approximate centre of the bed. 'You with me,' she pointed to Brigg. 'Him with Pearl.'

'You tossed for it,' guessed Brigg.

'Dice,' nodded Ruby beginning to take off her clothes.

'And you won?'

'I lose,' she shrugged.

She told Wilcox to turn to the wall while she undressed. He walked towards the kitchen alcove where Pearl was singing a Cantonese nursery rhyme over the coffee. Ruby smiled her childish Chinese smile at Brigg and he too began to undress. She was naked now, small and dark and beautiful, untouched by her profession, sitting dreamily on the side of the bed. Her small hands reached out and cupped him underneath. She ran her nose along his penis like a mouse going hunting. She smiled up at his expression. 'I win dice,' she admitted charmingly. 'I like Bligg.'

They slipped into bed like an accustomed married couple. Then, with an elaborate knock on the screen, Wilcox appeared around its side, bearing two mugs of coffee. Pearl followed him with two more. Wilcox laughed when he saw them.

'What's so amusing?' asked Brigg ungraciously. 'Haven't you ever seen a man in bed with a Chinese knocker before?'

Wilcox said: 'It's just . . . well, it looks so funny. She's so small against you.'

'Yours is the same size,' retorted Brigg. 'And let me tell you something. They may be eighteen, and tiny with it, but they know more about what goes on than the pair of us put together. The Army doesn't look after *them*. They have to look after themselves. That one is old enough to be your mother.'

They drank the coffee, unspeaking, strangely like a secure family in some dull, safe house. Pearl and Wilcox sat on the edge of the bed; Ruby had pulled the sheet chastely about her small bosom and Brigg, conscious of his exposed chest, was being careful with the hot coffee.

Wilcox finished first. 'Well,' he said glancing into Pearl's coffee cup. 'I suppose the wife and I had better be going. We're keeping you folks up. Come on wifey, let's go home.'

100

Pearl looked at him, her face pinched with curiosity. 'What you say his name?' she asked Brigg pointing her finger at Wilcox.

'That's Mr Wilcox, Mrs Wilcox,' grinned Brigg over his coffee.

'Wilcox,' she said, frowning. 'Wilcox.' He could see that she still did not believe it.

The others went beyond the screen and Brigg stretched in luxurious quiet with Ruby. He was lying full on his back, her round face at his shoulder, and the soft skin of her upper leg hooked across his hardened member. They listened like eavesdropping children to the others, the rustle of their undressing, the note of the springs as Pearl sat or lay on their portion of the bed. He and Ruby looked at each other and suppressed their juvenile giggles. They heard Pearl whisper: 'Oh, elephant!' Brigg and his girl forced their mouths into the flesh of each other to stop themselves laughing. Eventually, when they had calmed, the light on the other side was extinguished.

'Goodnight, Jumbo,' called Brigg across the silken wall of the screen.

Wilcox whispered an obscenity like a fond goodnight.

'He funny,' giggled Ruby in Brigg's ear. 'If him sexy like he funny, my sister happy.'

As though to dismiss the subject of Wilcox she ran her tongue into Brigg's mouth and turned it like a little worm tail around his teeth and gums, finally letting it rest on his tongue. She was so small he was able to reach right underneath her from her front to the fold of her back side. For a while she rode on his

101

arm like a girl on a swing. He let his middle finger move sweetly down the trench of her buttocks until it was enveloped with the damp nest of her underneath. His fingers toyed with her, feeling her already pliable place beginning to respond to his touches.

She put her hands to him and began to pull him beautifully through her palms and fingers as though she were gently feeding a rope. He arched to his knees so that she could do it all the more and worked his mouth into her pink breasts. She wriggled and stirred. His hand went down and between her thighs again and he cupped it and flattened it and cupped it again keeping time with a throbbing that was as distinct as a heartbeat.

'You sleeping, Briggsy?'

The voice whispered theatrically across the screen. Brigg grunted with annoyance.

'Sorry, Briggsy,' croaked Wilcox amiably. 'I thought you might have dozed off.'

'I haven't,' replied Brigg raising his mouth from Ruby's nipple.

'This Pearl's got bloody great long fingernails,' said Wilcox.

'Tell him to shut up, will you,' whispered Brigg to Ruby.

'Bligg say shut up,' bawled Ruby immediately her aware self again. 'Ruby say shut up, also.'

'Sorry,' said Wilcox cheerfully. 'Hope I didn't interrupt anything.'

'I'll interrupt your life in a minute,' threatened Brigg.

'Aw, sorry. Goodnight, Briggsy.'

Brigg said nothing but lowered his body into the heart of Ruby's open legs. She still had him in her small hands and she now, piece by piece, fed him into her. He was glad they had taken their time and not been upset by Wilcox. He was fully buried within her now and she shifted beneath him showing in her round sweet face the full experience. He could not believe she was pretending as she did with all the others.

He began to move and Wilcox began to move a moment later. The bed creaked like the overworked engine of an old paddle steamer, first one side and then the other, as their opposite movements began to gain determination. Ruby was making little gasps and her sister was making small cries on the other side. The screen between them began to rock and wave adventurously. Brigg rested, unwilling to go through to a climax immediately, and put off by the clumsy waving of the screen.

Wilcox stopped too. 'Have you done, Briggsy?' he whispered.

'Wrap up,' grunted Brigg.

'Sorry, but I was all put off by the noise from your side. She sounded like she was suffering. Are you sure you've not got it in crooked?'

'I'm going to kill you soon,' said Brigg.

There was no immediate response but then, abruptly Wilcox's cheerful head was thrust up above the screen.

Ruby squealed and Brigg looked over his bare shoulder. 'Oh for Christ's sake,' he said.

'Look, sorry,' protested Wilcox. 'But you've got to admit this is not all that satisfactory.'

'It was until you started fucking about,' snorted Brigg.

'Well, *I* didn't think so. And I'm paying half, after all.'

'I'm *not* swopping,' warned Brigg.

'I wasn't going to suggest that we did,' sniffed Wilcox. 'I doubt if mine would anyway.'

'What do you want, then?' Brigg moved himself on to his elbows and pulled the sheet carefully about Ruby who was watching Wilcox with amazed interest.

'It's all this rock and roll business. First your side and then mine.'

Brigg stared at him. 'What do you want me to do, wait until you've finished?'

'No, no. Nothing like that. Don't get so shirty, Briggsy. I thought that we could coordinate it a bit better that's all.'

'Coordinate it?'

'Yes, start off together and try to keep time. At least we'd get an equal movement and this bloody screen wouldn't flap about like the sail of a ship.

Brigg looked down wearily at Ruby. She had lost interest in the exchange and was examining her red nails. She looked up at Brigg, sulky under the sliced lids of her eyes. Wilcox emitted a short exclamation. 'God, she's tugging,' he said glancing down at Pearl. 'Well, what do you say?'

'All right,' agreed Brigg. 'Anything. But stop buggering about, will you?'

Wilcox disappeared beyond the screen like a marionette. Brigg smiled wanly at Ruby's half-closed almond eyes.

'You come back now?' she inquired sulkily.

'I'm back,' confirmed Brigg.

'Still good?' she inquired.

'Still good,' confirmed Brigg. He moved into her and felt the closeness, the well-being, flood through him. It was like a workman going home to a warm kitchen. His loins pressed to her, their stomachs rubbed, their legs were locked, her breasts sniffed at his ribs. Brigg kissed her with tenderness and she came out of her sulk and responded.

'Are you ready, Briggsy?' inquired Wilcox from beyond the screen. Brigg realized he had meant it.

'Ready,' he moaned.

'Right. Start from now. Ready, steady, go!'

Ruby said nothing and Brigg began obediently, timing his thrust and the creaky give of the bed to the like movement from the other side. The springs twanged heavily and then relaxed, twanged again and relaxed. Brigg was breathing strongly, his chest now forced down on the girl's breasts. Her face was contracted and her eyes screwed up. He went on his journey, moving purposefully now, in and out, in and out, forgetting all about the timing and the idiot Wilcox. In and out, in and out. Then he was riding free and away from any restraint, his engine running away with him. The girl was dribbling, silvery from the side of her mouth, and rocking her head to and fro.

Brigg was half conscious of a similar generation of pace and force from the other half of the bed. As he increased his pressure and persistence so did Wilcox with Pearl. The bed was bouncing like a raft in a storm. Suddenly the screen toppled on to Brigg and

105

Ruby. It made no difference. They were on the way home. So was Wilcox.

His voice howled delightedly across the Chinese room: 'Race you, Briggsy! Race you!'

7

On Sunday mornings the camp slept late. The ritual changing of the guard on the main gate took place at a Sabbath shuffle, there being no inspecting officer and the Colonel could be expected to be in his billet and bed two miles away. The only other movement, as an early and repentant sun flooded the landscape of the New Territories, was an engineer major who wandered down to view the tank embedded in the wall of the Chinese eating-house, and Joss and Wilberforce, the horticultural queens, who delved in the square formal garden outside the guard-room. They were not on punishment fatigues. They were being given bonus money for tending the garden since they had both the aptitude and the creative desire.

On this Sunday they called to each other in pleasant voices about the progress of the shrubs and flowers and hopped about, crouched like wallabies, tending to plants and rooting out weeds which had shown themselves during the week.

They were watched with professional gloom by Sergeant Billing of the night guard, itching irritably after hours in a sagging camp cot, and Sergeant Rolph of the day guard who was in an ill-disposition at having to rise and shave so early on the day of rest.

'*They* seem to get up early enough,' commented Sergeant Billing.

'Getting paid,' grunted Sergeant Rolph. '*And* it comes out of the amenities fund. Christ, in the old days they'd have found some reason to put them on a charge, couple of bum boys like that, so that they'd be doing it anyway. All for nothing.'

'The old man's always pleased as hell with this bit of garden,' yawned Billing. 'He says how nice they do it. Every Monday he takes a special look. He says they've got green fingers.'

'Brown fingers with those two,' said Sergeant Rolph unfeelingly.

'Ha! You're dead right there, Herbie. I'll be away then now. Don't let those nasty yellow Chinese come over and capture the camp now, will you?'

'They wouldn't do that on a Sunday,' said Sergeant Rolph. 'Too unsporting.'

'Cheerio, then,' yawned Sergeant Billing. 'See you in the mess.'

'Right, Dicky. Off you go.'

Sergeant Billing retreated at a tired march. Joss and Wilberforce looked up from their horticulture and wished him good morning. He snorted in return. They returned to the earth.

By nine-thirty the sun was benign, but intermittent having become entangled in some clouds that were coming in from the islands of the China Sea. Lance-Corporal Ferris emerged warily with his secret dog and took it for a surreptitious walk. He only did this in daylight on a Sunday, knowing that the camp would be asleep, all his other walks with the animal taking place under cover of darkness.

Colonel Simmons was out unusually early on his unofficial horse on this Sunday morning, for he had invited officers and senior non-commissioned officers to a midday drink at his house. By ten o'clock he was prancing across the watercolour countryside, urging the horse on, jumping hedges and demolishing walls which Chinese peasants had patiently built. Ferris and his mounted Commanding Officer almost collided on the perimeter of the camp, the lance-corporal guiltily trying to conceal his dog behind his legs. The dog barked at the Colonel's horse and the Colonel waved cheerfully.

At ten-thirty Private Treacle Thompson clad in a small scout-master's uniform led a parade of Chinese wolf cubs through the back alleys of the camp, between the moribund ranks of asbestos offices and corrugated workshops. Their infiltration was predictably easy and unchallenged. Mrs Murdoch, weeping alone on her bed because her husband was with his Chinese schoolteacher, saw them, but only through her Sunday tears. Her mixed mind, revolving with anger, vengeance, nostalgia and remorse, failed to acknowledge the strange sight. Farther along the row of married quarters Violet Love, on cue, stood in the front room window massively blocking any view her father might have had of the invasion. Her father snapped at her. Her mother called: 'Vi, get out of the window. Your dad's trying to read the paper.' Violet sniffed massively and moved aside like an obliging storm cloud.

By this time Treacle and the Hooded Falcon patrol had sidled by. He led them with shiny chin up, pimples glistening, blue eyes sharp and steady. His uniform, with its array of badges and emblems, its lanyard and whistle, felt more significant, more protective, than his everyday army denims. Today he had three stripes upon his sleeve. Today he was the commander.

Sturdily, but with an occasional prudent glance around an exposed corner or up at a dangerous window, he led the patrol. He blushed the colour of his own pimples when he saw the vast Violet occupying the window of her house, and, hoping that she still watched, he held up a ginger-haired hand at the corner by the transport sheds and the cubs halted while Treacle pushed forward with stealth to reconnoitre.

The Chinese cubs stumbled behind their leader. Undersized children, with trusting almond eyes, and naked feet, they wore uniforms provided from his own pocket. Some were unsure of the object and usefulness of what had surprisingly become a regular weekend matter in their own village, only interrupted by the leader's absence on British Army business, which, in truth, usually meant he was labouring in the tin room. But their village parents recognized that the uniforms brought by the strange, tiny, soldier, were far better quality than anything the boys wore during the week. Although Treacle shrewdly gathered them together and took them away at the end of each meeting, it was felt that sooner or later the village boys would gain them for their permanent possession.

Skirting the flank of the barrack square bordered by the deserted transport sheds, the wolf cub patrol flicked along the shadows of a grove of miserable military trees and emerged at the door of Treacle Thompson's own barrack block. He again raised a flat hand in the manner of a commander of US Cavalry, moved forward himself and then called the patrol to follow him. They trooped, low but sturdy, into the sleeping barrack room, among the zombie beds of soldiers thick in sleep after a traditional army Saturday night.

'Pat-roool, halt!' It was a low, nervous, piping order from Thompson, but determined too. The voice of a man who has convictions but generally fails to communicate them to his fellows. The ten pairs of bare feet padded on the floor. There were seven sleeping soldiers in the barrack room, some buried in sheets and blankets, others draped and dropped in odd and occasionally unseemly attitudes.

There was a discernible tinge of stale beer and hopelessness about the atmosphere. The Chinese children looked around, their leaf-shaped eyes nervous and surprised, each Oriental mouth with a droop of apprehension.

'Form a circle, lads,' said Thompson blinking encouragement. His tone was reduced but dogged. The Chinese understanding the motion of his hand more than the words, grouped themselves in a ring in the clear area near the door. They did so with tenuous trust in their leader, still eyeing the silent soldiers over the green shoulders of their wolf cub jerseys.

Treacle went to the centre of the ring and put up two fingers of each hand to the side of his ginger head like the erect ears of a rabbit or an owl. The cubs were now watching him, knowing the familiar sign. He

111

lowered himself, knees going outwards, sitting back on his heels. The cubs, like a circle of animals, copied him. None of the sleepers had moved.

'*Ark-a-la! We'll do our best!*' incanted Treacle.

'*Ark-a-la! We do our best!*' copied the cubs with difficulty.

Still nothing stirred in the room.

'*We'll dyb, dyb, dyb,*' recited Treacle more surely in the traditional wolf cub way.

'*We'll dob, dob, dob,*' answered the cubs in singing tones.

Hairy Harrison, foul with sleep and ill-remembered beer, lifted himself on to a thick elbow. Uncomprehendingly he watched the ceremony.

> '*We'll dyb, dyb, dyb.*
> '*We'll dob, dob, dob,*'

recited Treacle and the little cubs.

'Fuck me,' breathed Harrison thickly. He levered his gross body up on to both elbows, squeezed his eyes tightly into their hair-hung sockets. He opened them minutely and, seeing that the vision was still intact, then fully. 'Fuck me,' he said again.

Not taking his eyes for a moment from the incanting circle he reached out blindly to his left to touch the bed of Wilson.

'Nancy. Nancy,' whispered Harrison tugging at his sheet.

'I'm watching it,' replied Wilson quietly. 'The little cunt's gone potty.'

Treacle heard their whispers and his eyes flicked towards their beds, but he bravely continued with the

112

ceremony. *'I promise, on my honour to do my best, for God and the Queen . . .'*

The sheet shrouded forms around the room were now moving. Men blinked, sat up, and fell backwards again, then looked. Men's hands went to their mouths convinced that the dreaded sot's hallucinations had started, that their imaginations were rioting.

> *'. . . to help other people at all times,*
> *And obey the Wolf Cub Law!'*

Corporal Bainbridge, a simple soul, crossed himself and muttered, 'Dear Jesus in Heaven.' In the next bed, Pardoe, hoarse from the night's singing, croaked, *'Dyb, dyb, dyb,'* to himself as though trying to recall some magic rhyme from far forgotten childhood. All the soldiers in the room were now awake and watching. Had they been covered by an enemy armed with machine guns, they could not have remained more still, more impotent.

Eventually Bainbridge took command. His habitual dusting of himself with talcum powder each night before retiring caused it to fall from his service pyjamas like dandruff as he left his bed. He went uncertainly towards the circle, leaving a white train running from his pyjama leg dragging along the floor.

'Thompson,' he asked. 'What's going on?'

Treacle dropped his rabbit fingers from the side of his head and motioned the boys to do likewise. The cub patrol rose from its crouch and turned to watch the powdery Bainbridge with awe.

'Well, what?' demanded Bainbridge.

Treacle faced him bravely. 'It's cubs,' he said.

He looked squarely at Bainbridge as though the corporal, enlightened, should now return to his bed.

'Cubs?' said Bainbridge. 'What d'you mean, cubs?'

'Wolf cubs,' extended Treacle.

Pardoe began to laugh. Then came a hoot, and soon all the soldiers were rolling and howling in their beds. The group in the centre floor remained frozen faced.

'I will report you for this,' said Bainbridge inadequately.

'For what?'

'Cubs. Having cubs in the barrack room.'

Thompson looked at him strongly. 'It's my hobby,' he said.

'I don't care what it is. You can't have bloody cubs in the barrack room.'

'I can,' said Treacle. 'On Orders last week it said that because of the closure of the hobbies room in the canteen, hobbies may be carried on in the barrack accommodation.'

'Come off it, Thompson. That means reading and matchbox collecting and that stuff, not this sort of caper.' He pointed at the cubs. 'Besides which, they're Chinese!'

Treacle looked at him like a persecuted saint. 'What difference does that make?' he asked, small but full of dignity. 'The boy scout and wolf cub movement is worldwide. It doesn't take any notice of races.'

'Well, the bleeding British Army does,' snarled Bainbridge. 'You can't just bring a whole lot of fucking Chinks into a military camp. You'll be having their mums and dads up here next.'

'I'm hoping that will come,' sniffed Treacle.

114

'Oh, Christ,' said Bainbridge. He looked down and saw he was standing in a snowfield of his own talc. The Chinese boys were watching it with amazement. 'Look, get out of here, and take these kids with you. Otherwise I'll get the sergeant of the guard. I bet you never came in the gate, did you?'

Treacle knew he was caught. With dignity he ordered: 'Hooded Falcon pa-trol. Right-turn! Follow me.'

The Hooded Falcon patrol was suitably confused by the order, but once their leader made for the door they followed him with a rush. Great howls and foul echoes of laughter followed them from the barrack room, the uncouth sounds spreading across the empty parade ground. Treacle kept his little chin high. He marched them from the camp by the way they had entered. On the way they passed Ferris and his secret dog returning from their walk.

Ferris, from habit, inadequately hid the dog behind his legs as the oddly attired Thompson came around the corner. He nodded recognition and then stepped back in astonishment as the file of wolf cubs followed. They marched by gamely, not looking at him or the half-concealed animal. Ferris watched them troop around the next block, his dog had a squirt against an Army sapling, and Ferris, full of stupid wonder, walked back to the awakening garrison.

8

At noon the medical officer Major Stevens and his
wife rang the off-key musical chimes on Colonel
Simmons' door. They were the first guests to arrive
and Mrs Stevens, a well-intentioned but agitated
woman, set about helping the stoic Mrs Simmons to
add what they liked to call European touches to the
cocktail party arrangements made by the Chinese
servants. This added nothing, neither in taste nor in
practicability, but they liked to do it.

A Sunday party was unusual, particularly with the
senior NCOs and their wives also invited, but the
Colonel had his reasons.

Although their wives were friends, the Colonel and
his medical officer had never been wholly comfortable
in each other's presence. Colonel Simmons had never
fully trusted him since he heard that he, an officer, had
requested a record on *Family Favourites* and that the
BBC had actually played it. It was not the sort of thing
he wanted to recall, so he poured the Major a sherry
and hoped the other guests would hurry.

'Is Sergeant Billing's girl all right now?' inquired
the Commanding Officer who could think of nothing
else to say. 'It was she wasn't it who was hypnotized at
school by Brigg's lad?'

'As far as can be seen, she's all right again,' said

Major Stevens gloomily. 'Dangerous business though. Little devil put her right under. I couldn't revive her at all.'

'The lad himself brought her round, didn't he?'

'Under severe pressure,' grumbled the medical officer. 'Little devil was all for leaving her in a trance until his own safe conduct had been guaranteed. Indeed that's what we had to do in the end, promise him no punishment if he brought her round. Little bastard, if you'll excuse the expression.'

'What expression?' asked the Colonel absently.

'Well . . . er . . . little bastard,' Major Stevens reminded him lamely.

'Naturally, naturally, old chap. Very tricky from a medical point of view, I suppose. Bright lad though. I thought he might be the star turn of our concert when the Defence Minister is here. Be a bit different, don't you think? We'll have to do something to keep that bastard entertained, if you'll excuse the expression.'

'Yes, of course, sir. But I feel that to encourage young Brigg in these practices is trifling with the unknown.'

'*He* seems to know what he's doing,' commented the Colonel tartly. 'He brought the girl and the other kids out of their trances, didn't he?'

'Oh, yes, sir. But one can't tell about the long term effects of an experience like that. I've told Mrs Billing that if she sees her little child going glassy-eyed at any time to send for me.'

'Better to send for young Brigg!' chortled Colonel Simmons.

To the medical officer's relief, as well as that of his superior, the door played its tune again. It was Major

Fortune, and three other single officers from the mess.

'Not got that tank out yet, sir,' said Fortune cheerfully. 'Still stuck. I bet Command Workshops will be hopping. They lost their football final too.'

'Serves them right,' said the Colonel unfeelingly. 'Leaving a tank stuck in somebody's house. Damn thing will be obsolete before they get it out.'

Regimental Sergeant Major Love arrived next, with Mrs Love hanging somewhat excessively on his arm. His boots were brilliant; they pushed outwards in a sturdy 'V' as he stood, the roots of a pink unimpressive figure. The long-windowed room was filling now and the Colonel and his wife moved about dutifully handing out little parcels of small talk, polite with the officers, particularly polite with the NCOs.

But there was a detectably awkward feeling about the party, not only because the caste system made it impossible for anyone to enjoy themselves, but also because very few knew why the function had been called in the first place.

The Commanding Officer watched the sherry decanters with casual but well-judged glances, like a man under siege counting his ammunition. When he thought it was time, he tapped a Ministry of Defence supplied table and gained the sort of silence only achieved when everyone is waiting for it.

'Ladies and gentlemen,' said Colonel Simmons, leaning back against the table and then, distrustingly, testing it for his weight. 'I've taken the unusual course of asking you to drag up here today, when you undoubtedly have tons of other things to do, because I need the help of each and every one of you, wives as well as officers and NCOs, to ensure the success of something which will be upon us in a few short weeks – namely the visit of Her Majesty's Secretary of State for Defence.'

There was a politely concerned rumble and some shifting of feet and glasses in the room. The Colonel sighed. 'I had hoped . . . No, that is the wrong way to put it . . . I had *expected* that the visit of the Minister would be of only a few hours' duration, just a matter of a parade and his being shown around the garrison, but now I find that he will be our guest for an entire weekend, Friday evening until Sunday evening. We must, therefore, do something to entertain the wretched man.' He looked up benignly, anticipating the sporting laughter that greeted the remark. Then he continued: 'On the Saturday morning we will have a parade and inspection, and I know that everyone will be working hard for that and that the men will be at their very peak. In this direction I propose to increase the drill periods to four a week from next week. We seem to have become a little, er . . . rusty in that particular department. It's no great secret among us that two squads actually collided last week. This unit cannot afford to let that happen again.

'On Saturday afternoon we shall have to put on some sort of manoeuvre or exercise for the Minister, and if anyone can think of anything impressive in this direction then I, for one, will be grateful.

'On the other hand, and I hope it will be the other hand, he may simply ask to be conducted up to the border to have a peek at Peking.'

A puff of laughter greeted the pun. The Colonel did not look displeased. 'On Sunday we shall have a church parade, with some good singing, I hope, Padre . . .'

He glanced fiercely at the Reverend Captain Church-Smith who swallowed and then said courageously: 'I will need volunteers for the choir, sir. The present system whereby men on punishment fatigues either work in the kitchens or sing in the choir on Sundays is not adding to the singing standard.' He paused, then decided to say it all. 'Indeed, sir,' he went on, 'this system brings entirely the wrong type of man into the choir. Only this morning I distinctly heard them singing their own obscene and unofficial words to the anthem.'

'Right,' said the Colonel decisively. 'Mr Love.'

'Sir,' beamed the RSM.

'Make sure we have some good singers for the choir. Surely we've got a few Welshmen in the place.'

'They're cautious, sir, the Welsh,' replied the RSM defensively. 'Last time we asked for Welsh volunteers they thought they were going to sing and we had them peeling leeks.'

'They've lost confidence, eh?'

'I think that's the case, sir.'

'Well, get them anyway. We must think of some inducement to get men in that choir. I want the Defence Minister to hear some good hymn singing even if the drill is not so hot. That really leaves us with Friday night and Saturday night to fill. Well, I suggest that we have an officers' mess dinner on the Saturday and possibly an all-ranks' concert on the Friday after the Minister has had a bite to eat here.'

He leaned forward, like a pointer. 'What I want to impress on you is . . .' Behind him, on the table the telephone rang. The adjutant moved impressively behind his chief and took up the instrument. He listened, then said: 'This is Major Fortune,' and impatiently listened again. A professionally stern look set into his young face. 'One moment,' he ordered. 'Stay on the line.' He moved closer to the Colonel.

'There appears to have been some Chinese infiltration of the garrison, sir,' he said importantly but quietly. 'A patrol of uniformed men.'

'Good Christ!' exclaimed the Colonel. 'When? Here, give me the phone.' He took the receiver. 'Hello, Sergeant. Yes. What has happened? . . . Yes . . . Yes . . . What time? God, that's an hour ago. Mrs Murdoch saw them? And Mrs Brice. Both . . . separately . . . Yes, Sergeant. Call out the guard. Sound the general alarm. I'll be there in a moment.'

He straightened dramatically and faced the people in the room. 'There appears to have been Chinese in the camp this morning,' he said sternly. 'Uniformed, according to two witnesses. I want every man back with his platoon and every woman back with her family. Make sure that no one touches any strange object which may be lying around. It could be a mine. Now . . . Let's get to it quickly!'

There was an impressive rush from the room. Some glasses were knocked over and one of the women began to whimper. Jeeps and cars were started up outside.

'Will you be taking your horse, sir?' inquired Fortune with solicitous stupidity. The Colonel scowled at him. 'For God's sake get your jeep, man, and stop asking bloody silly questions. That's a ceremonial horse. This could be a war! Come on, man, move!'

Fortune ran out, the last of the general rush. The

Colonel kissed his wife and went after him. Mrs Simmons and Mrs Stevens looked around the sherry-smelling room. The Chinese servants began to sweep up the broken glass and empty the ashtrays.

'I do wish Mr Love would not wear those enormous shiny boots,' sighed the Colonel's wife. 'Everyone else wears shoes, and it *is* Sunday. I'm always afraid he'll damage the floor.'

'Do you suppose it's serious?' Mrs Stevens inquired conversationally. 'The emergency, I mean.'

Mrs Simmons blew out her cheeks. 'Not a hope, dear.'

'Jack's been in the Army for years,' sighed Mrs Stevens, 'and he's not once heard a shot fired in anger.'

'My husband has been in twice as long,' said the Colonel's wife. 'And he has never so much as heard a shot fired in a fit of pique.'

By one o'clock, the emergency was over and the truth was abroad. Brigg and Wilcox with other sergeants in full battle regalia clattered clumsily into the mess. Wilcox bought the beers and Brigg began to laugh.

'Cubs,' he hooted. 'Chinese cubs!'

Wilcox grinned. 'Not many of this lot think it's funny,' he said. 'You should hear them at the bar. They all want to put the poor little bugger in front of a firing squad.'

'Poor, poor sergeants,' murmured Brigg. 'Had their Sunday lunch messed up and missed their messages from loved ones at home on *Family Favourites*.' He mimicked: 'Dear Enid, miss you all very much and we're looking forward to the summer of 1978!' He drank some beer. 'Having to put on all that strange warlike clobber and get out those nasty dangerous guns. Poor souls!'

Wilcox laughed into his beer and made it bubble. 'Holy Jesus,' he chortled. 'I think I'll remember till I kick it, the way the little chap . . . what's his name . . .?'

'Thompson,' said Brigg. 'Known as Treacle.'

'Thompson, Treacle Thompson,' repeated Wilcox, savouring it. 'God when he trotted out and said it was his wolf cubs, I thought Love was going to knock him down and stamp on him right there and then. And the Old Man nearly had a seizure.'

Brigg nodded sagely: 'I think he deserves immediate promotion, not jankers, which is what he'll get. That will be no change for him anyway, the poor little devil is always washing up in the Tin Room. God, he's the first one in this crappy unit for I don't know how long who has shown the least initiative in any direction. He's also the only one who has ever made any kind of friendly contact with the local Chinese. And, what's more, he's shown once and for all what a joke the security is in this camp. I think he ought to be given a bloody commission.'

'He'll get jankers,' said Wilcox confidently. 'He'll be in the Tin Room for the next month. I don't think I've ever noticed him before.'

'Well, let's face it, he's not exactly riveting,' said Brigg. 'Poor scrabby undersized sod. I think they keep him more or less hidden away because he's not much of an advertisement for the British Army. Mind you, he's got to be pretty terrible for them to do that.'

'He hardly looks like one of The Professionals,' nodded Wilcox. 'Professional midget, maybe.'

'He's very determined, though,' said Brigg. 'He's not strong, but he's determined. We had a sort of exercise over on Stonecutters Island one Saturday. One of those divisional things where everybody from Hong Kong is involved. One of the things we had to do was go across a creek on a rope. You know, the usual dangling business. It was quite hard, because everybody thought they were bloody commandoes that day. Half of this lot couldn't walk for a week. But old Treacle stuck it. He got half way over the creek, his little monkey hands around the rope and with all his heavy equipment festooned around him, and then the rope sagged. Some joker on the far bank probably slackened it purposely, I don't know. But Treacle just disappeared under the water, with just his arms and hands and the muzzle of his rifle sticking out. His hands were round that rope and he was going hand over hand like mad. Gradually he got towards the other bank and he came up like a submarine. He couldn't have been far off drowning. But would he take any help? Would he hell! He just crawled up the bank and staggered up to where his defensive position was supposed to be. And he got down there and cleaned his rifle and he was sicking up dirty water all the time. He's the sort of soldier who gets the Victoria Cross, our Treacle.'

Wilcox yawned. 'All this warlike activity. I'll be in my kip this afternoon,' he forecast confidently. 'The twins' bed wasn't exactly Slumberland, was it.'

'It's not really meant for sleeping,' agreed Brigg. 'I should think it gets too much banging about for that.'

'Really it's not the answer, you know,' said Wilcox reflectively.

'What's the question?' asked Brigg.

'No, I mean, going off like that and paying for it from a couple of tarts.'

'Don't say you want your money back.'

'No, nothing like that. I was *well* satisfied on the night, believe me. It's just that the business I told you about before keeps coming into my mind. You know, with the American tourists.'

Brigg smiled indulgently: 'Ah, yes,' he remembered. 'You were going to be the Army's first gigolo. Chatting up and charming all those rich, blue-haired, Yankee ladies who tour the world just looking for a British Army sergeant with a big dick and a bigger ego.'

'I think it could work,' said Wilcox earnestly. 'I had a look around yesterday afternoon. There's masses of them just wandering about looking at the sights.'

'Has it struck you that it could be those American ladies actually *came* to look at the sights?'

'But they *must* want something a bit more exciting than gaping at bleeding sampans. There were whole clutches of them in some hotels, and nearly all women. Just sitting around, drinking martinis, looking bored as hell. I think we ought to be in on it.'

'We!' argued Brigg. 'Willy, you've got a nerve. Don't you get *me* involved in your foul bloody schemes, mate. If you think I'm going to get some rich old duck . . .'

'They don't have to be *old*,' argued Wilcox. 'Some of them were in their forties. That's only as old as you.'

'I'm thirty-nine,' corrected Brigg. 'And while they

125

may be as old *as* me, they're a damn sight too old *for* me. Understand? So forget it. Do it yourself if you want.'

Wilcox rose and finished his beer with a flourish. 'I was just offering you a profitable partnership, that's all. Great Britain Gigolos Incorporated. You want the best pricks, we have them. What are you doing this afternoon, taking the boy out?'

'Probably. We'll go over and kick his football about for a while, I expect. He thinks it amuses me.'

'He wants a mother,' said Wilcox piously.

'He's had a mother,' said Brigg.

'No offence. I just thought that a nice, loving, wealthy American mum is just what the lad needs.' He moved towards the door and sniffed up at the sky. 'You won't be playing football, anyway,' he forecast. 'It's starting to rain.'

He went out, putting his beret on at a slightly jaunty angle. Brigg finished his beer, drew the outline of a house with a tree in the garden in the beer on the table, got up, and went out into the already thickening rain.

9

The boy did have a mother once. Sometimes, before the thing went really bad, Brigg and Glenda had days when they were happy. In the July after the boy was born they borrowed an old car from an Army mechanic in Aldershot and took it to East Anglia. The baby was carried like luggage in a carry-cot, dutifully between them, as they walked through streets, staggered laughing over collapsing sand dunes, or sat watching the ships on the glazed summer sea. They then turned from the coastland towns and explored the circumspect counties, full of inner quietness. In Suffolk the dry North Sea wind followed them, its hands sorting through trees many miles inland; but Norfolk was still and hot, its expansive fields stretching out like sheets drying in the sun, its villages somnolent, its crouched lanes perfumed as old ladies.

They were very much alone and together, apart from the random noises of the travelling baby. There, far away from Aldershot, he was able to join Glenda in her ever-extravagant mood, laughing at her grandness; leaving behind with the mother-army most of his own uncertainties and lack of adventure. Once they got drunk in a village pub and went singing outrageously down the sleeping street, swinging the bawling baby wildly between them in its canvas receptacle.

'I don't know why you had to be a soldier again,' she said when they were between the sheets in their lodgings for the night. 'You're much better when you're like this, away from all that Army rubbish.'

'The Army's an adventure,' he recited solemnly. 'Don't you read the advertisements?'

'About as much adventure as a bloody butcher's shop,' she giggled. 'Even less. At least in a butcher's you've got a chance of lopping off your finger.'

'I'm a soldier because we've got to eat,' he told her, wagging his finger beneath the cover. 'I was no good at anything else, was I? I couldn't add up in that accountant's office, I couldn't sell insurance, nor door-to-door brushes. I had to go back because there was nowhere else to go.'

'There were certainly a lot of things you couldn't do,' she admitted ruefully. 'But, God, things get so dreary at Aldershot.'

'Maybe I'll get a posting abroad soon.'

'You *know* that will be exactly the same. Everywhere you go with the Army is the same. They seem to shift a lump of Aldershot with you and that's it.'

'I don't see any signs of Aldershot around here,' he said stretching in the big, aged bed. She moved tenderly against him. They could hear a light wind, like a young inexperienced ghost, moving jerkily across the dunelands beyond their window. There were mushroom-shaped shadows bruising the ceiling.

'No, it's not here,' she sighed. 'It's nice to be in a place where there's no Aldershot, no Army, no Army wives and kids. Just our luck that you can't do something else.'

'I *could* try again, if you want,' he said uncertainly.

'Surely there must be something. I'd have to buy myself out, though.'

'I don't want to think about it any more tonight,' she said. 'I'd rather do something else. I'd rather make love.'

'I haven't got any,' he said.

'Love?'

'No. You know, the other things.'

'Oh, Christ,' she said. But she laughed before she went to sleep.

The next day was the hottest of that summer. The sun burned the Norfolk plain as though it were a prairie. It was uncomfortable in the car and the baby was fretting. They pulled into a deep lane, ten miles from the sea, had their picnic lunch, and then walked, the baby in its oblong carrier between them. Glenda saw a stile, choked with wild summer growth, and decided they should go that way.

'It might be private,' said Brigg almost automatically.

'I hope it is,' she shrugged. 'That's exactly why I want to go. Let's see what's the other side of those lovely trees.'

He climbed the gate cautiously. He could feel it curling like a bow beneath his weight. Blackberry brambles and honeysuckle reached out for him. He stood in the field and she handed the carry-cot over to him, then easily climbed the gate herself.

The field had once been ploughed, probably the winter before, but it was now left fallow, ridged under its tufty grass and sprouting with free weeds. They walked unevenly across it, the baby slung between them, swinging easily from their hands. The sun was intense. Glenda lifted her face to it and smiled at its luxury. A few conscientious birds sounded in the hedges of the big field and the Norfolk sky, cleaned by its frequent wind and today polished by the sun, covered the visible world. From somewhere across their landscape they could hear an out-of-hours cock crowing, and for a minute or so a lofty and invisible aeroplane whined. But these sounds were soon vanished. They were left alone in the big field in the sun.

Brigg looked down at the baby. He was gaping unbelievingly at the unchanging rolled-out blue of the sky and reaching for it expressively with his miniature hands.

'He wants the sky,' Brigg laughed.

'Why don't you get it for him, you mean thing?' she said. 'Depriving your child of something like that.'

They reached the fringe of big trees, and saw that they were at the ramparts of a thick wood, swollen with the uncaring growth of July, sounding loud with insects and hidden birds. Glenda went first into its coolness and Brigg followed. They bore the baby on the slant, because of the narrow path. Twigs and brambles touched and scraped along the canvas sides of the cot and the child looked up questioningly as though someone were knocking on his travelling room.

The wood was three hundred feet at its fullest girth. Eventually the sun, like a signalling mirror, began to flick in through the branches and they could see large fields of sky again. They walked out almost at the water's edge of a fat, deserted, lake, sprawled out among the trees like a man asleep; flat at its shores, chopped by an unsuspected breeze at its middle. They were in one of its enclosed bays, two peninsulas jutting out a hundred feet away. Beyond that the lake expanded and extended into the darkness where, even on that bright day, the trees were dark.

'We're the only people here,' said Glenda.

'It's private. It must be private,' said Brigg.

'That's why we've got it all to ourselves,' she insisted. 'They must have known we were coming. It's beautiful, isn't it?'

'Very pretty,' said Brigg. 'Maybe we had better go back.'

'Oh shut up,' she said quietly and without anger, still looking at the lake. She giggled: 'If anyone catches us we'll say the baby came in first and we followed him.'

He shrugged and responded to her tug on the carry-cot like a pony responding to its bridle. They skirted the lake, making for the right hand peninsula where a duck had appeared and was now watching them along the deck of its beak. It was a fine duck, its feathers a jigsaw of royal turquoise and purples. It acknowledged them with a quack, and another duck, this time a tame brown, joined it on the bank, waddling up from the far side of the peninsula.

Glenda laughed at them and Brigg, a little reassured now, laughed too. They tipped the cot at a steep angle so that the boy could see the ducks, but he continued to spit small bubbles and to consider the sky with amazement.

On the far side of the peninsula was a boat. Glenda saw it first as she mounted the bank. It was a rough catamaran, a flat deck rigid between two fat metal hulls. It moved on the shallows turgidly like a feeding hippopotamus.

'It's home made,' said Brigg.

'You can tell it didn't come from the Boat Show,' said Glenda.

'Those are two fuel tanks,' he went on. 'From an aeroplane, I'd say. Doesn't look all that safe, does it?'

'I think it looks great,' she argued. 'It looks very exciting to me. I wouldn't mind having a ride in it.'

'You go,' said Brigg. 'I'll stay here and look after the kid.'

'Oh, come on, cowardy,' she said. 'Let's have a look at it. Those things on the flat bit must be paddles. It would be marvellous to go for a sail, wouldn't it . . .?'

'Glenda . . .' he began warningly.

'I know, I know,' she pouted. 'It's private. Don't be such a wet. We'll just go out a little way, and if anybody comes we'll say we sat on the boat and it drifted off with us.'

'What about the baby?'

'Put him on the flat bit, the deck. He'll enjoy that. He can see a different lot of sky.'

Brigg sighed. 'It's you who ought to be in the Army,' he said. 'You'd be starting wars all over the place.'

'That's what the Army is for, isn't it?' she replied blithely. 'It's not supposed to be the Women's Guild.' She was already moving along the edge of the lake, along some crunching stones, to where the painter of the ungainly boat was tied. They put the baby on the bank and Brigg helped her to pull the craft towards them. It was heavy and reluctant, but they coaxed it to

132

the shore. Glenda was about to step aboard, but Brigg touched her arm and gallantly went first. With despondency he saw that, as she had said, a pair of paddles were tied to the tail of the deck.

'You were right,' he sighed. 'Paddles.'

'Good, then there's nothing to stop us,' she replied.

'I wouldn't like to trust this thing very far,' he cautioned. 'Especially with the baby.'

'The baby wants to go for a trip just as much as I do,' she said. 'Come on, bring him over. It will be lovely.'

Brigg hoisted the cot from the bank. He placed it carefully on the deck boards. The ducks, now joined by two others, fidgeted and watched from the bank.

'Goodbye, ducks!' shouted Glenda. 'We'll see you when we get back.'

'If we get back,' muttered Brigg.

'If we get back!' shouted Glenda at the ducks.

Brigg loosened the painter and gave the boat a resigned shove with his foot; it heeled sleepily and turned out into the water. The horizon swung around and they were pointing out into the lake, the trees on the distant bank as dark and confused from that distance as any along the Amazon.

The baby was balanced on the elementary deck between the fat aluminium floats, lounging in the cot, still absorbed with the sky. Glenda took one of the paddles and, immediately assuming command, handed the other to Brigg. The boat was sluggish and reluctant like some old horse rudely ridden from sleep. They paddled unevenly and Glenda saw that he was looking pessimistically at the banks on either side.

'Expecting an ambush?' she asked.

'I'm expecting something,' admitted Brigg. 'Like a keeper with a gun.'

'What can he do if he does arrive? Pull your end round a bit, can you, we'll hit this mudbank otherwise. That's better. Yes, what can he do?'

'Well he can have us for trespass and theft for a start.'

'Listen,' she said. 'How can we be *stealing* anything? This is a lake, isn't it? It's not a river nor a sea. The bloody water doesn't actually *go* anywhere. So we can't be stealing because as long as we're on the water we will still be *here*!'

'And "here" is trespassing,' he put in.

'Oh, arseholes! What's trespassing? What have we done? Pushed down a few blades of grass with our feet and the baby's blown a few bubbles into somebody's private air. See if that will stand up in court.'

He laughed at her and she turned and grinned at him. They were making better headway now. The boat had woken up and they were getting the feel of the paddles. All around them the sun flooded the lake and touched their faces and their bodies. The baby said something to the sky.

'I'm going to take my things off,' decided Glenda. 'Nobody will see us out here.'

'Oh, for Christ's sake,' pleaded Brigg. But she had already started.

She put down the paddle and he stopped too, and watched her. They began to drift. Crossing her arms before her she took hold of the sides of her flowered summer dress and pulled it over her head, shaking her thick hair as it emerged from the sheath. They had been on a beach the day before and her arms and shoulders and upper chest were brown.

'For Christ's sake,' Brigg repeated.

'I wish you wouldn't keep bringing Christ and His sake into it,' she said rubbing her hands down the heavy breast swellings hung in her brassiere. He was always moved by the sight of her full body and out there in the sun and the air it excited him more. She was astride of the float, her pants a rigid pink triangle, one leg dangling in the lake, the other bent on the wooded deck at the side of the cot.

'It will just look like a bikini from the shore,' she said.

'Okay,' he said reflectively, still looking at her. 'I suppose it will.'

'Take your trousers and shirt off,' she encouraged. 'Go on! Nobody will know the difference with you either.' She was obviously surprised when he did. He straddled the float again in his underpants.

'You've got the horn, you dirty rotten beast,' she laughed. 'Look at it sticking up inside your pants! Lie on your back and we'd have a mast and a sail!'

The sun was heavy on his shoulders and back. He took up the paddle and put it down again. He leaned towards her, across the baby, and kissed her, putting his hands all over the flesh of her breasts, thrusting the fingers into the hammock of her bra and finding the soft coin of her nipple. She reacted immediately. Sex took her quickly like a drug, transforming her liveliness to a slow, thick, heat of anticipation. She reached over and took his penis from inside his pants. She ran the palm of her hand over the extended helmet.

'I'd like to report a leak, Captain,' he said.

'It's already been reported,' she replied. She had grown quiet and full of warmth now. He knew she had wanted him more than she told the previous night. 'It's leaking worse,' she added. 'Why don't you come over here and let me repair it?'

The baby was looking up at their bodies, arched across his cot, with mild annoyance.

'We'll unbalance the boat,' said Brigg. His head was down on her shoulder now and his tongue was lapping along the root of her breast. They were clinging to each other like people in dire distress.

'Move him over,' she said sleepily. 'I don't believe in letting children get in the way of their parents' screwing. Put him on this float. This side, darling. It's plenty wide enough. Then we can lie on the boards.'

Brigg hesitated and she saw it. 'He'll be all right,' she encouraged slowly. 'There's plenty of room for the cot. I'll keep one hand on it.'

'You promise,' said Brigg. 'About the hand?'

'Yes,' she nodded, her head still drooped. 'I promise, love.'

They were strangely weak in that sun on the lake. Brigg remembered that well, afterwards. The heaviness, the weakness, like a luxurious sickness upon them. They moved the cot to the float on which Glenda had been sitting. It sat there comfortable. He held it while she knelt in the middle and took the rest of her clothes off, and then pulled his pants away from him.

'God, look at the size and colour of that thing!' She regarded him through slit eyes. 'I think it's going to burst.'

136

'It probably will, too,' he murmured. He rubbed her flesh with his free hand, pressing the nipples, expanded now like pink bruises. She bent then as though worshipping him and put her full, warm tongue to him.

'I think you had better lie down,' he said, pushing his fingers into her stormy hair. 'And don't forget to hold the baby. I mean the one in the cot.'

She giggled like someone in a comic dream. They had never been like that before with each other, so full, so spontaneous, so free. Brigg glanced up and saw that they were drifting into the middle of the lake. The banks, quiet and indistinct in the afternoon heat, seemed almost as far away as the sky.

Their bodies were bursting with the sun and with their contact. There was a sheen of sweat on her stomach. She was soft and ready. He lowered himself to her and they coupled. As he moved into her he watched her face and saw it crease and then miraculously clear so that it shone like their child's when he smiled. Her right hand was firm on his backside, pushing him urgently into her and her left held the side of the canvas cot. The baby was gabbling brilliantly, but they did not hear him.

'I wanted you,' she said. 'I always do, you know.'

'We're taking a risk, you know,' he whispered. 'Do you want me to take it out if I can?'

'Do that and I'll kill you,' she said. 'I want every last inch and every last drop of it. I want to feel that monstrous thing gobbling up my insides.'

He was too occupied to answer. He moved to and fro, his hands cushioning her buttocks from the wooden deck. They knew that this was the great free moment of their lives together. No setting of alarm clocks, no thinking of early morning duties, nor the discomfort of a French letter. No artificial warming up. No wondering if it were *really* all right. This time they knew.

Glenda began to make little sobs every time he leant into her. The colour had almost faded from her eyes, she sucked through her barely opened lips and her breasts had hardened to boulders. Their orgasm came from both fonts at once, like rain pouring from two chutes into one. She writhed under him, and he used all his strength to hold her like some prisoner, feeling a great, joyful, surprising, power over her. He ground once more at her very centre and trembled as he jerked again. She cried out as if he were throwing stones at her. Then she collapsed and he fell on to her. She was quiet and finished, like a bale of silk beneath him.

Eventually she opened her eyes and said: 'Thank God, darling, that your one extravagance is between your legs.'

Brigg blinked the rivering sweat from his eyes. 'That,' he said, 'was the best ever.'

'The best ever,' she nodded. 'Not just for us, but for everybody else who has ever done it.'

With that she embraced him with real, momentary, love, throwing her arms about his naked shoulders, and at the same time carelessly releasing the baby's cot, which she had held bravely throughout her passion. The cot slipped deftly over the side and into the lake like a small ship being launched.

They both grabbed at it at the same moment, but it was gone. Brigg shouted and Glenda screamed.

Before he had gained his knees the canvas carry-cot ten feet away was floating easily, with all the joy of a little boat. She grabbed him as he was about to attempt a frantic dive over the side.

'No!' she spluttered. 'No, you damn fool! Gently. You'll turn it over if you don't.'

He stopped and patted her arm. Their eyes were staring at the buoyant cot. A tiny, derisive, pink foot appeared kicking above the edge for a moment. Brigg let out a terrified squeak. He slid into the water without a tremor and felt its deep coldness clutch his hot body. He went towards the cot like a frightened man swimming through a minefield. He reached it and, turning, touched it like a feather, pushing it back towards Glenda. He could hear her crying and then gradually drying up as he neared the float. Then she began to giggle and laughed and finally, when they had hoisted the cot and the mystified baby from the water, she collapsed in a fit of wild mirth and tumbling tears.

Brigg crawled carefully over the other pontoon. He looked down at the baby.

'Dry as a bone,' said Glenda. She felt. 'Even his nappy is.'

She gave Brigg a handkerchief to dry himself. He used that and his vest. Then they began to put on their clothes. They paddled towards the place where they had found the boat. They were exhausted and silent.

Brigg pointed to the distant bank, around the main curve of the lake. A man, waving one arm in the air, was cycling at a rush to reach the landing place before they could get there.

'Looks like the gamekeeper, Lady Chatterley,' said Brigg.

'Bugger him for a start,' said Glenda. 'I nearly lost my baby in his lousy lake.'

'We may need to run when we get ashore,' continued Brigg practically. 'Do you think you can manage it across the fields and back to the car?'

'I'll give it a try,' she agreed. 'If he catches us we'll jump him.'

Brigg grunted. 'Sometimes,' he said as they paddled faster, 'I think I'm a bloody sight safer in the army than with you.'

He knew she was laughing and he laughed too. They knew it was the best day they had ever had. Or ever would.

10

After the fiercest night of freak rain that Hong Kong had known that winter, a ten-ton recovery vehicle from the Command Workshops, a great brutish, snub-snouted thing, went to the Chinese village to recover the tank from the eating-house.

Thunder and vivid lightning had been in turmoil over the Cantonese hills all night, but at dawn the lightning paled, the thunder retreated to some secret fastness, and another Monday, wringing wet, spread over the New Territories.

The driver of the recovery vehicle and his companion, both sleepy and irritable with the early duty, drove stupidly along the main road, past the garrison and on to the village. At a point opposite the imprisoned tank they turned their monster off the road. They drove spectacularly into a newly born morass of red mud, progressed a few yards by brute force, and then, watched by a quickly assembled group of fascinated Chinese, sank axle deep into the slime. The man at the controls of the giant, from sheer temper and embarrassment, flung the engine into a frenzy, and the Chinese scattered as the gobs of wet earth catapulted from the ten churning wheels of the huge lorry. It sank deeper, like a smitten whale, grovelling and grinding, until the very lip of its great boxed engine housing was dipped into the mud. It was still thirty yards from the tank. The driver and his colleague sat back, lit up cigarettes, and discussed the positions of their respective teams in Division Three of the Football League ten thousand miles away.

At eight-thirty Colonel Simmons, driven by Turner towards the garrison came in sight of the catastrophe.

'Stone me, they've got another one stuck, sir,' remarked Turner with satisfaction.

'What is?' asked the Colonel with minor irritation. He was thinking about the Defence Minister.

'Command Workshops, sir.'

The Commanding Officer leaned forward and Turner slowed obligingly. The ten-ton recovery vehicle, sadly scuttled, was surrounded by utterly silent and unmoving Chinese villagers. The two soldiers were still comfortably conversing within the cab like wrecked but calm mariners awaiting rescue.

'Good God,' said Colonel Simmons. 'How the hell did they manage that?'

'Didn't use their loaf, I'd say, sir,' suggested Turner sagely. 'Didn't think about all the rain last night. Turns this lot into a bog. He looks like he's going to be there for good.'

'They appear to be forming their own scrap yard,' muttered the Colonel. 'I'm damned glad I'm not their CO.'

'How would they have managed on the beaches in Normandy, sir?' said Turner, who spent all the Second World War in Gloucester records office.

'How indeed?' agreed the Colonel who was also absent from Normandy. 'Or Burma.'

'Did you get to Burma, sir?'

'Er . . . no, Turner. Did you?'

'No, sir. Never made Burma.'

'Let's get on, Turner,' said the Colonel. 'I can't spend all day watching these clowns.'

Turner nodded his acknowledgement at the end of an unusually protracted morning conversation and accelerated towards the camp. As it was a Monday the Commanding Officer left the car at the main gate and, after a perfunctory look at the abject paraded guard, made a close examination of the geometrical garden which Lance-Corporals Joss and Wilberforce had tended the previous morning.

'By heaven, they do a great job, you know, Sergeant,' enthused the CO after bending close to each coloured patch.

'So I believe, sir,' said the sergeant without expression.

'I don't know how they get all the tiny weeds out,' said Colonel Simmons. 'They never leave one.'

'I understand Lance-Corporal Joss uses his nail file, sir.'

The Colonel glanced at him suspiciously, but detecting no change of expression, merely said: 'Certainly looks neat enough for that. Good chaps those two. They know their flowers.'

'It's their bent,' nodded the sergeant.

Once more the Colonel could find no malice in his face. He decided that the exchange was becoming unprofitable. Turning, he responded slightly sourly to the sergeant's properly stiff salute and re-entered the car. Turner drove slowly through the camp roads until they reached the boundary of the parade ground. He felt the Commanding Officer's touch on his shoulder and stopped secretively, as though they were taking part in some motorized ambush. The unit was drilling, another practice for the important day to come, its oblong platoons, under their awkward officers and mouthy NCOs, marched and wheeled and stamped. Arms swung higher and undernourished corporals screamed like battery commanders when the Colonel's car was sighted. From lemonade crates brought from the NAAFI shop and established at the point where the saluting base would be, RSM Love surveyed the militant gyrations. He tucked his stomach back in case it protruded against the colourless morning sky. His contralto orders sounded across the parade, each phrase with a piping squeak at the end as though he had been stuck with a hot pin. The Colonel ordered Turner to skirt the square to the saluting position.

'Pa–rade! Pa-rade, halt!' ordered the RSM as the Commanding Officer left the car.

'Pa-rade! Right turn!' he squeaked.

'Right . . . dress!' The entire garrison of some five hundred men performed, at the order, the most ludicrously embarrassing movement ever devised as a military spectacle, hands reaching out to shoulders, eyes swivelled sideways, and feet performing teetering chorus-girl shuffles on the wet parade ground.

Satisfied the lines were now straight, the RSM ordered the soldiers' faces to the front, approached the Commanding Officer and saluted him fiercely. His hinged arm vibrated like a spring.

'No collisions this morning, S'arnt Major?' said the Colonel blandly.

The RSM looked uncomfortable. 'No, sir,' he mumbled. 'Not yet, sir.'

'May I borrow your crate?' asked the Colonel.

'Crate, sir? Oh, yes, of course, sir.'

Love hovered as though wondering whether he should give the CO a hand up to the wooden perch. Colonel Simmons saw his intention and scowled him away. He stood carefully on the box and felt it wobble. He consoled himself that on the day of the big parade he intended to be firmly astride Melksham, his private horse.

He looked across the assembled, boxed, platoons, and then told the men, as he had told the officers and senior NCOs on the previous day of the extended visit of the Minister of Defence. As he spoke he looked over the heads of the parade, across the variously slanted berets and obediently attentive faces. When he had finished he called Love.

'S'arnt Major,' he said, tipping his head confidingly to one side. 'S'arnt Major, there appears to be a hole in the middle of one of the platoons.'

'Sir?' queried Love.

'A hole, Mr Love. In the centre of one squad.'

'Yes, sir,' said Love automatically. 'I'll see, sir.'

'Far right hand squad,' said the Colonel helpfully.

'Sir,' acknowledged Love. He saluted, wheeled as though his feet were activated by a powerful swivel, and bounced away across the parade ground to the extreme flank of the assembly.

Brigg, who was in charge of the squad, saw him coming and inwardly stiffened. The RSM stamped to a pompous halt three paces away. He knew the Commanding Officer was observing from his perch and that every eye within range, stiff and still, was sighted on him.

'S'arnt Brigg,' growled Love.

'Sir?'

'There's a 'ole in your squad.'

'A what?'

'A 'ole, S'arnt. An hopening, an haperture, an horifice.'

Brigg felt contempt rise within him for this man who wanted to play the stage sergeant major.

'There isn't,' said Brigg confidently.

'There is, S'arnt,' insisted Love. 'From where the Colonel is standing he can see an 'ole.'

Brigg looked squarely at Love. They did not like each other.

'Perhaps you could point out the hole, sir,' Brigg said.

'That's why I'm here,' said Love. 'The Commanding Officer is not keen on 'oles in the middle of platoons.' He strode bumptiously along the front rank and almost at the middle stopped and pointed with his cane. 'There,' he said triumphantly. 'Third rank back, slap in the middle. An 'ole.'

'That's correct, S'arnt Major.' The Colonel's shouted voice floated across the parade ground. 'That's the place.'

Brigg did not need to look. 'It's not a hole, S'arnt Major,' he said steadily. 'It's Private Thompson.' He ordered Harrison, in the front rank, to step one pace sideways and then motioned Love to examine his explanation. The RSM pushed his head into the squad like a man looking for something in a thick hedge. There in the heart of the tight formation was Treacle Thompson, a head shorter than the surrounding men, his pimpled face and blue eyes turned up apprehensively to the pink, unpleasant face of Love.

'So it is,' grunted Love withdrawing and looking at Brigg. Then, below his breath: 'That maggoty little bleeder. As if he hasn't caused enough bother.'

'He can't avoid being short,' Brigg pointed out. 'And he's got to march somewhere. He looks ridiculous in the outside ranks. When he's at the back he can hardly keep up with the rest and when he's in front he looks like a mascot. The only thing to do is to hide him – surround him by tall men.'

'All right, S'arnt Brigg,' said Love nastily. 'I wanted an explanation, not a lecture.'

'That's the explanation, sir,' said Brigg quietly. Love sniffed as though thinking of something further to say, changed his mind, did his hob-nailed pirouette, and marched back to the box on which Colonel Simmons was still mounted. He saluted apologetically. 'Sir,' he said. 'It's not a hole. It's a particularly small man, sir.'

'Good God, he *must* be small,' said the Colonel. 'He looks like a hole from here.'

'No, sir. I mean, yes, sir. But it's Private Thompson, sir. His platoon sergeant says he is attempting to hide him.'

'Well he's hiding him so effectively he doesn't look to be there at all. Thompson? Is that the Thompson who is on a charge today, concerning this Chinese Wolf Cubs nonsense?'

'The same, sir.'

'Can't think how a man like that actually got into the British Army,' murmured the Colonel sorrowfully. 'Right, then, carry on. Try and think of something to do with him when we have the big parade. We simply cannot have a man in the middle of the squad who looks like a hole.'

'Sir!' acknowledged Love. 'I'll attend to it, sir.' He saluted and the Colonel walked back towards his car. Before he had driven away the Sergeant Major knew what he would do about Treacle.

Each day in the life of the garrison was like a day's work in a factory that produced nothing. The routine, the machinations went on, letters and memoranda were written, read, signed, passed on, filed, lost, rediscovered, re-read and inadvertently thrown away. Men oiled and greased the unit transport and on this Monday the two Ferret armoured cars were given their weekly run to the railway junction at Sheung Shui and back. They went out from the camp at a frantic rate like their animal namesakes kept too long in confinement.

Soldiers, a section of ten men at a time, reported to Sergeant Wilcox at the armoury so that the various maladies touching their rifles and other small arms could be treated, and not a dissimilar parade of a dozen men lined up in the dun, dull afternoon outside the office and surgery of Major Stevens, the medical officer.

In the records office and the pay section, military clerks, bent of back and inky of finger, crouched over deal tables deeply illustrated by years of pen and penknife, with their memories, their dreams and their reflections. Jung himself might have been glad to spend an hour or two examining these subconscious patterns, these ships in gallant sail, arrows shot into the air, women with three breasts, bespectacled moths, booted caterpillars and addresses in careful illuminated lettering of small, cold, indifferent terraced houses ten thousand miles away. Army psychiatrists never gave a thought to inspecting them, content merely, on their sparse visits, to question the occasional and obviously lunatic soldier about his nocturnal habits and aspirations.

In the family quarters skirting the camp Monday was still washing day. It took more than half a world and the magic of the Orient to change that. Some military wives proudly insisted on boiling their own sheets and other whites, hanging them like flags of identification on the washing lines behind their houses. Others left it to the Chinese home help which the Army thoughtfully provided, and leaned back to enjoy and occasionally to criticize.

The army children were in school, their piping, confused voices issuing over the garrison road with the mixed incantations of the nine times table, and the twenty-third psalm. Mothers, passing on their way to the NAAFI supermarket with their afternoon bags, paused and strained to listen for the individual tone of their choice infant.

On their journey to the shop they passed the short parade of soldiers outside the Medical Officer's surgery and although the women went by unconcerned, deep in their own chatter, the waiting men were visibly discomfited and turned their faces away from the wives.

'We didn't ought to be made to stick out like this,' moaned Harrison. 'It's bloody embarrassing.'

'It's only a general going-over,' pointed out Pardoe. 'Nothing to be ashamed of, Hairy.'

149

'But *they* don't know that, do they,' returned Harrison. 'It's the *wrong* time of day for sick parade. They know *that*, don't they? Stands to reason they'll think we're on the pox parade or something.'

'Run after them and tell them that we're not,' suggested Pardoe. 'See if they care.'

'I bet they'd care if they saw one of their buggering husbands in the queue. *Then* they'd want to know what it was all about. Anyway, I don't see why we've got to stand out here. Who's in there now? He's been hours.'

'Treacle,' muttered Renwick from the front of the line.

'That accounts for it,' said Harrison. 'He's got things wrong with him what's unknown to medical bleeding science.'

Inside the surgery Major Stevens had the same misgivings as Harrison. He stared at the small and extraordinary figure of Thompson, stripped to the waist, before him. He had weighed and measured the soldier and now he sat and merely gazed at him.

'You *could* get a discharge, you know, Thompson,' said the MO from across his desk.

'Discharge, sir?'

'Yes. You'd have no difficulty at all. You could be out of this mob and back in the UK in a couple of weeks at the most.'

'But I don't *want* a discharge, sir,' replied the astonished Treacle. 'I'm a professional.'

'When did your shoulders get like that?' asked the MO at random.

'Like what, sir?'

'Like they are. They sort of dip quite dramatically

between your arms and the top of your spine. It looks like you've spent your life carrying a yoke and a couple of pails.'

'I've never noticed it,' said Treacle. 'Unless it's all that work I get given to do in the Tin Room. Stretching into the sink after the meat tins and suchlike.'

'You do that a lot, do you, Thompson?'

'Nearly all the time, sir. The Colonel's given me another fourteen days confined to barracks this morning, sir. And Mr Love is bound to put me in the Tin Room, because he always does.'

'That was because of the farce, yesterday, wasn't it?' nodded Major Stevens. 'Well you can't grumble at that, Thompson. God, you had the whole damned place on War Alert. And Sunday lunchtime, too.'

'Yes, sir,' acknowledged Treacle.

'Your hair seems to come out a lot,' pursued the major.

'Lumps do,' admitted the soldier. 'But it seems to sprout again, sir.'

'Oh,' said the medical officer. He seemed disappointed. 'Has the dentist seen those teeth?'

'One did, sir.' Thompson bared his teeth.

'What was his report?'

'I don't know, sir. He was that dentist that shot himself in the lavatory at Kowloon.'

'I remember,' sighed Stevens looking at the teeth from his distance. He breathed resignedly. 'All right, Thompson. Let's have a look at your bits and pieces.'

'My what, sir?'

'Take your trousers down, man.'

'Sorry, sir. Never heard them called that before.'

He obligingly dropped his trousers and looked up to meet the doctor's profound stare. He looked down at himself as though to ensure that the officer had not spotted something he himself may have missed. Major Stevens began to write hurriedly. 'Well, Thompson,' he muttered grudgingly. 'You seem to be A1 in that particular region.'

'Yes, sir.'

'Perhaps the fact that the rest of you is so undersized makes it look all the bigger. Get dressed. Tell the next man to come in.'

Thompson dressed, saluted miserably, and marched out. One day, he thought, *someone* was going to give him credit for *something*.

11

Brigg's afternoon was interrupted first by the arrival in his office of a whistling corporal with the tickets for the monthly football pontoon, and then by the tea trolley, manoeuvred by a NAAFI employee who claimed to have driven a tank in the desert during the war. He relieved the tedium of his duty by swivelling the trolley in the traditional manner of a twenty-tonner, and by swinging the steaming tap on its urn to various points from which he apparently needed to repel enemy attacks. If he thought no one was within hearing he made childish staccato noises like the firing of a gun. His journeys with the metal trolley, its urn standing like an armoured gun turret, were aggressive and occasionally damaging. He was careful with Brigg's door, however, since he had torn it violently from its hinges on a previous raid.

Brigg's third visitor of the afternoon was Major Fortune. Brigg was surprised to see him for he was rarely bothered by officers during his working hours. At the moment of the major's entry his feet were resting in the open drawer of his desk and he was peeling an orange. He awkwardly disengaged himself from both activities and gave the adjutant an embarrassed salute.

'Caught you on your NAAFI break, Sergeant,' said

the young officer amiably. It was a relieving statement not a question.

'Yes, sir,' agreed Brigg. 'Having my quiet five minutes.'

'Sorry to interrupt. We all need to pause now and again.' Brigg saw he was looking at the picture gallery around the office.

'People you know?' asked Fortune.

'Failures, sir,' admitted Brigg lamely. 'People who have failed in life. I collect them.'

'How super,' enthused the young man. 'What a jolly notion.'

'Thank you, sir.'

'Yes, I really think that, Sergeant. Most original hobby. If you could get some of the other chaps interested, get them collecting too, you could have a sort of failures' club and swop among yourselves.'

'Good idea, sir,' said Brigg solidly. 'Perhaps I'll give that some thought.'

'Anyway, I'd better tell you why I've dropped in,' continued Fortune. 'I was coming by anyway, and the CO asked me to talk to you.'

'Yes, sir?'

'Couple of things, mainly. He's very keen on that lad of yours doing his abracadabra stunt – you know, the hypnotism – at the concert when the Defence Minister is here for the weekend. The old man seems to think he'll be the hit of the evening.'

Brigg shrugged. 'I'm a bit worried about the idea, sir. He's only dabbling in it, after all. And so far, you might have heard, he's caused more bother than entertainment.'

'That business at the school?'

'Quite.'

'Well, between us, Brigg, I think the Colonel was more amused about that than anything. I shouldn't let that worry you.'

'But *who* is going to be hypnotized?' insisted Brigg. 'After what happened at the school I can't see any of the ranks here shoving their kids forward.'

'I think Colonel Simmons is thinking of having the men as er . . . victims . . . er . . . subjects,' said Fortune doubtfully. 'He wasn't thinking of children. . And if there's any lack of volunteers, we can always press a few by other means.' He brightened: 'We could get those on fatigues to volunteer.'

'He's quite a small boy, sir,' argued Brigg. 'And he has to stare into their eyes when he puts them under.'

'In that case he'll have to stand on a chair,' said the adjutant decisively. Then, indicating that the matter was finished, he said: 'Tell him to get a bit of an act together, will you. And if you need time off to help him rehearse then that will be fine. He'll probably need a couple of afternoons off from school, won't he?'

'I expect so, sir, if that's all right.'

'The Old Man's word is my command,' smiled the major. 'And, by the way, I was also told to tell you that the man in your platoon called Thompson, the scrawny little chap . . .'

'Yes, sir?'

'He's not to march in the middle of the squad. The Colonel says he looks like a hole.'

'What's he got to do, then, sir?'

'He can't march behind, I gather.'

'No, sir. He can't keep up.'

'Well, fix it so that he marches up and down at the side of the square during parades. Then he won't mess up anyone.'

'By himself, sir?'

'I think it's a good idea, don't you, Brigg? It won't sod up the parade and it will keep him from running to fat. Anyway, whatever happens, the Colonel doesn't want him looking like a hole in the squad.'

'No, sir. All right, I'll tell him.'

'Right. That's that, then. Oh, there was something else. I'm supposed to ask everyone who went into Hong Kong on Saturday. Were you?'

'Er . . . Saturday? Yes, sir, I was.'

'Somehow the Military Police have got some story that two men from this camp put the boot into a couple of civilian businessmen at somewhere called the Jiggery Pokery Club. Dare say they asked for it, and they've left Hong Kong now anyway, but they made the complaint. Some waiter, or someone, said the men were from this unit.'

'Jiggery Pokery Club?' said Brigg, his hand going reflectively over his mouth.

'Never heard of it, myself,' said Fortune.

'Well, I've *heard* of it,' admitted Brigg.

'Ask around your lads, will you?' said the major. 'Just routine.'

'I will, sir. I'm afraid it was sausage and chips at the YMCA for me last Saturday.'

There were still growling thunderstorms in the inland hills that night and a troubled sky covered the fingers of the mainland which touched the sea. It was electric railway night in the garrison and fifty enthusiasts of all ranks stood around a model of green English country-side in a disused barrack room and watched with rapt delight while miniature British Rail expresses clicked on their tiny travels through paper vales and plastic villages.

The camp debating society was in early uproar due to a hand-to-hand fight breaking out between two drunken privates during a discussion on the existence of God.

Every blatant barrack room light thrust out over the square while soldiers lay on their beds, dozed, dreamed, watched Hong Kong Television, wrote letters, or played darts. The NAAFI was scarcely occupied, it being Monday, the only two dozen patrons were with RSM Love and Mrs Love at the camp cinema. Lights on the married quarters fringe of the garrison were subdued, far less obvious than the curtainless barrack blocks, the soldiers and their families occupying themselves behind their prim suburban drapes.

Two crossed floodlights splashed white across the area of the guardhouse and the main gate. The sentry did his clockwork evening walk, his only amusement watching the irritable lightning over the distant mainland and the brilliant lamps which Command Workshops had set up around their tank and their tank recovery vehicle to prevent their theft during the dark hours.

The administration and workshop section of the garrison was in mute blackness and so was the adjoining cookhouse apart from a single weary light issuing from the door of the Tin Room. It was a light thickened, gasified, by the wandering steam that

157

issued from the same opening. From within came the tinsmith sounds of Treacle at his menial, metallic labours. His sixpenny face damp with sweat, steam and grease, he launched the last of the night's meat tins into the thick lake of the sink.

Weary though he was, there was a certain lightness in his manipulations of the floating tins, and a half-whistle then a half-smile kept coming to his lips. He disposed of the tin quickly, hoisted the plug and let the water regurgitate down the drain. Then he wiped his face and hands in a foul tea-towel, and thrust an optimistic comb through his soggy hair. He switched off the light and went like a commando through the night.

The dulled light through the curtained windows of the married families' quarters caused him no anxiety, but at Mrs Murdoch's garden fence he bent tightly and went like a kitten through the shadows, for she stood, as she frequently did, against the curtains, just ajar, looking out into the solitary darkness.

He scampered through the back gate of the Loves' house. Violet was watching for him at the kitchen window. She opened the rear door before he could put his hand to it and he skipped in joyfully. The little man and the fat girl clutched each other sweetly in the blackness of the kitchen. By extending his toes he could elevate himself to her lip-level, but their kiss was limited by the time he could maintain the elongation.

'They've gone,' Violet whispered.

'They've definitely gone to the pictures?' asked Treacle. 'They wouldn't go anywhere else and suddenly turn up, would they?'

'There's nowhere else they would go,' she said

confidently. 'Come on through, love.' She led him into the living room. Two glasses of sherry were poured ready on the table. He saw them and smiled self-consciously at her.

'Your old man wouldn't get fed up with the film and come out, would he?' he said anxious once more. 'It would be terrible if he came back. Because . . . because you promised tonight, didn't you?'

'Look,' she said forcefully, putting her thick arms around his wasted body. 'We're going to do IT tonight and that's all there is to it, darling. He won't come out of the pictures once he's paid and he's in there. He's too bloody mean.'

They stood looking at each other happily. Then she released him and he said: 'Let's have our drinks.'

'Good idea,' she said. 'I had to water his sherry, but he won't notice that. He doesn't know what he's drinking half the time, silly bugger.'

'We're definitely going to do it, then,' he said taking up his glass.

'Definitely,' she promised. 'I've made up my mind, Robin. I've hardly been able to do anything right in the shop today, just thinking about it. I knocked a bag of flour all over Mrs Anstee's baby. There was a terrible commotion over that, I can tell you.'

'I love you,' he said firmly, raising the sherry to his lips.

'I love you,' she echoed. Her glass rose up past his face and they drank together. 'I'll put some music on,' she said. 'Which group do you like?'

'Group? Oh, group. I keep forgetting you're a teenager,' he said. 'You're so much bigger than me that I forget. I mean, I'm thirty next month.'

She looked at him genuinely. 'Does it make any difference to you?' she asked.

'Difference? Not a bit. You're seventeen and I'm thirty. But so what?'

'No, I mean the difference in *sizes,*' she said. 'I'm a good deal bigger than you, Robin. Some people would find that a barrier.'

'Barriers are meant to be got over, Vi,' he told her blushingly.

'Let's go upstairs,' she suggested daringly. 'Right now. Don't let's bother to mess about down here with music and all that. Let's go up. My bed's all ready.'

'Vi,' he whispered looking at her sternly. 'Now, you really *mean* it, don't you, Vi?'

'I *mean* it,' she affirmed putting her meaty hands around his ears as a mother might her child. 'I'll show you how *much* I mean it.'

He put down his glass purposefully, missed the small table and dropped it on the floor. It broke but she did not seem to notice. Their eyes were transfixed with each other. She put her arm around his thin waist and his arm went optimistically half way across her broad back. They stumbled up the stairs together. She brought him round like a dancing partner and pushed him into the bedroom. The curtains were drawn and a bedside lamp with a woodpecker on its shade gave a soft light.

'Well, here we are,' she said, suddenly awkward. He pressed his head against the massive flesh below her sweater. 'Do you want me to undress you, darling?' she asked.

'I think we'd better each do that ourselves,' he said prudently foreseeing the pitfalls.

160

She made no move, but looked at him seriously. 'I've got to tell you something,' she said, as though making up her mind on the difficult matter. 'I'm not all there.'

'You're not . . . ?'

'I'm not a virgin,' she said firmly. 'It got lost.'

He smirked. 'Neither am I, Vi. I didn't tell you before, but I was married.'

Her great face expanded with astonishment. 'Married? Good gracious, Robin! You didn't tell me. You're not *now*, are you? For God's sake say you're not!'

'I'm not,' he confirmed obligingly. 'She went off. I always knew she would. She just went.'

'Take your things off,' said Violet decisively as though she were afraid someone else would claim him. 'Let's get bare and start from there. You can tell me all about it afterwards, Robin. And I'll tell you about me.'

The two strange, ugly, people undressed before each other, shyly, but lovingly. Eventually they stood there, his blue boyish eyes feasting on the shining marrows of her breasts, her cow gaze descending from his scarlet face to his sexual trunk dangling between his spidery legs.

'You're lovely, my darling,' he blurted out sincerely.

'And you are, too,' she answered.

Treacle pushed out his hand and felt it go into the cushion of her stomach. His touch made her topple back on to the bed like a large rolling cargo. Her face looked up between the piled flesh of her chest. Treacle found the edge of the bed and began to

161

advance nervously. She took hold of his stiffened member like a bargee pulling a tow rope and brought him towards her. Gratefully he found the place and sank into her body. They made splendid lovers. For him she was completely comfortable, wide and lush, a whole landscape of womanhood with a new horizon every time he chose to move his eyes. For her he was small and exquisite, like a little boy, manoeuvring about her, pressing into her and making her glow like a big bonfire. They made three separate loves, because he was very strong and she was enduring, then he lay, still sprawled across her stomach, sweat running into his screwed up eyes and matting his scrubby hair.

'I told you,' she said eventually. 'I told you I wasn't.'

'I'm glad,' he said sincerely. 'I probably wouldn't have known how to go about it with a virgin.'

'Tell me about when you were married, Robin,' she said. 'I was so surprised you could have knocked me down.'

'I did,' he said manfully. Then, caution returning, he added: 'Don't you think we'd better get up in case your mum and dad get back. I can't say I fancy him walking in here right now.'

'Neither do I,' she giggled. 'But the big picture won't be halfway through yet. We're all right. Let's stay. I feel very comfy. Tell me about being married.'

'All right,' he said lifting his chin and letting his face rest on her breast like a pillow. 'Her name was Jean and she said I made her laugh. But making her laugh wasn't enough because off she went with some other chap and I joined the Army and she got me for desertion. Funny, when you think about it – joining up and being done for desertion. Been divorced three years now.'

'I'll tell you about my virginity,' she said. 'I was only fifteen and I went to this party with this boy soldier in Aldershot. I might as well tell you it was a pig party.'

'What's that?'

She looked sad, but not embarrassed. 'I might as well give it to you straight,' she said. 'All the boys get together beforehand and put some money in a kitty and the one who takes the ugliest girl to the party gets the prize.' She paused and looked at him. 'Mind you, my boyfriend didn't win.'

'He must have been mad to make a bet like that,' said Treacle. 'How could he hope to win with you, my darling.'

'I've got a moustache,' she said. 'A bit of one, anyway.'

'Moustache!' he exploded. 'I can't see it.' He leaned over as though he were looking for it.

'Anyway,' she said decisively. 'It was there that it happened.' They lay quietly for a while. Then he said:

'I think we've told each other everything now. Don't run off with anybody else, will you? Not like Jean.'

'You know I won't, Robin, I love you.'

'And I love you, Vi. Nothing can happen to us now.'

'That's all right, then, isn't it.'

12

The Buller Barracks record-player was relaying 'Lights Out' over the subdued garrison when Treacle, bursting with the jauntiness of his love, went back to the barrack room. He whistled a thin, patriotic air as he marched strongly alongside the barrack square.

He was whistling and marching, his gnomish figure making a Disney silhouette across the wider lights of the doors and windows of the barrack blocks, when he saw Brigg standing quietly, regarding him from the shadows.

'Evening, Sar'nt,' said Treacle cheerfully.

'Evening, Treacle,' said Brigg. 'Having a practice march?'

'Who me? Oh, I see. No, Sar'nt, just marching along and whistlin', that's all.'

'How's life in the Tin Room?'

'Up and down, Sarge,' said Treacle. 'Baked jam roll tonight, though. The meat tins are bad enough, but that baked jam roll needs a grenade to shift it.'

'I'll try and get Sergeant Wilcox to requisition some grenades for you.'

'Ha! Thanks, Sarge.'

Brigg made to turn away.

''Night, Sarge,' said Treacle cheerfully.

'Goodnight,' said Brigg. He hesitated. 'Oh, listen a minute.'

'Yes, Sarge?'

'Umm, I wanted to see you about something.'

Surprise widened on the soldier's face in the half-dark. 'Me?'

'Yes. The RSM wants you to march up and down at the side of the square when there's a parade in future.' He waited awkwardly. 'Instead of in the squad.'

'At the *side* of the square?'

'Yes. More or less like you were doing just now. I thought for a minute that he'd told you himself and you were having a bit of a practice.' He said it lightly with a difficult smile.

'No. Nobody said anything. Why have I got to do it?'

Brigg said slowly: 'Well, it's just that he wants you to, that's all.' Then he said: 'You know what a mess they've been making of the drill movements . . . well, the RSM wants to have somebody of more or less average stride . . .'

He could see the stubbly face crack into a satisfied smile at the thought of being considered average. The troll head nodded with sudden eagerness as Brigg continued: 'He wants you marching up and down so he can use you as a measure to see if some of the others are overstriding or slacking. He'll keep an eye on you and he'll time the whole parade by you.'

'Honest, Sarge?' Brigg looked away from the expression of pleasure on the boyish man's elderly face.

'That's right,' said Brigg. 'You'll be like one of those

things they put on top of a piano to keep in time with.'

'A metronome!' exclaimed Treacle. '*We* had one of those when I was a kid.'

'That's it. You'll be a sort of marching metronome.' Brigg, half regretting beginning the fantasy, nodded at him sagely. 'And you start from tomorrow. Okay?'

'Righto, Sarge. Goodnight, Sarge.'

'Goodnight, Treacle.' Brigg as he turned heard Harrison's foul laugh coming from within the barrack room. He waited, on instinct, loitering in the shadows. Treacle, whistling more shrilly, threw out his arms and legs and strode towards his bed.

His jaunty march was stopped at the barrack room door. He stood fixed in the light. Harrison, Wilson, Bainbridge and the others were formed in a circle in the middle of the floor, crouching, their fingers upright at their ears. Pardoe was at the centre. At the moment he arrived they began to incant:

> '*We'll dyb, dyb, dyb.*
> *We'll dob, dob, dob.*
> *Arh-ka-la! We'll do our best!*'

Then they disintegrated and rolled yelping on the barrack room floor. Ferris' secret dog howled in reply from beneath his bed as its sleep was broken by Wilson's descending elbow. It sniffed out disdainfully.

Treacle turned quietly and sadly towards his bed, unbuckling his webbing belt as he did so. He rubbed the grease clinging to his short forearms.

'Come on, Brown Owl,' shouted Harrison. 'Come and have a fucking dyb, dob with us!' Treacle was facing away and did not look around. Harrison rushed from the others and grabbed the small man around the waist, hosting him and swinging him round and round like an infant. Finally he threw him brutally to the centre of the floor.

Harrison went after him. 'Come on you little pimply cunt,' snorted the heavy Harrison. 'Let's see you do a dyb, dyb, dob.' The others backed away not laughing now. Pardoe said: 'Drop it now, Hairy.' Wilson stepped forward and pushed Treacle towards Harrison.

'*I* don't want him, Nancy!' shouted Harrison, pushing him heftily back. Wilson returned him with another shove. This time Treacle, choked and spluttering, struck out at the big Harrison, missed and found himself grasped around the waist once more. Harrison picked him up cruelly, easily, and flung him around and around again, shouting 'Wheeee!', spinning in the middle of the floor, and finally throwing him into a corner. Treacle lay with his forehead against the cooling wall. 'Tell him to pack it in, Bainbridge,' said Pardoe. 'You're in charge.' Bainbridge said nothing but reached for his tin of talcum and powdered his pubis.

Treacle sensing Harrison leaning over him again, turned and swiftly hit the big man in the mouth with his fist. Harrison fell back, recovered, and came at him spitting and roaring like a large lunatic. He caught both Treacle's arms just below the elbow and tugged, intending to pull the little man to the centre of the room again. But the limbs that had spent so many hours submerged in cookhouse grease gave him no hold. As he violently tugged so his hands slid the length of Treacle's forearms and astonished

167

he stumbled back under his own weight, bowling over Pardoe, and striking the foot of one of the iron beds.

Pardoe was shouting from the floor: 'Pack it, Hairy. Come on, pack it. A joke's a joke but sod a pantomime.' Harrison stumbled to his feet and pushed Pardoe easily away. His fat eyes were on Treacle transfixed at the end of the room, his arms still out before him as though in supplication. 'They're all *greasy*,' he explained agonisingly in Harrison's direction. 'That wasn't my fault. It wasn't . . .'

Harrison began to advance, his face mad, his fists out before him. 'Bastard!' he screamed. 'I'm going to fucking well kill you!' He rushed abruptly, but his run was interrupted by a boot that appeared from the side of a locker, tripping him so heavily and spectacularly that he dropped like a bull and slithered half the length of the room. He lay against the wall for a moment and then turned his big watery face up to see Brigg.

'Sorry, Harrison,' murmured Brigg. 'Fancy you tripping over my foot like that.' Nobody spoke in the room. Harrison's face screwed up in a delayed whimper. Brigg said: 'Didn't think a big chap like you would be rushing about so fast. You must be pretty light on your feet.'

'Sarge . . . Sarge . . .' said Harrison malevolently.

'Let me give you a hand up,' said Brigg solicitously. He reached down and pulled Harrison to his feet by one arm and the collar of his shirt. With exaggerated concern he swung him on to the nearest bed.

'My head,' complained Harrison. 'I've cut my head. Behind.'

'Thompson,' ordered Brigg. 'You're supposed to be the boy scout. Get some water and a towel for Lance-Corporal Harrison's head.'

Treacle went without a word to the ablutions at the rear of the barrack room and returned with a fire bucket and a towel.

'Let's see,' said Brigg briskly. He turned Harrison's head about. 'Ah, yes, bit of a graze just at the back of the nut. Let's have the towel.' He took the towel from Treacle, dipped it fully into the dirty bucket water, and splashed it violently against Harrison's head, soaking the big man.

'That's my bed, Sarge,' protested Pardoe.

'Sorry,' said Brigg with full concern. 'Better get him on the floor.'

'I'm all right,' whinnied Harrison. 'Really, I'm all right now, Sarge. I don't need no more.'

'That's the stuff,' enthused Brigg. 'Now you're quite sure, old chap?'

'Quite sure, Sarge,' said Harrison eyeing him. 'Quite.'

'Right,' said Brigg. 'Well, I'll be off. If Harrison needs any more attention, you, Pardoe, come and call me. Keep the bucket and the towel handy. We don't want him having a relapse, do we? Very nasty fall, that was.'

Brigg was facing his squad on the fringe of the parade ground, the sun clear and lofty in the Hong Kong sky, warming the earth and the soldiers after the spell of poor weather. He felt uncomfortable in the thick prickly winter khaki and the men fidgeted.

'Stop wriggling about,' growled Brigg. 'McBride,

for Christ's sake! Renwick! You're like a load of bloody hula dancers.'

The squad stilled itself obediently. Its faces shone in the sun.

'We're going to march to the armoury,' said Brigg. 'The CO is having everybody's rifle checked so that when the Defence Minister arrives we don't have bolts dropping out and bayonets clattering all over the place. Sergeant Wilcox at the armoury is also going to demonstrate to you the new army instructions to replace the practice of boiling out the barrels of rifles. The British Army has been doing it one way since Water-bloody-loo. But now top scientists after years of research have discovered it does not really need hot water at all.'

The squad smiled dutifully. Brigg thought that Harrison's smile was too full and fixed for too long. He continued: 'Everybody is also being issued with nice new pull-throughs and clean bits of four-by-two. So many of these have been lost recently that the Colonel has decided to grant a general amnesty, which means you can all start from scratch. But anyone who loses his nice new pull-through from now on is going to have to pay for it. Understood?'

An assenting groan came from the squad. Brigg surveyed them with a professional short sniff. 'Finally,' he said. 'You will see posted on Orders during the next couple of days an instruction regarding the placing in rifle magazines of Coins-Rattling-For The Use Of. We all know that a bit of small change in the magazine makes a nice smart rattle during well-executed drill movements. The present-arms never sounds better than when there is some silver or copper currency clanking about inside the weapons. Unfortunately the rifle drill of this particular unit has failed to reach a satisfactory standard of coordination and the use of coins, as you might have noticed makes the whole thing sound like a collection for the Salvation Army. So there's going to be no more coins. You'll just have to bash those rifle stocks a bit harder, that's all. Right . . . Squad! . . . A-ttention! Squad, right t-urn! Quick march!'

He surprised them by wheeling left instead of right at the far corner of the square and turning up the road towards the married families' quarters. He had not intended the diversion but he was reluctant to return to his office that afternoon. The sun was full and the day quiet and he thought that, carefully handled, the visit to the armoury, plus the NAAFI break, would fill in the time to five o'clock.

Wives and small children were in their gardens. Hilda Harvey waved idiotically from her open window and Doris Boswell, who had manhandled an armchair out of doors to squat in the sun, shouted so long and so loudly that Brigg had to bring the marching squad to a halt.

He left them, stood at ease in the road, like a milkman might leave his cart, and wandered over to the scanty garden fence to converse with Mrs Boswell. The widespread, honestly ugly woman, a thick mail order catalogue in her lap, was enthroned in her armchair among the garden weeds, with white bedsheets, recently washed by the Chinese servant, flapping all about her in the sun.

'Yes, Mrs Boswell?' asked Brigg from the fence.

'Yes, what?' asked Mrs Boswell cheerfully. The

Chinese woman had come out with an armful of other washing and Doris Boswell pointed mutely but imperiously to the end section of the washing line where she wanted it hung.

'I thought I heard you calling,' said Brigg knowing he had.

'Oh, I was,' sighed Mrs Boswell happily from her chair. She let the shiny catalogue pages of bedding, garden rollers and electrical appliances flick over like a peepshow in her lap. 'I was just shouting that it was a bit unusual to see the Army in these parts. Unless it's got its feet up on the sofa, if you see what I mean.'

'Oh, yes,' acknowledged Brigg unsurely. 'How is Phil, by the way? Never see him in the sergeants' mess these days.'

'Never goes there unless he can help it,' said Doris haughtily, ignoring the first inquiry. 'He likes his home, my Phil. There's a few in that mess he's tempted to give a dose of sennapods to, I can tell you. Present company excepted, of course.'

'I should hope so,' gossiped Brigg. He nodded at the sheets. 'Nice drying day.'

'At last,' sniffed Doris. 'We're getting the sodding rainy season a few months early, by the look of it. You never know when to get the girl to do it. Still it's nice today. I'm enjoying it. Where are you taking that lot?'

'Which lot?'

'The big, brave soldiers. Is there an invasion?'

'Not that I know of. Just a little walk-about. Thought we'd show the flag up here. Just to reassure you.'

'I'm more reassured when I *don't* see the mob we've got here,' said Doris frankly. 'You ought to have seen the lovely unit we had in Berlin . . .'

172

'Never mind, love,' laughed Brigg. 'As long as we've got your Phil, we've got hope. I'll have to be going now. See you.'

'Bye-bye,' said Doris heartily. 'How's that kid of yours?'

'Just the same,' said Brigg over his shoulder. He heard her back-street hoot of laughter from behind. He marched the glowering squad away leaving her sprawled in her chair among the billowing sheets. When they had marched to the rising ground before the armoury, and he could look back down to the valley of the family houses, he turned and saw her still there like some unkempt Queen Victoria enthroned on the deck of a ship in full sail.

His plodding squad continued to attract attention among the Army wives. They turned from their tasks or their pastimes, looked out of their windows or hurried to their picket fences when they heard the sound of the boots, looking puzzled as people do hearing a familiar sound in a strange context. Soldiers! Marching soldiers! Pre-school-aged children held their breaths and stared at the men as they might have stared at an occupying army. Mrs Brice, who had spotted the Chinese on the previous Sunday, screamed: 'What yer looking for now Sergeant? Girl guides?' She bent double with self-inflicted laughter over a food-hung high-chair in which her pale youngest child was imprisoned.

Mrs Murdoch called Brigg over to her fence, but he let the squad march on this time, although they looked distrustingly over their shoulders at him as they went, like nervous cattle being sent on ahead by a dallying cowherd.

173

'If you see my old man, tell him to be home early tonight because I've got a steak and kidney pie for him,' shouted Mrs Murdoch. 'Tell him not to hang around in the mess.'

Brigg looked at her with quick pity. She was a thin, desperate woman with a mass of splendid black hair tipping over one side of her high boned face. 'I'll tell him,' he said awkwardly, knowing that he never would. Nor would Sergeant Murdoch be homing to steak and kidney that night. Chicken, bamboo shoots and rice, perhaps.

Brigg was about to turn when she called again hopefully. 'Why don't you come over one night and have a chat with him?' she blurted out. 'He'd like to do that. He only watches the television. And you're by yourself, aren't you?'

'Thanks,' swallowed Brigg. 'I will one night.'

'Don't forget. He would enjoy it.'

'Right,' said Brigg. 'Must go. I'll lose my troops. Bye!'

'Bye, Sergeant!' called Mrs Murdoch. The cheerfulness died on her face the moment he had gone. He did not look back but sprinted after the squad who had already marched by one left turn he had intended them to take. They were almost at the junction of an alternative road when he puffed up beside them and ordered them to change direction. They did so with surprise and relief like the passengers on a runaway bus when the driver has once more managed to take control.

They reached the armoury and Brigg halted them. Wilcox, a soiled apron around his middle, sleeves rolled up, and a large pair of pincers in

174

his hand, emerged from his workshop.

Brigg approached him. 'You look like the bleeding village blacksmith,' he said quietly.

Wilcox glowered. 'I thought you'd got lost,' he grumbled. 'This lot should have been here twenty minutes ago. It's nearly NAAFI break.'

'Timed it perfectly,' confessed Brigg. 'I took them on a bit of a route march. All around. Places where no white platoon has ever set foot before. Along the married quarters and all that area.'

'Showing the flag, eh?'

'Sort of.'

'Who did you show it to?'

'Let's see. Doris Boswell.'

'Christ, the sennapods queen. That's what I call time well spent.'

'She's all right,' said Brigg. 'Then there was Mrs Brice. That stupid cow wanted to know if we were looking for girl guides. And then I had a chat with the lonely Mrs Murdoch.'

Wilcox grinned. 'Ah, yes. I did a recce on her when you told me about her old man living with the Chinese school-marm. She's not bad, you know. Yards of black hair.'

'Why don't you pop in?' suggested Brigg. 'She asked me to call around one evening to see her husband who isn't there. She'd probably prefer you to me.'

'Bound to,' agreed Wilcox considering it. 'I may take her up on that. Right. You'd better get your mob off to have their tea. Tell them to be back here by ten past three.'

Brigg gave the instruction to his squad and dismissed them. They clattered away along the camp

175

road, back to the canteen outside which they had begun their afternoon's march. No one seemed to think that the march had been at all pointless. It was the way the army did things.

Nor did it occur to Brigg and Wilcox as they sauntered back in the same direction, like tutors who had dismissed their pupils.

'You should go and see Mother Murdoch tonight,' prompted Brigg. 'Apart from anything else she will have steak and kidney pie.'

'Chucking in all her trumps, eh?' smiled Wilcox. 'She'll probably be panting for it by the time I get around there.'

'She asked *me*,' Brigg pointed out. 'But as I'm a decent family man, anyway, and I've got Ho-Ho to cook my dinner, I'll willingly step down in favour of you. I'll be interested to hear what the pie was like.'

'We can't go tonight, anyway,' said Wilcox. 'We've got something else on.'

'*We* have?' Brigg stopped and carefully scrutinized Wilcox as though he had suddenly revealed himself as an enemy agent. 'How do you mean – *we*?'

Wilcox put a reassuring hand on Brigg's shoulder. 'I've done it,' he said looking straight and steady into the other man's eyes. 'I've done it; I've fixed it. Tonight we start in the gigolo business.'

Brigg's face contracted then widened blankly. 'You stupid bastard,' he breathed. 'Now what have you gone and done?'

'Nothing,' said Wilcox innocently. 'Merely fixed it, that's all.' He looked hopefully at Brigg. 'But I want you to come, Briggsy. I don't want to keep such a good thing to myself.'

13

Inverted triangles of light from Hong Kong city showed through the clefts in the hills. The warmth of the day still pervaded the evening for the Oriental spring was in the air. Brigg sat miserably beside Wilcox in the taxi.

'I can't believe this is happening to me,' he groaned. 'I can't believe that I'd let *anyone* – *anyone* – talk me round to this sort of caper. For God's sake, I've got a bloody kid at school. And here I am going out poncing on a couple of middle-aged Yankee ducks.'

Wilcox looked at him bitterly. 'There are times, friend,' he said, 'when you sound dead left wing. Poncing on middle-aged Yankee ducks! Put it that way and it *does* sound nasty. It's bound to. Look, as far as I'm concerned, we are acting as professional escorts to two lady tourists who happen to be Americans. We're doing them a service that's damned near invaluable. They'll be able to go to places and see sights they'd never be able to if they were on their tod.'

'Why don't they get their own men to take them?' Brigg complained.

'Because they haven't got men.'

'Let them get some, then.'

'I doubt if these two could.'

'Christ, this sounds better all the time!'

'Look, you won't have to sleep with yours if you don't fancy her.'

Brigg glowered: 'Thank you very much, master. I didn't bleeding well intend to, I can tell you. God, you'll have me flogging my hole around the YMCA next.'

'This will be much more satisfactory,' Wilcox assured him. 'I know you're going to like it. Look, they're very nice, clean, civilized women. The hotel porter told me when I fixed it. All we do is go out to dinner with them, amuse them, flatter them, and then take them back to the hotel – and *they* pay! It's beautiful – and perfectly normal. Professional escorts operate all over the world these days. It's a godsend to lonely unattached women like these. They spend all their cash touring the world, and then they have to skip half of it because they haven't got a man with them. And as white folks we're going to make a bomb, old mate, because most of the professional male escorts in Hong Kong are Chinese and American women don't like them because in the backs of their minds they think they might be Commies.' He leant forward: 'Briggsy, we're on twenty quid a night!'

'Well, I'm *not* going to bed with mine, and that's for certain,' sulked Brigg. 'I'm not prostituting my body for anybody.'

'Tell her you've got a period,' said Wilcox putting his hand gently on Brigg's.

Brigg took his hand roughly away. 'Do we tell them we're in the Army?'

Wilcox looked at him anxiously. 'God help us,' he said. 'I don't think you're going to be all that good at this.'

'Let's go back then.'

'No you don't, mate. You promised to give it a try. But we mustn't let them know we're in the cake, whatever we do. They might not take to that idea. It doesn't sound very glamorous to say you're a British Army sergeant, does it?'

'Make out we're field marshals,' said Brigg simply.

'We're professional escorts,' insisted Wilcox. 'That's our job. We don't do *anything* else.'

'We sleep all day and romance all night,' suggested Brigg nastily. Wilcox smiled and nodded.

Brigg regarded him sorrowfully but could not say anything. Wilcox felt he had to reassure him. 'Listen,' he said. 'This could be just the beginning. There can't be many Europeans doing this in Hong Kong, and half the tourists seem to be unattached American women. These two might recommend us to some of their pals, and then there could be more who want to join in. We'll sub-contract work to other blokes at the camp.' He chuckled and warmed to his idea. 'We'll charge a fiver for a no-hoper, like what's-his-name, Treacle, and twenty quid for somebody like that Charles Atlas twit and fifty quid for the Colonel.'

'You would too,' sighed Brigg. 'You'll probably be getting that mangy dog of Ferris' to screw their bloody poodles for a quid a time.'

At midnight the Sikh hall porter at the Sunrise Palace Hotel heard a female noise in the street and went unhurriedly to the main door. The two middle-aged American ladies who had caused so much trouble in the hotel with their drinking and their men friends, were hung out between the two English soldiers who

179

had called for them earlier that evening. The porter had known they were English soldiers because he would recognize the haircut anywhere. His colleague on the day shift had told him that some Englishmen were interested in the two American ladies, but this did not surprise him except that it constituted a departure from Portuguese, Dutchmen, Koreans and Chinese.

Brigg and Wilcox, the women slung about their necks, like a brace of brightly arrayed albatrosses, looked up pleadingly at the Sikh porter, but his only assistance was to ceremoniously open both glass doors of the hotel to admit the party. The Englishmen seemed to be in a distressed condition, perspiring and quarrelling with each other and with their burdens. Both women were singing heartily, but with their eyes tightly clenched and apparently from the depths of a heavy sleep.

The Sikh, casually, picked up a pair of keys from the board behind his desk and led the four people to the lift. 'Gentlemen,' he said in his rich Indian voice. 'I think you had better drop them in.'

Brigg met Wilcox's eyes despairingly.

Wilcox gave a short, savage nod of agreement and they half-pushed, half-heaved the two women, into the lift. They stopped singing. The porter, as though he were well accustomed to such a duty, sat them on the single cross seat where they lolled horribly open-mouthed against each other. Then he bowed with pleasing ceremony to the two Englishmen and closed the doors by hand as part of the same movement. The lift was in an open, gilded cage. It rose regally, leaving Brigg and Wilcox helpless on the ground floor. They heard the howling sound of wild female laughter, helpless, unsmothered laughter, from high above them.

They remained, stranded, standing there. Brigg did not look at his companion. But he said: 'All right, Casanova, when do they pay?'

'Be patient,' pleaded Wilcox unconvincingly. 'We'll shaft them before long, you wait.'

Brigg bristled: 'The only shaft you are going to see, clever bugger, is the one that fucking lift is in.'

'It went a bit wrong,' admitted Wilcox miserably.

'A bit wrong to the tune of two weeks' pay,' retorted Brigg.

'We'll invoice them,' said Wilcox firmly. 'Send them a bill. That's what a normal escort bureau would do.'

'A normal escort bureau would get the money first, I think,' said Brigg. 'Then it wouldn't *matter* if the clients got pissed out of their minds.'

'You can't just ask a woman for money before you take her out,' Wilcox argued. 'It's too difficult. I'm bloody sorry, Briggsy. The whole thing went up the spout from the very start. I suppose we *should* have got the cash first. I suppose there's no chance of us getting down here in the morning to see them . . .'

'Tomorrow they won't remember,' groaned Brigg. 'Christ, why did we have to go to that floating sodding restaurant? That stupid cow of yours threw half her dinner over the side. And champagne! *Why* did it have to be champagne?'

'They wanted it,' muttered Wilcox wretchedly. 'It was only Chinese champagne.'

'I don't give a monkey's dick if it was Abyssinian!' exploded Brigg. 'It was champagne!'

The lift came down in its golden enclosure. The Sikh smiled through the bars with white teeth like slabs and performed his Indian bow as he came out. 'Very comfortable,' he assured them. 'All most nice.'

'Thanks,' said Wilcox.

'We were worried,' muttered Brigg.

The Indian made short hesitant steps about their vicinity and Wilcox finally and reluctantly reached into his pocket and handed him a note. The man gave a subdued eastern hum and retreated behind his hall porter's desk where he became engrossed with a ledger and apparently forgot them entirely.

'Have we got a taxi fare back?' inquired Brigg patiently.

Wilcox shook his head in panic. His eyes quickly moved towards the hall porter. 'I gave him the last droppings,' he said as he realized.

'I thought you had,' said Brigg, still quiet. 'We're walking back to camp I take it.'

'Murdoch?' said Wilcox in a contrite whisper. He looked at Brigg from beneath his lowered eyebrows. 'He'll give us a lift, won't he?'

'Good old Murdoch,' said Brigg. 'Friendly old Murdoch. A few hours ago you were all for screwing his wife. He'll give us a lift at seven. It's now quarter past midnight.'

'Yes, Briggsy. I'm sorry, Briggsy.'

Brigg lifted his thoughtful chin from his chest and at once found himself looking into a face he knew. She had come in through the main door and they had not seen her then. When Brigg saw her she was taking a key from the porter. She glanced at the two men, smiled, uncertainly, then certainly, and then walked forward.

Brigg went back to the Sunrise Palace Hotel at six the next evening, taking the first possible train into the city after getting out of the camp. He had gone early, taking the easy unofficial exit, through the perimeter, and leaving a cigarette burning on the ashtray of his desk. He did not smoke, but it always worked. They always thought he would be back.

Barbara Finch was waiting for him in the hotel lounge. She was sitting in one of the silk-embroidered Macao armchairs reading a magazine. The same Sikh porter was at the back of the rounded reception desk in the attitude of a man behind a barricade. His face fluttered when he saw Brigg come through the door in uniform. His hand half rose but then he saw who it was. Brigg jogged his head at him and walked into the lounge.

She glanced up, smiled, and put the magazine on the table in front of her. He could see it was Chinese.

'That must be interesting,' he said. She was wearing a careful red woollen dress with a Victorian choker and pin at her throat.

'Certainly is,' she agreed. 'Please sit down.' She looked at the magazine and gave a shrugging laugh. 'It takes you right back to childhood. Before you could read – when you had to look at the pictures to figure out what the story was all about.'

She talked on engagingly, making tight but elegant hand motions. He thought her wedding ring looked too heavy for her. He nodded quietly and watched

183

her. When he had sat beside her in her car in the New Territories he had only been able to see her face when she turned to speak to him, and then she had been too close for him to look properly. Now he was able to study her. Her hair was dark and simple, parted across her face and gathered behind her neck. It framed a serious face made beautiful by the extraordinary eyes, grey-blue, full of lights and expressions. Her figure was slight but assured; she looked cool, comfortable and easy in the exotic chair, her slim arms, brown from the few days of springtime sun, resting on its extravagant brocade.

'Thanks for your help last night,' Brigg said. 'We were completely up the chute. Stranded.'

She laughed again: 'You were most welcome. I've never seen two people looking so forlorn and lost. Just like two small boys. If you'd been holding hands I think I would have burst into tears.' She paused, 'Is it too late for tea for the British?'

'Never,' he said.

She raised her hand to a Chinese waiter and ordered tea. 'Was it gambling?' she inquired. 'Or is that an impertinent question?'

'Since you paid our taxi fare back to camp, I don't think any question is impertinent,' shrugged Brigg good-naturedly. 'Gambling? Yes, I think you could say it was that. In a way.'

'And you lost,' she said.

'Oh, we lost, all right,' grinned Brigg. 'I'll tell you all about it some time.'

He realized immediately the intention of what he had said; that the words implied that they would meet again after that evening, that they would know a relationship where they would be able to exchange things that could not be disclosed to casual friends. He felt immediately annoyed with himself and he looked up apologetically. She showed no sign of having noticed the unconscious meaning. The waiter returned with the tea and she leaned forward and began to pour it easily into the fragile flowered cups.

'I guess this will be a little different to British Army tea,' she said. 'It sure doesn't look too robust.'

'I have a Chinese housekeeper,' he said. 'She makes it her way.'

'Ah, I see. How is your son? He's pretty lively.'

'Too lively sometimes,' nodded Brigg. 'He's what you could call an outlandish sort of kid.' He leaned back with his tea cup, strangely at home with her, and told her of Charlie's hypnotism at the school. Her smile deepened as he recounted it, and eventually she had to put down her tea cup and laugh into her slim hands.

'For heaven's sakes,' she giggled. 'What a marvellous kid.'

'He is until you have to clear up after him,' said Brigg. 'I spend half my time apologizing to people. Ho-Ho, my housekeeper, thinks he's in league with the devil. If she walks out we're sunk.'

She smiled at him across her hands, touching now before her chin, her eyes lively, her face composed. Their conversation had reached a full stop.

'When is your husband coming from Vietnam?' said Brigg abruptly.

At once she seemed embarrassed that he should have asked. 'I still don't know for sure,' she said unhappily. 'I guess I shouldn't have come to Hong

Kong. It was a crazy thing to do. He's got involved with something in the Demilitarized Zone and his leave can be fouled up at a few minutes' notice. He may be here next week. But I really should have stayed in New York.'

Brigg had difficulty in thinking of something to say. 'It must be expensive,' he said eventually. 'Waiting around here.'

'Certainly is,' she sighed. 'But now I'm here, I just have to wait, that's all. Leaving now would be a bigger waste.'

'What do you do?' he asked. 'I mean, do you get out a lot?'

'I wander around a little,' she said. 'Just sightseeing. Last night I went to the movies around the block. I had that little car for a period, but I thought that was too much of an extravagance. So I just walk around and wait. That's all I can do. I just hope he hurries up.'

Brigg hesitated and then leaned slightly forward. 'On Saturday,' he said. 'I usually take Charlie on some sort of outing.'

'I know,' she smiled. 'That's where I found you.'

'Well, I don't know whether this appeals to you. Please say if you don't want to do it. I'll understand . . .'

He waited again and she said good humouredly: 'Well, tell me.'

'It's only that on Saturday I said I'd take him out, up to the Peak or somewhere like that. Sergeant Wilcox, the one last night, has given him a camera and he wants to take some pictures, so I'm taking him up there, and if . . .'

186

'I'd love it,' she said quietly. 'I truly would. That's if you were about to invite me.'

'I was,' swallowed Brigg. 'It won't be much. Just . . .'

'Just up to the Peak,' she said. 'I know. I'd love to come. Maybe he can hypnotize me.'

'Don't encourage him,' grinned Brigg. He felt a gush of excitement, a gallon of joy, surging through him. Thank God for Charlie.

'Do you have to go back right now?' she asked looking at her watch. 'Do you have to get back to Charlie or have you got to guard anything?'

'No,' he said. 'No, I haven't. Charlie's doing his homework, or he'd better be, and we haven't got a lot worth guarding. It's not my job anyway.'

'Well,' she went on hesitatingly. 'You may have other plans . . .'

'No. Nothing.'

'Well, it's just I've always wanted to walk along the harbour in the evenings,' she said. 'Do you think we could do that? It's sometimes a little embarrassing for a woman to take a stroll like that on her own at night. I'm taking advantage of you, I know, but I need an escort. Do you think . . .'

'You couldn't have done better through an agency,' said Brigg. 'Every service rendered.' He rose and held out his arm. He closed his eyes as she rose and wished for a single moment that Wilcox could have been there.

They walked out and the sad, musky, evening smell of the city touched them. It was mild in the air, with the last ribbons of the day flying from the inland hills. An inevitable ferry laboured across the gold-washed harbour, the many ships were lighting their evening lamps, and the bright falling stars of an airliner descended across the long tongue of the airport runway thrust out into the sea.

Thick traffic moved noisily along the quay, but in the street where they first walked, by the harbour railings, there were only the tinkling sounds of sampans moving in the mild water below them.

Barbara said: 'I've never known a place so crowded and yet where it's so easy to be by yourself. One moment you have a million people all round you and then you turn a single corner and there's nobody.'

'It always seems crammed out down here to me,' said Brigg. 'Everybody just about falling over each other and tipping into the water . . .' He moved to the railings and together they looked down curiously at the nestling sampans and the people in them, cooking on aromatic stoves, crouched in shadowed corners, singing, walking acrobatically about, and calling to each other. A stretching dog on one houseboat rail howled across the evening and received an answering call from over the bronze water. Brigg went on: 'Up in the New Territories it's so empty, as you saw. There's more ducks than people. But they all crowd down here and live up in the town hills in those tin shacks. I suppose they're not keen on the countryside.'

They strolled along the pavement. A squatting Chinese asked them to buy sweetmeats from his candlelit tray. Brigg waved his hand at him quietly.

'We don't come down here a great deal ourselves,' said Brigg. 'The men from the camp, I mean. I get into town more than most because I bring Charlie down here and I sometimes get down at night.' He hesitated. 'To see friends. But the rest don't. It's a strange thing about the British Army. It likes to keep to itself. It gets into a lot of foreign places, but it doesn't like the foreigners very much.'

'Maybe it doesn't trust them?' she asked.

'That, I suppose. But I don't think it really knows what to say to them.'

'So it keeps to itself. I wonder if the US Army is like that?'

Brigg immediately detected a wife's question, so he shook his head non-committally. 'When I was eighteen I was a conscript in this army,' he remembered. 'We were all shut up in a garrison in Singapore. We shut ourselves up really. We hardly went anywhere outside. Everybody was hungry for sex, but not many would dare go out and find it. Instead they saved up their pennies to buy civilian suits so they could look smart for the girls in the dance halls when they got home.'

'Eighteen?' she said. 'And no sex?'

'Sounds incredible these days, I know,' said Brigg. 'Quite honestly I was nearly nineteen before I discovered the delight. I was scared stiff one of the Communist bandits in the jungle would shoot me dead before I knew what women were all about. There wasn't even much likelihood of that. Getting shot, I mean. Nineteen. And I would bet that half those kids came home at twenty – and still virgins.'

'It sure sounds quaint today,' she agreed. 'I guess now it comes along a good deal earlier than that. And even now, you say, the Army doesn't . . . er . . . come out . . . very much.'

He laughed at her. 'That's very carefully put.'

189

'I intended it to be,' she smiled.

'It's a bit different now,' said Brigg. 'It was just kids in those days, straight out of insurance offices and that sort of thing. And even outside the Army they hadn't heard of this permissive society. Now, there's a lot of old sweats – old timers – and married men who cart their wives and kids around with them wherever they go in the world. The single ones manage.'

She laughed out loud. Three ragged Chinese children looked up at her questioningly from the pavement and she stopped, 'Why are you still in the Army?' she asked him as though it had suddenly occurred to her.

He screwed up his face. 'I suppose you could say I "dropped out", in a way,' he lied. 'I got fed up with the way things were going for me, so I dropped out. But I didn't go looking for any guru, and I didn't grow a beard and wear rags. I did it the comfortable way. I came back to the Army after I'd been out of it for seven years. I only just made it. Unless you're a scientist or a good footballer they don't normally let you back in after twenty-seven. That's when I got back in.'

'But that's not dropping out,' she argued. 'Dropping out is dropping out. You have work, duties, to do.'

'Not much, if you're careful,' he said. 'I'm not exactly proud of it, but it's a fact. And it's a comfortable way of keeping out of society, except for the early mornings. You get fed and clothed and housed and you're given money to buy sweets, and you don't have to work very much. You just have to look as though you're doing it.'

190

'It doesn't sound right to my conformist mind,' Barbara said. 'But if you say so . . .'

'An army is unproductive, right?' said Brigg spreading his hands. 'They're always telling us that our job is keeping the peace. You do that just by *being* here. You don't go around actually *keeping* it. Telling people or warning people. As long as you're here it should be kept – people more or less behave. It's only when you actually have to start *doing* something – like fighting – that you've failed in your job. Right?'

'I suppose so,' she said doubtfully.

'So we sit on our backsides and do our job. Every now and then we shoot a gun or two, but there's not much excitement otherwise. We've the most peaceful occupation on earth in the Army.'

'Somewhere,' she said slowly. 'There's a hell of a flaw in that reasoning. I know it but I'll have to take time to work it out. Anyway, you're a "drop out".'

'Definitely,' said Brigg. 'And I don't intend to drop in again for a long time. Until I'm on a pension.'

'I've spotted the flaw,' she said after they had walked without speaking for a while. 'What happens to your thesis if the Chinese invade?'

'We wouldn't have a chance,' said Brigg simply.

They walked the entire evening, stopping at a Chinese eating-house for a while, and then going back to the hotel. Through all the time and all their talking she did not once speak about her husband, nor he about his dead wife.

When he was walking away from her he remembered the money. He turned and ran back to the hotel. She was still in the foyer, taking her key from the Sikh porter. She turned in surprise.

'I forgot your loan,' he laughed handing her the money.

'I thought you'd never mention it,' she smiled.

He touched the back of her hand with his fingers before turning to go again. 'I'll see you on Saturday,' he said.

'I'll see you then,' she said.

14

Eight solid soldiers marched across the square to the main gate, wheeled wearily left onto the road and continued until they reached the patch of rubbery earth where cadaverous sacks were suspended from wooden supports and an obstacle net hung forlornly from a wooden frame so that it looked like a long lost goalpost. This was the garrison battle-school where the standard arts of personal war were taught to troops, some of whom had been going through the same routines with bayonet and bravado since the summer of nineteen-forty.

The men trudged in single file, their heads only diverting from the front when they progressed by the Chinese village where a Command Workshops jeep was slotted into the mud, making a sad formation with the sunken tank recovery vehicle and the tank still nuzzling deep into the Chinese eating-house. It had rained again in the late night after the daytime sun, strong, unusual rain, and the driver of the jeep, blatantly ordered on by a dawn officer who believed the ground had dried out, had scuttled his vehicle alongside the others.

Each of the marching octet swivelled his eyes and smirked at the accumulating catastrophe. The staff sergeant who strode at their side was a stranger and frowned uncomprehendingly at the mechanized mess. Various lethargic British soldiers and an expressionless but constantly entertained Chinese village population stood in the vicinity like fishermen viewing flotsam on their beach.

'What's happened there, then?' asked the staff sergeant from the corner of his mouth. Pardoe, who was marching parallel, said sideways: 'The tank broke a track, staff, and crashed into the chop-chop house, then the big thing went down to pull it out and got stuck in the mud. The jeep's a new one on me. Haven't seen that one before.'

'Looks like a blooming amphibious operation,' said the staff sergeant.

Pardoe squinted at him suspiciously. The new staff sergeant, the unarmed combat expert they had been promised, was on secondment from a unit at Kowloon. He was unlikely looking, short with a bright bucolic face and a stomach hammocked in his webbing belt. Pardoe had never heard a soldier say 'blooming' before.

They turned from the road and trudged up the short slope to the battle training ground. The staff sergeant halted them and then turned a pained, distasteful look on the apparatus spread across the field. He sniffed and turned directly on Pardoe. 'And how often,' he asked acidly, 'do those sacks have the benefit of your warlike bayonets?'

'About once a month, staff,' said Pardoe. 'Sometimes on Saturday mornings we come up here with bayonets and that, and other times we're on the firing range, and sometimes we dress up like trees and we have to find each other.' He looked at the NCO apologetically. 'That sort of thing, staff.'

'How about training films? Do they ever show you training films? Unarmed combat? Any unarmed combat?'

'Now and then, staff. They're usually about fighting in the jungle or the desert, of course, which don't apply around here. Then they have these films to tell you to go to the lav regular, and how to find out if you've got the clap.'

'Right, that's enough,' bawled the staff sergeant suddenly and surprisingly blushing in the cheeks. 'I didn't ask for all that.' He let the colour settle in his face and then regarded the squad. 'My name is Staff Sergeant Parsons and I've had the misfortune to be brought here to give you out-of-condition bunch a crash course in unarmed combat because you've got to do something fierce to entertain the Secretary of State for Defence when he turns up next month.'

He had large indefinite blue eyes, like bruises in his ruddy face. He went on: 'As you have doubtless taken respectful note from my shoulder flash, I am in the East Anglian Regiment which is made up of the three best line regiments in the British Army, bar none. The Essex Regiment, the Suffolk Regiment and the Norfolk Regiment. It, therefore, gives me a good deal of pain and inconvenience to have to come to an odds-and-bods blooming garrison like this even for a short time. But where my country, God bless her, wants me, that's where I will be.'

The necks of the eight soldiers extended forward in wonder as though he had unasked commenced an impromptu music hall turn for their entertainment.

He regarded them with the agricultural contempt

of a farmer examining a poor herd. 'And right at the start, I had better give you bunch a word of warning. I am a member of The Norwich Wayfarers.' He leaned back, portly, full-faced, waiting for the reaction which never came. Parsons's small smile fell into a scowl. 'You,' he pointed at Burgess. 'What are The Norwich Wayfarers?'

'A football team, staff?' suggested the body-builder hopefully.

'No!' roared Parsons. 'The ignorance these days! The Norwich Wayfarers is a religious order – and a very strict order too. In my own unit at Kowloon I am known as Parson Parsons, and I'm not a little bit ashamed of that title. So just watch your language when I'm around. Understand?'

They all understood. 'Right to work then,' said the staff sergeant. 'Unarmed combat. If everybody followed the teachings of Our Lord Jesus Christ then we wouldn't need unarmed combat. And we wouldn't need a blooming army either. We could all pack up and go home. Unfortunately this happy state is a long way off and so I propose to demonstrate today such basics as the two-fingers-up-the-nose, the upward jab neck splitter and the thumb used as an eye-gouger. These are not the names from the manual, but I prefer to call them by the less fancy handles. Let's see . . .' He looked along the line. Each man looked away, as much as he was able. Parsons said encouragingly: 'Many are called, but few chosen. Matthew twenty-two, verse fourteen. You – come here.'

He pointed at Burgess the Bodybuilder, who rolled his shoulders and stepped forward slowly, muscularly, an uncertain smile on his simple face.

Parsons regarded him with pity. 'You're a great big chap,' he said sadly.

'Weights, staff. I do weights.'

'Right,' said Parsons. 'I want you to punch me in the face.'

Burgess, a head above Parsons, blinked: 'Punch, you, staff?'

'Punch me, lad. It's an order,' said Parsons looking up at him.

Burgess eyed his comrades with a growing smirk, turning almost bashfully from the staff sergeant and then wheeling swiftly, swinging a vicious fist towards him. The portly little man seemed to shrivel like a suddenly released balloon. Burgess flailed at the air and was then caught with a pulverizing chop under the ribs and a second swiftly on the shoulder blade. He lay on the red mud trying to get his eyes focused and the other men laughed in line. Pardoe exclaimed: 'Oh, bloody hell!'

Parsons revolved with ceremonial slowness and his bruised eyes settled on Pardoe. A silence like death fell over the squad. 'I heard you,' said Parsons.

'Yes, Staff,' mumbled Pardoe. 'It was me.'

'What's your name?'

'Pardoe, Staff.'

'You're Welsh. You sound Welsh.'

'Yes, Staff.'

'Very religious people, Welsh people,' said Parsons almost dreamily. 'Why aren't you God-fearing, Pardoe?'

'Don't know, Staff. Been away a long time, I s'pose.'

'Well, I told you about blasphemy, didn't I? I *did* explain about The Norwich Wayfarers?'

'Swearing. Yes, Staff.'

'Come here.' The voice was chilly and ominous.

'Didn't mean it, Staff. It slipped out.'

'Don't worry,' said Parsons. 'I am not going to paralyse you with one touch of my big toe today. Just come here in front of the squad, son.'

Suspiciously, nervously, Pardoe moved out of the line. Burgess was still looking up from the ground where he had prudently remained. The squat staff sergeant put a steely hand on Pardoe's shoulder and he jumped fearfully at the feel of it.

'Now,' said Parsons. 'Since this is our first day, I am going to be charitable. Without charity I am as a sounding brass or a tinkling cymbal. Am I not, Pardoe?'

'Yes, Staff.'

'So I am not going to paralyse you. But so that we can bring home the fact that the Lord is with us everywhere: "Where two or three are gathered together, there am I." So that we can really *feel* that, I think that you, Pardoe, will now sing a chorus.'

A startled look added itself to Pardoe's expression. 'A chorus? What sort of chorus, Staff? I can't sing.'

'Of course you can sing, Pardoe. You're Welsh, boy! Now, let's see . . . *Build on the Rock . . . Happy day . . . Pull For The Shore, Sailor.*'

The Welsh soldier shook his head miserably. 'Don't know them, Staff. I only know a few, like . . . pop songs.'

'Pop songs!' bellowed Parsons. 'You had better think of something better than that, Pardoe.' He leaned closer, threateningly. 'Or would you prefer the paralysis?'

'No. Not that, Staff.'

'*Jesus Wants Me For A Sunbeam*, then?' suggested Parsons. 'Everybody knows that.'

Pardoe swallowed. 'I can't remember it all, Staff.'

'Start,' said Parsons.

Pardoe croaked the little song, hesitating, stumbling, looking at the staff sergeant fearfully, like a threatened pony. Burgess looked up from his position on the ground, a smile of inexpressible enjoyment filling his face.

> '. . . Jesus wants me for a sunbeam,
> A sunbeam, a sunbeam,
> Jesus wants me for a sunbeam.
> I'll . . . I'll be a sunbeam for him.'

The squad were rolling with laughter, unable to hide it, until the staff sergeant roared them to order.

'Now we'll *all* blooming sing it!' he snorted. He motioned to Burgess. 'You, get up. Now raise your voices. Ready – go!'

They all began to sing in ragged attempted unison, at the middle of the muddy field, the curious chorus drifting over the road and down to the Chinese village with its trapped army vehicles. The Command Workshops men and the attendant Chinese turned at the strange childish sound and saw the group of soldiers above them, singing against the Oriental sky.

Their voices stuttered to the end of the chorus and they stood dumb and fidgeting. 'I will sing praises unto the Lord,' incanted Staff Sergeant Parsons with satisfaction. 'Now, let us commence with the upward jam neck splitter.'

*

Colonel Simmons had returned from lunch in the officers' mess and was elongated in private quietness behind his desk. The sun had come out for the third time that day and was flooding the barrack square and flying through the windows where the soldiers worked.

For God's sake, why did the Defence Minister have to poke his Whitehall nose into *their* garrison? If he had to travel then why couldn't he travel somewhere else? Aden. No, not Aden. Probably running out of places. Pulling the flag down everywhere. Still it was so inconvenient. Everything, from the drill to the fire hose nozzles, had to be polished up. Soldiers who had never before damaged a fly were having to be taught the rudiments of unarmed combat and a Grand Camp Concert had to be arranged. The Colonel sighed. He prided himself that all through his military career he had never shrunk from answering the call of the bugle even if the result of the summons had incidentally, but nevertheless invariably, been total anti-climax. But when he retired, he thought, fondly, he would buy a house within echo distance of an army camp and he would listen to the bugle blowing while he was pruning his roses or writing his memoirs. He had often thought of writing his memoirs, tame and peaceful volume though it might be.

But then they could blare their teeth out on their bugle and he would only be required the effort of a smile and get on with whatever he was doing. The picture was a satisfying one, but his comfortable head-nodding in time with the dream was interrupted by Major Fortune.

The adjutant came apologetically through the door with two oblongs of paper. 'Sorry to disturb you, sir . . . er . . . at this time of day . . .'

The Colonel brought himself up from the lounging position into which he had slipped during his reverie. 'No bother, Fortune,' he growled guiltily. 'Twenty-four hours a day one is on duty in the British Army. That's what the men are always told, isn't it?'

'Indeed, sir.'

'On the other hand, if you can give me an hour to myself after lunch, I'm always grateful.'

Fortune gave a short, understanding, bow. 'Naturally, sir.'

'We all have to recharge the batteries, Fortune.'

'Yes, sir. But there's a couple of urgent things, and I thought you would want to see them.' He moved forward with the papers. 'Security arrangements for the Defence Minister's visit, sir. From Military Police and Special Branch, sir. And, more important, the provisional list of acts for the camp concert.'

'Oh, yes,' agreed the Colonel. 'Glad we've got the concert launched. Who's in it?'

'Let's see,' said the captain. 'Sergeant Major Love is the comedian.' He looked up to catch the pre-dictable doubt born on the face of his commander.

'Love? The comedian?' whispered Colonel Simmons unbelievingly. 'Is this a joke?'

'I hope it will be, sir. "Frank Love – You'll Love Him!" That's how it's listed here,' he said dolefully.

'That's going to be the character act of the century, I should think. I didn't know he even *knew* any jokes.'

'Apparently he does, sir. But he wants a man with a

blackboard to stand in the wings, so that he can remember the first lines.'

The Colonel sighed tiredly: 'I suppose that gross daughter of his is going to do a fan dance.'

'No, sir. She's singing a selection of pop songs with the camp group, Brod Perkins and The Ding Dongs. Let's see, she's jotted them down, sir. *Blue, Blue, My Love is Blue, Eleanor Rigby* and *I Can't Get No Satisfaction.*'

'The last sung from the heart, no doubt,' muttered the Colonel. 'All right. What else?'

'Room B, Barrack Block Two, are doing their version of *Charley's Aunt*, with that coloured lance-corporal, Forster, as the aunt.'

Colonel Simmons brightened. 'That's more promising,' he nodded. 'I like the sound of that.'

'Staff Sergeant Parsons, the secondment from Kowloon, the unarmed combat instructor, is singing *I Know That My Redeemer Liveth.*' Fortune looked up and stared with mute challenge at the Colonel, who scratched his teeth uncomfortably. 'Is he . . . like that, then?' he asked.

'Like what, sir?'

'Well, Messiahish. Religious.'

'It looks like it, sir. Shall I try and put him off. Perhaps we can get him posted back by then.'

'No, no. Let's not be too hasty. Could add a bit of class to the show. A slice of Christ after Sergeant Major Love's jokes might go down well. What about the wonder child hypnotist? Brigg's lad.'

'He's all right, sir. But he says he can't always guarantee to put the subject into a trance. He says he can do it to about one in three. So he wants half a dozen volunteers on the stage, so that he's absolutely

202

sure of getting somebody he can put under.'

'That can be arranged. But why can't he try a few out before hand, then he'll know who is who?'

Fortune shook his head: 'The men are most reluctant, sir. Even on the night of the concert I feel we will have to hold out some inducement.'

'Or threat,' added the Colonel. 'Right, half a dozen hypnosis victims, wanted.' He made a scribbled note on his pad.

'Subjects,' corrected Major Fortune carefully.

'Oh, all right, subjects, then. What other delights have we got?'

'Me, sir. I thought of doing something.'

The Colonel was surprised and gratified. 'Very sporting of you, Fortune. What on earth can you do?'

Fortune coloured, but then mumbled modestly. 'Well, it's a sort of pastiche, sir. I'm supposed to be a pre-war British officer posted in the Far East. You know, puttees and everything. Swagger cane. All that.'

The major paused, but the CO nodded for him to go on. 'It's all Kiplingesque stuff,' he continued. 'Honk-ers, Rang-ers, Bang-ers, Sinkapoops.'

'Good God, what's that?' asked the Colonel.

'Pre-war slang, sir. Honkers is Hong Kong, and the others are Rangoon, Bangkok, and Singapore.'

The Colonel seemed doubtful. 'Sinkapoops is Singapore?' he said unclearly.

'Exactly, sir.'

'Sounds hilarious,' said Simmons unconvincingly. 'Work on it, Fortune. Work on it.'

'I certainly will, sir. There will be some more acts volunteering before the night, sir, I'm sure. A prize of seven days' extra local leave is being offered for the best.'

'I see. In that case we'll have more on the stage than in the bloody audience.'

'We'll be doing some stiff auditions, sir. Don't worry. Now, do you want to see this thing from the security people about Military Police deployment during the Minister's visit?'

'Those clowns,' grumbled the Colonel. 'All right. Give it to me. Let's see what they have.'

Fortune handed the paper to him. He was reading down it when the sound of singing filtered with the sunlight through the open office window. The Commander looked up and screwed up his mild face.

'Singing, sir,' said Fortune as though confirming a rumour. He moved towards the window. The Colonel joined him and they witnessed Staff Sergeant Parsons swinging alongside the marching single file of the unarmed combat squad. The cherry-faced instructor was striding and strident with his song:

'Marching beneath the banner,
Fighting beneath the cross.'

The soldiers, loud but glum, sang with him as they strode around the barrack square. Faces abruptly blocked half the camp windows. Colonel Simmons turned sadly to his aide. 'Looks like The Messiah has arrived,' he said.

'Looks like it, sir,' nodded Fortune.

'Just our luck,' said the Colonel. 'As though we haven't got enough arseholing trouble.'

*

'Party! Paaarty . . . load. Party . . . five rounds application . . . in your own time. Fire!'

Wilcox bawled the orders across the backs of the prostrate soldiers. Their legs were wide, their toes pointing outwards; the set position required only of basic sexual intercourse and firing a British Army rifle. Ferris fired first, jerkily and without controlling his breath. A rotund crow rose ill-temperedly from a jasmine and turned muttering away into the blameless Saturday morning sky.

Brigg walked steadily up the muddy path to the firing range. It had rained with unseasonal enthusiasm once more in the night and rumour was around that the Commanding Officer of Command Workshops now had his staff car sunk in the slime at the Chinese village and had actually drawn his revolver on his driver. Sightseers from the garrison had gone down to witness the growing calamity when they were free after the morning tea break.

'Keeping the class after school?' said Brigg to Wilcox.

'Had some little bits of trouble,' said Wilcox eyeing the men.

'Shooters still not right?'

'A bent nail here, a bit of string there,' grunted Wilcox still not turning. The soldiers were firing spasmodically. 'But it's not the rifles I'm worried about, it's them that's got 'em. Look at Burgess, the muscle bound bugger. Every time he presses the trigger his bum jerks up. You'd think he was shooting his load, not his gun. And have a look at Blackie there.'

'Fucking Forster!' he bawled. 'Squeeze it gently. You're shooting at white men, man!'

Brigg put his hands in his pockets. 'Not much cop, then?'

'These are the only troops I've ever seen where the butt party could lie down and sunbathe in perfect safety, right in front of the bloody targets,' commented Wilcox grimly. 'Ferris killed a fieldmouse this morning.'

'That's not bad shooting,' said Brigg.

'It was seventy yards in front of the intended target,' grunted Wilcox. 'I think if the Old Man reckons on having range firing as part of his pantomime for the Defence Minister he'll have to arrange for somebody to go up and poke a few pencil holes in the targets first.'

The squad had finished firing. 'I think the kiddies have exhausted themselves,' said Brigg nodding towards them.

'At ease,' muttered Wilcox at the men. They relaxed upon the ground.

'No Jiggery Pokery Club tonight?' asked Wilcox quietly.

'No. I've . . . promised to take Charlie out.'

'Tonight?'

'Well, no. But we'll be late getting back.'

'Who's after a pretty little Yankee tail?' whispered Wilcox.

Brigg scowled at him. 'We're just going up the Peak that's all,' he said.

'Is that what it's called now?'

'Well you'll have the rest of the field to yourself, mate, won't you,' pointed out Brigg. 'Give both the twins the benefit of your physique, but avoid all silver-haired dolls from North Carolina.'

'Bollocks,' muttered Wilcox amiably. He called the men to their feet. 'Everybody unloaded?' he inquired. They grunted and nodded and said, 'Yes, Sarge.' Wilcox sniffed. 'Just point the nasty end of the weapons in the air, will you, lads,' he suggested. 'That's it. Everybody. You too, Burgess. Right, now, from the front, by number, pull the trigger. That means, you to start Forster. Ready! Squa-ad, by numbers!'

'One!' answered the dark Forster, clicking the trigger of his rifle.

'Two!' Click.

'Three!' Click.

'Four!' Click.

'Five!' Bang!

It was Burgess. The body-builder, sheet-faced, eyes aghast, stared at the sky into which the bullet had gone. Then he dropped his petrified gaze to Wilcox.

'Down!' blared Wilcox as though in terror. 'Everybody down!'

Irrationally the soldiers flung themselves flat. Wilcox and Brigg stood and watched them, sprawled, hands clasping necks.

'THAT BULLET IS COMING DOWN AGAIN!' bellowed Wilcox. 'It's coming down. It's descending! Here it comes. Wheeeeeee!' Some faces looked up shame-facedly from the earth.

'Get up you troop of ponces,' ordered Wilcox. 'Burgess, you're on a charge. I knew you still had a round there, but you didn't, did you? And *I'm* not the one who is supposed to count, lad. Report to me as soon as you open your darling little eyes on Monday morning. At the double. And, now, because you've given all your comrades such a nasty shock you can carry every other bugger's rifle back to the barracks. And that's at the double too.'

15

At eleven o'clock that night Brigg, standing close behind her, put the fingers of his right hand anxiously, irrevocably, against her neck. She was looking out of the window of his house. The barrack square, with its built-up sides, the barrack blocks, looked like a great fishtank in the yellow lights. A bugle calling the Last Post unwound its sound over the camp.

Barbara allowed his fingers to remain and rest. 'No genuine, nice girl should be in an Army camp at Lights Out,' she observed.

'It's not a genuine, nice, Lights Out,' returned Brigg. 'We haven't got anyone who has enough puff to blow a bugle, so they play a record.'

She gave a laugh, a light chuckle, but he felt it vibrate tenderly through her skin. She was still facing away from him, the lights from the square, as always ignoring the bugle, washing lightly over her face.

'I think Charlie enjoyed today, don't you?' she said. 'He said the China Sea was shining like a dragon. He could be a poet.'

'He used up three rolls of film,' said Brigg. 'It will be cheaper if he *is* a poet. He had a good time though. Did you?'

His fingers remained flat, but not pressing, against her. 'I had a beautiful day, thank you,' she said calmly.

Brigg said: 'Do you mind being here?'

Her head shook and her hair rolled slightly against his face as he stood behind her. 'If I did, I wouldn't be here,' she answered. 'I am that sort of person. But I am in a house and there's a child asleep upstairs. Shall we say it's a long, long time since I felt so secure?'

A quartet of drunks came into view across the window, squaddies attempting the difficult voyage from the NAAFI to their beds. One of them had fallen down in a pool of lamplight and the others pawed and stumbled over him, trying to pull him to his feet. They shouted and croaked and eventually hauled him upright and dragged him along between them.

'The fallen comrade,' muttered Brigg.

'They look like they're in battle,' she agreed. 'Listen, they're singing. I can hear them.'

'It's probably something it's best not to hear.'

'Listen,' she whispered. They remained still in the window and the men sang blatantly.

'It's *Goodnight Irene*,' said Barbara. 'There's surely nothing wrong with that.'

The words filled the Saturday night now. The men were stumbling and slipping just across the road from the house.

> '*Sometimes I live in the country,*
> *Sometimes I live in the town,*
> *Sometimes I take a great notion*
> *To burn the old shithouse down . . .*'

She turned, laughing, with her hands against her mouth. She looked joyfully at him over her fingers.

'I told you,' he said. 'Soldiers are all the same.'

210

'You're a soldier,' she said immediately quietened. 'So is Paul.'

'I wondered when you were going to mention him,' sighed Brigg.

'It's so long I've almost forgotten him,' she said, turning and walking concisely into the room. 'That country, that war, are so far away. Every day he doesn't come back to me a little bit of him vanishes.' She looked up at Brigg. 'Do I sound like I'm making excuses?' she said. 'Because I guess I am.'

'For what?' asked Brigg.

'For being here with you in this house,' she said. 'I know we took Charlie out to the Peak for the day, and we brought back the food, and Ho-Ho is away visiting with her grandpa, but it's late, Sergeant, it's very late. I can't get back to the city tonight. You and I both know that. And I haven't even mentioned going, have I? And when you touched me just now, with your fingers, I didn't take your hand away, did I? Nor did I remind you that I am spoken for. Nor did I holler for the guard.'

'No,' said Brigg, his voice low and suddenly cumbersome. 'No, you didn't do any of that.'

They were still standing three feet apart. 'I knew, and I know you must have known too,' she said simply as though explaining some ordinary thing. 'From the second time we saw each other, anyway, that there would be something for both of us in this.' She glanced at him with a sort of serious amusement. 'Are you scandalized?' she said. 'I guess you think I'm shameless.'

'No, no,' he stumbled. He was looking full into those remarkable eyes now, dark in the room but moving with lights like the sea at night. 'I'm just amazed. I'm not generally very lucky, that's all.'

She smiled at his inelegance. 'Things like this don't happen to me very often,' she said. 'Maybe I'm not too lucky either.'

'There doesn't seem much else I can say,' he said awkwardly. 'Except it's an unexpected pleasure.' They each took a pace towards each other. Even then Brigg merely looked into her face. His hands hung at his sides as though afraid to touch her. He saw her soften before him and in that instant they were clutching each other so fiercely that they might have been lovers parted for years instead of lovers who now held each other for the first time. Her body relaxed against the thickness of his chest. His arms were protectively about her, as though he feared she might vanish. Her mouth came jerkily to his; his clumsily to hers and they somehow achieved a distorted kiss. They did not care. He felt a great crashing throughout his body. She let herself be quiet against him.

'Oh, Sergeant,' she croaked into his neck. 'Oh, I've been so goddam lonely. I just can't wait for him any more. I don't *know* him, I don't *want* him any more. He's gone too far from me. And you are here, Sergeant darling, you are right here with me.'

With his bent face he began to nose against her blouse, feeling the softness beneath give easily against his movements. His hands fell helplessly down the slope of her back until he held the skirt at her small buttocks tight against his palms. She lifted his face with one hand and kissed him tenderly but with a consuming hunger. He took her and held her to the kiss.

'Charlie,' she asked. 'Is he asleep?'

'He's a very good sleeper,' said Brigg, his nose against her neck again. He lifted his hands to the pearl buttons on her blouse and began to undo them unskilfully.

'Let me take these things off,' she whispered. 'I know where everything is.'

'I'm clumsy,' Brigg confessed. 'It's a long time since I was married. Two years.'

'Me, too,' she smiled busily. 'These are little devils to get unhooked. But I know how . . .'

Together, like dancers in a slow ritual, they took away some of their clothes. She stood in front of him in a pale half slip and her brassiere. He was still wearing his trousers. Barbara smiled at him. 'Not bad for strangers,' she said as though seeking to reassure him. 'Would you like to take a stab at this.'

She touched the thin straps across her brown shoulders. 'The curtains,' he mumbled. 'I'll just see to the curtains.' He went across the room and pulled them together.

'I can't see you,' she said.

'I'm here,' he replied. 'These are my hands on your shoulders.'

'I can feel them. Rub my neck with them.'

He stroked her neck feeling her hair falling like satin tendrils across his hands. Then he pushed his rough fingers down into the cleft of her back and easily, gratefully, found the hook. He felt her small, half awake breasts slip forward in surprise when they were released. He wanted some light then, so he could see them. It was very dark in the room. He ran his hands up to her ribs until he had them laid against the lower slopes of her breasts. He rolled the swellings sweetly in his palms, feeling his body heating and his senses rushing.

'My turn, Sergeant,' she whispered. The slim touch of her fingers came to the flesh of his belly and she let them drop at once against his trousers, pressing against the urgent swelling beneath the cloth. 'Someone's awake,' she said. She opened his trousers and with sudden impatience pulled them away from his thighs and legs. Naked he moved against her and felt himself slide up the front of her half slip. He retreated and did it again, the two textures, the skin and the nylon, running together. Her body, in his clasp, was warm but shivering.

'I think I'll lie down,' she said in her matter-of-fact way. 'Down here on this rug. Is it soft?' She looked at him through the dark.

'I don't know,' he choked. 'I honestly don't know.'

She lowered herself elegantly like a gymnast in slow motion. His eyes were used to the dark now and he could see her lying below him. Somewhere, far away in the camp, in another world, he caught the sounds of *Goodnight Irene*; the clock that had been a wedding gift for Glenda and him, clicked loudly on the mantelshelf; and Barbara was motionless on the floor. Brigg dropped to his knees and bent and kissed her legs, her hands moved out in the dark and her cool fingers found his loins and closed so that she held his penis like a bird she did not want to hurt. He stumbled forward on his knees, and she arched her back. He caught the nylon about her waist in his anxious grasp and pulled it all away from her body. She opened herself to him.

214

'Come on, my darling English Sergeant,' she said. He could see her eyes, bright slithers of steel in the dark. 'Come on,' she repeated. 'Now. Jesus, if you only knew. Inside this good clean all-American girl, there's a screaming sex maniac fighting to get out.'

Brigg planted himself within her, hesitating at the first entry, but finding her so warm and welcoming that he went all the tender way. He heard her gasp as though he had punched her. He was conscious of his stone-hard stomach grinding against her soft belly. He pulled himself away on the first long feeling and he felt her wriggle frantically beneath him. Then he re-entered her and felt himself driving through all the filigree folds.

'Barbara, oh, Barbara,' he breathed. 'Oh, Christ, Barbara.'

'You're like a velvet dragon,' she said. 'A dragon from the dragon sea.'

'And you have a secret cave.'

'Take that damned dragon out of my private cave and run it in again.'

'Here he goes. Come on, dragon, out of the cave.'

'And in again, sweet Sergeant. In again.'

'It's going. It's snorting in again.'

'I know. Jesus, what a long, long dragon!'

'I think it's dripping wet in this cave.'

'It is a damp cave, Sergeant.'

'And muddy. Very muddy . . .'

'The dragon is muddy. God, what a nasty tacky dragon. Where has that dragon been?'

'DAD! DAD! ARE YOU DOWN THERE?'

They solidified on the floor. The boy's voice was from the top of the stairs but he was coming down. In

215

the dimness the man and woman looked at each other in a frenzy. He pulled himself from her and they scampered like monkeys across the floor to the long curtains at the window. They stood, shivering and ridiculous behind them, their backsides to the glass.

'DAD!' shouted Charlie again. They could hear him sleepily toppling down to them. Brigg realized that their clothes were on the armchairs and the rug. But it was too late now.

Charlie put his head into the room and asked 'Dad?' without hope, once more, but he did not turn on the light. He withdrew again and staggered along the passage outside towards the kitchen. They heard him taking a drink from the tap and then returning and complaining tiredly, but loudly to himself as he made his way back to his bedroom. 'Gone,' his small voice complained. 'One minute they're there, the next they're gone. Some people think they can just bugger off . . .'

16

Brigg remembered it later in the night. 'Gone. One minute they're here and the next they're gone. Some people think they can just bugger off . . .'

Some people do. Glenda for one. So quickly it's all over before the surprise begins.

The coroner's court, that distant but still distinct English day, reminded him of the schoolroom he had once known; dust floating in whirls like midges in the window-sun. A cold-dry, senile room, unkempt, uncaring. A room aching in every joint. You almost expected to hear its nasty cough.

The benches were comfortless wood against the backside. A globular iron stove stood in one corner, its chimney pipe sticking into a hole in the ceiling like a man with his finger up his nose. It was unlit that morning even though dead leaves were all along the gutters from Aldershot and the sky was distended with cold.

It was an odd little pantomime. There were three inquests that day and the families and witnesses and the other people involved sat on the benches, mostly self-consciously, some making whispers, some fearfully clutching on to their own woollen gloved hands, some staring straight at the coroner's desk, raised importantly above them. The jury looked more apprehensive than the others.

A bright young man and a girl with a long scarf came in together, both red from the chill of the day, and sat chattering cheerfully in the little choir stall labelled 'Press'. They nudged each other as though they were in a niche of a dance hall or a pub, and he told her at least two jokes. Brigg thought they behaved like that because they were accustomed to inquests, hearing and writing down the details of other people's hideous deaths.

Beryl Pollock, the widow of Staff Sergeant Pollock sat on the bench behind Brigg. She was a bulky untidy woman with a hare lip. Brigg had never given much thought to her; she was just one of the uglier wives at the Aldershot camp. But now he wondered how a man who had apparently been attractive to Glenda, *his* Glenda, could have, in the first place, married such a woman as Beryl Pollock. She was with an elder woman he thought must be her mother. He did nothing more than nod to her, an acknowledgement she returned sourly, sardonically, as though immediately asking him what sort of man he was to allow his wife to die with someone else's husband. They had nothing to say to each other; there was no sympathy. Two failures never made for even one minor success.

He conferred for a moment with a black mackintoshed man who had walked with theatrically resounding steps through the seats and eventually sat down beside him.

'Have you been before?' asked the man as though it were a clinic.

'No, I don't think so,' said Brigg.

'You wouldn't know when they bring the bodies in then?' asked the man, looking straight ahead then, rabbit fashion, quickly left and right as though unwilling to miss anything.

'Bodies?' repeated Brigg, a nasty sensation settling within him. 'They don't bring the bodies in, do they?'

''Course they do,' whispered the man convincingly. 'That's why we're all here, ain't it? That's what an inquest is all about. They've got to have bodies.'

'No,' said Brigg. 'I hope not. I've seen mine once.'

The man looked immediately interested. 'You've *seen* yours have you?' he said. 'Actually seen it. What was it like?'

'Like my wife. A bit,' answered Brigg.

'Oh, they're *bound* to have them,' reaffirmed the man. 'Bound to. I'm here for my Uncle Bernard. I fully expect them to wheel him in.'

Brigg leaned over and touched the arm of the uniformed court officer who was progressing along the benches like some veteran usherette. 'Excuse me,' he said. 'They don't actually have the bodies in here, do they? I mean, we won't be seeing them, will we?'

The officer regarded him with dislike. 'You people always ask that,' he admonished as though Brigg attended regularly. 'The answer is, no. It's not some form of entertainment, you know.'

'No,' agreed Brigg. 'No, it's not that, is it.' He turned coldly to the mackintoshed man who continued to look ahead with a simple, sure, smile.

'I bet they do,' he repeated. 'I bet they wheel them in.'

The court official had shuffled to the door at the back of the room now and Brigg heard the door open and felt the quick draught.

'Rise, please!' croaked the usher. Everybody stood

up, Brigg's neighbour glancing with undiminished expectancy over his shoulder in case the robed coroner might be followed by a procession of bleeding cadavers, trolley-borne, or possibly even carried across the backs of additional court assistants. But the coroner was alone. He smiled a professionally sad but reassuring smile at the people and the court official called theatrically: 'Oyez! Oyez! Oyez!' and followed it with a strange recitation about all the good people of the land coming forward to give evidence to Her Majesty's Coroner for the County of Hampshire, touching the deaths of Frederick Noone, Bernard Phillip Conway, Staff Sergeant Ronald Pollock and Glenda Rose Brigg . . . Brigg even remembered the other dead people's names.

'Mine's second,' whispered the man next to Brigg. 'Bernard Phillip Conway. That's my Uncle Bernard.'

'I'm glad mine is last,' said Brigg defensively. 'Everybody will have gone then.'

'I'm going to stay,' contradicted the man. 'I've got the morning off work anyway. I might just as well stay. After all this isn't the sort of thing you get a chance to see every day, is it?'

Brigg added nothing. He watched and heard the ritual touching, as they poetically put it, the deaths of Frederick Noone and his immediate neighbour's Uncle Bernard. Both were suicides and nobody cried. The witnesses gave their evidence, dry words, as though resenting the lack of consideration of their deceased relatives. The coroner nodded and wrote in short dashes. Brigg watched it remotely, like a man standing in a winter street watching a drama on a shop window television set.

He could feel the eyes and the hare lip of Beryl Pollock on him when they began the case of Staff Sergeant Ronald Pollock and Glenda Rose Brigg. The names, once uttered by the coroner, seemed to hang about in the old air of the room. The thought crossed Brigg's mind that they would never have liked their names to be linked in public. He saw the boy and the girl reporters with their heads touching, the girl checking the names from the young man's notes.

'Call John Brigg,' said the coroner. It was an official drone.

The coroner, a creased, elderly man, blinked from his pulpit desk like a captain steering a small tugboat.

You don't have to call me, I'm here, thought Brigg as he stood up and pushed past the man in the black mackintosh. He trod roughly on the man's feet and turned apologetically. The man nodded a smiled encouragement as though Brigg were going up to sing or recite.

'John Brigg!' shouted the usher unnecessarily when Brigg was three feet away.

'Here,' said Brigg into the man's old smelly face as he went by towards the witness stand.

He held the unfamiliar Bible like a hand grenade. His tardy tongue spoke the odd words of the oath and followed it with the admission that he was Sergeant John Brigg and he was the husband of the deceased.

'When did you last see your wife?' asked the coroner, adding hurriedly: 'Alive.'

Brigg said: 'On Monday, sir. In the afternoon when she brought the boy – our son – back from the school. I was off-duty early and she came back about four-thirty.'

'Did she say anything to you?'

'Just the usual. She'd been to the library and she had a book, *Make Your Divorce A Happy One*. It was one of those American things, I suppose.'

'Were you contemplating divorce, Sergeant Brigg?'

'*I* wasn't.'

'I see. She might have been?'

'She didn't say anything. But you could never tell with Glenda. I think she'd just got the book for a laugh.'

'Yes, it sounds an amusing title. Did she say she was going somewhere that night?'

'She said she was going to baby-sit for a friend of hers in Farnborough, a Mrs Allen.' He heard Beryl Pollock snort nastily as he said it. He half turned and then changed his mind and looked back at the coroner again. The coroner did not appear to have heard anything.

'Baby-sitting,' murmured the coroner. 'I see. She said nothing about going anywhere else? Anywhere with friends, or a friend? Staff Sergeant Pollock, for example?'

'No, sir. She said she was going to baby-sit.'

'Did you know that she and Staff Sergeant Pollock were friends?'

'No, sir. Not friends like that.'

'Like what, Sergeant Brigg?'

'Like they were.' He was tempted to add, 'Fucking friends.' But he stopped himself.

'Nothing had ever been drawn to your attention?'

'No, never.'

'And you had never noticed anything yourself?'

'Nothing,' said Brigg. 'I knew they knew each other,

of course. Everybody knows each other on the camp. I saw them dancing at last year's Christmas party in the mess. But that was all.'

'Did your wife tell you very frequently that she was going to baby-sit for er . . . Mrs Allen?'

'About once a week.'

'What time did she used to return?'

'Quite late, sometimes. I was usually asleep.'

'You have spoken to Mrs Allen about this? Since the accident, I mean?'

'I telephoned Mrs Allen the next day.'

'And what did she tell you?'

Brigg felt himself choke. He dropped his head and he heard the coroner tell him softly not to worry, but to take his time. This is what they called 'touching the death of' was it? The two reporters were writing and it occurred to him for the first time that the boy would read it in the papers and so would the others in the Army school.

'Are you all right now?' asked the coroner with formal kindliness.

'Yes, I'm fine,' said Brigg. 'Mrs Allen told me that Glenda had not been baby-sitting that night before.'

'Had she ever been baby-sitting for Mrs Allen?'

'Only once, so Mrs Allen said, about a year ago, when we first were posted to Aldershot.'

'So her story was a fabrication? An excuse?'

'Yes.'

'After the police had told you about the accident, did you see the body of your wife and identify it as such?'

'I did.'

'Thank you, Sergeant Brigg. I think that is all I need

to ask. I would only like to offer my sympathy to you on this sad occasion.'

'Thank you,' said Brigg. He walked down from the witness stand and the usher, revengefully, called, 'Mrs Beryl Pollock!' very loudly in Brigg's ear as he went by.

'I knew they went out together,' said Beryl Pollock strongly. 'I knew for about a month before this. I was just waiting to scratch her eyes out in front of the Commanding Officer.'

'I see,' murmured the coroner.

'I would have done it at the wives' night in the sergeants' mess next week. That's all I was waiting for.' She looked hard and coarse. Brigg watched the prow of her hare lip rising and dipping sharply.

'What excuse did your husband make for being absent from home? Did he say he was on duty or something?'

'He reckoned he was taking a course at Frimley. To do with preparing himself for civvy street.'

'What was that course? Do you know?'

'Intercourse, I should think,' rasped Mrs Pollock. Brigg was surprised to see her crumple and begin to sob. She was a strong woman, with a hard face and she looked as though she never cried.

The coroner remained calm. He waited then asked her: 'How long do you think this intercourse had gone on?'

'Long enough,' she said, her face still in her hands. 'Army camps. Brothels, that's all. Brothels. Dirt . . .'

The coroner persisted: 'You last saw your husband alive on the evening of Monday, the twenty-first,

when he left home saying he was going to his er . . .
course . . . at Frimley.'

'Y-yes, that's right,' she stammered.

'And did you identify his body . . .?'

'No,' she said hurriedly. 'I sent my brother. I didn't
want to see him when he was dead.'

A thin man in an expensive blue suit arrived in the
court and came between the seats, bent over like a
Red Indian on the trail. He gave a little apologetic
bow to the coroner and then sat in front of Brigg.
Brigg saw that he was doodling with a red ballpoint on
a pad set on his knee. The man drew organs of the
body, a stomach and a heart and lots of curling pipes,
running all over the pad. He then sketched a small
pair of lungs and a spleen. Then the coroner called for
the pathologist and the man got up, gave his bow
again, and went to the witness stand.

'This was the body of a well-nourished female, two
months' pregnant,' he said. 'My examination indicated that there was no sign of natural disease. In the
vagina there was a quantity of semen, recently
deposited, and I formed the opinion that she had
recently had sexual intercourse. Death was due to
fractured skull, ribs, and other multiple injuries. And
shock.'

Brigg heard Beryl Pollock say: 'I bet.'

The policeman who stood to give evidence was a soft,
thin, unsteady young man. The sort, thought Brigg,
that the drill sergeant would like to have banging the
square for a month or so. He was trying to think about
anything but Glenda being pregnant. He had not

made her pregnant. But the pathologist had said she was two months gone, and any man who could doodle hearts and spleens and lungs like that could hardly be mistaken. He fixed his eyes at the back of the man's head. The pathologist's hair was fair and under-nourished and the pink skin showed through at the back. Brigg thought: 'Well, I'm looking into *him* now. Right in through the back of his nut.'

For this was the fellow who had experienced the final and, physically, the deepest intimacy with Glenda. He had messed about with her body, probed where no man had been before, not even her husband, not even Staff Sergeant Pollock, until he had discovered that there was a baby inside and a quantity of semen in her vagina. And he simply turned up and informed all the world about it. Even the two young reporters. What a job. What sort of a life was that for any man?

'I was called to a lay-by on the Ash Road, at eleven thirty-two on the evening of the twenty-first.' The constable had a voice like his body, soft and thin. He squinted at his notebook as though experiencing difficulty in recalling the details out of a mass of deathly accidents he had attended that week.

'What did you see there?' asked the coroner.

Inside Brigg's head a rhyme was revolving.

> *'Constable, constable. Where have you been?*
> *I've been up the road to the accident's scene.*
> *What did you do, when you got there?*
> *In the back of the car I found a fine pair.'*

The coroner's eyes travelled up. 'Is someone humming?' he asked surprised and sharp.

'WHO'S HUMMING?' shouted the court usher.

'I think it was the sergeant who gave evidence,' said the policeman like a school sneak.

Fuck you, for a start, thought Brigg. Toadying, tell-tale, copper. 'Yes, it was me, sir,' he admitted, standing to face the coroner. Everyone in the comfortless room had their face to him. The mackintosh man, next to him, was smiling. He heard Beryl Pollock snort through the jug of her hare lip.

'Why were you humming?' demanded the coroner. The elderly usher moved towards him with a threatening stagger.

'I was trying to cheer myself up,' confessed Brigg. 'I'm very sorry.'

'I should think so,' said the coroner, not indicating whether this was a comment on the first or second sentence of Brigg's admission. But he said it more softly. Then he said: 'This is my court and we are investigating a serious matter. It is not a place to cheer yourself up. If you feel a desire to hum then would you be good enough to go outside.'

'I'm sorry,' repeated Brigg. 'I won't hum any more. I'd finished anyhow.'

'Good,' said the coroner. 'Then perhaps we can get on. Now . . . Constable?'

The policeman was looking at Brigg as though marking him down for future reference. He jerked around to the coroner and mumbled: 'Yes, sir. Sorry, sir. Never heard anyone humming in court before. Not coroner's court.'

'Neither have I,' agreed the coroner. 'Please go on.'

'Yes, sir. I arrived on the lay-by and I saw that an articulated lorry had been involved in a collision with a Ford Prefect. I noticed that the rear of the Ford was trapped beneath the front of the vehicle and that two people were trapped in the rear seat of the car.'

Fine observation, thought Brigg. And an *articulated* lorry. Perhaps they would call *that* to give evidence. Better than this copper. He glanced around, carefully, at Beryl Pollock. Her lip was protruding and dry, like a small horn, and her eyes were closed, not peacefully but with the eyeballs bulging under the thin-skinned eyelids as though they wanted to be released. He saw that her mother was quickly knitting something black.

'I waited until the fire brigade and the ambulance arrived,' continued the constable. 'The two people were extricated and taken to Aldershot District Hospital where they were found to be dead on arrival.'

'Did the driver of the lorry say anything to you?'

'Yes, sir. The driver . . .' He put his eyes closer to his notebook, 'Mr Henry Adams of Prescott Avenue, Huddersfield, was treated for shock. I have a full statement, sir, which I took from him on a later occasion . . .'

'Read that in a moment,' said the coroner a little impatiently. 'Did he say anything to you at that time? At the scene of the accident?'

'Yes, sir. As you wish, sir. He said: "I never saw them. I drove into the lay-by and I didn't see the car until I hit it. It had no lights".'

'Did you check the lights, constable?'

'I did, sir. The switch was in the "off" position.'

'You examined the car when the ambulance men had taken Mrs Brigg and Staff Sergeant Pollock away?'

'I did. I made a list of the loose contents, sir. It's not very long.' He ran his finger down his list. 'One key ring and keys with Royal Artillery Old Comrades badge on the fob. One copy of *Soldier* magazine. One ladies' handbag. One pair of ladies' tights and one pair of ladies' knickers . . .'

Brigg got up and imitated the pathologist's jerky bow to the coroner, then, smiling in turn at the jury, his mackintoshed neighbour, the usher and Beryl Pollock, he squeaked on tiptoe out of the court.

Outside the day was still and ashen. The world itself looked near death. A pale lank of sun crept along the stone wall of the coroner's court, pausing against a trio of empty trees, and then vanishing. Brigg felt it touch his face as it passed him. When it had gone he walked around to the side of the court into a blank alley, wet with weeds and leaves. He leaned his head against the wall of the court and then, as an afterthought, relieved himself against the dull stone. He returned to the front of the building and loitered there. The court usher shuffled out and said officiously: 'You musn't go away, you know. The coroner may want to recall you.'

'I'll wait,' promised Brigg. He waited, pushing the round toe of his army boot into the dun gravel outside the door. Presently the man in the mackintosh came out, smiling like the first patron to emerge from a cinema after the end of the performance.

'Don't worry. It's all right,' he assured Brigg. 'Accidental death. Both.'

'Thanks,' said Brigg.

'They're just paying out the jurors. Do you know, they pay them out right there in court so that everybody can see it's all fair and above board! They

229

have a properly made-out list and they all have to sign. Fancy getting *money* for it! That's not bad, is it?'

'Not bad at all,' agreed Brigg. 'If people got killed a bit more often they might even be able to make a living wage.'

'That's *not* a very nice thought,' said the man disapprovingly. 'Think of my poor Uncle Bernard, slitting his throat like that. I find it very difficult to sit on that toilet now, I can tell you. I can just see him doing it.'

'Well,' shrugged Brigg. 'Some go one way, some another.' He wondered if it would matter if he strangled the man now. He kept his hands behind his back. The man's face brightened.

'Well, your two were accidental death, anyway. That's something. It always *looks* better, I say. Well, I must be getting back to work. It's been all very interesting. Goodbye.'

'Goodbye,' murmured Brigg sadly. 'See you next time, perhaps.'

'Hah!' said the man setting off jauntily. 'I hope not. I jolly well hope not. Goodbye.'

Brigg got away from the court before anyone else came out. He met the bus coming in the opposite direction and he got aboard. From the platform he saw Beryl Pollock and her lip and her mother emerging from the coroner's court. Behind them was the wispy haired pathologist and the pale policeman talking impressively to a clutch of eager jurors. The young reporters, the girl now holding the youth's hand, went off down the cold street, still leaning together in their happy chatter. Brigg wondered if she had a quantity of semen, recently deposited, in her vagina. He sat down heavily and watched the dim country and then the dismal town reel by the window of the bus. He wondered whether the heart and the spleen and the other things the man was drawing were just general, or whether they belonged to anyone in particular. Glenda's perhaps.

He got off outside the Army school and waited for his son. The boy came out scuffling in a knot of three. He saw his father and stopped. They walked together down the road.

'I went to the inquest thing,' said Brigg eventually.

'Was it all right?'

'Yes, as far as those affairs can be, it was all right.'

'We had two periods of jogga this morning.'

'Jogga? What's jogga?'

'Jogga. You know. Different countries, rivers and all that sort of terrible stuff.'

'Geography,' said Brigg.

'That's what I said. Why did you come and meet me? The others will think I'm in the infants or something. It's only the little kids get met outside the school.'

'Sorry,' said Brigg. 'I was just going past, that's all. Shall we have some fish and chips?'

'I wouldn't mind. Can we eat them in the shop?'

'All right. How would you feel about going to Hong Kong?'

'I wouldn't mind that either. Can we go?'

'I think so. I think they will fix me with a posting pretty quickly.'

'And *I* could come, too. You wouldn't have to leave me here, would you?'

'No, I'd make sure you could come, too. I don't

think the Army stops children going on foreign postings, even if they haven't got . . . a mother.'

'All right then,' said the boy. 'We'll go. It's all right with me.'

'What are you doing this afternoon?'

'Are you going to take me somewhere?'

'No. I meant at school. You can't just skip school.'

'Oh, I see. I thought you were going to get me an afternoon off, or something. We're doing maths and biology this afternoon. Worse luck.'

'Life's hard,' agreed Brigg.

'I'll say it is,' said his son. 'Maths and double jogga in one day.'

17

'Look Barbara,' he said. 'I think I can work three days' leave, Monday, Tuesday, Wednesday. At this end of the year I think we could get one of the small houses on the sea for that time.'

'Yes,' she said in her uncomplicated way. 'That sounds fine. What time will you pick me up?'

'I'll come to the hotel about ten tomorrow.'

'Will we have a telephone?'

'Oh, yes. I see.'

'Well, I must know.'

'Yes, of course you must.'

'You understand that, don't you?'

'I understand. What else could you do? I'll see there's a phone.'

'Sure, Sergeant,' she smiled. 'I'll come and play house with you. We'll have a great time. But they must be able to tell me when my husband arrives.'

On the Sunday afternoon some of the married soldiers in the garrison with the traditional Sabbath guilt of the British family man took their wives and children down to the Chinese village to witness the tank stuck in the chop-chop house and all the other vehicles of the Command Workshops sunk in the mud. It had rained, hard Hong Kong rain, every

233

night for a week, and the days had been touched with a drying wind from the sea and widespread sun.

The freakish combination of weather had resulted in the heavy vehicles sinking more dramatically each night and cementing themselves in each drying day. So far only the officer's jeep and the Commanding Officer's staff car had been rescued, ignominiously pulled out by a team of morose New Territories' oxen, normally used in the paddy fields. The farmer who owned the oxen scrutinized the tank and the tank recovery vehicle for several minutes, his parched expression watched hopefully by the British engineers. But eventually he had committed himself to a long, hopeless Oriental shrug and driven his oxen away. So the armoured casualties remained, embarrassing for their owners, the source of derision from every other section of the British Army, and the unspoken delight and interest of the local Chinese.

The Sunday afternoon crowd took on considerable proportions, the spectators spread in a well-flung circle, like people at a strange frozen circus, watching the vehicles for some miracle or movement that never came. The British troops who had been detailed to guard the wallowing monsters (for the suspicion was rife that somehow the ineffable Chinese would find a method of removing them if they were not watched) stood with the slightly embarrassed stance of attendants at the prehistoric mammal section of a museum.

The mishap had, however, afforded the garrison inhabitants the opportunity of an outing that did not require the trying ritual of boarding a foreign bus or an alien train, and was on familiar territory. They trooped from the camp houses, heavy with the

234

Sabbath offerings of roast beef and Yorkshire pudding, tinned peaches and custard, and infinite cups of Lyon's tea; they went in the afternoon sun, walking the road like a large Sunday school outing. The soldiers were for the most part wearing their off-duty slacks, coloured shirts and relaxed expressions. Civilian nods were substituted for salutes when an officer was spotted, or a stiffening of the neck and a quick turn of the nose, as though the man were trying to rid himself of a crick, when a highly senior or an unfamiliar officer in uniform passed by. The wives, incarnations of the illustrations in Doris Boswell's club catalogue, wore their best suits and coats over their customary domestic stoop; some dared hats, and some had matching shoes and handbags. Gloves were carried in the hand not occupied with the husband's off-duty elbow or used in pushing along mouthy, fretful or reluctant children. The children, daily familiars at the military school, greeted each other with joyous or antagonizing calls now that they were in the unusual convoys of their families.

''Ello, Nooky, where you going?'

'To see the tank and the sunk lorry.'

'So's we!'

'My dad says it's a right balls-up.'

The women were cheerful, snide, or both, in their greetings to the other women. Some had trailed each other through the political outposts of the world, the background chorus to many a British catastrophe, and had never exchanged a considerate word since, perhaps, a snub at the sergeants' Christmas dance in Libya in 1963, or a dispute over the last packet of Shredded Wheat in the Nicosia NAAFI shop during

235 ·

the Cyprus fighting. Others called Sunday good wishes to acquaintances and then muttered gossip to their husbands from the last dropped half-inches of their mouths. The husbands nodded and added the slanders current in the mess.

But they were all going in overall good humour to view the Command Workshops' calamities. On arrival the children laughed and ran about machine-gunning each other, dying writhing deaths about the conversational legs of their parents. Men who spent their whole military life filling in ration allowance forms or requisitions for bed-springs, shook their heads in a manner which suggested they contained some secret wisdom which, if it were requested, or had been requested earlier, would have solved this sorry situation. Women pursed their lips and indicated with shaking heads that they were not the least surprised. Was it not the same demented Command Workshops who blew up the garrison boiler house so spectacularly the previous October?

Doris Boswell and Hilda Harvey with their retinue of children trudged together on the pilgrimage. Both their husbands were on guard duty that day. Doris, whose husband was generally excused such incon-veniences since he was responsible for the garrison food, ('responsible' being the term generally accepted among those who ate it) wore a quietly strained expression as though he had been posted missing in action. Hilda prattled and puffed at her friend's side, sympathizing with her indignation, and nodding patient agreement with the threats of multiple senna-pod dosing that was to follow the imposition on her Phil. She was, nevertheless, glad when they caught up with Mrs Brice, also without her husband, who was towing three unhappy children.

'Where's your Bill?' asked Doris aggressively.

'Putting his feet up. Having a rest,' said Mrs Brice solicitously. 'I wouldn't drag my Bill out. Not like some I know.'

Doris said bluntly: 'I reckon it would be easier to drag that buggering tank out than your Bill.'

'Oh, no,' protested Mrs Brice, but without vigour. She knew Doris too well to mix it with her on a Sunday afternoon. 'He likes his Sunday nap. Where's Phil, then?'

'On bloody guard,' muttered the aggrieved Doris.

'Doesn't get many, though, does he,' said Mrs Brice soothingly.

'Neither should he.' Doris stopped her heavy plod and glared at the other wife. 'Making vol-au-vents for the officers' mess one minute and guarding this dump the next. If the Chinese ever do invade he'll be there in the front line with a machine-gun, my Phil. Right away – even if he *is* in the middle of the bleeding goulash.'

'I don't expect they'll come today,' said Mrs Brice stupidly. 'Not Sunday.'

'Not while Bill's having his nap,' sniffed Doris.

Hilda, who could see a row developing, thrust her small nose between the women. 'Mrs Brice,' she asked benignly. 'What do people die of in your family?'

Mrs Brice paled. 'There's nothing wrong with my Bill,' she asserted. 'He's just tired, that's all. There's no question of him dying, Mrs Harvey.'

'No, no,' Hilda assured her. 'Bill's the *last* one to die, I know. What I meant – is there anything special

237

that *takes* them in your family? I was asking Doris the same the other day, wasn't I, Doris? It's *hearts* in our family. Edwin's Uncle Alex went the other day with it. Sudden.'

'Oh, I see,' said Mrs Brice, the relief settling with the realization on her face. 'Well, there's Bill's brother Percy. He was a fit man.'

They had continued walking now. The jogging Hilda looked with puzzlement first at Doris and then at Mrs Brice, as though the inquiry had still been misunderstood.

'A fit man, Mrs Brice?' she asked. ''Ow exactly do you mean?'

'Fits,' said Mrs Brice with expansive simplicity. 'He had *fits*. I've known him pass out like a light on the lav. That's 'ow he went in the end.'

'On the lav?' asked Doris unkindly.

'No. A fit. Top deck of a bus and the conductor was one of these blackies, so you couldn't expect *him* to know what to do.'

The other women nodded sympathetically. They had climbed to the road above the village now and joined the ring of other watchers, first taking in the armoured catastrophe spread before them with all the satisfaction of Army wives at the misfortune of other Army wives' men-folk. Then Doris turned her big broken face around the crowd, slowly, like a search-light. She focused eventually on the extreme right of the spectators, digested what she saw, and then nudged her companions. She said nothing but pointed with her nose and they looked where she indicated.

Wilcox was talking to Mrs Murdoch, standing with

customary familiarity beside her and saying something which was making her laugh. Brigg's boy,
Charlie, was standing beside them intent on the minor
happenings about the tank.

'Looks like the lonely hearts is going to stop
bleeding soon,' sniffed Doris.

Hilda and Mrs Brice smiled their thin women's
smiles. Hilda inconsequentially dwelt on the thought
that she had never before heard Doris use the word
'bleeding' other than as a swearword. 'Wondered
when something like that was going to come off,'
continued Doris sagely. 'He'll soon have his size tens
under her table.'

'Under her bed, more likely,' suggested Mrs Brice.
'See how he's got Sergeant Brigg's boy with him. I
suppose *his* old man's too busy with that Yankee
floozie who's got her claws in him.'

She stood, waiting, arms across her chest, scarcely
contained joy on her face, knowing triumphantly the
effect her words would have on the others. They
remained still, fixed like marble, like Greek peasant
women in a play. Then they wheeled slowly, with
wonder, upon her, as though she had confidently
claimed possession of the world's innermost mysteries.

'A Yankee?' whispered Doris. 'A Yankee? How
come I didn't hear?'

'I'm *telling* you, Doris,' said Mrs Brice happily and
uniquely on the ascendant. '*I'm* telling you now.
That's what he's got hold of. I know. He was seen on
the Peak with her. And last night she was here, in the
camp.'

Doris's mud-pack face had gone hard. Hilda
dipped her chicken head several times. 'You usually *do*

know, Mrs Brice,' she agreed. '*You* spotted the Chinese last week.'

'Mr Brigg has been up to his eyes in it,' continued Mrs Brice who had felt let down at the Chinese proving to be wolf cubs and preferred not to be reminded of it. Smugly she continued: 'Last night . . .'

'Yes, yes?' crooned Doris and Hilda together urgently moving their heads to her.

'Last night,' continued Mrs Brice like a conjuror keeping the suspense. 'After midnight they was standing *naked* in the window of his billet. They were seen clear as day by my Bill on his guard patrol.'

'In the window?' gasped Hilda.

'Naked?' asked Doris doubtfully. She was already discounting the other woman's story. 'What patrol was your Bill doing anyway?'

'He was on guard, wasn't he,' said Mrs Brice defensively.

'How long 'ave they been patrolling up near the married quarters, then?'

'It's not *official*,' said Mrs Brice testily. 'Bill does it himself. He's very conscientious, Bill.'

'Looking in windows,' mentioned Doris.

'They was *in* the window. Anybody could have seen them,' argued Mrs Brice indignantly. 'Naked in the window. The pair of them. He could see their bums against the glass!'

'Naked,' whispered Hilda enthralled. 'Naked.'

Doris gave her thin disciple an ill-tempered tug. 'Come on, dear, I think we'd better be off. I'm sure Mrs Brice has got a lot more people she wants to talk to.'

Hilda squeaked a startled agreement. Doris looked

stonily at the protesting face of Mrs Brice and began to stride away, pushing Hilda along with her.

'It's true,' Mrs Brice blurted out after them. 'Every word.'

Doris turned majestically. 'I'm sure it is, dear,' she said. Then she bent towards Hilda. 'No wonder her Bill wants to spend his Sunday afternoon in bed,' she said. 'Dirty bastard.'

The house on the Tolo Channel had a green winged roof and a wide bamboo window that looked out on the coastland, the sharp islands held together by the sea, and the heavy back of the New Territories mainland. On the rail at the foot of the stairs which hung almost incidentally to the side of the house was a Malayan parrot who rang a small sweet bell with its beak when anyone approached.

'Good, good,' bowed the caretaker as he led them up with his keys. All the way up he worked his head to and fro, like the parrot, and said 'Good, good,' half to himself, until finally he showed them into the house and bowed a final: 'Good, good.'

When he had gone Barbara said, 'Good, good,' with an imitation of his Oriental nod. She and Brigg stood, facing into the room, like a honeymoon pair, their two suitcases between them. 'I like it,' said Barbara. 'I like the bamboo mats and those little toy chairs, and the flowers and the lady painted on that screen. I just adore the rattan blinds at our window and I love the sea and the islands we can view from our window. And I like our sexy silk bed over there.'

'It's all right, then?' said Brigg inadequately.

'That's what I said,' she laughed. 'This is where we

live. Number One Mao Tse-tung Boulevard, Tolo, Tolo Channel, Hong Kong.'

Brigg bent to a low table by the door. 'And the phone number is 7728934. The exchange is Lai Chi Chong,' he said simply.

'The agent already told me,' she said not looking at him. Walking towards the kitchen she made a Chinese voice again: 'And this is where Mrs Bligg will make all nice things.' She turned and half ran, half walked back to him. She thrust herself against him and clutched him. 'Forget the phone, will you?' she said. 'Forget it's there until it rings. Okay?'

'Okay,' he agreed.

'Would it be asking too much of you if I told you that I wanted you to put me on that Chinese silk bed and give me the most almighty fucking ever an English sergeant provided for a needy American girl?'

'As you put it so nicely, I will,' said Brigg.

'Darling,' she said, kicking her shoes away. 'I mentioned this terrible weakness I have, and I want it like last night again – but without Charlie coming searching for his dad.'

'I don't think Charlie will find us here,' he said kissing her face and pulling his hard hands against her blouse.

'Lock the door in case he does,' she said. She was stripping as she spoke, taking her clothes off in haste, watching the small movements and lines in his face. Brigg turned to the door but laughed when he got there.

'No lock,' he said. 'I forgot, the Chinese hardly ever have them. They're too honest. Nobody ever breaks in.'

'It's not what they're going to *steal*,' said Barbara. 'It's what they're going to *see*, for Christ's sake.'

'The parrot will ring the bell if anybody comes to the stairs,' Brigg assured her. 'That's why he's there.'

'Do you think he will?'

'I think so.'

'Jesus, could you believe having to trust a parrot with your peace of mind,' she said. But she was still undressing. She was finished before he had taken off his shirt. She stood, brown-pink, slender and smooth, her nipples snouting out, her slender fingers rubbing back against her buttocks.

'I'll be expecting you,' she said, giving a brief, naked, curtsy. She turned quickly, using her feet like a dancer, and walked towards the low bed. She slid across the silk cover, laughing with the abrupt luxury of its feel, and then swivelled on to her stomach and waited for him. When he was naked he walked towards her and she reached out and caught him with one urgent hand, leading him like some mule on a bridle around the fringe of the bed until he was standing over her. She turned her eyes up to him, full of evil smiles, and put out a flat pleading tongue.

'That's very wicked,' he muttered.

'I warned you,' she answered. She then moved her head to him and did what she was going to do while he stood screwed up with the sensation she made.

Eventually he put his hands to her ears and levered her away from him. 'In ten seconds,' he said, 'you are going to ruin the whole thing again.'

'It was Charlie last time,' she said.

'They say women's tongues always make trouble,'

he said. 'But I thought they meant gossiping. Lie back. Make some room.'

He moved on top of her and immediately into her. Not waiting. Knowing she did not even want him to wait. Her face wrinkled at the forehead, the eyes, the bridge of the nose and the mouth, and then gradually cleared. Sweat oozed over her. Her eyes were tight and through her close teeth she said: 'Christ, I wish I didn't feel as bad as this. I just want you to smother me with it, feed me until I'm gorged. That's correct my darling Sergeant . . .' She opened her eyes for a moment, as though she were on the point of death. Then she closed them again making a deep breath. '. . . That's quite correct. God, I swear it's heading for my heart . . . I swear . . .'

There was nothing more from her. No words, only the inward sounds of her body, moving like a serpent. Brigg felt old and wooden on top of her. He struggled to contain her movement as she slipped on the silk cover. Once he tipped to one side and caught the malevolent eye of the embroidered dragon dented below them. He moved back, safe between her legs again. She drank him in like a thirsty creature at a deep water hole.

In the morning they heard the squawking of strange birds with deep voices, and woke in their bed with canes of yellow sun poking in through the rattan blind. Barbara slid naked from the bed and Brigg turned in his first moments of awareness and watched her with profound and happy satisfaction as she went to the window. Her hair dropped around the nape of her neck and she gathered it negligently in her fingers, as she walked, in the way an assured woman does. Her skin was almost orange colour in that early diffused light, her back was splendidly curved and her buttocks trembled as she walked from him.

All night he had held her, waking and then sleeping and then waking again, luxuriating in the close warmth of her skin. She had stirred several times, kissing him absently and then sleeping again. Once, when she had slid about in her dream, he had caught her with his forearms beneath her arms and his palms quietly rubbing her breasts. His hardness lay in the channel of her backside and his mouth was among her hair.

When she had reached the window and hoisted the blind she stood looking out with the sun flooding about her. She had folded her hands across her chest but she remained naked. She turned into the room, as though suddenly remembering him, and smiled. Brigg stretched his legs into the corners of the bed and watched her lovingly.

'I think they polished the world for us this morning,' she said brightly. 'Everything out there is shining, Sergeant.'

'Why do you call me Sergeant?' he asked as he stretched.

'Because that's my name for you,' she said decisively, walking back across the room to him. He watched the skin tight and flushing on her breasts. 'Millions of people are called John. And I don't want to . . . to . . . er . . . think of you as just one millionth of a great mass of humanity. So I call you Sergeant.'

Brigg pushed his hands behind his head and regarded her face, paying careful thought to her eyes.

They changed with the time of day. Now, in the morning, they were distant, pale. 'Just now,' he said, 'you were really going to say "I don't want to *remember you* as just one millionth part". But you changed it, didn't you? You said "I don't just want to *think of you*" instead. There's a difference.'

'Details,' she said, sitting on the bed. She kissed his open mouth. 'Little tinchy details. Lie back, Sergeant, I want to have a pony ride.'

'The pony wants his oats,' grinned Brigg childishly.

'He'll get that as well,' she smiled. She pulled the dragon cover away from him. 'Behold, what Chinese magic is there here?' she incanted. 'One dragon is taken away and another is revealed.' She joked and touched it with her finger, pushing it down and letting it spring up again. But he could see, for all her playing, how serious it was with her, how urgent her need, and how often. Now, he could see by her expression, she could not wait to have him within her again. He tried not to think priggishly about how she had survived all the months her husband had been in Vietnam.

Gently, but with honest eagerness, she straddled him, locking with him immediately and descending on him, fraction by fraction, her eyes tight, her lips half open in the formation of a silent scream. He thrust his urgent loins up at her and felt her cover him.

'My God, Jesus, that's a terrible hot spike you've got there, dragon,' she whispered, her eyes opening to slits.

'You said I was a pony,' Brigg breathed. 'Let's get the animals right.'

'A dragon,' she insisted, her head nodding now as though she were rocking herself to sleep. 'It's just got to be a dragon. No pony could have a spike like that.'

His hands held her strongly at the velvet valley of each leg with her trunk. She remained sitting upright, riding him in her own time, her face alternately at peace and then rent with a look of savagery. Her breasts were hard and shining hubs.

Brigg hardly moved, allowing himself only the easiest thrust of his lower muscles and letting his thumbs and index fingers rub into her groin on each side. He watched her face very intently, feeling each sensation himself and watching it transmitted to her mouth, her chin, her cheeks and the vivid signals of her eyes.

Abruptly her hair collapsed all over her face. Her mouth made soundless movements until she seemed to gather words and speed and she called to him urgently, 'Hard, now, Sergeant! Hard now! Jesus, it's breaking out!'

She pitched forward on top of him and he grasped her as though he had captured her in an ambush. They broke together rolling in the full storm of it, until she lay panting, but then matter-of-factly, on his chest, pulling at the hair behind his ears. Sweat slithered around between their bodies. She lay for a few moments longer, then she yawned and said: 'Let's get up and eat, and then go out, shall we? Christ knows what we're doing lying in bed on a lovely morning like this.'

18

The Malayan parrot at the foot of the stairs gave them a greeting on his bell as they walked down. Barbara laughed and talked to it lovingly. Along the beach the caretaker, who had let them in the previous day, was plodding, dragging a reluctant small boy by the hand. He nodded to them and said, 'Good, good,' and they returned the exact greeting. The boy stopped wriggling and regarded them with round-faced wonder. Then the man dragged him on again, scolding him in Cantonese.

There was a smell of flowers on the beach, touched with fishy spices from the village. Fishing boats like cobwebs were on the sea, against the sun, and cormorants flew hopefully down the estuary. On the far side of the channel the land lay flat as a hand but then seemed to gather itself in strength and rose powerfully until it formed mountains, far off, laced with morning clouds.

'How far is that?' asked Barbara. 'Is that Communist China?'

'That's it,' Brigg nodded. 'Doesn't look very dangerous, does it?'

'It looks like some sort of sleepy place,' she agreed. 'Sure doesn't seem to be doing any harm.'

'It gets nasty later on in the afternoon.' Brigg smiled

at her and she returned the smile, pleased with their game.

'Where's Chairman Mao?' she asked.

'He's just behind the mountain,' said Brigg. 'He's probably sleeping late.'

'I guess those clouds around the top are Chairman Mao's Thoughts,' said Barbara. 'Can you read what he's thinking?'

Brigg looked hard at the Chinese horizon. 'He's thinking what a cloudy day it is,' he grinned.

'Okay, okay,' she laughed. 'You win. I love to pretend like that. Sometimes in the winter in New York I take a walk along Riverside Drive and look over the river to the other side. All the river and the sky is black in the afternoon and when it's been snowing and I look across to all those wharves and things I think it looks just like the Arctic. It's white and silent with pieces sticking up and thrusting out, like the movies you see of the Polar ice cap. Have you ever been in New York, Sergeant?'

'No,' answered Brigg. 'I only travel where the Army pays for my fare, and they gave up the garrison in New York some time ago.'

'We beat you out!' she laughed loudly. 'We beat the damned British out!' She began to run along the beach.

'That's because I wasn't in the Army then,' shouted Brigg, making for her and catching her arm. 'They wouldn't have kicked me out, mate!'

'I wouldn't, mate,' she agreed smiling seriously into his face. 'You know I love you, don't you? You know that?'

The words came as a strange shock to Brigg. The

everyday way in which she said them; her honest, fair and loving look, that came while she waited for him to speak. He reached out and pulled her to him. He hugged her, not passionately, but with everyday love and relief. Roughly, like a man would hold his mother. Then he loosened his hold and kissed her like a lover. 'You knew about it, didn't you?' she said again.

'I knew. Of course I did,' he said close to her neck. 'I was just shattered to hear you say it, that's all. God, it was almost as big a shock as you telling me you *didn't* love me.'

She began to walk, along the beach. Some boys kicking a football near the village looked up and then went on with their game. Irritable dogs began to bark in the yards about the bamboo houses.

'You love me also, don't you?' she said looking at him uncertainly. 'Say if you don't. Just say it now and it will be okay.'

'I love you,' he assured her simply. 'I can't believe that it all happens like this, that's all. Not love.'

'I'll always love you,' she repeated slowly like a girl trying to learn a difficult poem. 'Always. And it won't change.'

He saw the shadow on her face, and felt it pass to him. They had reached the chop-chop house of the village now, its roof unintentionally straying over the beach. They went to one of the wooden tables and the Chinese man chased away a bright lizard which had been sitting glassy-eyed under the sun. They asked for tea. The man went away and brought it. The lizard re-appeared, scaling the leg of the table again, and walked on to the table like a determined

250

comedian going towards the centre of a hostile stage.

'What was Glenda like?' she asked.

Brigg was surprised that she should have retained Glenda's name. He thought he had only said it once.

'Great,' he said. 'Glenda was just great. Everybody thought that. Unfortunately.'

'How did she die?' she continued. 'If you don't want to say, don't say . . .'

'It's all right,' Brigg answered. 'I don't mind. We can't talk about Chairman Mao's Mountains all day, can we. She was killed in a car. In the back of a car, stationary in what we appropriately call a lay-by. A man called Pollock was killed with her. Very much with her. A lorry, a truck, hit them in the dark.'

'That's terrible,' she said.

'They probably didn't know what hit them,' said Brigg bitterly. 'At that moment each must have thought the other had provided something they'd never experienced before.'

'I'm sorry I asked you about it.'

'That's all right, Barbara,' he replied. 'Dead people are no bother. They can't interfere.'

She looked at him with concern. 'Let's walk back along the beach,' she suggested. He got up and they left the eating-house hand in hand and went back the way they had walked that morning. Big shadows of clouds were on the sea now, roaming like a school of whales. The China mountains had retreated into an indistinct horizon.

'Seems like Chairman Mao's having some bad thoughts,' said Barbara.

'We all do,' he said. He looked at her and saw how disappointed she was at his melancholy. Then he laughed and touched her hair and was glad when she laughed in answer.

'Sorry,' said Brigg. 'There'll be plenty of time for the miseries when this is over, these few days.'

'After the telephone rings,' she said, serious again.

'Right,' he said. 'After that.'

'What do you expect me to do?' she pleaded. 'Leave it off the hook? You know I could never do that. I'm sure I've never loved anybody like you, but he's my husband and he's coming back from a war.'

'All right, all right,' said Brigg. 'He was first.'

'I came here to find him,' she said looking down at the sand running across his feet, walking beside him like a child telling a man her problems. 'And by accident I found you. But I can't just eliminate him. He's a fact.'

The fishing boats they had seen like skeins on the channel earlier were inshore now, with the villagers unloading them.

Men and women were wading through the water and children carried boxes of fishes on their heads towards the patchwork huts.

'If we buy a couple of good sized fish will you cook them for dinner tonight?' Brigg asked her.

'Sure. I'd do something really special.'

'And we could have some Chinese rice wine.'

'Let's do it.'

'Right,' nodded Brigg taking her hand firmly. 'I'll get some from the fishermen.' He thought as he went: 'Funny if all we get out of it is a decent meal.'

They slept innocently in the late afternoon and when the last tatters of daylight were on the hills and reflected in the channel, she got up from the bed, leaving him, and began to prepare the meal. Brigg woke later and went to the village for the wine. He arrived back at the house with two bottles and smelled the scent of the fish before he had reached the lower stairs. The parrot gave him a coloured bow and obligingly dinged the bell.

'My God,' called Brigg as he came through the door. 'Smells like Saturday night in Aldershot. Splash a few bottles of beer around and start a fight and you've got the complete thing.'

'Is that a fish town, Aldershot?' she called cheerfully from the sizzling pans.

'All British towns are fish towns,' he said moving to the kitchen door. She had found an Oriental smock and she was wearing it over her dress. He kissed her over her shoulder. 'Fish and chips towns,' he said. 'It's our gift to the world. Fish and chips.'

'They've started them in the States,' she said. 'But I don't know if they're *truly* the American thing.'

'Of course not,' exclaimed Brigg. 'Christ, you lot have only been going a couple of hundred years. Twenty centuries of history, breeding, and what-have-you, have gone into the perfect portion of plaice and six penn'orth. It's part of Britain – like the Queen and Big Ben, and strikes and bad debts. All that sort of thing. It's our heritage.'

'I've never tried Chinese rice wine,' she said nodding at the bottles.

'Very sexy,' he warned her. 'Saturday night is rice wine night in the villages. Nothing moves except little Chinese bottoms going up and down.'

She laughed and went into the kitchen again. He

glanced at the telephone sitting like a black crab in the corner of the room. His temporary happiness drained from within him leaving him cold and hollow. What if it rang at this moment and the hotel porter said her husband was on his way from Saigon? Would she finish the fish?

Brigg wandered to the window. She had left the blinds up. There was a strong spring warmth in the air and an early moon, its light lapping over the channel. Haphazard lanterns hung like signals in the village, and across the sea were firm clusters of light sprouting from the settlements on the far bank.

'Beautiful night for fish and rice wine,' Brigg called to her.

'I'm cooking great penn'orths of chips,' she laughed. 'Just to make you feel at home.'

She served it on the bamboo table by the window. Just before they sat down they saw the caretaker still pulling the protesting small boy by the hand along the beach below them. Barbara called from the window: 'Good, good.'

'Good, good,' responded the man and then gave the child's arm a fierce tug to hurry him on.

'Where do you imagine he's taking that kid?' said Barbara. 'All the time he just drags him up and down.'

'Perhaps he's trying to sell him,' said Brigg. 'If we were staying longer perhaps we could buy him for ourselves.'

'The way we operate I just can't see us having to *buy* a child,' she smiled. 'We'd be getting them free all the time.'

'Oh,' he said, suddenly visited by his old craven

254

anxiety. 'How do we know that we haven't already . . . ?'

'Sergeant, you're old fashioned sometimes,' she replied. 'Don't worry about it. I've put up the "No Sale" on the cash register. Does that reassure you?'

'Sorry,' he said. 'I'm afraid I started my sex life in the days when you either pulled away or pushed a pram.'

'You foul bastard,' she said amiably. 'Is that the sort of talk for a romantic night, with fish and chips and wine.'

'Sometimes,' he shrugged, 'I'm just a low soldier.'

'Will you always be a soldier?' she said.

'Till I'm too old, I expect,' he said. 'I'm no good at anything else. I've tried and made a mess of everything. Insurance, selling, buying, general grind. That's why I joined up again. It's the only thing I'm fit for.'

'You told me you went back into the Army because it was your way of dropping out of life,' she pointed out mischievously.

'I lied,' he admitted simply. 'Life dropped me more than me dropping it. Do you know, meeting you and being here with you, is the only proper, definite, concrete, thing I've done in years. I wander along, losing a wife here and a bit of self-respect there, not bothering when I know people are laughing at me, or are sorry for me, which is worse. And dragging Charlie along with me. Jesus, I'm like old Good-Good down there hawking that kid along the beach.'

'You sound like you ought to read *The Power of Positive Thinking*. Maybe it was written for you.'

He poured the wine. 'I've glanced at it,' he admitted. 'Have you read it?'

'No. Maybe I should.'

'On the first page the author says something like: "When I wrote this book I little dreamed that it would sell millions . . ." Now there's a bit of positive thinking for you.'

She laughed delightedly. 'Is that so?' she said.

'It is,' he affirmed.

'Some men make a success of the Army,' she said. Then unsurely, 'Don't they?'

'Like your husband?' He felt angry with himself as soon as he said the masochistic words.

'Why don't you quit about him?' she asked. 'I didn't mean that at all. He likes it, or he seems to like it, he's always talking about it. At least, I seem to remember he was. If liking being a soldier is being good at it, then I suppose he is. But he'll never be a general.'

'He'll be here soon,' said Brigg the sensation of loss and loneliness already washing like a sickness within him. 'They'll be calling you on the phone.'

'Why don't you open the other bottle?' Barbara said. 'Is the fish really good?'

'Very,' said Brigg, forcing cheerfulness to his face. 'But you haven't got the British touch with the chips. They've got to be limp and soggy. As though they've been out in the rain. It's something you can't achieve in a moment. It's the thing I was telling you about. Our heritage.'

They drank the wine and ate the food. Then they walked in the weightless darkness along the shore for an hour, going the way they had gone that morning, the moon travelling alongside them through a ragged

256

sky, the village warm with lights, murmuring voices and broken evening music.

Their feet were muffled by the sand and they spoke little. The great welling of love he had for her was engulfing him. She pushed herself against him as they walked like a nervous animal seeking protection. The brushing of her breast against his ribs, the hint of her hair against his neck and cheek as she leaned to him, multiplied his gladness that she was with him now and the knowledge of the emptiness that was to follow on her going.

'We still didn't get around to that second bottle of wine,' she said. 'I forgot. Did you?'

'We'll keep it for our home-coming,' he said. 'When we get back in a few minutes.'

'Okay, Sergeant,' she murmured. She turned her face to him and hid against his shirt. He could hear her tears. 'I don't want to leave you. You know, I don't want to.'

'There'll be other times,' he said unconvincingly.

'No,' she sniffed like a girl and shook her head. 'No. I just can't see it. When he's gone, I'll go back and you will still be here. Imagine, you will be able to visit our house any time. And I'll be so far away.'

'Maybe the British will occupy America again,' he said. She gave a dry little laugh and they said no more, but walked again towards their house. They drank the rice wine, sitting by the window, looking out over the channel striped with moonlight. There were fewer lights in the estuary villages now, for it was late. They died one by one and eventually a slow wind began to move over the land and the sea like some elderly sweeper-up.

Wordlessly they left the bottle and the glasses by the blind and went again to the bed. They were both a little excited by the wine; they laughed and made silly jokes as they prepared for the night. Both were lean and naked, their bodies warmed by each other and their appetites. They rolled on to the dragon silk cover, sliding like fish through comfortable water. Their hands were on each other, all over and under and about their skin, their muscles and the giving places.

'Sergeant, Jesus, God, you are in a frightening condition tonight,' she muttered, her mouth running wet against his stomach. 'Is that what the rice wine does?'

'It could be *you* as well,' he said lightly, prodding her. 'This thing certainly feels weighty. It must be all the fresh air and exercise.'

'I think he's going to get damaged, bruised or something, banging about like that,' she said.

'What do you suggest?'

'I have many suggestions,' she answered. 'But only one final answer. But, even so, I want to taste him first.'

She bent into him and Brigg tried to grasp onto her body while she was doing it. He caught and clutched her breasts, her buttocks, behind her knees, in frantic sequence, and then desperately caught her hair in his fist and pulled her firmly away.

She turned like an otter and lay against the pillow, her eyes closed, tears running beneath the lids, her mouth still open, her head trying to turn from him as though she were ashamed and frightened. He took her strongly, put his arms and his hands about her, and deftly arranged her on the bed.

Their love was quiet this time, long-stroking, with pauses and few words. Their playfulness, their violence, was spent, and they travelled calmly, like contented familiars. Only when they reached the end did they run. Then they both dashed together, partners in a race, flinging themselves to the finish, jubilant and fine and then at the last, infinitely sad. He looked at her in the moon shadows and saw that she was quietly weeping. He leaned and ran his tongue up her cheeks, lapping the tears from their channels. He closed over her protectively feeling his physical love still disgorging and his spirit engulfing her.

Then the phone rang.

He felt her heave beneath him, then stiffen. He looked down and caught her suddenly frightened, pleading face, then watched it wash away, resigned, expressionless. It was the expression of a captured criminal.

'The phone,' she said.

Brigg said firmly: 'I hear it. Let it ring.'

'I can't! You know I can't!' It came from her in a trapped squeal like a creature caught in a snare. 'Let me up. Please let me up.'

He pressed firmly against her. '*Think*,' he whispered. 'Please *think*, Barbara. Please let it ring.'

'Let me go!' Barbara wriggled angrily, squirming to get away from him. Her loving hands hardened suddenly to fists and she struck him on the chest. 'Get out!' she demanded. 'Get away.' He saw her trapped face and at the same moment released her. The force of her endeavours and the silk beneath their bodies combined to send her tobogganning to the floor. She scrambled crazily towards the insistent phone, like a drunk making for a compulsive bottle, the first few feet covered on all fours as she started from her fallen crouch. Brigg watched her, as he lay back naked, sick and disgusted, yet with his hand involuntarily reaching out towards her.

'Hello.' She picked up the phone. She dropped to her bare knees the moment she did so, and knelt with her head leaning into the receiver. The moon was strong in at the window now, beaming in unchecked, and Brigg watched her body in its light and the wet shine of the continuing tears on her face.

'Hello,' she whispered again. 'Is that the hotel?' She bent closer. 'Who? Oh . . . oh, I see. Yes . . . okay . . . He's here.' Barbara looked up at him almost comically. 'It's for you,' she said.

'Me?' Brigg's insides felt suddenly scooped out. 'It's nothing about Charlie, is it? It's not Charlie?'

'I don't think so,' she said soberly proffering the phone. Brigg began to crawl from the bed. 'It's bloody late,' he said. 'Who is it?'

'Take it,' she said evenly. 'I'll make some coffee. Do you want some?'

'Yes, thanks. I'd like some,' he said automatically. 'Who is it?' He took the phone from her and said, 'Hello,' hoarsely, the pains of the last few moments still sticking into him.

'Hello, Briggsy!' shouted Wilcox cheerily. 'How are you?'

'Christ,' muttered Brigg. 'You bastard. Do you know what the time is?'

'Why, mate, are you the speaking clock?'

'Look, what do you want? I told you only to call me in an emergency, you lousy sod. You don't know what you've done here.'

'Sorry, Briggsy. Were you right in the middle of the old fast and free?'

'What do you want, Wilcox?'

'Well, it is a *sort* of emergency,' said the bright, slightly drunken, voice. 'But I didn't know what your programme was fuckwise, now did I? It's just that we've been having a chat in the sergeants' mess about a football game against the Engineers. They keep going on about it and we thought we'd take the buggers on. And we want you in goal for us. Will that be all right, Briggsy?'

'Wilcox,' said Brigg quietly.

'Yes, mate.'

'Piss off,' said Brigg. He put the phone down violently. She came into the room with the coffee, her robe about her shoulders. Brigg put his shirt on and they sat and drank it shamefacedly. They lay down then and slept and in the morning they awoke to the telephone ringing again.

This time it was her call.

The village taxi took them down through the New Territories and into the city. They were silent for most of the way, but as the backs of the city came into view on the seamost hills she said: 'Three weeks today I'll meet you, if you want. If you don't then it's okay. I'll understand.'

'Thanks,' he muttered.

'I'll be up on the Peak, where we took Charlie the other day. At six-thirty in the evening.'

'In the film,' said Brigg tartly, 'Cary Grant had to see her on the Empire State Building.'

'I saw it too,' she admitted dully. They had reached the Star Ferry Pier and Brigg tapped for the taxi to stop. They kissed once and she turned her face away from him as she quickly left the cab. He watched her walk busily along the harbour front towards the hotel like an office girl returning to work. The taxi slowly overtook her. Brigg reached for the window, but never put his hand to it. He did not look at her when he passed and she did not look up at him.

The taxi driver said he had to return to the village, so Brigg, for no reason in particular except his loneliness, went with him. He walked moodily from the village along the sand to the house and the parrot squawked and rang the bell. Brigg walked up the stairs. The house was his until tomorrow night. At the bottom of the stairs the caretaker appeared, without the boy, and croaked, 'Good, good.' Brigg waved a negligent hand to him and went into the house. 'Not so bloody good, good,' he said to himself.

The place was so vacant without her. Their bed stood cold as a slab, the table by the window where they had eaten and drunk and talked last night, was bare and speckled with uncaring sunshine. He went to the window and saw that the sea was alive with the light of the spring day. The fishing boats were working. It didn't matter to them.

He went to the kitchen and absently began to wash up the previous night's dinner dishes, their plates and cutlery and glasses. He put the two wine bottles together and placed the mouth ends to his eyes like binoculars, but it failed to amuse him.

They had told her that her husband was due at midday. He would be there now in the hotel, embracing her, feeling her, eager for her, and she would show, would pretend, she was eager for him. Dirty bastard! Probably been screwing every little whorey cow in Saigon, picking up all sorts of foul things. After all it was the Yanks who brought all the pox into Hong Kong, wasn't it? And then they expected to turn up and claim their wives. See the conquering hero comes! He probably would too. Many times.

She had told the hotel on the phone that she would keep the same room. 'That's right, four-o-four,' she had said while he lay and listened bitterly. 'Yes, sure, it's a double.'

Brigg finished drying the dishes. He wiped his hands down his shirt and went to the phone. He called the hotel. Sorry, sir, four-o-six was occupied, but four-o-two was vacant. He would have that? Fine. For one night only. Okay, sir. What is the name? Mr Good, oh, sorry, Mr Good-Good. Good hyphen Good. Okay, Mr Good-Good. We'll be expecting you.

He went timidly to the hotel after dark. He did not see her, although there was a young American man looking at the restaurant list in the foyer. Brigg turned his face away guiltily and went quickly upstairs. He told the bellboy to take his bag up first, and then, hurriedly followed and slipped into the room.

Two hours later they went into their room. He heard them talking in the corridor, heard her unmistakable tone, and then the door opening. When he listened at the wall their voices were close, although still indistinct. His bed was against the wall, longways, and he guessed theirs would be also. He stripped himself and lay naked against the wall, against the plaster, his forehead, his chin, his chest, his penis, his thighs and his knees against its bored indifference.

Their voices continued and he heard them both laugh. The bedsprings sounded. The great thing with these Hong Kong hotels was that because there was a shortage of water for making cement and plaster, the walls were always thin. As Brigg breathed heavily and pressed himself despairingly against the wall, he knew that only a few inches away was the lovely naked body of his Barbara.

On the other hand, he thought, with *his* luck, it might be her husband's hairy arse.

19

In the morning he awoke cold, naked, spreadeagled across the bed. Layers of sun came through the blinds and he could hear the traffic moving along the harbour road and children shouting from a school playground. He lay and recalled, illogically, children's voices from twenty years before. Chinese children too, calling at play, when he awoke to his first day without his virginity. Lucy was there with him then; dear Juicy Lucy, his first fully paid-up love. The one who took him and showed him the way. He smiled at her memory and then moved towards the wall. There came no sound from the other room. They must be sleeping.

He groaned. Twenty years and here he was again. Watching the morning bars of an eastern sun through a window blind, hearing the Chinese children, wondering where he was going from that day, if anywhere. When he was nineteen, that long morning after his deflowering, at last, so he thought then, he had become a man; he imagined that from that day he could stride through the snares and battles of the world's life all-knowing and unafraid. And here he was now, still the virgin soldier, laying naked and hungry on a bed in an eastern city. His hopes, small and diffuse, his marriage filed away forever, his gates closed, his love just powder. Only Charlie remained. That meant they were both lost. He scratched his backside.

He left the hotel that day, paying his bill like a man who has stolen the towels; jumpy with anxiety in case she should come down to the foyer and see him. Then he went uselessly wandering along the waterfront, watching the men making the steel tunnel which they were going to put under the harbour. The welders' sparks, the armoured clamour, the shuffling boats in the port, made him aware of his weightlessness, his aimlessness, all the more.

In the afternoon he went to the YMCA and sat in one of their wicker armchairs, reading *Motor Mechanics*, and treating himself to a pot of tea for two and synthetic cream cakes. At that point he had decided to return to camp in the evening, but he eventually went into the bar and in the course of the next two hours got massively drunk with a sergeant in the Catering Corps, a globular man with sore eyes.

'I'll show you something,' said this soldier confidingly when they had entered the second hour of drinking. 'It's not many that I'd show this to because it's private, but seeing as you're so screwed up about women I'll show it to you.'

'What is it?' asked Brigg hazily. 'What you goin' to show me?'

'My hobby,' said the Sergeant. 'My hobby as I've carried it on for twenty-five years in the mob. Ever since the end of the war.' He was wearing a civilian sports jacket and he reached with some ceremony for the inside pocket from which he brought a heavy wallet.

'Hair,' he announced quietly, looking craftily about the room. He laid open the wallet and Brigg bent forward to look into it.

It was separated into compartments, each one covered with a neat window of cellophane. The same type as Brigg remembered stamp collectors carried about with them for their specimens. In each of the compartments was a curly question mark of hair. Above each was neatly noted a woman's name with a date and a geographical location.

Brigg squinted into it, in his drink not comprehending. 'Very nice,' he mumbled. 'Some women have got lovely hair. My former Glenda had nice . . .'

'They're cut from the fud,' said the man without ceremony. 'Clipped right off the business district.'

Brigg choked and his beer bubbled. 'God, no,' he said. Horrified, he leaned closer: 'I didn't get it right away. God, so they are. You mean to say you . . . you . . .?'

'That's right, a little clip with the scissors when they least expect it, and pop! Into the album they goes. Look at that, the very first. Hilde – never got her second name – Hanover, Christmas 1946. Came into the camp looking for carrots and spuds. Being in the cookhouse you're always on a good thing when there's not much nourishment about outside. I only did it as a sort of afterthought, you know, when I'd had it away and she'd already got her hands on the veg. Didn't even wait to get her clothes on right, she just grabbed for the carrots. Bet she wasn't more than fifteen neither.'

Brigg stared at the man as though he had produced a collection of big toes. He felt he had to make some comment. 'That's a big one,' he said eventually, pointing to one specimen.

The sergeant tipped forward and squinted at it as though he had difficulty remembering. 'Yerse,' he breathed, his eyes went up piously, in thought. 'Yerse. Now she was a really shaggy girl. Arab bird in Haifa. All over her, she had hair like that. Not much of a specimen really. With all that choice I had to cut it off too near the arse.'

The man turned the wallet and showed Brigg his most recent acquisitions, three curls of greying hair, and Brigg excused himself and went to a bar down the street. Why did his former Glenda have to go off with Staff Sergeant Pollock and get killed like that? Or why couldn't he have kept his former Lucy, and they could have been happy forever, waking to the sounds of children playing in a Chinese schoolyard? Now, there was his former Barbara, not very much former, but former nevertheless, encased in that hotel room with her husband. He telephoned the hotel and learned that Room four-o-two was still vacant, so he went there and undressed again and heard them talking in beyond the thin wall. He heard their door open and shut and guessed they had gone to dinner. Drunkenly he crawled to the door to see if he could catch just a glimpse of her back but she was gone when he looked into the corridor. He closed his door again and kneeled against it, hanging on to the doorhandle like a man drowning.

He almost drifted into sleep like that, but his penis was on the floor and a sharp draught was blowing under the door and on the tender end of it. So he slithered away, ill and stupid, and pulled himself once more on to the bed. He went into a chilly sleep and when he awoke it was two minutes to midnight.

A thick physical feeling enveloped him, hot inside with a thin coating of ice laying across his face and chest. Almost involuntarily, like a spy who has slept on duty, he pushed his ear against the wall, but to silence. They would be back soon and again he would have to lie there, all through their indecent love-making, knowing that the thickness of the wall would be the nearest he and she could ever be again.

He sat up and put his shirt around his shoulders. Then he rang the Jiggery Pokery Club and asked for Humphrey, the barman.

'Humph,' he asked him thickly. 'This is Sarj Bligg here. Are the girls there? The twins.'

'Ah, Sarj Bligg. How you go?'

'Bloody terrible, Humph. Are they there?'

'Sure, sure. No customers tonight. Just sitting, drinking coke. Look most fucking bored.'

'Listen, Humph, tell them to come over to the Sunrise Palace Hotel. I'm in Room four-o-two. It's okay. They'll get in. I've seen various girls coming in here. Tell them to give something to the porter, will you. I'll settle with them. Room four-o-two.'

Humphrey whistled across the line. 'Say, Sarj,' he said. 'That's okay hotel. You won the races?'

'I win bugger-all, Humph,' said Brigg dismally. 'Will you ask the girls?'

'Okay, you wait Sarj Bligg. I go now. Make sure nobody else fixed them.'

Brigg waited. He tied the arms of his shirt about his neck like an embrace. Humphrey returned. 'Okay,

okay, Sarj Bligg. They come. Very bargain tonight, I guess.'

Brigg thanked him, put the phone down and waited. He lay like a corpse in the dark. He wished he smoked because it was a good time for a cigarette. Twenty minutes went by and he heard voices in the corridor and then the door of the next room opened and closed again. He heard her husband laughing wildly and thought with superior disgust that he must be drunk.

After five more minutes there was a tap like a mouse at his door. He slid across the bed and opened it and Pearl, beaming a childish expression of wicked delight, came delicately into the room.

''Lo, Bligg,' she whispered kissing him. 'You run away from army? You all hid?'

'No, no.' He smiled at her through his dismay and his weariness. 'Where's Ruby?'

Pearl patted him on his privates and motioned that he should lie back on the bed. She stretched beside him, easily, without complication, the silk of the Chinese trouser suit she wore lying against his skin.

'Ruby, she find work,' she explained patiently like a tender relative breaking bad news. 'But we figure anyway you drunk, so no can do two girls. One, maybe so. But no two. So you got me.'

He rolled towards her, laughing sadly, and kissed her with meaning and friendship. She reacted quickly, like a pleased child. Her silent arms went about his neck and she kissed his lips and throat. A thought seemed to catch her and she rose from the bed and went to the washbasin in the corner. She returned through the half-light with a flannel and a towel and

270

gently washed him down, his sweaty face, his aching body, his groin and his legs, drying him comfortably with the towel afterwards, as light and considerate as a nurse.

'Well, at least, you're not the *former* Pearl,' he mused aloud, the drink still rebelling within him.

'Former Pearl?' she repeated making lines in her face as she did when puzzled. 'How mean, former Pearl?'

'You're *here*, that's all, love,' said Brigg softly. 'And you're not somewhere else.'

'No, no,' she whispered, still not understanding. 'Pearl is here. This is me, Sarj Bligg.' She giggled. 'There, see, you feel.'

Tiredly he unbuttoned the front of her tunic and slipped it back against her shoulders. She was wearing a young girl's bra, white and clean against her skin made dark in the low light.

'Pearl do,' she whispered, remembering his particular clumsiness. She curled her left hand behind her back and unclipped the hook with a single press of finger and thumb. The scrap of white material dropped away like the sail of a toy boat.

He leaned towards her in the dimness. He was always glad to see her breasts, soft and impudent, and of no size. He laid his mouth against her and his hard lips became gentle and they closed over her nipple.

'Sad tonight,' said Pearl her lips forming the words against his forehead.

'No, love,' he answered quietly. 'Bit decrepit, that's all.'

'What that?'

'What? Decrepit. Oh, well, shagged out. You know. Old.'

'Why you come to hotel?' she said. 'Plenty room my house.'

'I know,' he said. The drink was still lurking in him. He began to sing softly:

> 'There's always room at our house.
> There's always room for you.'

'Now you sing song, for Jesus Clist's sake,' she said full of puzzlement. 'You want love or music?'

'Both,' he said grinning at her uncertain face showing through the half light. 'But love first.'

He could hear them stirring in the next room. The bed moving and the voices burred in conversation. He rolled himself away from the wall and lay half across Pearl. She began to wriggle out of her silk trousers, but he stopped her with a touch of his palm. Firmly, but with no effort, he turned her over on to her stomach. Her head swivelled round to him, her face looking at him expectantly.

'You want this way, first?' she inquired. 'No good this way to kick-off. Better after little time.'

He laughed dryly. 'God, don't you pick up some English,' he said. 'No good this way to kick-off. Where did you get that one? Bet he was an Everton supporter.'

He knew she would not understand so he spoke almost to himself. To her he said: 'Don't worry.'

He drew the waist of the trousers down over the little hill of her rump, taking with them the nylon underskin of her pants.

The velvet incision of her backside lay smiling up at him. He bent to it and kissed her along its clean valley, one hand stroking the slim plain of her back, running along the ridges of her shoulder blades and the gentle indentations of her spine. The other hand he tunnelled under the garments still caught about the tops of her legs, pushing his fingers into the crevice. He heard her make a subdued buzzing sound as he moved both hands and his mouth to her various parts.

'You play music on me,' she told him tenderly from her end of the bed. 'Make me like piano.'

He pressed his face to her bottom and laughed at her phrase. Then he rolled her over and she kicked her legs from the trousers and pants. Her legs arched professionally, but she watched him with a great interest, a look for a lover, not a customer. He found her, that night, as sweet and loving and luxuriously enjoyable as any woman could reasonably be.

Afterwards his hands found her fragile fingers and held them for reassurance. In the next room he heard the man begin to laugh and then the woman's laugh joining in. Sweat was channelling down Pearl's childish face and Brigg pushed his nose into it. His face was wet when he took it from her. She slid away from him and slipped on the switch of the bedside light. Her small orange face looked at him.

'Hot,' she said. 'All hot.' She wiped the sweat from her face with the back of her hand. Then she put the soft palm to his cheek and wiped his face also.

She giggled uncertainly, half-serious. 'Hot,' she repeated. 'All sweat. Jesus Clist, Sarj, you look like you cly.'

20

Now the sun was taking a firm hold on the sky. Each spring day it rose with increased confidence and claimed the sea, the islands and the mountainous land. Rain still came in the night, raiding down through the hills, but each morning was pale and innocent, and the days were increasingly fine.

Treacle Thompson, marching in solitary along at the side of the square, while the remainder of the garrison drilled and paraded at its middle, was more than aware of the growing heat. He, like the rest of the army was still in his prickly winter battledress, and it made his spots itch. But, believing that his wide-legged stridings at the fringe of the square were being watched and timed closely by the distant sergeant major he stuck uncompromisingly to it, full in the knowledge that he was an important factor in a military operation.

'Brigg,' asked Sergeant Major Love from his box on the far side of the parade ground. 'What's that little clockwork cunt Thompson supposed to be doing? Trying to rupture himself or something?'

'The Colonel says he's got to march at the side of the square,' said Brigg. 'And that's what he's doing.'

'Christ, does he have to march like that? His bloody arms will fall off.'

Brigg stared across the hot concrete square to the remote toyish figure. 'I think he thinks he's helping, Sarn't Major. He's marching because he's a soldier.'

Love looked at Brigg metallically. Brigg returned the look steadily. 'All right, Sarn't Brigg,' said the RSM nastily. 'That's all.'

'Thank you, Sarn't Major.' Brigg swung smartly and stamped back to his squad. He moved them to and fro, marching, wheeling, about-turning, eyes-righting and eyes-fronting, with incised commands spat out quietly with none of the blatant theatricalism of some of the other platoon sergeants.

The squads made patterns all about the square, the shouted orders bouncing against the impassive white walls of the barrack blocks. Large Oriental rooks fidgeted and jumped about the trees irritated by all the military noise and activity.

At one end, sweating on the unkempt grass where the parade ground concrete ended, Staff Sergeant Parsons, red as a country apple, shirt sticking to his low belly, looked over the unhappy unarmed combat squad with his impassioned pastor's stare.

'Today being the first Monday after Sexagesima, which marks, you will know, the beginning of Our Lord's teaching on earth,' he said. 'We have five days to make you into killers. When the Right Hon the Minister of Defence of Her Majesty's Government – God bless her, too – watches your blooming antics next Saturday afternoon, I want him to go back to the Prime Minister and order a cut in the amount of taxpayers' money expended on guns and other instruments of war. And why is that? I'll tell you why, though I know you, Harrison, for one, could tell me if I asked, now couldn't you?'

'No, Staff,' muttered Harrison.

'I knew you could, Harrison. It's on account of the Minister realizing, when he sees you perform, that the British Army don't need guns no more. That they can fight with their bare 'ands. Now, Harrison, rush at me to kill me.'

'Me again, Staff?'

'My goodness gracious, Harrison,' incanted Parsons. 'Don't disobey your favourite staff sergeant. Rush at me to blooming kill me, man.'

'But I'm *always* the one, Staff, who has to rush at you to kill you. I can't even move my arm from last Saturday.'

'Which arm, Harrison?' asked the instructor.

'Left, sir.'

'Rush at me with the right arm under-chop. And to *kill*.'

Harrison groaned. The remainder of the squad smirked and he trundled forward resignedly, then, hopefully, roared into the bulky body of Parsons. There was the usual extraordinary spring and jerk movement from the tubby instructor, and the usual despairing spin from the would-be killer. He lay on the tufty ground, grizzling, holding his right shoulder.

Parsons regarded him mercifully. 'O Lord,' he recited. 'By reason of the frailty of our nature we cannot always stand upright.' He beamed at Harrison and transferred it to the rest of the soldiers. 'The Collect for the Fourth Sunday after Epiphany,' he announced. 'Used in the Anglican Church, of course, but nevertheless applicable on outside occasions, as

276

we now see. Get up, Harrison, it seems to be NAAFI break.'

The garrison's unaccustomed activities extended through the evenings of the week. In the barrack rooms lights were mirrored in the rich, shining toe-caps of the soldiers' boots and in the golden brightness of their brasses and badges.

On the camp's outskirts the plastic, pointed windows of the chapel, with their multi-coloured St Jerome, gave their celluloid glow while the choir of pressed men sang away a dirgeful hour. Rehearsals for the concert were, by Thursday, steeped in pessimism. Pardoe refused to play the spoons unless they were specially issued since RSM Love had already made him pay for one mildly damaged set of cutlery. The Reverend Captain Church-Smith had to be told that his jokes were unsuitable for an adult audience and was replaced in the cast.

But throughout the week the light in the Tin Room, removed from the other inhabited places, still sent out its sickly yellow message that Treacle Thompson was at labour among the metal and muck.

On Thursday night he was hurrying with excite-ment. They were to meet again at her house, for Sergeant Major Love and Mrs Love were at an emergency meeting called by the Colonel to tie up the loose ends, military and social, of the Minister's visit. Treacle laid aside the last of the tins and let the water ooze down the plughole. Then, extinguishing the light, he went out and crept like a dwarf burglar into the shadows of the married quarters area.

Violet was waiting at the window curtain like a cow

at a gate. He could see she was there because the curtain bulged against the window. He skipped like an elf to the rear garden and the back door. She embraced him as he stepped into the house.

'My little darling,' she whispered in her elementary fashion. She kissed him fussily. 'They've gone. It's all right, my love.'

'I've been going mad waiting,' he said sincerely. 'They had a million pans tonight, or so it seemed like it. My hands will be a bit greasy, I'm afraid.'

'I won't slip through them,' said Violet poetically. 'We'll have some of his sherry first, shall we? We know each other now, there's not so much rush, is there.'

Treacle looked at the mountains of her blouse, and her plain face. Her doughy hands were holding his small-boned fingers. 'I've never known any woman like you,' he blurted honestly. 'I kept saying to myself in the Tin Room – only five more pans to go, only four, only three . . . All the time, just dying to get here.'

'You haven't met anybody else, then?' Her voice was sincere.

'No,' he said. '*You* haven't, have you?'

'No. Honest,' she smiled. She led him maternally into the lounge. Taking the sherry decanter she poured two small, medicinal, glassfuls. 'Just to get us in the mood,' she said, the smile settling like a thrown rope across her face. 'It's only a drop, but I don't want that miserable bugger to notice.'

She handed the glass to him and they toasted each other with genuine love. 'Oh,' she said suddenly, almost biting on the glass. 'I nearly forgot. He was on about you tonight.'

278

'Your dad?' said Treacle, a small, immediate tremble touching him. 'Me? What about?'

'Don't worry. It was only about the concert, you know, the camp concert for the Government bloke that's coming. He's doing an act and he wants you to help him.'

Treacle gaped his astonishment. 'Me! No. Honest, Vi? He wants *me*?'

'That's what he said.'

'What sort of act?' he said, suspicion draining the enthusiasm from him. 'What's he going to do? Saw me in half, I bet.'

'No, love, no,' she giggled. 'He's telling jokes. He thinks he's funny, even if nobody else does.'

'He'll be wanting to chuck whitewash over me or something,' forecast Treacle morosely. 'Otherwise he'd have somebody else.'

'No, he won't,' she said. 'He wants you to hold up his blackboard at the side of the stage. He has all his jokes written on it, or the first lines anyway. He can't remember them otherwise, bloody fool. Every posting we've had he does it. Same old jokes. There's some in this camp that's heard them four or five times.'

Treacle grinned. 'That's all right, then,' he said. 'I won't mind doing that. Just holding a board up for him. He might even get to like me a bit.'

'*I* like you a bit,' said Violet her big eyes shining.

'And I think you're marvellous, really,' he mumbled moving towards her. 'You're the only thing that makes my life anything at all.' She leaned across her own breasts and kissed him. He pushed his pitted face into her flesh. 'There doesn't seem a lot of love around, otherwise,' he said.

She said: 'But if you wanted to come up and do it now, then I'm ready. But take your time over the sherry.'

Treacle who had only a smear of the small sticky drink she had given him remaining in his glass said: 'I've had enough, thanks, Vi. I'm not one of those who needs alcohol before sex.' They closed together and with her thick arm about his weedy neck and his bony fingers seeking a purchase on her widespread waist they went with difficulty up the carpeted stairs.

'The funny thing is, I think your dad's got a sneaking regard for me, Vi,' said Treacle thoughtfully when they reached the landing. 'For one thing he's using me to pace out and time the whole parade while they're practising for this Minister of Defence thing. He picked me specially for that, Sergeant Brigg told me. And on Saturday when they actually do the drill he's got a *special* job for me. He said.'

'But that's fabulous,' she said in her teenage way. 'That really is. Maybe you'll get your stripe soon.'

'Then I'd really feel that it's all been worthwhile,' answered Treacle. 'I'd know then that the Army really wants me.'

'I want you,' she said, jumping in again. 'Very quickly too. *And* – listen to this – I want to do it in *their* bed.'

Treacle went cold. 'Their bed?' he said. 'You mean your *dad's* bed? Your *mum's* and *dad's*?'

She giggled. 'Yes, that's it. Don't worry, they're not royalty or anything, you know.' She became strangely shy. 'And I'd just like to do it, that's all,' she said.

'But why? What's the matter with your . . .?'

'Nothing. But I just want to. I want to get my own

back on them, see.' She looked at him as though she knew he would not understand. 'I really would,' she whispered. 'I'd like it all the more in there.'

'All right, Vi,' he said, still unsure. 'If you think they won't find out.'

'They won't,' she enthused. 'And the thought of *us* doing it in *their* bloody bed, is fabulous. Honest.'

They went into the large bedroom. Treacle was still frightened, but once he had undressed the carpet felt comforting under his feet. There was a photograph of her father in full dress uniform on the dressing table and another of her parents on their wedding day. Violet had stripped and now she stood enormously, white and bulging, looking fondly at his pixie face. 'Get in,' she invited. 'Get in between the sheets, darling.'

Treacle glanced at the picture of the RSM, gave it a nervous nod, then pulled the covers back, and, still looking at her, half afraid, half joyfully anticipating, he climbed in, like a small boy going to bed. She was about to follow him, her swollen breasts hanging like clouds, when, as an afterthought, she went to the dressing table and brought the pompous wedding day photograph to the bedside cabinet.

'Mum and dad,' she said formally. 'I'd like you to meet my boyfriend, Private Thompson, who is about to give me a good rogering. He's very nice, and he's got a much bigger dicky than dad, and I'm going to enjoy it twice as much as mum. So watch carefully.'

'Vi, you're terrible,' whispered Treacle admiringly. 'Come on in.' She went into the bed with him, sliding weightily along the nylon sheets, until her large thundery body was against his undernourished frame.

He pulled himself up, using her shoulders as levers, so that their faces were as near as they could manoeuvre them.

'I *have* got a moustache,' she said, suddenly miserable. 'I've watched it growing. It's bad enough being fat, but having whiskers as well! It doesn't do much for a girl. I sometimes curse God, I honestly do.'

'You haven't,' he said kindly. 'You haven't at all. I don't know how you can think that.' He laughed. 'I wish I could grow a bit of hair. Mine keeps coming out in handfuls.'

'You feel huge down there,' she said changing the subject mistily. 'All your strength seems to have gone to one place. A lot of men would envy you.'

'They would if they knew I had you,' he said gallantly. 'I can't believe it's me – not lying here like this with you, naked in the sergeant major's bed.'

'It's you all right,' she said, her voice melting. 'Nobody else could be like *that* in bed. God, it feels like there's two of you.'

He climbed between her legs and connected himself carefully and considerately to her. She gave a long, fat groan as he did so and he kissed her on the neck, which was the highest point he could reach. 'I love you, Vi,' he said. 'I love you, my beautiful.'

'My man,' she answered lazily working her thighs like slow pistons. 'You're my man.'

As they had found before they were able to make love for a long period, changing the movements and the rhythms, but knowing it was impractical to consider changing positions. 'I'd like to ride on top of you, dearest,' she said, but added sensibly, 'but I don't think you'd be able to breathe.'

He wanted her to try, but she refused, and they sailed along on their happy journey together, until they knew that the conclusion was not far off. Treacle, his cheeks brick red, shifted himself up her body, like a man on the back of a dray horse seeking a safer seat. Now they were ready to go. Violet's eyes were closed and excited bubbles blew from her mouth. He quickened his pace and she moaned with each scrambling movement. Even in his ecstasy Treacle had the feeling he was a beetle trying to scramble up a wall.

Then, when they were seconds away, a door opened downstairs. They heard it bang and swing noisily. Treacle almost screamed with fear. He pulled away from her on impulse, throwing himself across the bed, and splendidly ejaculating all over the blue nylon sheet as he did so.

'Oh, Jesus Christ,' he moaned. 'Look what I've done.'

'Hush,' Violet ordered, taking hold of the situation. 'Push your things under the bed and get into the wardrobe.'

'Anybody home?' The woman's voice pleaded from downstairs.

Violet sighed. 'It's all right,' she whispered to Treacle. 'She's from next door.' She padded to the landing pulling on a dressing-gown about her. 'Coo-ee,' she called over the rail. 'That you, Mrs Billing?'

The woman's face trailing a body behind it like a tadpole stared up from the hallway. 'Yes, dear. Oh, it's you, Vi. Are they out?'

'Gone to the Colonel's meeting,' said Violet. 'Did you want something?'

'I couldn't go,' said Mrs Billing. 'Dad went, but some friends have turned up from Hong Kong. Quite unexpected. Have you got any custard powder? I've got to give them something.'

Violet grimaced, but descended the stairs. 'Been cooking, Vi?' chatted the other woman. 'You're quite red in the face. And there's a smell of cornflour. Have you been making cornflour? I love it, but my husband . . .'

'I'm having a bath actually,' said Violet sliding past her, twitching her nose to detect the cornflour smell once she was heading the other way. She found the custard powder with the three birds on the tin in the kitchen and gave it to the neighbour. 'There you are, Mrs Billing,' she said moving her towards the door and adding sweetly: 'Hope you have a nice custard.'

'Thank you, Vi, dear,' said Mrs Billing, her puzzlement plain on her face. 'I'm sure we will. Now I come to think of it I could have made some cornflour. Still if dad doesn't care for it . . .' She reached the door. 'Well, then, thanks dear. Give my regards to your mum and dad. 'Night.'

''Night, Mrs Billing,' said Violet. She closed the door thankfully, then pulled aside her dressing-gown and looked down to where Treacle had left a streak of himself on her fat upper leg. She bent and had a sniff at it. 'Cornflour?' she wondered to herself.

It was eleven when Sergeant Major Love and Mrs Love returned from the Colonel's briefing. In their bedroom Mrs Love said with satisfaction: 'Well, you certainly showed them.'

'Somebody had to,' he agreed generously.

'Somebody had to pawn them out. The Old Man was chuffed, though, wasn't he? That *I* was able to tell *them* how to stop the Minister seeing their balls-up.' He stopped speaking and undressing. 'There's a funny smell in here, Suze.'

His wife sniffed. 'I can't smell it,' she said.

'I thought I could,' he said, sniffing again, but then continuing with his trousers. 'But Command Workshops owe me a few beers now, don't they?'

'I'll say,' she agreed loyally, undressing the other side of the bed. 'A pipe band! Who would have thought of it?'

'I did,' her husband said smugly. 'Have a pipe band playing on the bank of the training ground right opposite where their bloody tank and the rest of their rubbish is stuck and make sure the Minister looks at the pipe band when he's driving by. Then just steer him clear of the place after that. When he leaves it will be dark anyway. It's all so bloody simple. Are you sure you can't smell anything?'

'Well there is a bit of a funny smell,' she said. 'It's like cornflour. Where did they say they'd get the pipe band from?'

'Kuching,' he said.

'Is that far?'

'Sarawak,' he answered. 'Christ knows what they're doing there, but that twat in Intelligence says there's one there, so they can fly them up here. Anything to stop him seeing their bleeding . . . You know, that's a funny smell. I can still smell it. But I can't place it. It's not the sort of smell you get very much. But I've certainly smelled it before.'

'Maybe Violet's been cooking something for her

285

supper. You know what concoctions she makes.' They climbed in opposite sides of the bed, kissed perfunctorily and turned their backs on each other for sleep.

The sergeant major's nose continued to twitch over the sheet and drowsily Mrs Love wondered why her wedding day photograph was staring at her from the bedside cabinet.

21

Because of an unexpected, special priority air movement, the Minister of Defence was kept waiting in the
sky for half an hour before being allowed to land at
Kai Tak Airport, Hong Kong. His Royal Air Force
transport was obliged to describe an annoyed circle
over the colony, the clouds and the cluttered islands
while the captain kept up an ill-tempered exchange
with the military controller in the airport tower.

The transport plane from Kuching, Sarawak,
having nudged into Kai Tak by a nosewheel before
the Minister's aircraft, discharged a puzzled Gurkha
pipe band which, with its equipment, was taken on to
Army lorries and rushed away even as the Ministerial
Canberra was coming into the rudely projecting
tongue of the peninsula runway.

An hour later, all the senior handshakes over, the
Minister, Mr Harold Pomeroy, was being driven from
Hong Kong to the New Territories to be greeted at
the village just short of Buller Barracks by a huge
Chinese crowd entirely concealing a howling Gurkha
bagpipe band.

'Good heavens, what a turn-out,' said the Minister,
patently pleased. He leaned towards the car window.
'All these Chinese! Just shows whose side they are
really on, doesn't it. What's all that wailing?'

'Pipers, sir,' said his worried escorting officer. 'Over here on the left. Unfortunately you can hardly see them for the crowd.'

Nevertheless, the subterfuge had been achieved, the official car had sped by the ignominious tank and its disgraced companion, and on to the garrison gate where a guard of honour was formed before the furled flag and the flower beds.

Colonel Simmons, pink with the occasion, saluted and shook hands with the visitor, who then inspected a guard of honour so shining and blazoned, creased and crackling, that the garrison had never seen the like. Apart from three undone fly buttons bright as medals on the front rank marker it was a gallant display.

A borrowed bugler from the artillery unit at Kowloon blew a greeting and the Union Jack was broken at the mast head. The Colonel, who had not noticed the miserable fly buttons – although the Minister had – described with flushed anxiety and enthusiasm mixed, the programme they had planned for the following two days. The concert, the parade, the display of military training.

'I think, sir,' he admitted with formal military modesty, 'you're going to find it is *quite* a weekend.'

For once in his life he was right.

Later that night it occurred to Colonel Simmons that the camp concert was the closest he had ever been to a real military disaster, although even that milestone was soon to be superseded. From the start it had not gone well. The night was sweaty and the cinema where they assembled was tight as a tin box. He sat by the Minister and watched with sideways concern as the caterpillars of sweat wriggled down the Whitehall neck. He and the medical officer, Major Stevens, and their wives who flanked the front row visitor, fanned themselves energetically with their programmes, but someone had forgotten to give the Minister his and no one noticed the omission.

'My adjutant, Major Fortune, is doing a little act in the show,' said the Colonel conversationally. The Minister glanced enviously at the vibrating programme. The Colonel did not notice. 'A pastiche, I think he called it. Very sporting of him, I thought.'

Major Stevens leaned with morose satisfaction across the Minister. 'He's not doing it now, sir. He gave it up.' He fanned enthusiastically and the Minister leaned tentatively forward trying to filch some of the draught.

'Gave it up!' retorted the CO. 'Why, for heaven's sake?'

'Nobody laughed,' said the doctor brutally. 'At rehearsals everybody just stood around looking glum. They said they didn't understand it.'

The Colonel swallowed his annoyance with a smile. 'Probably under-rehearsed,' he said diplomatically.

'That as well, sir,' pursued Major Stevens. The Colonel's warning swivel of the eyes reminded him that the Minister was his neighbour and he smiled with embarrassment. 'He's still in the show, however,' he said trying to recover. 'Master of Ceremonies.'

'I thought that was going to be the padre,' put in the Colonel.

'He couldn't think of any suitable jokes, sir. So he backed down.'

The Minister took out a large handkerchief and towelled the sweat from his neck. He was aware that men and their wives in all the crowded rows behind were trying to catch a glimpse of him, straining forwards in their seats, standing up and even blatantly pointing. He heard a female voice say: 'That's him, wiping the sweat off now.' He smiled stoically.

'Sounds like the good old army concert,' said the Minister managing a slippery smile through lips wet with heat. 'It *will* be all right on the night!'

'I jolly well hope so,' said the Colonel fervently wishing that he had kept a closer eye on the arrangements. 'Well, we shall soon see. Here we go.'

The lights fell and the curtains shrank away as though cringing from the assault of Brod Perkins and The Ding Dongs, the garrison pop group, gyrating heavily in serge firemen's uniforms and big rubber waders. Their panic-striken overture to the concert accomplished, they bowed stiff-legged, from the hips, to near-hysterical applause and the curtains dropped. Nothing happened for three minutes. The Colonel leaned to the Minister and said: 'Pretty enthusiastic, don't you think? The group, I mean.'

'Yes,' mumbled the Minister. 'Why were they dressed as firemen? They're not firemen, are they?'

'Oh, no,' the Colonel assured him. 'They're Army personnel. Our own lads. It's their professional image, I suppose you'd call it. It's because they're called The Ding Dongs. Ding-Dong – like a firebell, you see, sir. Sometime during the performance they actually ring a brass bell, don't they Stevens.'

The Medical Officer nodded and the Minister said a little absently: 'I shall look forward to that.' No movement was apparent on the stage, so the Minister turned to the Commanding Officer once more. 'If they're military personnel, how is it they're permitted the long hair? That one in the front has hair on his shoulder.'

'Wigs,' said the Colonel triumphantly. 'They wear wigs. They don't feel it's in keeping with a pop group to display the regulation short back and sides. Ah, here's Fortune now. Late as usual.'

Major Fortune's pink young head poked through the curtains, a wildly worried grin impaled on his face. As though reassured, he stepped through to the footlights.

'Good evening, ladies and gentlemen,' he blurted. 'That was The Ding Dongs, and jolly good they were too, weren't they?'

It was a rhetorical question which the audience did not feel impelled to answer and they did not. Fortune shivered against the indifference. Then he asked: 'I wonder if you've heard of the cannibal who *passed* his friend in the street?'

Most of them had, and, through the restrained laughter of those who had not and still understood it, came the strong tones of Doris Boswell, 'Dirty bugger.'

Colonel Simmons dropped his face resignedly into his programme and by the time he had raised it again the stage was completely filled with Violet Love, her form and her strong honest voice. She wore her large Snoopy sweater and tubular jeans. Quickly she dealt with two popular songs. What she lacked in finesse she accounted for with technique, a truly remarkable movement, hips one way, breasts the other and head revolving at the centre. Beyond her The Ding Dongs pop group were occasionally glimpsed in the background.

Almost demented enthusiasm was generated by this performance and by the subsequent songs. Violet had set the concert on its feet.

The remainder of the show, until Charlie Brigg's hypnotism act, went lame. Staff Sergeant Parsons, a questionable alto voice issuing from his rough bass face, sang *I Know That My Redeemer Liveth* and *The Trumpet Shall Sound*, the single taps of The Ding Dongs' drummer, head suitably bowed, substituting for the more customary trumpet solo.

The bugler, begged from the Royal Artillery, Kowloon, for the weekend, declined to volunteer for the trumpet voluntary normally associated with the piece but had offered to play Lights Out very softly to Handel's masterwork if Staff Sergeant Parsons was willing to take the chance. He wasn't.

RSM Love ('And here is Frank Love – You'll Love Him!') stood solidly and told mixed jokes to mixed reception until some off-stage emergency, unseen by the audience, brought his act to a sudden, confused, unsatisfactory conclusion. The comedian's wicked grin fell quicker than the curtain and his violent boots were heard stamping across the boards. As an emergency stop-gap his daughter was launched into the lights for another frenzied ten minutes with The Ding Dongs.

The Ding Dongs concluded with two sagging solo numbers, and the group, slowed to exhaustion with the heat and their firemen's kit, began the second half of the show and then continued by accompanying yet another return of Violet Love. 'By popular request,' according to Major Fortune, whose nerve had cracked under the back-stage pressures.

The hysteria which greeted his desperate introduction was the voice of people who feared that things could get much worse. By this time the heavy young girl, soaked with sweat, was croaking protests in the wings. She bent and coughed like a heavyweight boxer who had taken a low blow, but the pleading of the half-demented adjutant and an ill-tempered push by her father sent her spinning into the limelight again. She sang two more songs then rolled off like a bag of damp laundry to tremendous and sincere applause.

Charlie appeared for his hypnotism act in what he and Ho-Ho imagined a wizard would wear, a long-pointed Christmas hat and a coloured robe adapted from the dress of his dead mother which Brigg had given to the housekeeper.

Brigg closed his eyes when the boy appeared at the footlights. Wilcox sensed his reaction and mistook it. 'He'll be all right,' said Wilcox from the next seat. 'He *must* be good after the others.'

Forcing the sick unhappiness away, squeezing it out, and letting the sympathetic laughter all around him dilute it and wash it from him, Brigg nodded. 'He'll be fine. Sometimes he's just like his bloody mother on the big occasion.'

Wilcox glanced at him strangely, but Brigg was smiling a straight smile and watching the boy on the stage. That dress. That multi-coloured memory. Why did he still remember when she had been such a shit?

It had been right at the back of the wardrobe, something she had not worn since that summer, that day of
that summer, when they went to Norfolk and the baby
– this very boy – had floated away on the lake. What
a hot day that had been. All her other clothes had
gone, taken quickly from the house after her death,
when he found it. Now he cursed himself for dragging
it half way around the world. Why did he do that?
Why did he want it? Just because they had been happy
that day? Jesus, it was bad enough seeing the bones of
the shuffling Ho-Ho showing like lumps through it,
but to see it draped so hideously about his son! If
Glenda, his former Glenda, bastard that she was,
getting killed with Sergeant Pollock like that . . . if she
could see their son now. The boy's confident, funny
voice penetrated through the pleased laughter all
about. Would she recognize her Leofric? Would she
recognize her dress?

Charlie was serious, addressing the audience: 'I've
already explained to my dad and the Colonel that I
can't put absolutely *everybody* in a trance. Not for dead
certain. Sometimes it won't work. So to save time I'll
have six volunteers on the stage and try it out on all of
them. There ought to be at least a couple I can do it
to.'

The audience floated into laughter at his serious-
ness. Doris Boswell was weeping copiously and
muttering, 'No mother. Poor little bugger. No
mother.' The Minister settled back and seemed to be
enjoying himself at last; the Colonel sat with a
growing smile and only the Medical Officer scowled.
Fussily he pushed his doctor's bag forward indicating
that he might be needed at any moment.

294

'So I need six volunteers,' pleaded Charlie.

Half a dozen suspiciously gloomy men rose simultaneously from one row and with a common fatalism went towards the stage.

'That was quick!' exclaimed Charlie with genuine surprise. The audience bellowed. All the other concert participants, apart from RSM Love and Treacle Thompson who were outside the building in the dark, crowded the wings to watch the act. Brigg could see that Charlie was nervous because his voice kept leaping an octave and the startled boy had to tug it back again. But no one else noticed. The volunteers had now reached the stage and were arrayed in an unhappy line like men about to be shot. Charlie looked at their general height doubtfully. 'I think I'm going to need the box,' he called to the wings. A lemonade crate was pushed on to the stage and Charlie stood on it, measuring his eye level against that of his first subject.

The laughter increased and swelled on, broken by the renewed sobs of Doris Boswell, now joined by the sentimental Hilda, incanting in turn: 'Motherless.' 'Crying shame.' 'Poor little bleeder.' Wilcox was falling over on to Brigg's shoulder. Brigg smiled for the boy, but he could not take his eyes off that coloured dress.

The drummer of The Ding Dongs, encouraged by his success with *The Messiah,* now gave Charlie a roll of snaky sound and the boy mounted his lemonade crate before his first subject, a stolid lance-corporal in the garrison pay section.

A grave silence now occupied the audience, with Doris bravely upright and shiny of eye and Hilda minutely snivelling. Charlie looked around once, as though seeking Brigg, but then he returned to the subject and looked deeply into the soldier's dull but suspicious eyes.

Charlie took a small medallion on a chain from his pocket. Brigg recognized it at once as a swimming medal he himself had won when he was sixteen. The boy let it swing like a pendulum in front of the lance-corporal's distrusting eyes, repeating in a young dream-like voice, 'You are going deep into a deep, refreshing sleep . . . deeper and deeper into a deep refreshing sleep . . . deeper and deeper . . . deeper and deeper.'

The man merely stood, not stiffening, not moving, relaxed and, from the audience's view, apparently unaffected. Charlie looked at him uncertainly, then moved his box along and began on the second subject. The words were said and the medal swung and again there was no apparent reaction. The two men stood, still and unblinking, and Charlie went on to the third and then the fourth.

When he was in the middle of his ritual with the fourth subject the first man toppled spectacularly from the stage and landed in the lap of the Minister of Defence. There were shouts and screams. Then the second fell on to his knees and face-out on the stage boards. Charlie panicked and ran to the third man, who was just toppling, trying to push him upright, shoring him up with his small arms.

'Dad! Dad!' howled the boy and Brigg and Wilcox went at a run down the aisle through the erupting pandemonium. The fourth man, only half into the trance, was crawling like a sheep about the stage. The remaining two subjects had run away. Brigg took the weight of the toppling third soldier from his son now almost crushed beneath it, and laid him out, stiff as a tree, on the boards.

The Minister of Defence had remained fixed in his seat, the pay office lance-corporal in a kneeling attitude before him, the large head on his knees, the reddened uncomprehending eyes staring up into his governmental face like those of a dead bloodhound. Everyone in the crammed hall was on their feet to see what was happening. Great foghorns of laughter were coming from Doris Boswell.

Major Stevens and the Colonel combined to try to pull the prostrate soldier from the Minister's legs. But he was a dead weight and the space was limited between the seats and the edge of the stage. Helpers got in each other's way and only men in the deepest trance could have failed to be disturbed by the noise.

Brigg on the stage was in a hot panic. Wilcox was sitting on the lemonade box heaving with laughter, uncheckable tears furrowing over his cheeks. Brigg kicked the box angrily. 'For Christ's sake, what's so bloody funny?' he demanded. 'Give me a hand with this one.' Wilcox shook helplessly through all the rescue operation. The hall looked as though someone had tossed an accurate hand grenade. Brigg saw the soldier who had fallen first being finally disengaged from the Minister, dragged like a finished bull from a ring. Some fools had begun community singing and Charlie, in tears, came to his father and said: 'I couldn't help it. Honest. I thought I was going to get them all under. I didn't mean them to fall down, Dad.'

'Look, Charlie,' said Brigg tersely, 'just bring them round, that's all. And damned quick too.'

'All right, Dad, I will.'

'And take that ridiculous bloody dress off,' said Brigg.

22

The first eyebrow of the new day was only half raised when the garrison lights began to show and the soldiers made their preparations for the big parade. A real bugle call honked across the dawn. The married quarters were buttoned with squares of bilious yellow light.

Sticky-eyed RSM Love rolled from his bed after a night of grinding teeth. 'Today,' he promised himself as he dug his fingernails into his pubic area, 'Today, I'm going to crucify that little shitface.'

'What's the matter, dear?' stirred Mrs Love. 'It's very early, isn't it?'

Love scowled at her. 'Not when you've been awake all sodding night like I have,' he said. 'It's all right for you, you've been snoring like a sow.'

'Thanks very much,' she muttered rolling over the side of the bed and trying to find her slippers with her feet. 'Take it out on the right one, will you, kindly. Take it out on *him* not *me*.'

'Take it *out* on him. That's mild to what I'm going to do, Suze. I'll age that puny little bastard ten years in the next week. Only a feeble fucker like that could hold the blackboard the wrong way round – and then when he turns it about he's rubbed all the jokes off with his pissing knees.'

'Language, please,' his wife complained mildly. 'You're not in the mess.'

'Oh, shut up,' he told her. 'Get some tea for Christ's sake. It's Human Bloody Comedy Day today. The big noise wants to see all the brave British soldiers marching up and down.'

'I'll make the bed first,' she said firmly. 'Violet did it yesterday and she never does it properly. Tell her to get the tea.'

'Right,' he agreed. 'It wouldn't hurt that lazy cow. Chucking herself around like a fat camel in front of the Colonel and the Minister last night. And not once but half a dozen times. Every time I looked there she was banging about the stage. Violet! Violet!'

A sound like the approach of a small breeze eventually came along the corridor and Violet appeared in her long, comfortable, nightdress. Her father glared at her and her mother stared. 'Glad you could manage it,' said the sergeant major. 'Perhaps the camp sex-*pot* wouldn't mind putting some tea in the tea-*pot*.'

Violet looked at him with distaste. She wasn't afraid of him. 'At least I didn't need a blackboard to tell me which bit of filth to tell next,' she said bluntly. 'And then take it out on the man you picked to do your menial work.'

'He's going to have some more menial work today too,' said Love with nasty satisfaction. 'He's going to shovel up the dung behind the Colonel's horse. That's what he's going to do.'

Violet stared at him. Her face filled with unreleased tears. 'You wouldn't do that to him,' she said trying to keep her voice straight. 'You *couldn't* break somebody like that. Not when he thinks he's a soldier . . .'

300

'Break him? Break him?' shouted her father. 'I'm going to bloody-well disintegrate him. I'm going to squash him down and smash him up, I'm going to kill him, I'm going to take him bit by . . .' He stopped and looked hard at her. 'What's it to you, anyway?' he frowned. 'What do you know about him? How do you know . . .?'

'Frank,' said Mrs Love quietly. 'Have a look at this.'

He turned to tell her to shut up again. Then he saw what she was showing him. The sheet. The blue nylon undersheet stained with Treacle's ejaculation, a seminal map of a jagged peninsula with a large island blobbed on its end, and an archipelago of other islands trailing away to the edge.

'Who did that?' snorted the RSM. Then he realized. 'That smell,' he whispered. 'That's what the smell was. I *knew* I remembered it from somewhere way back. Spunk! It's Human Spunk!'

'Frank!' gasped Mrs Love. Violet stood like ice.

'Somebody's been in our bed,' said Love. His voice was hoarse, unbelieving.

'Somebody's been in our bed,' acknowledged his wife bitterly. She looked towards Violet. 'And they couldn't change the sheet because we haven't more blue ones.'

Love did a slow pirouette, like an exaggerated drill movement. '*Somebody's* been in our bed,' he whispered at Violet. 'Now who could that be?'

'Goldilocks,' suggested Violet. She was stiff with fright now.

'You dirty little cow.' His voice was still low and threatening. 'You dirty little pig. I thought I knew that smell. And it was you. You and *who else*?'

301

Thoughtfully he went to the back of her and closed the door. 'You and who else?' he repeated going around to her marble face again. 'Who's going to fancy *you* anyway?' He looked at her thick breasts under the nightgown.

'Tell your father,' demanded her mother, leaning stiff at the edge of the bed. 'Tell him.'

'Tell him what?' asked Violet. 'Tell him who it was, or who is going to fancy me anyway?'

Love hit her then, bringing his heavy hand up from the waist and heaving it at her face. The blow caught her full on, sending her staggering back with a frightened cry.

'What have you got to say?' said her father.

'What have you to say to us?' said her mother.

'Fuck off. That's what I've got to say to you. Fuck off, both of you.'

This time her father hit her with the other hand, closing it to a fist as it flew at her, striking her on the cheek and the ear. She fell against the door and he ran at her like a madman, grasping the nightdress at her neck so that it tore in a great long shred. He pulled her up by her arms and her hair, then struck his right hand across her face again. Her nose began to bleed.

'It was that worm Thompson, wasn't it?' he demanded. 'Tell me! Tell me! It was, wasn't it?'

'Worm?' she sobbed. 'You're the worm you sodding bastard. Nobody could crawl lower than you.'

'You had sex!' her mother screamed at her. 'You messed up *our* bed!'

'Well, *you're* not likely to mess it up, are you?' sobbed Violet. She drew herself up bravely against the door. The blood from her nose was dribbling over her white mouth and she could taste its saltiness. 'Not you two,' she wept. 'I doubt if you've got a decent fuck in you – either of you!'

They both rushed at her this time. A madness seemed to have seized them. But as they charged, Violet lowered her big head and butted her father in the face. The collision knocked her dizzy, but she looked up and saw him staggering away. She laughed wildly and put her fat hand in the distorted face of her scratching mother and pushed her powerfully across the room. The woman screamed as she hit the corner of the bed. Violet picked up their wedding photograph, put a great gob of spit on it, and threw it after her mother. Her father was coming back at her now. She opened the door and staggered towards the stairs. He caught her two stairs down, brutally put his foot in her back and sent her tumbling down the rest of the flight.

Violet sat up on the bottom stair and leaned against the wall at her side, crying softly. Her father came down to her, menacingly. He stood above her. 'It *was* him, wasn't it?' he said. She could feel he was spitting in his rage. Bullets of spit were hitting the side of her face.

She put her hand to her head waiting for the blow. 'Well, was it?' he demanded again, moving one step down.

'I'm seventeen,' she mumbled.

'And you're a big girl,' he finished mimicking her voice. 'We all know that, you great lardy lump. It *was* him. Tell me it was.'

'If you touch him I'll tell the Colonel,' she said simply. 'I love him. If you can understand that.'

'Love him!' he snorted. 'He's been in every poxing whore house in the world. Dirty little snide. I'm going to see that he gets just what's coming to him. And you too.'

Her mother was at the top of the landing. 'Lock her in the toilet,' she breathed over the banister. 'Lock her away. Go on, Frank, do it.'

Violet stood up and pressed her fat face to the wall. If only she could see him now. If only he could be with her. She didn't want her father to touch her again so she turned of her own accord, like a surrendering prisoner, and walked towards the downstairs lavatory. She took the key from the lock and handed it to her father, not looking at him. Then she closed the door. He locked the door with the key.

Violet leaned against the cool lead pipe. Then she leaned forward and was sick down the pan. She flushed it away, waited for the cistern to fill and then flushed it again, putting her head over the pan and washing the blood from her face with the water.

Brigg walked out onto the square, felt the sun fill his face, and from habit stamped his boots on the concrete. It was supposed to make the creases fall into place. It seemed a very empty, unfilled morning, with no clouds, not even herded on the hills, and the square, which had been swept by a hundred men with a hundred brooms on the previous midnight, white as icing.

There was no one on the parade ground then, but the soldiers, despite themselves, charged with the juvenile expectant excitement of a military occasion, stood burnished and buffed on the concrete balconies of the barrack blocks and looked out, waiting for the bugle call.

Wilcox, stamping professionally also, joined Brigg in the sun. 'Don't you feel good to be one of the Queen's soldiers, on a morning like this?' inquired Wilcox sniffing the air. 'Just think, you could be a poor, bent old sewerman in Stoke-on-Trent, instead of being here, all tarted up, the guardian of an Empire on which the sun hardly ever rises.'

'Most of my squad *ought* to be sewermen in Stoke-on-Trent,' answered Brigg. 'I'll tell you how I feel after it's all over, friend. If they'll only keep more or less in step it will be something, I suppose. You can bullshit the rest by shouting loud. Hello, here's the Messiah.'

Staff Sergeant Parsons was moving at what he liked to call a good Christian pace along the fringe of the square. They exchanged greetings and good wishes for the parade.

'We'll all be getting upped in rank after this, I expect,' joked Wilcox. 'Once the Minister goes back and tells Her Maj. What a lot of lovely soldiers she's got.'

Parsons' face seemed polished in the sun. 'Promotion cometh neither from the east, nor from the west, nor yet from the south,' he quoted. Wilcox raised his forehead towards Brigg.

'Blooming Book of Psalms,' said Parsons unasked. 'Psalm one-twenty-five.'

'I'll look it up,' promised Wilcox.

'Set not your horn on high,' continued Parsons, 'and speak not with a stiff neck.' He smiled at that. 'Same psalm. Previous verse.'

The borrowed Royal Artillery bugler, all shining buckles and red sash wrapped about him like a dressing on a nasty wound, marched with short loud steps to the side of the square. He made a great performance, raising the bugle to his lips as though it were a bottle of a rare and delicate vintage.

'The one who sets his horn on high,' Wilcox pointed out.

'And here comes the one who speaks with a stiff neck,' put in Brigg nodding across the square where a small posse of senior NCOs were approaching with RSM Love at their front.

The bugler blurted out his summons, the demanding notes of the On Parade. Although they had been awaiting it, its sudden rending clarity, cutting brilliantly through the vacant air, startled them. The sergeants drew themselves instinctively upright, sterner and taller. Such was the note of the bugle. From each of the barrack blocks channels of soldiers moved out to their positions on the parade ground, clattering down the stone stairs, each one stamping on the side of the square as though unsure that it would bear his weight.

They formed their echelons and their blocks, each man knowing, by now, the final inch he would occupy on the square. A detailed squad carried the saluting base like a coffin to the chalked out area designated for it. Then the platoon sergeants began calling their orders; the right dress, with its chorus girl shufflings, the eyes right and eyes front; fussy platoon officers looking down a rank of noses, adjusting and measuring like surveyors.

It was a sight to stir in the Hong Kong sunshine, the

bright-faced barrack blocks, the dazzling square, the Union Jack confident against the blameless blue sky. And, at one corner, so miserably ashamed he was almost hiding, was Treacle Thompson, dungman of the day, parading with the implements of his duty, a bucket, a shovel and a small rake. He watched the sharp splendour with an isolated, childlike, sorrow but, still determinedly soldier-like, gave the bucket a wipe with his sleeve. At least he was an individual, he consoled himself, a lone operator, not merely a cipher to-ing and fro-ing to squeaky orders. He had burnished his equipment that morning, working as hard as any other man worked with his brasses or rifle. If he had to shovel shit then he would be the most shining shit-shoveller in the whole of the British Army. He was a Professional.

Violet continued sitting in her lavatory prison until she heard her parents slam the front door. Her lip curled when she thought of her mother wearing her new pink costume and her pink hat to sit in the families' stand at the parade.

'Like a bleeding prawn,' she told herself squatting on the pan belligerently. 'And that bastard . . . I hope he swallows his own spit and chokes himself.' She began crying softly into her folded arms. She knew her face was swollen and her nose left a crimson imprint on her forearm. 'Oh, Treacle,' she whispered. 'Oh, darling, what a bloody life.'

She had intended getting the sheet from the bed at the first chance, somehow sponging it and putting it back before they could notice. Her mother had been hanging around the house with a change-of-life expression all the previous day. Violet had made the bed and she had planned to do the sponging this morning, making some excuse for being late on parade. But now it was too late. Mean cow, only having one pair of blue nylon sheets.

She was not worried about being in the lavatory. She had been glad of the respite, the separation from them; glad to put the door between herself and her father's fists and grateful that she would no longer be tempted to put her own girlishly powerful hands about the saggy skin of her mother's windpipe.

Now, she decided, it was time to leave. The fear, and the fury, the cold shock she had known when her father told her what he had planned for the day for Treacle – in a way greater than the blow to her face – was now setting hard inside her, an icy anger. Yes, it was time to go, to see their arseholing parade and to make sure that it was a memorable occasion. Only in *her* way.

Violet stepped back to the wall by the pan. Then she ran and threw her meaty shoulder at the door. The governmental lock was never equal to her propelled fourteen stone. It broke and gaped with a tearing protest. The door sagged. She leaned back and flung it open with her planted foot. Then she went upstairs and put on her jeans and her favourite Snoopy sweater. She wanted everyone to get a good view of her.

23

Afterwards, when he was in military custody awaiting his court martial, Brigg would lie on his bunk and think over what had happened that day, and still find it difficult to credit that it was true.

Initially the parade patterns had gone splendidly, with the men swinging their arms a fraction straighter and higher, the marching in good unison, the orders curling on the morning air, the rifles slapped and shivering. It had been suggested that a selected squad of the best men might attempt the most difficult of all rifle drill sequences, the Queen Anne's Salute, a propeller movement accomplished with a spinning and twirling of the rifles, but the nightmare thought of a mass clattering of fallen weapons onto the ground had wisely given way to its abandonment.

Eventually the RSM's voice, flying through the air like the summons of some irritable muezzin, stilled the entire parade. It solidified under the sun, platoon on platoon, each with its officer and sergeant, that most hypnotic of all military sights, a battalion in suspense, on a feather-end for the next order.

Then the Colonel, lofty on his private horse, trotted onto the square; a figure from Kipling, khaki, leather, brass, with elevated, set, expressions on the faces of both mount and rider. The horse crapped plentifully at the edge of the square when it saw the troops. Wilcox, who witnessed the golden discharge, nodded sympathetically as he stood at the front of his platoon. 'I know how he feels,' he said to himself.

Treacle Thompson emerged swiftly, at a running crouch, like a bomb disposal expert, and swooped the steaming buns from the concrete. A thrust with the shovel, a quick movement of the rake, and the pile was captured in his bucket. He darted back to his hidden corner just as the open car bearing the Minister of Defence and Major-General Farlfax, the General Officer Commanding the district, turned through the garrison gate. 'Does that pipe band play on that bank *all* the time?' inquired the Minister. He was not in the best of humours. His knee was deeply bruised from the chin of the tumbling lance-corporal at the previous night's concert. 'Every time I go by they're up there blowing their insides out and surrounded by a million Chinese.'

'Can't say I've noticed them before,' said the Major-General truthfully. 'Must be a new posting. Gurkha chappies by the look of it.'

The car took a silent curve around the fringe of the parade ground. Colonel Simmons had wanted the band on the square for the marching, but the Commander of the workshops, fearful that his sunken tank and recovery vehicle would be exposed, had insisted that the band remained where it was doing the best job.

The other musically endowed units in Hong Kong had refused to lend their bands to the garrison, reasoning that they needed them for their own ministerial parades. The borrowed bugler was the best they could do.

Now he blew a welcoming voluntary for the distinguished guest. The ranks stiffened from the *Easy* to the *At Ease*, at the echoing of the Sergeant Major. Then, as the Colonel reached the front of the echelons, and the black car rounded the last corner of the square, there came the echoing command. 'Parade! Pa–rade! Atten-tion!' They stamped together majestically. Love smiled his bitter broken glass smile and wheeled on his corkscrew whirl to salute the Colonel.

The tableau of greeting was acted out, salutes and handshakes between men who had seen each other frequently during the past twenty-four hours. The Minister was clad, the Colonel was disappointed to see, in a grey lightweight lounge-suit, which, however, he rescued by the addition of a bowler hat.

Mounting the dais the Minister faced the soldiers. Then the marching began, the solemn convolutions of armed men, a khaki-coloured ballet of stiff arms and stiff legs. It was a scene beloved of the British, stamped out over half the world for two centuries and more. Men and arms, moving to orders, under a blue foreign sky.

Brigg sweated alongside his squad, squinting down at their mechanical feet, black boots hitting the concrete like the feet of a great centipede. His beret was tight across his forehead, the band digging into the sweat. Had her husband gone back to Vietnam yet? To his war? Were they happy, filled and fulfilled with each other now? Had he delved and probed into her and unburied her buried love? Would she go back now, to New York, and wait for him? For her Paul?

Brigg marched and thought of the Chinese house a few miles away on the Tolo Channel, the bright parrot and his bell, and Barbara perspiring sweetly in his arms through the luxurious night. 'Right . . . wheel!' He remembered in time. He was a soldier too. Perhaps not a soldier who rode in a gunship helicopter, or set fire to a Viet Cong in a bunker, or wept over comrades dead after ambush, or from bombs dropped from friendly but myopic aircraft. But he was still a *soldier*. He was a *British* soldier. A *marching* soldier. 'Left, right, left, right . . . A-bout turn . . . Left, right . . . Eyes . . . right!' Let her go back to New York, to Riverside Drive, or wherever the bloody place was, and gaze out on the winter to see the other shore looking like the Arctic. Why did he remember her saying that? Well, he wasn't going to make every kind of fool of himself going up to the Peak to keep their rendezvous. He wasn't Cary Grant. He wasn't going to stand up there pretending to enjoy the view and know that she would never be coming. That she was sitting looking out on Riverside Drive. Waiting.

No woman who laughed, as she had laughed that final night on the other side of the wall at the hotel, who had sounded so free and loving, would ever want to meet him on the Peak. And he wasn't going just to stand around and look at the China Sea and the islands and then descend, crushed, to his old life again. What was the point of a risk like that? His former Glenda showed him that, didn't she? And he was *married* to her. He was just a stop gap for both of them. Something until something better came along.

'Left, right, left, right. Right . . . wheel! Left, right, left, right . . .'

For God's sake, this is where it was safest and best. Marching with the Army. At least you felt you were going somewhere, even if it were only around a concrete square. 'Squad . . . halt!' Now, this is it. 'Right, turn!' Were they on the right chalk mark? Yes, there it was by Harrison's foot. Thank Christ for that. That bloody horse had crapped again. Just backward of the saluting base. What did they feed it on? Prunes? God, and there was Treacle, creeping in like a goblin guerrilla, with his bucket and shovel. Surely he wasn't going to try it now? But he was! Oh, Treacle, you blind little cunt, they didn't mean you had to pick it up while it was still hot! But he's done it. Unbelievably he's breached the security. He's shovelled it up behind their backs, the Minister and the Commanding Officer and all the others, Love and the special military police as well, and nobody noticed. There, he's off with his stinking load, the little raider! The horse crap commando!

Brigg glanced at his own squad again. A wasp had settled on Wilson's nose. Hell, *not* a wasp. *Not* on Wilson! The bulky, lily-pale, soldier, went fearfully cross-eyed as it strolled up his nasal ridge, watching it, almost eye-to-eye, extra sweat oozing out over his unhealthy face. Brigg, his eyeballs stretched to the right and half behind him, muttered: 'Don't move.' Wilson did not. The wasp reached the bridge of his nose and then about-turned and tramped down the slippery parapet again, Wilson's marbled eyes following its every step. On the tip of the nose the creature stood, balancing, like a daring tourist looking out from a promontory. Then, leaning over a little more it discovered the soldier's hairy left nostril like a half concealed cave under its front feet. The wasp went exploring immediately, curling over the rim of the nose and walking boldly up into the nostril. Wilson was stiff with fear, desperately trying to control his trembling, his eyes bulging and blatantly crossed. The wasp reappeared from the nostril, stood on the nose again for a moment and then buzzed away. Wilson fainted, a buckling at the knees followed by the dull plop of his puddingy body on the square; his rifle toppled, striking with a clatter, louder it seemed on that silent square than any report from its muzzle.

Brigg saw Love's head screw around angrily, and the Colonel peered genteelly from his horse, like a huntsman at the view. But the Minister, on the platform now, and rustling the notes of his speech, did not look up.

Brigg's immediate concern was for the soldier. He swore quietly at Love for his facial rage, but had scarcely time to move before two eager stretcher-bearers came homing on their first casualty of the morning. They rolled Wilson onto the litter and whisked him heavily away. Brigg ordered the ranks to close.

The Minister, with a mild cough and a sly glance to see that the disturbance was now over, was ready to make his address to the troops. Love bawled out the orders to bring the entire parade to the *Easy* position. The soldiers did so gratefully.

They faced the dais and the Minister and in the background were three barrack blocks in a row, the expansive sun directly on them.

314

It was on the middle balcony of the middle block that Violet Love appeared. 'It has been a pleasurable duty,' the Minister was beginning, 'to come to this Crown Colony of Hong Kong . . .'

Only a few of the soldiers saw her at first. She was standing, naked to the waist, on the balcony, her great lard-coloured tits resting on the concrete ledge. She remained motionless, before the parade, and above it, like some fertility goddess looking out on a gathering of her people. Her long hair was parted at the middle and lying across both shoulders like a roof over her breasts; her round face set and serious as though she was indulging considerable thoughts.

A few at a time, a handful, then a rank, then a squad, saw her with widening, unbelieving eyes. The Minister went on, '. . . It is our duty, the duty of not just soldiers but politicians, families, everyone, to put forward the best that we have, to show ourselves . . .' Eyes were switching up to the girl on the balcony, dozens of eyes, then hundreds. Soldiers drew astounded sucking breaths, blinked, and looked again. Even in the farthest rank they could see her nipples standing out like targets.

In the special stand set up for the soldiers' families, Mrs Love leaned forward uncomprehendingly, and then fell back, her teeth chattering, her pink hat fallen to the back of her head. The women were straining their eyes and gabbling with excitement. 'It's *not* Violet. It's not her.' The words tumbled from Mrs Love. 'Not *our* Violet.'

'It *is* her Violet,' confirmed Doris Boswell with deep and nasty satisfaction. 'Nobody else has got bristols like that.'

In the stand reserved for the garrison children excitement was rife. Little boys stood on their seats to get a better view, Mr Winter, the headmaster of the military school and his two women teachers tried to recover order with threatening whispers.

Winter, at first, did not spot Violet on the barrack block balcony. Fiercely he demanded to know what excitement had captured his pupils.

'On the balcony,' Charlie told him suavely. 'That girl. She's got all her . . . lungs hanging out.'

Every man's eye on the parade ground was now on the girl, except those of the party around the saluting dais who were facing the other way. Gasps had given way to fruity male grins, and a seething noise went through the troops, making the Minister look up questioningly and the RSM bristle under his hat.

Brigg, dry-mouthed, sensing the inherent tragedy in the extraordinary sight, could feel his squad fidgeting like schoolgirls. 'Shut up,' he whispered angrily. Then, optimistically: 'Any man who looks will be charged . . .' He looked up again himself and sickly closed his eyes. Within him was a deep pity for her. God, who had sent her mad like that?

Now there was no stopping the quivering confusion. Major Stevens, the Medical Officer, who was facing the barrack block, began to march tentatively forward. The Colonel, still not understanding because he was looking the wrong way, scowled at him. The Minister stopped speaking and blinked, lost and bewildered, glancing first left and then right for an explanation. Then Major Stevens pointed a shaking finger at Violet and said in the Colonel's direction in an attempted whisper: 'Sir . . . There appears to be . . .'

Everyone, the Colonel, the General Officer Commanding, the Minister, and Sergeant Major Love, turned and saw her then. 'Good God,' said the Minister quietly, almost devotionally: 'How very extraordinary!' The Colonel all but tumbled backwards from his saddle, giving the reins a prodigious tug and causing his horse to whinny and rear.

Violet's father staggered back on his heels. His mouth opened like a red cave but, for once, nothing emerged. It dropped into a droop. He waved his cane impotently in the general direction of his daughter.

'Hello, Daddy! Hello, RSM Love!' the girl joyfully shouted. She began to wave like an excited child from a train. In the families' stand Mrs Love was mouthing into her hands and her handkerchief. 'I'll kill her. Her father . . . Her father . . . Oh, God, I'll kill her.' She could hear Doris Boswell and some of the others tipping sideways with their coarse laughter.

The children's stand was all confusion. Some of the little girls were crying.

'Get her,' muttered Love venomously to no one in particular. As he said it, the girl began marching along the balcony, doing a grotesque imitation of her father's voice: 'Left, right, left, right, left, right . . . about turn . . . left, right.' She thrust out that swollen naked bosom as she marched, like a big brass drummer thrusts out his drum in a parading band.

'Get her!' Love exploded it now in a horrified squeak. Wet at the mouth, he pointed to the squad of red-banded military police, standing as transfixed as all the five hundred and more men on that square. 'Move!' he squealed. 'Get her!'

The six policemen shook their heads from their

daze and loped off uncertainly, three going one way and three the other. Violet saw them coming and called: 'Halt!' to herself. She turned smartly so that she was facing the square and all its many open mouths and astounded faces. Then she raised two sausage fingers in a long and derisive salute to the entire assembly, and followed it with a shorter, but jerkier gesture to her purple-faced father. The military policemen were coming heavily up the concrete stairs now, so she turned and ran through the barrack room, tears rivering down her face. Her breasts bouncing she went like a bull through one barrack room and out to the balcony at the back of the building. A soldier, confined to his bed for the day with tonsillitis, sat up as though activated by a loaded spring when she streaked past. The policemen were nearly on her now. She managed to make the upper stairway before them and reached the balcony at the back and at the top of the barrack block.

She stood, trapped at the centre of its concrete length as she saw them come up the stairs, three at each end. 'Halt! Stay there!' shouted the leading man.

'Bollocks,' answered Violet quietly. She climbed heavily on to the parapet. She glanced at their distance from her again and then let herself tip over. She fell forty feet, striking the paved path below with an unhuman thud that was heard on the other side of the barrack block, on the square. When they ran around to her, and turned her over, face upwards, they saw the great bloody squashed breasts, and the quiet look on her young face and they knew that she was dead.

*

The Colonel, dazed and idiotic, but with some sub-conscious notion that the show always went on, turned to the Minister. 'Would you like to go on with your speech now, sir?'

'I think enough has been said,' returned the Minister caustically. 'More than enough . . . I think, perhaps, it might be better to dismiss the parade.'

'Yes, of course. Commonsense really,' mumbled the Colonel. He turned around to find the RSM. 'Love,' he barked. 'RSM Love!'

The sergeant major strode from somewhere at the back of the square, his stick under his arm, his face the hue of rotten fruit. He threw up an arm in salute.

'Sir.'

'Dismiss the parade, Sergeant Major.' The voice was cold, toneless. So was the face.

'Sir,' acknowledged the sergeant major. He hesitated, and trembled. 'I'm sorry, sir. Her going and doing that.'

'Dismiss the parade, Sergeant Major.'

'Sir.'

Love wheeled to face the now ragged assembly of soldiers, their eyes fixed on the stretcher being carted from the barrack block to a military ambulance, inside which the fainting Lance-Corporal Wilson was just sitting up after his experience with the wasp. He had lain forgotten there during the crisis. Now the stretcher bearers opened the ambulance doors and Wilson stood shakily. They looked up stonily at him from either side of their burden.

'I feel all right now, thank you,' mumbled Wilson. 'I had a bit of a nasty turn, but I'm all right now.' He nodded at the stretcher which he could only sectionally see. 'Somebody else fallen out?' he asked.

'Yes,' answered one of the orderlies truthfully.

'Looks like it's the day for it,' said Wilson.

RSM Love felt his voice tremble and break as he made to give the dismissal order. But he reinforced it and shouted across the square: 'Parade! Pa-rade! Att–en–tion!' The ranks snapped to his order. The ambulance was pulling away now leaving Wilson standing puzzled at the side of the square.

'Pa-rade!' bawled Love. 'Pa-rade . . . Dis . . .'

. Three shots exploded from the centre barrack block. Three sharp, distinct, unmistakable, rifle shots. The bullets whistled over the soldiers causing immediate and fantastic panic. Men flung themselves flat on the concrete, lying there with palsied hands behind their heads, or arse-up, comically crawling to any shelter at the fringe of the square. Others uncompromisingly ran, clattering across the parade ground, leaping like untrained hurdlers or tripping and falling over prostrate comrades.

The Colonel's horse bellowed and stood on its hindlegs. Colonel Simmons, showing considerable agility and improvisation, slid backwards from the frightened animal, over its rump, and landed gratefully, if without grace, on two feet. Someone had pulled the Minister down below the level of the saluting base, and he crouched there, with the GOC's head behind him thrust intimately against his trousers, like a miner leading other miners along a low tunnel.

'Dear Christ,' said the Minister unhappily over his

shoulder. 'This sort of thing doesn't go on all the bloody time, does it?'

'No, no. Of course not,' said the Major-General. He felt like adding: 'Bloody fool.'

'You've got your head up my bum,' said the Minister testily.

'Dreadfully sorry,' grunted the GOC equally irritable. 'Someone's jamming into me, I'm afraid. Pushing me in the seat. I suppose we must be short of room or cover or something.'

Two more shots exploded and furrowed the morning air across the parade ground. Those many soldiers prostrate across the area either cowered lower, forcing themselves harder against the immovable concrete, or with mad bravery, straightened up and ran blindly away from the shots, as though trying to outdistance any further bullets. Ferris's secret dog could be heard howling with consternation. Its owner, face down to the parade ground, prayed that it would stop. From somewhere came the ghostly call of the bugle.

Mr Winter and his two teachers were lying flat among the pupils between the legs of the chairs. Charlie, pressed against the end of the improvised stand, elevated his eyes to look out at the embattled scene.

In the families' stand, some of the women having run around the edge of the square to see what had happened to Violet, only a frightened section remained, lying low in their best clothes, hats, handbags and gloves all scattered. The girl's mother was hiding, as much from the other women as the bullets, crouched bitterly, as though praying, against the wooden upright in front of her; weeping savagely, hitting the wood with her thin fist and mouthing: 'I'll kill her. I'll kill her.' She had not looked up and did not see the stretcher going to the ambulance.

Brigg was on one knee when the second brace of shots sounded. He could see they were coming from the sergeants' room at the left hand end of the middle barrack block.

'Treacle,' he muttered. 'Stupid little bastard.' He jerked up and ran across the exposed space, flying clumsily over soldiers lying in rows like the dead from some strange orderly massacre. He took a wide curve to the left as he neared the barrack building, then zig-zagged, and finally, breathless, reached the bottom stairs. He paused then ran heavily to the middle floor, went through the stocky wooden door leading onto the balcony – the same balcony on which Violet had paraded – turned and bolted it behind him. Then he hurried to the extreme end of the balcony and bolted the door there. There were two more doors, at the back of the building. He raced through, watched by the petrified tonsillitis patient, cowering at the side of his bed, and bolted the two doors at the back. Now he had Treacle to himself.

He ran to the door of the sergeants' room and pulled at the handle.

'It's locked,' Treacle's voice came calmly from within.

'Treacle,' said Brigg, crouching close to the door. 'It's Sergeant Brigg here.'

'Oh, hello, Sarge,' answered Treacle quietly. 'How are you?'

Brigg was stunned by the question. 'I'm

unwounded, Treacle,' he said eventually. 'What in the name of fuck are you doing?'

'Shooting, Sarge. Shooting out of the window.'

'Listen, how many rounds have you got left?'

'Two,' answered Treacle. 'I'll shoot another now.'

Brigg heard the report from inside the small room and closed his eyes helplessly, pressing his head against the door.

'Now I've only got one, Sarge. And I'm keeping that.'

'Treacle,' muttered Brigg. 'Open this bleeding door, son. Open up. That's an order.'

'No,' said Treacle still in the matter-of-fact tone. 'No, Sarge. I'm not opening it. Not even for you. Not yet. What happened to her? She's dead, isn't she?'

'I don't know,' lied Brigg. He had seen the ambulance blanket over her face.

'She jumped,' said Treacle. Then he added, as innocently as a boy: 'That rotten lot. Her mum and dad had been at her. She told me this morning, Sarge, while I was round the side with my bucket. But I didn't know she was going to do anything. Not like she did.'

'Come on out, Treacle,' said Brigg firmly.

'I'm in a bit of trouble, I suppose,' said the voice through the door.

Brigg winced. 'A bit,' he agreed. 'You scared the shit out of the Old Man's horse.'

'Wonder he had any left,' replied Treacle. 'I thought I'd shovelled it all up this morning.'

Brigg heard boots on the concrete stairs. The door was hammered.

'Is that them after me?' asked Treacle.

'It's not the NAAFI with your bloody tea,' said Brigg. 'I'll go and talk to them, son. Don't go away.'

'I won't,' promised Treacle. 'I'm not jumping from the window, if that's what you think. It wouldn't be far enough for me. She was a big girl, you know, Violet.'

'Wait,' said Brigg. He ran to the balcony door. He knew it was the visiting military police. He put his mouth to the door. 'Listen,' he shouted. 'This is Sergeant Brigg. Let me handle this. He's in my platoon. Let me sort it out.'

'Open this door, Sergeant,' bawled a voice. 'That's an order. Open up.'

'I've had the Colonel's permission to do this,' lied Brigg. 'So sod off, will you, and give me a chance.'

This worried them. He knew it would. He heard one of them go banging down the stairs. Then, for some reason crouching as though he were under fire, Brigg hurried back to the door.

'Treacle,' he said, his mouth so close he could feel the wood against his lips.

'Yes, Sarge?' replied the small private quietly. Then, with optimistic innocence: 'Have they gone away?'

'For a few minutes, but not for long. Listen, son, you've got to come out of there.'

'I've still got this round up the spout, Sarge,' answered Treacle.

'What does that matter, for God's sake? You know how to get it out of the spout, don't you? You're a soldier.'

'I'm glad *you* think so, Sarge. Nobody else did. Everybody treated me like I was some sort of skivvy. With leprosy.' The voice suddenly became lighter,

324

more hopeful: 'Did I actually *hit* anyone out there, when I was shooting?'

Brigg closed his eyes again. He pushed his forehead against the door. 'No. I don't think so, anyway. Thank God. If you come out now it won't be so bad. You and I can do our cell time together.'

'Oh? What have *you* been up to, Sarge?'

'Well, for a start, I've just told the military police to fuck off,' said Brigg. 'The Army gets a bit touchy about that sort of thing. Unreasonable, but there it is.'

'Sarge, you shouldn't have got yourself into bother because of me. I know what I'm doing. It's been worth it just to see the Colonel and all the rest of them falling over and scattering when I was shooting above their heads.'

'Right,' agreed Brigg. 'You've had your fun, now come out.'

'It's not on without Violet,' said Treacle simply. 'I know she's dead, so you don't have to try and kid me. Nobody as big as her could jump that far and get away with it. She really hated them, you know, Sarge. She hated every bit of their guts. And there was a terrible rumpus in their house this morning. Her father punched her in the face. Fancy a man doing that to a young girl. You should have seen how swollen it was. And there was blood on her nose and her lips. And it was all because of me. The one person I'd ever cared anything about, Sarge.'

'Our Regimental Sergeant Major is a crap-faced fool,' said Brigg fervently, against the door.

'Don't let him hear you,' said Treacle sincerely. 'You'll be in more trouble. But I must say, I agree with every word.'

'Treacle, why don't you fire that last round off? Give the silly tits another scare. Shoot it up in the air. Go on, son, give it a go.'

'Ah, no, Sarge. I realize you think you're doing it for the best, but I can see through you. I'm keeping it.'

Brigg ran out of patience then. Desperately he stood and launched himself against the door. It would not give.

'Stop!' shouted Treacle from inside. 'Stop it, Sarge, or I'll shoot. And not you either.'

'Listen you stupid little bugger,' panted Brigg. 'Open this door right away and come on out. I can hear them coming back up the stairs. Come on, Treacle, for Christ's sake.'

'I'm not, and that's it,' came the quiet voice from within.

'Do you think Violet would have wanted you to do this?' pleaded Brigg. 'You don't believe that, do you?'

'No,' agreed Treacle. 'She'd have wanted me to put this last round right between her old man's eyes. But I don't think I'm going to be able to manage that.' There was a pause from inside. A hammering began on the balcony door and Brigg looked around anxiously. Love's voice came bawling from the outside.

Brigg scampered, again at a monkey crouch, to the far door. 'Sergeant Major,' he called politely against the door. 'Will you let me handle this?'

'Brigg!' The voice was choking with rage. 'You are on a charge! Open this door – and now!'

'This man will take his life,' said Brigg, still composed. 'You can't let that happen.'

'Open this door, Brigg,' Love's voice was low and

nasty now. 'I'm going to bust you, mister. I'm going to have you crawling on your belly.'

Brigg lost his temper. 'Isn't one death enough for you in one day, you plum-faced cunt?' he shouted. 'Bust me if you like, mate, but if this kid kills himself, I'm going to kill *you*! Just get that straight!'

'Brigg!' the voice was apoplectic against the door. 'Brigg! Open up! Open up! We can break it down.'

Brigg scampered back to the inner door. 'Treacle,' he called. 'This is it. You've got to come out now, son. They're all after us.'

'Ha! I've never felt so wanted, Sarge. It's very decent of you, getting yourself in trouble because of me. I wouldn't let you do that for anything because you've always been all right to me. But it's funny to be wanted. I had a wife once, you know . . .'

'So did I,' said Brigg quietly. He thought they might as well talk.

'Mine was called Jean,' Treacle continued. 'She was so bloody clever that she used to write off for jobs – for me. This is civvy street, of course. She'd write off for these jobs, and she made me sound so fantastic in the letters that I always got an interview. They thought it was *me* writing, you see. And the bull she used to give them! And then every time I went for the interview they took one look at me, and that was that. Her letters were a million miles better than ever I could even pretend to be. She would have had me in jobs like the Managing Director of Walls Ice Cream, Chairman of ICI and Chancellor of the Exchequer all rolled in one. But I never got through the interviews. They didn't want me, and she didn't either in the end. Even when I find somebody who really wants me she goes and jumps off a balcony. Now all this mob want me! That's a laugh, for a start.'

'I know how you feel,' said Brigg truthfully. 'Listen, Treacle . . .'

There was a heavy concerted ramming against the balcony door. He turned and saw it swelling as the men outside charged against it. The bolt creaked and strained. Once. Twice. Next time it must break.

'Treacle,' called Brigg urgently at the door. 'Listen, for God's sake, son. Fire that round off.' He added hurriedly, 'Out of the window. Go on give them another scare. Try and hit the Old Man's horse.'

'It's not there now,' Treacle called back. 'He's taken it away. The square's all empty. It was funny seeing them all crawling away on their bellies.'

Brigg heard the men hit the door again. At the first heavy charge it almost gave. The screws from the bolt fell appropriately like spent bullets onto the concrete floor. They went at it again and this time it burst violently and three military policemen fell in, followed by three more and RSM Love.

'Wait!' pleaded Brigg hopelessly. 'Give me one minute. Just one.'

'Arrest that man!' boomed Love, striding along the balcony.

'Treacle!' bellowed Brigg going back to the door, pushing his face against it. 'Treacle!'

'Don't worry, Sarge . . .' called the small soldier. The report of the rifle was short and final. It stopped the military police in mid-pace. Brigg felt cold, angry and tired. He stood up and looked at Love.

Love said: 'Get in there after him.'

'He's dead, Mr Love,' said Brigg. 'You've bagged

two in one day. I bet that's your best score since you fucking well joined up.'

Love was only two yards away from him. The military police were still frozen. Brigg stepped forward and smashed his fist into Love's face.

24

Wilcox's face, parcelled up into the neat barred square of the cell door, looked through at him. Brigg sat up on the bunk while the locks were undone. Wilcox thanked the sergeant of the guard effusively and was pushed in.

'At home to visitors today?' he inquired.

'I was thinking of going sailing or maybe having a day at the races,' said Brigg laconically. Then he asked: 'Why did he shove you in like that? They don't do that to visitors.'

'He is a rough man,' grinned Wilcox.

'You're in trouble,' said Brigg eyeing him. 'Why are you in here?'

'Because the other cell has got a damn great hole in the wall, or something. Dry rot, I think. They're going to brick it up for me and put me in there when they're done. I think they're worried that it'll be too draughty.'

'Oh, come on,' said Brigg impatiently. 'Tell me what's going on.'

'A slight discussion in the mess at NAAFI break over . . . er . . . recent events,' said Wilcox. 'There was a bit of a set-to and the bar and several tables and chairs were destroyed.'

'You haven't got a scratch on you,' Brigg pointed out.

'They missed,' shrugged Wilcox.

'What's the charge?'

'I'm not too sure. Wilful damage, I suppose. That's one. Assaulting Sergeant Murdoch. Something like that. I won't know until they've sorted him out in the hospital.'

'Murdoch! You're a bloody fool, Willy,' said Brigg. 'Getting in here on account of me.'

'You? Bollocks. Nothing to do with you. You're not the only one who has things happening to him, you know. I've been chatting up his missus now and again and after all the confloption on Saturday she came up to me, just like that, and invited me up to have a nibble of her steak and kidney pie and whatever else was going.'

Brigg grinned: 'And old Murdoch walked in while you were having whatever else was going?'

Wilcox shook his head solemnly. 'No. As a matter of fact the rotten bugger, having fallen out with his Chinese schoolteacher, chose to return home when I was right in the middle of the steak and kidney pie. And *that's* really embarrassing. I mean if he walks in on you screwing his wife, then that's it. There's no getting out of that and everybody knows exactly where they stand. But when he finds you munching into his wife's pastry, sitting there with your feet under his table and a big smug smile on your face, that's different. That's real trouble.'

Brigg sat on the bunk and laughed. 'Go on, burst your seams,' grumbled Wilcox. 'I didn't think it was funny. There was I with my gob full of pie, a plate of steaming spuds and sprouts in front of me, trying to talk myself out of it. All three of us were sort of tip-toeing around each other like some pansy ballet.

'I couldn't even say I'd got an urgent appointment and clear out. That would have meant leaving my dinner half-eaten and I'd have looked as guilty as hell. When the husband comes in and you've got your cock in his wife's mouth, then you're supposed to quit, and quick. But when her steak and kidney is in your mouth you have to go on to the bloody bitter end. All three of us sat down in the end and finished off the pie. It was like one of those plays. Conversation was muted, shall we say. I went as soon as I decently could, bowing and saying how nice it was of them – not *her*, *them* – to invite me and all that crapulence.'

'So you waited until today for the fight?' said Brigg.

'Well I could see he was sort of gunning for me. Naturally nothing was said about the steak and kidney pie, but while everybody in the mess was talking about Saturday's battle he came out with some rubbish to the effect that it was a pity the rifle didn't blow up in poor old Treacle's face. And, as you know, I've had every one of those weapons checked and adjusted.'

Brigg shook his head and grinned. 'You silly sod,' he said.

'I'm not that stupid,' said Wilcox suddenly serious. 'Not like you, you half-daft twat. It's enough those two having a suicide wish. But you . . .'

'Maybe I have,' shrugged Brigg. 'Now you come to point it out. What's happening outside?'

'Preparations for the burials. After the inquests, of course. They'll call you as a witness.'

'I'm experienced,' said Brigg.

'So you are, I forgot. Well, there's that. And the

sorrow-wracked Mr Love has been given compassionate leave to prepare for the funerals.'

'Funerals? He hasn't got the fucking cheek to go to both! Going to one is bad enough, the murderous bastard.'

'He's polishing his brasses and shining up his boots for one, so I suppose he thinks it's a waste of bullshit not to go to both.'

Brigg put his head forward on his fists. Then he glanced at Wilcox. 'How's Charlie?'

'Great,' said Wilcox. 'He'll probably be coming to see you – us – in the next few days. The army is a bit funny about letting kids visit their dads in the nick, but I think things are working in that direction.' They sat in friendly silence for a few moments, pensively on the opposite bunks of the cell.

'You know that bugler they borrowed,' said Wilcox eventually. 'He actually sounded The Retreat when all the shooting started.'

'He didn't!'

'Too right, he did.'

'I suppose they'll keep him on to do the Last Post at the funerals.'

'That's the idea, I gather.'

'He's turned out to be very useful one way and another. What else have you been doing?'

'There was something about Charlie.'

'What about him?'

'Nothing special. Oh, yes. I saw him helping Ho-Ho to carry the groceries up from the NAAFI shop.'

'The kid's reformed,' said Brigg.

'Looks like it. And the girls send their love. The twins.'

'You've been down there,' said Brigg. 'Pity we couldn't smuggle them in here. It would pass the time.'

'They're a bit concerned about you. They read it all in the papers.'

'Yes, I suppose it would be in the papers,' said Brigg. 'I hadn't thought about that.'

'Not just in Hong Kong either. We've had blokes from the *Daily Express* and the *Mirror* and the Associated Press and a couple of dozen others up at the camp. You're famous, mate. With any luck you might get off with three months for striking old Love. I reckon I'm in for at least as long as that. What with the bar collapsing in the mess and one thing and another.'

'The twins are okay, then?'

'Just the same. But, listen, there's something I wanted to sort out with you. Something they told me.'

'What was that?'

'I didn't know you went to the Sunrise Palace Hotel, you crafty sod. I thought you were supposed to be with Barbara over on the Tolo Channel. Pearl said you were screwing *her* in the hotel.'

Brigg was annoyed. 'Well bloody Pearl *shouldn't* say,' he grunted. 'Can't they stop twittering for a minute.' He sighed: 'All right. What happened was that Barbara's husband turned up from Vietnam while we were out at the house. She had to go to him. We only spent one night together.'

'That was a bit rough,' said Wilcox.

'I thought so too. I didn't tell you because I didn't feel like it.'

'I thought you went a bit ghostly when you got

back,' said Wilcox. 'You didn't want to talk about it so I shut up. She went back to him, eh?'

'She had to, didn't she?' shrugged Brigg. 'That's why she was in Hong Kong. Not to make *me* comfortable.'

'The twins only told me because they thought it was a joke, that's all,' continued Wilcox.

'How? What sort of joke?'

'You sent for *both* of them, right? From the hotel.'

'That's it. I phoned Humphrey at the club.'

'Only Pearl turned up, right?'

'Yes. She said Ruby had got some other work.'

'That's right,' grinned Wilcox. 'What she didn't say was that she got the work *right outside the hotel* when they were coming to you. Some chap picked her up just about at the front door.'

Brigg shook his head indifferently. 'No, she didn't say that. I thought somebody fixed her at the club. So what, anyway?'

'What made them laugh was that the bloke who picked her up came out of the hotel – and he took Ruby into the very next room to yours.'

Brigg felt his stomach turn. 'The next room?'

'Yes,' laughed Wilcox uncertainly, puzzled at the reaction. 'Pearl saw her go in there, before she came into your room. They could hear each other through the wall.'

Brigg dropped his head into his hands. 'Jesus,' he said. 'Why the bloody hell didn't she say . . .'

'You're the one who says they should keep their mouths shut about their business,' said Wilcox.

'The three weeks are up today,' said Brigg to himself. He looked up at Wilcox. 'Thank God you told me.'

'You're welcome. What's it all about?'

'Willy,' said Brigg. 'I've got to get hold of young Charlie.'

Doris Boswell marched formidably towards the guardroom, sweating steadily, her coat on one arm, a heavy straw shopping bag over the other. The sergeant of the guard had gone to the orderly room for conversation and coffee and Lance-Corporal Ferris, large and benign, was left in command.

''Morning, Mrs Boswell,' he beamed.

'I've come to see Sergeant Brigg,' said Doris immediately.

'Can't do, Mrs Boswell,' said Ferris with his aching grin.

'Can bloody-well-do!' snarled Doris. 'The Adjutant says it's all right, so it's all right. Let me in.'

'Oh, the Adjutant,' mumbled Lance-Corporal Ferris. 'He said, did he?'

'That's what I've just told you.'

'Did he give you a pass or a chitty or anything, Mrs Boswell?' asked Ferris waveringly.

'No, he didn't. He told me.' She regarded Ferris carefully. 'And I had a mind to have a little word with him about that hulking great dog of yours. Every night I see it pee-ing up against the cookhouse, or the surgery or my garden fence . . .'

'Dog? I haven't got a dog, Mrs Boswell. Nobody's allowed to have a dog . . .'

'Oh, come on, for Christ's sake, man. Everybody in the camp knows you've got that foul farting thing. Everybody . . .'

Ferris stared at her. 'Well, if the Adjutant says it's all

right, then it's his responsibility . . .' he murmured.

He turned sulkily and Doris followed him into the guardroom and to the cells at the rear. At the cell door, he glanced at Doris and then, awkwardly, knocked on the heavy door and went in at Brigg's shouted invitation.

'Two of you!' exclaimed Doris when she walked into the cell.

'He couldn't be away from me,' said Brigg nodding at Wilcox.

'Ah,' nodded Doris understandingly. 'I heard there was a bit of a dust-up in the mess. I was waiting for my old man to come home to tell me what it was all about. Who went off in the ambulance?'

'Sergeant Murdoch,' said Wilcox dropping his head. 'God have mercy on his soul.'

'Good for you, son,' said Doris stoutly. 'Been meaning to do something about that two-timing bastard. But a good fist is better than a dose of sennapods any day. Are you all right?'

'Well, apart from being in the clink, I'm all right,' said Wilcox. 'Nice of you to come and see us.'

'Yes, it is,' said Brigg. 'Have you seen Charlie?'

'That lovely kid,' said Doris wistfully. 'He's coming. That's why I came up. I told him to skid off at dinner break in the school and run over here and I'd get him in to see his dad.'

'You've bribed the guard?' grinned Brigg.

'It's only that bun-faced bugger Ferris,' sniffed Doris. 'I don't take "no" from the likes of that. I've brought you some mince pies and some toffees. You'll have to have half each now. I didn't know the place would be so crowded.' She explored her shopping

337

bag. 'Ah, and I thought you might like to have a look through the new Littlewoods' catalogue while you've got nothing better to do.' She produced the massive coloured volume. 'I can get everything at special forces rates. Even things like lawn mowers and that sort of gear.'

'I could use a lawn mower just now,' said Wilcox.

'Not so much lip,' said Doris amiably. 'I was only showing an example of the goods what can be sent. And you don't notice the money when it's weekly. That's what I tell all the sub-normals around here anyway. And they believe it.'

Brigg was flicking through the shining pages of the catalogue. Wilcox looked across his shoulder. 'Oh, that's not so bad. There's some pictures of women's underwear. All nice colours too. We can look at that.'

'You would,' admonished Doris.

'Better than lawn mowers,' said Wilcox.

There was another apologetic knock on the cell door and Brigg could see the face of Ferris, standing slightly away from the small barred window, like a fading portrait.

'Charlie,' said Brigg almost to himself. 'Come in.'

Charlie came in smiling, Ferris just behind him. 'He says he has the Adjutant's permission,' said Ferris doubtfully. 'He was told to ask for Mrs Boswell.'

Doris took a look at the small boy and tears began to flood down the cracks of her face like rivers in autumn spate. 'Poor little kid,' she trembled. She kissed him roughly and Charlie smiled uncertainly at her, wiping her tears from his face.

'I'll go now, because you'll want to be alone with your dad,' said Doris illogically discounting Wilcox.

338

'I'll wait on the road outside, son, just to make sure none of the big, brave soldiers gives you any bother.' She went with their thanks.

'Why don't you escape,' said Charlie immediately, looking around the cell. 'It wouldn't take you five minutes to spring from this place.'

'Charlie,' said Brigg gravely. 'There is nowhere Sergeant Wilcox and your dad could run. Only China. So we think we're doing the right thing staying here. Now listen, son. Tonight I want you to deliver an important letter for me. You remember that day we went up to the Peak?'

' 'Course I do,' said Charlie.

'Can you remember how to get there? I mean, could you go on your own?'

' 'Course I can. I'm not a little kid.'

'I'll write the note. It's for Barbara . . .'

'I remember Barbara,' said Charlie pointedly as though forestalling a question.

'But, listen, son, you've got to be up there by six o'clock. Which means starting right after school. You'll have to catch the half past four train. Make sure you're on it because the next one will get you there too late.'

'Can't I stay off school?' suggested Charlie hopefully. 'I'd be sure of getting there then. Just for the afternoon. It's only jogga and sums.'

'Do your jogga,' instructed Brigg. 'But make sure you're on the four-thirty train.'

'Right-o, Dad,' said the boy. 'I'll be on it.'

When the boy had gone, Brigg said: 'He's never been to Hong Kong by himself before. I hope he's okay.'

339

Wilcox was leaning forward thoughtfully. 'You fixed up to meet her on the Peak at a certain time on a certain date?' he said.

'That's right,' answered Brigg.

'I saw the film. But it was the Empire State Building.'

'Cary Grant,' said Brigg.

'That's right,' nodded Wilcox. 'Cary Grant. Silly sod. Got knocked down by a cab on the way, or was it the bird?'

25

Charlie returned to school in the afternoon eating a Chinese sandwich that Ho-Ho had made for him. It was bread with bean shoots and pork balls spiced with soy sauce. He enjoyed it as he trotted along the garrison road to the school. His father's letter was in the back pocket of his trousers. The soy sauce wriggled down his button chin.

The army school was a prefabricated building, erected on the edge of the garrison where the ground dropped steeply towards the road and the village. There were four classrooms in one block and the cloakrooms and lavatories in an annex block. Charlie arrived two minutes before the afternoon bell. He wiped the sauce from his mouth with the back of his hand and went into the lavatory. He urinated into the trough, throwing the spout up and down the Shanks pottery, wriggling it in patterns, pretending he was a fireman at a blaze. He was joined almost at once by Nooky Brice, the unkempt son of Sergeant Brice, who began to pee also.

'Your dad's going to get ten years,' said Nooky confidently.

'He's not,' said Charlie with finality.

'My old man says ten,' insisted Nooky. 'He'll be a convict for ten years.'

Charlie calculated that his bladder held just about enough liquid for the revenge that came immediately to mind. He swivelled at the hips and pissed all over the other boy's legs and boots and socks. Nooky howled with distress and staggered away so frightened that his own urine dried up and he was unable to retaliate. He looked down at his leaking legs and then screaming ran from the latrine. When Charlie walked quietly into the classroom, the icy, knowing smile was set on the face of Mr Winter, the headmaster, who was also Charlie's teacher. Brice trembling with tears stood under his protection, thin wreaths of steam drifting up from his soaking boots and socks, a small pool about his ankles.

'The Briggs seem to be trouble-prone,' said Mr Winter. He pointed down with his ruler. The crowded class was sharp with excitement and suppressed giggling. Those at the back were standing or intruding into the aisles for an improved view.

'Well, Brigg, what have you got to say?'

'It was an accident, Mr Winter,' replied Charlie calmly. 'He just said my dad was a convict and I turned around to tell him that he isn't a convict, and that's what happened. I forgot what I was doing at the time.'

The class howled at this and the headmaster turned on them savagely. 'What's so funny?' he demanded. 'This sort of behaviour is not laughable! It's the sort of thing which seems to be catching in certain families in this garrison! I'll say no more. Brigg, you will stay in after school. I'll deal with you then.' He looked down at the smelling feet of the other boy. 'You'd better go home and get your mother to do something about that,' he said. 'Tell her I'm dealing with the culprit. Brigg, sit down.'

Charlie dejectedly went to his desk. He raised his hand. 'Sir.'

'What now?'

'Can I stay in tomorrow instead of today? I've got to do a message for my dad tonight.'

'I'm afraid I find it very difficult to accommodate either you or your father, Brigg. No. You will wait after school.'

Charlie sank low over his work that afternoon, his wet eyes close to the tributaries of the Ganges, the Himalaya foothills, and, later, the mysteries of long division. The others, with the endemic cruelty of children, goaded him as they left at four o'clock. He remained in his desk. The headmaster went from the room and Charlie could see him talking to a woman in the playground; Brice's mother, he guessed.

The window on the opposite side of the classroom looked out on to the steep, shale-covered hill that descended to the main road. It was coated with outbreaks of hairy grass and stunted bushes holding on to its sides. Charlie had climbed down it many times on Saturday afternoons, going steadily, hand over hand, down the incline. Now he eyed the drop from the window and judged how far the force of his fall would tumble him down the hill. He glanced at the window on the playground side and saw that the head's face was still away from him, bobbing up and down like a pecking hen as he consoled Mrs Brice.

Charlie climbed onto the window sill. His foot immediately dislodged the class mustard-and-cress garden which fell to the floor, earth and tender green

343

shoots spreading widely. Frightened, he looked towards Mr Winter's back again. It was still there. The open window, a fanlight on a swivel, was a section above the sill and he had to climb to it. He levered himself up, his thin elbows and knees working at angles, his fair, serious face set with the effort. He reached the fanlight, pulled himself outside, and keeled to the left until he hung by his fingers. The drop looked enormous from there, red-earth slanting far down to the road. There was ten feet before his feet would hit the earth. If he could keep his balance as he landed, keep on his feet and control his fall, it would be better.

He tried. He saw Mr Winter about to turn around in the playground, waving a conciliatory hand to Mrs Brice. That was the time to go. Charlie dropped, hit the ground and tried to control his fall by letting his knees give as springs.

He almost succeeded. But the shock of hitting the ground and the looseness of the shale sent him tipping over down the slope, rolling and bouncing and sliding until halfway down he caught a strong root, which swung him to a stop. He lay face-down on the incline, the wind knocked from him, scratches grooved into his face, his knees and his elbows. He closed his eyes, his nose pressed against the loose red earth. When he opened them and looked up Mr Winter's white plate face was against the school window, glaring down at him. They stared at each other for twenty seconds. Then Mr Winter's face vanished and Charlie knew he would have to hurry.

He turned over on to his back and went at a scarcely controlled slide, on the seat of his trousers, down the remaining incline to the road. Then he began to run, hobbling as he went, towards the village. He looked back and saw that Mr Winter was standing, four hundred yards back, where the more orthodox exit led from the school to the road. He was milling his hands and bawling. Charlie continued on. When he again looked back the headmaster was gone. Another glance two hundred yards later and he saw Mr Winter was on his bicycle and coming after him.

At the village a newly-erected barrier was set across the road and two military policemen, their red caps and armbands ominous, were on duty. For a terrified moment Charlie thought the trap was set up specially for him. Then he saw the crowd of Chinese civilians and British soldiers gathered on the higher bank, and the powerful, dark-blue, tugging truck with 'Royal Navy' on its side. They were pulling the tank and the recovery vehicle from the village mud.

Charlie staggered on. With wooden officiousness the military policemen held up simultaneous hands to inform him that the road was closed. They failed to notice the mud, the blood on the bruises, or the boy's hunted eyes. He looked back. Winter was pedalling on. Charlie ran feverishly up the bank to the spectators, and hid among them, looking at the dismounting headmaster through the bodies like a fugitive animal through trees. He saw Winter wagging his head at the military policemen and then pointing towards the crowd. Charlie hid and waited. The headmaster was obviously determined to hunt him and to get him. Face stretched with the exertion of his bicycle pursuit, Winter turned towards the crowd. One military policeman found himself abruptly holding a pair of handlebars and the headmaster strode and sweated towards the hidden boy. Charlie trembled and tried to crouch deeper in the crowd. Among the soldiers' uniforms he realized he was conspicuous and he moved towards a bundle of Chinese boys, making his eyes squint in a childish hope of being assimilated. The man who stalked him was now sorting through the people, moving determinedly and methodically among them like someone counting goods in a warehouse. He was only yards away. Charlie could see his mouth working and the savage expression in his eyes.

'Shit,' muttered Charlie. 'Oh, shit.'

Then Staff Sergeant Parsons, the rosy Parson Parsons, saw the searching headmaster and caught his arm with enthusiasm. 'Saw you coming on your blooming bike, headmaster,' he bellowed. 'The driving is like the driving of Jeru, the son of Nimshi, for he driveth furiously. Second Kings, chapter nine, verse twenty.'

'Really,' said Mr Winter. His eyes still swivelled through the crowd. Charlie ducked lower and began to make his way to the lower edge of the spectators once more. Parsons still had his ripe hand on the headmaster's arm as though planted to begin one of his debilitating unarmed combat throws. Winter smiled at him nervously and moved his arm away.

'I've been told I'm going to stay here for a while, headmaster. They feel there's a need for an unarmed combat instructor on the permanent staff.'

'After Saturday's farce,' said Winter still looking about him, 'I think a machine-gun instructor would be more to the point.'

346

'Could be, could be,' laughed Parsons jovially. He put his hand back on Winter's forearm again and Winter once more took his arm away. 'Man is born into trouble, as the sparks fly upward. Book of Job. Forget the chapter now.'

'What do you want?' asked Winter brutally. He knew he had lost Charlie now. He glared at Parsons. 'What is it?'

'Well, as I'm here permanently I thought I might run a Scripture class for the schoolchildren. Let them hear the word of Our Blooming Lord!'

Charlie sidled through to the fringe of the crowd looking back through the shirts and seeing Parsons now with a friendly, ever-threatening, hand on the headmaster's shoulder. The boy reached the last of the spectators. The barrier was here and the military policemen, one still holding the bicycle like a groom at the halter. But they were looking out over the barrier to the manic efforts of the great Navy recovery vehicle as it tugged and inched the Command Workshops embarrassments from their cavities in the drying village mud.

The boy ran quickly across the road. There was only one way now and that was through the village. He had never been in the village, nor did he know anyone, apart from poor Treacle, who had. It frightened him, with its close houses of wood and bamboo and corrugated iron; its alleys and fires and extraordinary music.

From the road he ran along a rutted and overgrown track and then, with just a moment's hesitant nervousness, he turned right and jumped down a bank behind one of the Chinese houses. Wide-eyed and panting he ran along the thin fringe of the place and turned into an alley full of thick smells and strangely drifting smoke. He walked at first, his eyes going left and right and at the openings to each house, his nose stuffed with the aroma of burning wood and unknown food. Then he turned a corner and almost fell over an old woman leaning over a little pot on a fire.

'Sorry,' said Charlie, very frightened. The old woman reached out a hand like a claw of a chicken towards him and he started with terror and began to run blindly. Down one narrow way and along another. A woman with a baby at her breast screeched after him and he heard a confusion in the dark of the house behind her. But most of the people, he realized, thankfully, were watching the recovery operation.

Not all though. He ran out into a small central area in the village and almost collided with a moon-faced toddler poking a stick at a dog. Then, immediately, he saw a gang of boys, all about his own age, about six of them, at the far end of the open area, walking from the direction of the recovery operations.

They saw him at the same moment. The sight stopped them with astonishment, as though he were some planetary invader. Then with odd cackling cries they ran instinctively at him. Once again he had to run, his face stiff with fright, his lungs blown up inside his chest, his heart vibrating.

Through a long alley he went, along bamboo and rattan laid over a stinking drain that sploshed in time with his running feet. The boys screamed behind him. He turned a sharp corner and hurdled a surprise cooking pot sizzling on a fire at his very feet. They were still close behind, and he knew they must catch him before long. He was stumbling with the effort of his running. Then, abruptly, he was in the open, away from the village, dragging himself across a dirt field with goats feeding and ravens calling in the peaceful trees. He looked behind and saw that the Chinese boys had stopped at the limit of the village houses. Thankfully he slowed down, walked exhaustedly to the bank leading up to the road again, pulled himself up to the top and turned in the direction of the main road junction and the railway station. Behind him was another barrier on the far side of the recovery operation. He knew he had got away from them. All of them.

Charlie did not have a watch. He pushed his tired legs to run for the last stretch to the station and he got there just as the clock reached twenty minutes to five. The train had gone.

The boy stood hopelessly on the platform and watched the Indian porter piling up some newspapers. He stumbled to one of the station benches and stood staring ahead of him until his eyes became fused with his own tears.

26

On the morning of Brigg's court martial the newly-demoted Lance-Corporal Wilcox went early to the garrison guardhouse.

'I heard they had the firing squad practising over on the sports field this morning,' he said amiably to Brigg. 'I've arranged for various parts of your body to be given to science and the Chinese twins have asked for your dicky to be pickled and sent to them.'

Brigg grinned wryly. 'I'm glad you're so bloody confident about the outcome,' he said. 'I hate to disappoint you, mate, but my defending officer, the prisoner's friend don't they call him? – well he reckons the most I'll get is three months and by the time the *Daily Express* get to work on the sentiments of the British public I'll be sprung in about two weeks. So stuff that.'

'He's quite right,' agreed Wilcox. 'You'll have public sympathy behind you. Mums all over the world will boo-hoo at your story. You'll probably get off a damned sight lighter than I did.'

Brigg said: 'You do look a bit naked with only one stripe on your arm. I hope you've reformed and you're working your way back up in rank again.'

'I quite like it down here,' answered Wilcox good-humouredly. 'For one thing I don't have to listen to the change-of-life ladies' club in the sergeants' mess. That's worth loss of pay and privileges for a start. And there's a lot you can do as a lance-corporal. I actually had a twist of that great nose that sits on the face of the unspeakable Hairy Harrison yesterday. I couldn't do that when I was a sergeant. By the way, there was a letter for you.'

'A letter?' said Brigg. 'From America?'

'That's right. Could be Alistair Cooke.'

'Bollocks. Let's have it.'

Wilcox grinned and handed it to him. 'See you in court,' he said. 'I've got a job as one of the ushers.'

'See you then,' returned Brigg absently. He sat down on the bunk and opened the letter.

'Darling Sergeant,' it said.

'Darling English Sergeant,' it repeated. 'I went up to the top of the Peak, as arranged, and you didn't come so I figured that we were washed up or a taxicab had got you like it got Cary Grant (or was it the girl?). I went straight to the hotel and then to the airport and here I am staring out over Riverside Drive, as previously described, with the other bank looking like the Arctic.

'Christ, how I love you. I couldn't think that I would never see you again. I stood on top of that bloody Peak crying like a fool and I flew all the way back here feeling like I wanted to hit somebody. You, maybe.

'Shit, how I love you. Today, through my tears (well, maybe not actually *tears*, but misery anyway) I read in the *New York Times* about you having a private shooting war with the British Army and being arrested and the rest. They spelt your name "Brugg" but I knew it was you because nobody else could be so crazy. Anyway nobody is called "Brugg". At first I figured I ought to send you a cable or flowers, or something, but then I thought that (a) I don't have the money for cables or flowers and (b) from reading the newspaper account, it seems that you won't be going anywhere without leaving an address for a while. So I saved and sent this letter instead.

'Love, how I love you. I went, that day, to meet Paul and we went to dinner and so to bed, as scheduled. But I didn't want his dinner or his bed. I tried but they both choked me. I don't know how he felt, but he said he wanted me, so I suppose he did. After the first night in the hotel we wandered around for the next day like two strangers. No, not strangers, because strangers have something to say to each other. But we didn't seem to have anything worth saying. It was awful and I really felt sorry for him because, after all, he'd come from the war and he kept looking hungrily at all the Chinese girls. I felt so sorry for him. All day the storm warnings were flying and at dinner we had the storm. I quit and packed and went back to our house – yours and mine, Sergeant – on the Tolo Channel. But you had flown. I tried to call the garrison, but I couldn't get any sense out of them. (Jesus, I hope your British Army never gets a four-minute warning over the phone!) Anyway, you weren't there. I went to sleep in our bed under the big Chinese cover, naked and wanting, and trying to pretend you were there. But my finger is a poor substitute for what you've got. (I'm a disgusting jerk! And even that could be a sexual pun!)

'By my finger – how I love you! Anyway I slept there and got a few raised eyebrows from old "Good-Good" and that Technicolor macaw. The next day I went back into the City and I saw Paul sitting alone on a bench by the harbour, just staring out at the ships. And I felt so tender towards him, and so ashamed, because he *is* my husband and he *did* come from the war to meet me. He even paid for me to be there and to meet you, etc, etc. I sat alongside him and we talked and I went back to the hotel like a good loyal girl. We had a good time together, in the end, and I think we ended up better than we had ever been. We were friends. I don't think we will ever see each other again. He went back to his war and I came back to Riverside Drive.

'By Cary Grant, I love you, you big-thinged thing. I'd be there now watching as they sentence you for years and years, and quite happy because years and years is not like forever, which it was before. But I can only just afford the stamp for this letter. (It's a pretty stamp, isn't it? Special issue, they said, for Do-Your-Own-Thing Week) so you'll just have to understand that I'm personally and actually in the envelope with this message. Kiss me once. Tomorrow I start a new job and I guess by the time I've saved my fare you'll be out of the calaboose.

'Goodnight, darling Sergeant. I'll kiss my finger for you.'

As Brigg folded the letter the Military Police Provost Sergeant opened the cell door. 'Time to be on parade,' he said haughtily. 'Get yourself moving. And I should wipe that bloody grin off your face, Sergeant, because there's nothing coming to you that's going to give you cause to grin.'

Brigg smiled on. He pinched the policeman's face playfully. 'I wouldn't bank on that,' he said. 'Cheeky.'

The Virgin Soldiers

Leslie Thomas

'It rained a lot, and steamed when the sun shone. It was always hot. But it was safe . . .'

One way or another the Communist guerilla war in Malaya kept a whole British army occupied from 1948 until 1952. They were the virgin soldiers. Idle, homesick, afraid, bored, oversexed and undersatisfied.

A young virgin like Brigg had to grab his fun while and where he could – in the Liberty Club, in Juicy Lucy's flat or up in Phillipa's room – in one frantic attempt at living before he died or got demobbed . . .

'Scenes rivalling the best of D. H. Lawrence' *Daily Telegraphy*

'Truly exciting' *Daily Mail*

arrow books

Stand Up Virgin Soldiers

Leslie Thomas

The worst has happened. On the eve of their return to Blighty, Brigg and his fellow National Servicemen find themselves sentenced to another six months in Panglin Barracks . . .

Many of the surviving characters from *The Virgin Soldiers* live again in these pages: dogged Tasker, the odious Sergeant Wellbeloved, the vulnerable Colonel Bromley Pickering and the comically touching Juicy Lucy.

But we encounter new characters too: the fanatical and demented Lieutenant Grainger; the endearing Welshman, Morris Morris – strong as a horse but vagglingly buxom; US private Clay – mysteriously lost in transit by the American Army; and last, but not least, Bernice Harrison, the sporting nurse who threatens to replace the wayward Lucy in Brigg's affections . . .

'Ribald and rich in comic invention' *Daily Mail*

'Splendidly conveys . . . compassion, excitement, entertainment' *Evening Standard*

arrow books

Waiting for the Day
Leslie Thomas

Midwinter, 1943. Britain is gripped by intense cold and in the darkest days of the war. It is six months before D-Day and the battle to liberate Nazi-occupied Europe.

RAF officer Paget is heading home for Christmas, back to the resurrection of a passion he thought was long over.

In a freezing hut on Salisbury Plain, Sergeant Harris is training his troops for landing on the shores of Normandy, but his mind is occupied by thought of just how his young wife is coping with his absence.

Lieutenant Miller has arrived at an all-but-derelict mansion in Somerset where his American division has set up its head-quarters. His affair with an Englishwoman is both bittersweet and potentially dangerous.

Cook Sergeant Fred Weber is enjoying fishing off the coast of occupied Jersey. His calm is soon to be shattered as his war takes on a violent twist.

Each man is heading inexorably towards the beaches of France, where the great battle will commence . . .

arrow books

The Magic Army

Leslie Thomas

The war, they said, would be over by Christmas. That was in 1939, and it is now January 1944. An exhausted Britain faces another year of conflict.

Meanwhile, small coastal villages in Devon are facing an invasion from an army just as foreign as that of the Germans. The Americans are smart, well-fed and well-equipped, and they have swept the bewildered citizens of South Devon from their homes in deadly earnest rehearsal for D-Day.

As the beaches echo to the sound of bullets and the local church to the sound of Glenn Miller, Americans and English are thrown together with sometimes hilarious, sometimes painful and puzzling results.

arrow books

THE POWER OF READING

Buy *Leslie Thomas*

**Order further *Leslie Thomas* titles
from your local bookshop, or have them delivered
direct to your door by Bookpost**

☐ **The Virgin Soldiers**	0 09 949003 X	£6.99
☐ **Stand Up Virgin Soldiers**	0 09 949004 8	£6.99
☐ **Waiting for the Day**	0 09 945719 9	£6.99
☐ **The Magic Army**	0 09 946917 0	£6.99
☐ **The Dearest and the Best**	0 09 947422 0	£6.99
☐ **Dangerous in Love**	0 09 947423 9	£6.99
☐ **Dangerous by Moonlight**	0 09 942170 4	£6.99
☐ **Dangerous Davies and the Lonely Heart**	0 09 943617 5	£6.99

Free post and packing
Overseas customers allow £2 per paperback

Phone: 01624 677237

Post: Random House Books
c/o Bookpost, PO Box 29, Douglas, Isle of Man IM99 1BQ

Fax: 01624 670923

email: bookshop@enterprise.net

Cheques (payable to Bookpost) and credit cards accepted

Prices and availability subject to change without notice.
Allow 28 days for delivery.
When placing your order, please state if you do not wish to receive any
additional information.

www.randomhouse.co.uk/arrowbooks

a r r o w   b o o k s